Knightess

J.A. Stein

JA Stein Publishing

Cover design by VenomCo

Edited by Gail Delaney

Map by J.A. Stein

ISBN: 979-8-9864908-0-9 (paperback)

ISBN: 979-8-9864908-1-6 (ebook)

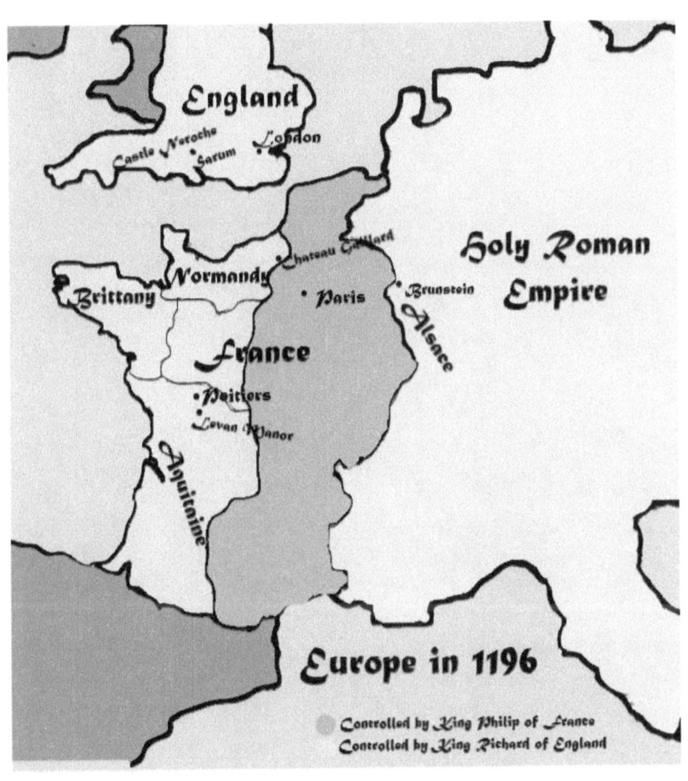

England
Castle Neroche
Sarum
London
Normandy
Brittany
Chateau Gaillard
Paris
Brunstein
Holy Roman Empire
Alsace
France
Poitiers
Levan Manor
Aquitaine
Europe in 1196
Controlled by King Philip of France
Controlled by King Richard of England

Chapter One

The frosted grass crunched beneath her feet as she picked her way around the edge of the knights' encampment. She breathed in the crisp air, laced with the sweet smell of campfire smoke, exhaling slowly to steady her nerves. Like a phantom on the edge of the meadow, she skirted the tents, noting every pennant, every crest. The first rays of golden dawn cut the smokey haze, lighting the white-plastered stone of the castle behind her like a shimmering torch. Ella lengthened her stride, impatient. She had to be sure.

The knights had risen now, the faint chink of their chainmail in the air as they donned their armor. Somewhere across the meadow a horse whinnied. The tournament field rose before her from the misty dawn, the platform for nobility to her right. With the last few hasty steps, her eyes relented in their darting quest. She had reached the end. They weren't here.

She leaned against the arena's wooden rail with her elbows, the cold sweat of her fear now cooling down the back of her plain gown. How many tournaments had she witnessed? Dozens? Perhaps a hundred? It should be easier by now. She shouldn't lose sleep and have to check every crest, every colored pennant, with this feeling of dread in her gut. She sighed and rubbed her forehead, wishing the tension away.

"You crossed an ocean to get away, you fool," she whispered to herself in her native Langue d'Oc. Instantly correcting herself, she switched even her thoughts back to English. *They will never find you here.*

The crunch of the frost alerted her, but Ella didn't flinch. Slowly, she straightened and turned toward the man two horse lengths behind her. Her eyes narrowed as she took in his ruddy complexion and looming stature: a typical knight. His green tunic was embroidered with a black bird. Unfamiliar. Unimportant.

What she wasn't prepared for was the look of astonishment on his face, laced with a note of recognition. She took an involuntary step back, the rail of the arena blocking further retreat. She glared at him. She was sure they had never met. She would recognize the crest on his chest; she would recognize him. His expression softened slightly as he noted her reaction; now he showed both curiosity and the all-too familiar lust newcomers to Sarum often tasted when they first saw her. He would learn to stay away soon enough. The trumpets sounded from the castle not a moment too soon, announcing that the Lord and Lady of Sarum were en route to the tournament field. With a long, brazen stride, Ella put distance between herself and the gawking man. She again forced herself to exhale her nerves, charging ahead with the resolve to get through this day like all the rest.

The lack of footsteps behind her told her he didn't follow.

Ella let her stride lengthen once again, not in apprehension now but because she was late. She had promised her lady she would return to the castle before the grand procession. She had not. She bent a knee, bowing her head gracefully, as the Lord and Lady of Sarum passed by. Lady Gwen ignored her. Ella winced. Perhaps she would be in trouble after all. All because she *had* to come down to the field early. She simply *had* to look for the crests of knights that were an ocean away.

As the noble entourage passed, Ella straightened and fell into line with the rest of the household. Her friend and fellow maid, Helin, stepped up to her.

"What took you so long?" she whispered as she handed Ella half of her heavy load of wine goblets and decanters.

"I'm sorry," Ella replied.

"I know I owe you from a few weeks ago, but Lady Gwen is furious. She likes *you* to arrange her hair."

Ella peered over the growing crowd toward Gwen, whose ankle-length golden hair was woven into an exceptionally elaborate braid down her slender back. "She looks beautiful as always, Helin."

Helin frowned. "I'm telling you, she's mad. She'll probably have you emptying chamber pots."

Ella's face fell, but she said nothing. It wouldn't be the first time she had done such lowly tasks. Oh, thank God her parents were dead, and spared the shame of how far their daughter had fallen.

Helin shot a sideways glance at Ella's darkened expression and laughed. "I'm joking, Ella. She's only a little mad, and she would never make you do such a menial task. She values you too much."

Ella raised her eyebrows at Helin but stayed silent. Her young friend did not know what it was like to fall in status, much less fall from nobility to nothing as Ella had. She squared her shoulders. She had worked her way into a good life, a good position, in an incredible household. It was going to be fine now.

It had to be.

A hand grabbed her arm and Ella flinched, almost dropping the decanter. Every nerve fired at once, making her heart pound as she braced herself to fight or flee.

"Sorry, Ella," Lord Gawain's manservant said gently. "Lady Gwen asked if you'd get her cloak from the castle."

Ella nodded, exhaling the tension that again flared in her like a thousand hot needles. She handed the decanters to the man and ran a shaking hand across her brow.

"You alright, Ella?" he asked.

"I'm fine. Yes, I will be right back with her cloak." She looked to Helin. "Did she bring down her fur mittens?"

Helin shook her head.

"She'll want those, too." Ella nodded again, more to clear her head than in reassurance. She turned and made her way back to the castle. Every step of the way, she wondered why she was so on edge. It was an ordinary day, an ordinary tournament. *They aren't here*, she reminded herself yet again.

Cloak and mittens successfully retrieved, though likely to be rendered unnecessary by the warm sun that now spilled over the plain, she edged her way through the thick crowd that now surrounded the tournament arena.

"What are you hiding, little maid?"

Ella jumped and spun around to face the man who had spoken, but he was merely strolling along behind her, adjusting his gauntlets. A knight. And the same green-tunicked one as before no less.

She ignored him and carried on.

"If you fail to answer me, I'll have to report you to the Lady of the Castle as a thief."

She spun to face him again. "It is *you* who *I* will have to report. For delaying me in my task for 'The Lady of the Castle'."

"Ah, so you *are* Lady Gwen's maid."

"One of them," Ella said quietly. She turned to go.

"Is she the type to be offended if I should offer to win the tournament for her?" The man had stopped, ready to turn off toward the entrance of the arena. "Or is she the type to revel in the attention?"

Ella narrowed her eyes at the man, taking in his sharp features. He was younger than Gwen, but older possibly by several years than Ella herself. Dark haired, dark eyed, with only a faint bristle of facial hair, many would consider him handsome. His mail seemed new . . . expensive. But his worn boots and frayed linen pants did not speak of the same wealth. A knight-errant trying to win his way to status by tournaments, perhaps?

"You would be a fool to win for any lady but Gwen while at her manor," she said in a quiet tone.

The man's lips curled into a lopsided smirk that made Ella's stomach clench. "You don't think she would take kindly to me offering to win the tournament for you then?"

She froze, her eyes narrowing. "Why would you even say such a thing?"

The man chuckled and walked into the arena.

She stared after him in shock. Heart pounding for reasons she did not understand, she pushed into the crowd and back to Gwen.

She had just handed off the cloak when trumpets again blared, this time directly in front of them. A herald cleared his throat and began, "Lords and Ladies of England, welcome to Sarum, as we join this day in tournament!" The crowd cheered. "Today, we will have four events! The Sword! The Club! Wrestling! And the Joust!" The roar of the crowd on the last word made it clear what the spectators' favorite event was. "Today our brave knights fight to a yield in all but the joust!" A hush swept across the field. "Today, the joust will be a challenge of the rings!" A few of the commoners booed.

"I knew they wouldn't like it," Gwen said to herself. She glanced at Ella. "I insisted to Gawain that this year we run the rings. I want to be able to watch at least one event with my eyes open."

The herald continued over the unhappy spectators, even louder now, "The joust will begin with the knights charging and lancing the largest ring. Each round will proceed to the smallest!"

Ella glanced to the familiar beam anchored in the center of the arena, its wooden arm stretching over a groomed dirt path on which the horses would charge. The largest ring was four palms wide, while the smallest of the five would fit merely the tip of a lance.

"The tournament champion will be he who wins the most events! The joust counts for double!" the herald shouted, then bowed deeply to the nobles before stepping aside.

A young lady toward Gwen's left said indignantly, "How is that fair if the event with the least danger counts *double*?"

"Shh," her mother hissed. "The joust always counts double."

"But—" the girl protested.

"I make the rules!" Gwen interjected, and the entire platform of nobles went silent. "And who could imagine a victor who can't handle a bit of power between his legs?" She smiled then, her features lighting in amusement like the sun itself. The entire crowd laughed with her, to the expense of the still thoroughly flustered young lady.

Gwen winked at Ella and waved her away, thoroughly engrossing herself in the unfolding competition as the noblewomen around her gossiped and drank the sweet wine brought from the castle. With relief, Ella sank onto the bench next to Helin in the back of the platform.

The crowd around them gasped as one of the knights in the sword arena fell, his opponent's sword at his neck. He raised his arm to yield.

Helin looked away, muttering in Ella's ear. "At least that round wasn't bloody. I hate this event."

"They have on their mail. And there are certain maneuvers that aren't allowed. It's not as brutal as battle." A minute later, Ella flinched as the next two opponents struck metal to metal with a clang that echoed across the arena over the voices of the spectators. The knight on the offensive had dealt a solid blow to the other's head, and it was clear the man was stunned. A step later his knees gave out, and he crumbled into the mud.

She conceded, "Alright, it is pretty brutal."

Helin still avoided looking at the arena, though Gwen and Ella watched every movement. "Just tell me when the joust starts. At least that I can watch."

"You have a long day ahead of you."

As the sword competition continued on, the knights entered in the joust began circling by. Lord Gawain rode in on his great destrier and stopped in front of Gwen. "My lady, my love, my Lady Gwen . . . I will win this tournament for you!" He bowed toward her from his saddle, smiling. Gwen smiled back and rose with elegant grace, pulling a single bright red ribbon from her hair and tying it around Gawain's lance.

"Best of luck, my lord," she said and blew him a kiss.

Gawain nodded and rode off toward the end of the field.

Another, older knight rode up to Gwen. "My most lovely Lady, with a smile like the sun itself, striking warmth to my old soul . . .with lips like the petals of a dew-dropped rose, with a heart like a saint . . . my Lady, should I have the exceptional privilege to win this tournament, I do so in your honor."

Gwen laughed, her smile beaming. "Lord Cenric, you flatterer. Be safe today."

Cenric put a hand to his heart in mock ecstasy. "And the fair one knows my name . . ." With a wink at Gwen, he rode back toward the other knights.

One after another, the other knights rode by and pledged their undying devotion to their Lady of the Tournament, the fair Lady Gwen. They spoke poetically of her beauty, sometimes comically so. Her light laugh filled the stands, even as the knights competing in the lessor events fought bloody battles before them all. The parade of "love stuck" amours paused only when the crowd let out a loud cheer as the champion of the sword event laid the last blow on his opponent and strode before them, his arms raised in victory. Ella narrowed her eyes in curiosity as she realized it was the same man with the green tunic who had spoken to her outside the arena. She couldn't catch every word the herald shouted over the noise, but she heard "Earnblaec." At least that explained the black hawk on his tunic.

Hardly anyone among the nobility paid the victor notice. They were busy drinking and chatting as they waited for the joust to get underway. Ella watched the man glance toward the platform. Her heart pounded as she thought of his threat to win the tournament for *her*. He was only joking, surely. His eyes locked with her own, and his lip curled into a half-smile yet again. Heat rose to her cheeks, and it wasn't until he walked out of the arena that she realized she had been holding her breath.

"How does she stand it?" Ella whispered to Helin, eyeing the line of knights vying for Gwen's attention.

"She loves it. For as long as I've known her. Even when I was a child, and she was even more stunning then if you can imagine it, she would joke with each and every knight, accept their praises, and flatter them in return."

"I've never seen her give a token to any man other than Lord Gawain."

Helin went quiet. "Of course she wouldn't. He is her husband."

Ella looked at her friend's frown. "But?"

Helin shook her head. "There once were rumors, but I have never seen any of this be more than the fun, chivalric show that it is. And that is all it is. A show."

"Of course," Ella said, watching Gwen laugh as yet another knight made a joke.

By high noon the joust was ready to begin. The excitement in the crowd was palpable now, both in the stands and around the field. Ella couldn't help but be sucked into it. She stood now, Helin with her, both of them peering over the high chairs and heads of the nobility to watch as the knights charged across the field on their destriers, galloping one at a time down the list in a show of horsemanship. Everyone caught the largest ring. The beauty of the horses' rippling muscle drew cries of awe from the crowd; the sound of hoofbeats made the very earth tremble with the percussion of horse and man in unison. They proceeded to the second largest ring, then the third, each round getting progressively harder, with fewer knights continuing on.

A cheer went through the crowd. Someone had rung the second smallest, the ring secured to his lance with its ribbon fluttering. He slowed his horse from the gallop. Ella leaned forward, realizing it was once again the newcomer. He rode a great bay horse that shone with an expert's care. The man turned and trotted past Gwen, nodding his head in respect to her. Even from under his helmet Ella caught the faint smile on his lips, framed with unshaven stubble of a beard.

"My, there's a fine man," Helin breathed.

Gwen overheard. "And one of few who has not promised to win this event for me. Who is he? It must be far away . . ."

"Earnblaec," Ella chimed in before she could catch herself. "He just won the sword event, too."

"Right you are, Ella," Gwen replied, still staring after the man. "But he is not the old Sir Alfred Earnblaec. He, I knew."

"His son?" asked Helin.

"He must be," Gwen said. "He's a knight-errant now if he is. Sad story. Ella, go invite him to dine in the castle with us tonight." She smiled slyly.

Ella gritted her teeth. This "Earnblaec" was the last knight she wanted to play messenger to, much less have in the castle that night. Obediently she rose and worked her way through the crowd, listening as the joust escalated to its dramatic conclusion. To the credit of the herald, she could hear even from her position deep in the crowd, "And our tournament champion is Sir Alec Earnblaec!"

Ella quickened her stride, intent on catching up to him as he left the arena, before he was back in the encampment.

"Ah, the English Winter comes to visit us at last," one of Lord Gawain's squires said to a friend, elbowing him in the side. Ella ignored them, keeping her face impassive as always.

"No such luck my friend. Some ice never melts." The teenagers laughed.

Ella waited anxiously at the end of the busy tilting yard until Alec trotted up, triumph on his face. When he saw her, his smile grew even broader.

Ella lowered her eyes, watching his horse's hooves. "Sir Alec, Lady Gwen requests your company at the banquet this evening. Will you be able to attend?"

Alec leaned toward her from his horse, the movement drawing her gaze back to him. "As my lady requests, I will." Then he sat up with a chuckle and a grin to his squire, who took his lance from him. The lean, lanky teenager smirked at Ella as if he and Alec had some secret joke between themselves.

Ella nodded and turned to leave. She was ready to be out of the crowd.

"What is your name?" he called after her.

She sighed and stopped. This man was terrible at reading body language. "Ella, sir."

"Your accent . . .you're from France?" He dismounted and handed his sweaty horse to his squire.

Ella exhaled through her nose. Her accent was so faint now, how could he have possibly caught it? "Yes, sir."

"Which Dutchy?"

"I'm a bit of a wanderer."

"Would you like to take a walk? Tell me about home?"

No! her mind screamed. Ella glanced around, noting several of the other knights watching in interest. "I'm sorry, sir. I'm really rather busy." One of the knights listening laughed. The words *English Winter* reached her ears once again. Ella blushed as she turned to leave, her eyes on the ground.

She didn't have to turn to know he followed.

Ella relented as Alec came level with her, matching her stride for stride. He was persistent, she'd give him that. If they were both going to the same place, what could it hurt?

Some people headed back out to the local farms and nearby manors, others up the path to the village and the castle on its motte where select competitors headed to celebrate with a feast. The sun was setting, throwing its shadows and red rays across the field.

As much as she wished to resume her quick, purposeful stride, Alec lagged behind, commenting on the sunset. She slowed her pace with a sigh, instead glancing up at the vibrant colors streaking the sky. It certainly was stunning. Golds and reds were haloed in a vibrant yellow as the last rays shot across the plains below them. How often did she take the time to watch such a masterpiece unravel? They stopped and watched in silence a moment.

"Dawn was stunning this morning as well, was it not?" Alec said quietly.

"A perfect morning for a tournament," Ella agreed.

"You looked like something was bothering you . . ." Alec let his voice trail, perhaps hoping to encourage her to talk, but she remained silent. "I apologize for my initial reaction."

"I'm curious. What did you see?"

"The rawest beauty I have ever seen."

Ella frowned deeper. She suspected there was only half-truth there. "Save your flattery for Lady Gwen, Sir Alec. I know what I am. I know what you are."

The revelry already in progress in the main keep reached their ears.

"And we're both late," Ella said with mild alarm. "My lady will see you at the banquet, aye?"

"May I see you again, Ella?"

She didn't answer as she jogged up the rocky path ahead of him. Helin stared from the manor doorway as Ella quickly brushed past her into the kitchen. Ella ducked her head to hide the flush of her cheeks, but a glance at her friend's amused smile revealed it was too late. The emotion was noted. Thankfully the work preoccupied them enough to divert Helin's questions, as least temporarily.

During the feast, Ella caught sight of Alec seated next to Gwen, laughing and joking with her. Gwen's delicate laugh echoed across the hall. Lord Gawain listened with rapt attention from Gwen's opposite side, smiling but draining his cups a bit faster than usual. Carefully, Ella refilled goblets at the head table. When she got to Alec, he held out his cup to her. Their eyes met for the briefest moment, and Ella had to once again force herself away from him, her heart pounding.

She knew what he was all right. He was another snake in the grass, just like them all. But if she was the prey, he was the first in this nest of vipers that had actually seen her.

Chapter Two

The bubbles splashed to the ground in the early afternoon sun as Ella and Helin, sleeves rolled to their elbows, dunked and scrubbed a few of Gwen's choice gowns. The lady did not trust anyone but them to handle certain fabrics. For some reason, despite the exhausting tournament the day before, she wanted the maids to get them clean *today*. Ella yawned and wiped her forehead with the back of her hand.

"You had nightmares again last night, didn't you?" Helin asked quietly.

"I didn't sleep well at all." Ella stifled another yawn as she fished another item from the washtub.

"Will you ever tell me what it is you dream about? All I hear is you thrashing about."

"I'm sorry. I try to hide it."

"It's always worse when there's a tournament, isn't it?"

Ella kept her eyes averted. Helin was full of questions today. "Yes."

"Won't you tell me why?" Helin prodded.

Ella gave her friend a hard glare. "It's nothing, Helin. I'm sorry if I woke you."

"You spoke Sir Alec's name last night. That's the only word I've ever been able to understand in all your mumblings. What is that other language you speak, anyway?"

Ella went still and pale. Apparently, she'd need to start sleeping alone if her subconscious was going to be so vocal. "Langue d'Oc," she answered. "I said his name?"

Helin perked. "Yes! What were you dreaming?" She giggled. "Do you fancy him?"

Ella shook her head. She vaguely remembered Alec in her dreams last night, but she hadn't been sure if he was friend or foe. He wasn't part of the nightmare at least. The fact that he'd reached into her dreams at all was concern enough. She had not dreamed of anyone she had met in the past eight years . . . years that she had been alone in a sea of new faces. Lost to her own thoughts, she ignored Helin's incessant chatter.

Dunk and scrub. Ella swirled the clothes with a wooden paddle and fished another item out to be soaped.

"Ella," Helin whispered, nodding toward the stables in front of them.

Ella looked up directly into Alec's gaze as he led two horses toward her. One, the unmistakable bay stallion. The other, one of the manor's lessor palfreys tacked in a sidesaddle, an awkward chair-like contraption that women like Gwen sometimes rode in, always with an escort. The maids quickly dipped a knee as he came to a stop in front of them. With a polite nod in Helin's direction, he focused fully on Ella. "Ride with me," he stated.

Ella felt a twinge of resentment and fear at the command. She eyed the palfrey with longing but shook her head. "I'm sorry, sir. I have work to do."

"I've already asked permission of Lady Gwen. She thought it would do you good. Come."

Ella looked at him with no small degree of doubt. Lady Gwen's aversion to horses was strong enough for Ella to resort to sneaking into the stables on occasion just to smell them. There was small chance she had approved of such a venture as riding. Particularly with a knight.

Alec held out the reins to her with an impatient shake. "I have work to do, too. I'll have you back in less than an hour. I just want to talk. We will stay within sight if the castle."

Ella looked to Helin, whose expression was a conflict of bewilderment and amusement. Helin motioned toward Alec with her chin. "You better go."

Ella looked back at Alec, shaking her head. "If you spoke with Lady Gwen, then where is proof of her permission?" She didn't like the way his smile turned into a kind of smirk, the kind a man wore when he held a secret. He pulled a piece of folded paper from his pocket and handed it to her. Hastily she opened it and read before she could stop herself. It was scrawled with a hasty "See if you like him" and signed by Gwen's unmistakable signature. Eleanor folded it back up and shrugged at Alec. Maids were not supposed to be able to read. "This bears her mark, but it could say anything."

"It says you may come for a short ride with me."

Ella wondered if Alec himself could read, or perhaps he had not seen the note. She glanced from him to the horses. Oh, how she missed horses.

Again she looked to Helin, who again motioned for her to go.

Ella was a fool, and she knew it. She nodded and with a last apologetic glance toward Helin, set the clothes down, wiped her hands on her skirt, and accepted Alec's help up onto the horse. The chair-like saddle left her feeling somewhat precarious and dependent on Alec's lead. She wished to throw her leg over and ride astride like him, but the awkward seat made such a thing impossible.

Alec mounted once he saw Ella was relatively stable.

"Not for long please, sir," she said quietly, then nudged her horse forward with her leg.

The palfrey was an uncomplicated mount. Ella gradually relaxed and followed Alec out into the fields. At first, he led her horse, her reins always within reach of his grasp. He chatted amicably about the weather and the tournament, receiving mostly simple answers in response. When a pheasant shot out of the brush and spooked the horses, Alec instinctively reached for the palfrey to steady the maid, but already Ella was cantering off, laughing. She was as solid in a saddle as any man.

Ella shot him a glance as they rode, Alec's silence both a relief and a worry. He was regarding her with furrowed brow, his sharp eyes taking in her every action. As their gaze met, he pushed his horse faster, and Eleanor allowed the palfrey to charge ahead, keeping pace. She smiled to herself, reveling in the glorious freedom a good canter offered.

It was an hour later that the pair returned to the manor. Ella's cheeks were flushed with joy and exertion. It had been so long since she rode . . . too long. Her hair was wind-tossed out of its neat braids. Alec was in much the same condition, though the furrow in his brow remained regardless of the fact that he was smiling at her. Ella gritted her teeth, reminding herself that most women couldn't keep pace with a knight on a destrier. But for the physical limitations of the now exhausted little palfrey, Ella would have. Obviously, Alec had noticed.

As she looked toward the central keep of the castle, her face fell further. Everyone stopped what they were doing and stared at the two. Helin, still scrubbing laundry, had an amused look.

They dismounted and led the horses into the stone building outside the great manor keep. The smell of the horses filled Ella's nose with memories and a yearning for things long past. She had only rarely been in the stable at the manor. Gwen did not think it was a place for a woman and hated the smell. Lord Gawain's stable, however, was beautiful. Clean, as everything else on the property, and well taken care of. Two rows of magnificent horses filled the stone and wood structure. Each horse was tethered in a three-sided stall, quietly resting or munching on hay. Alec tied his own horse. She followed his lead and led the palfrey into its own stall and tied it, stroking its velvety neck with gratitude for the moment of temporary escape.

Suddenly, she felt Alec's heat as he stood behind her, the masculine scent of leather, pine, and sweat filling her nose. She glanced up and turned, once again her attention on him.

"Why does it bother you to be seen with me?" he asked.

"Their looks, Sir Alec. They are assuming the worst."

"The worst?"

"Yes."

"And what would you call the worst?"

"We should have gone with an escort. I should not have gone at all." She blushed. "We have no business being together. It's improper. It's against all chivalric virt—" She froze as he took another step toward her. *Too close, too close.*

"Ah, but there is no lady here to offend." His breath warmed her neck as he said, "That code of chivalry is rather overrated, I find." His thumb brushed her wrist ever so lightly.

Ella stepped back in sudden panic, memories flashing behind her eyes. She stammered to cover her reaction, embarrassed. "Sir, do not think light of that code. You swore into it."

"What would you know of the oaths of knighthood?"

"My father taught me well," she continued inching away from him, now distrustful. "He was a . . . blacksmith. Worked for a lot of knights." She hoped he hadn't caught her slip of the tongue and the lie to cover it. "Why are you wasting your time with me when so many others swoon over you? Though I do appreciate the ride, why did you take *me*?"

Alec ignored the question. "Why are you so afraid to be near me? You were not repulsed by me an hour ago. I was only going to kiss you, nothing more. You are a bit old to act so innocent and prudish. A normal maiden would not show fear, but interest. But here you cower."

"I am not cowering." Ella's mind raced, and she forced herself to look at him and stop backing away. Her back was now in the corner of the stall anyway, with the palfrey on her left, and Alec blocking the way into the aisle. She focused on his strong, surcoat-clad chest, avoiding his face.

"Yet still you do not show the interest of the innocent."

Ella's bottom lip trembled ever so slightly. Willing herself to the present, she pushed her shoulders back and lifted her chin. "Why did you take me out today?" She finally forced herself to meet his intense, dark eyes, letting her gaze turn to a glare.

Alec laughed at her brave posture, and stepped close to her, so they were no more than a foot apart and she could feel the heat from his body enveloping her, forcing her pulse to pound in her ears. He looked her in the eye, smirk on his face, and said softly that only she could hear, as if telling a secret in a crowded room, "You came highly recommended from Sir Lezay."

Ella froze as loathing and fear resurfaced in her even stronger than before. Her last remaining joy from the ride vanished and dread settled in the pit of her stomach. Her eyes blinked rapidly, still locked on Alec's. She knew then that she had shared too much. How? Her trust had been violated once again. Her mind spun as she heard her voice say almost independently, "I have not heard that name."

Alec smiled at her discomfort. "I believe your reaction leaves no doubt who you really are, and that you *do* know that name."

Ella took a shaky breath and gave up the lie. "You know Lezay?" The breath left her in a whistle.

"Aye, m'lady, and more. He's been searching for a girl of your description."

"He must not find me," she whispered to herself. Her thoughts moved through a hundred terrifying memories and the work she had done to hide herself. The struggles she had been through. The humiliation.

"Ah, really now? And how much is not finding you worth? Your name is everywhere in France."

"Is there a reward for me? You would turn me in to Lezay?"

"I *could*. They offer a high bid for you. Enough for me to pay my knight fee for the next few years."

Ella leaned back against the wall of the barn, amongst the horses that were oblivious to her distress, and closed her eyes. "What gave me away? Other than my foolish trust . . ."

Alec leaned over her, an arm against the wall on either side of her head. She felt him and her eyes flew open, defiant, but she didn't move.

"Your face matches the description—those sharp blue eyes, and I'm sure that hair is richly brown colored under that dusty grime. You don't act like a commoner, as hard as you try. You have a desire to do more than just scrub clothes. You can ride well, like a lady or at least like one schooled by a master. And of course, your 'father taught you well'. You are Sir Lezay's wife, Lady Eleanor, in all but name. But really, 'Ella' is not a far stretch. I would have chosen something more interesting if I were in your position."

Ella studied Alec's face as he said all this, cursing herself as she tried to think of a way to halt Alec's plans. "What will ensure your silence? Surely there is something, or you would have revealed me by now."

Alec smiled, and now Ella realized how hideous of a smile it was. His eyes had a gleam to them and his lip curled up a little more on one side, revealing his straight teeth like an animal.

"I must admit, I am no fan of Lezay myself. But that is a story for another time. Perhaps you and I could come to a form of . . . partnership. The enemy of my enemy is my friend, right?"

Alec still stood over her, watching as Ella wrestled with his words. "Stop the acting. Stop the innocence." His eyes narrowed as lust crept into his eyes. "I plan to ruin Lezay, and since you've been hiding from him all these years, I get the impression you wouldn't mind that. Would you?" Ella trembled as she held his gaze. "All I want from you is one night. One night that allows me to despoil the bride he claims to hold so dear."

The edges of her vision blurring in panic. "What?" Her voice asked of its own volition, her mind whirling.

"Lie with me."

Ella's heart pounded and for a moment she couldn't think.

He dared to brush her arm with his fingertips. "Surely, after all these years on your own, I wouldn't be the first. I can compensate you if you'd like. And I will be discreet to all but Lezay himself. I am good—"

"Compensate?" Ella spit out, shaking her head. She had fled Lezay all these years, and for what? To be offered up as a chunk of meat to a different man? Neither was an option. She pinched her eyes shut for a second, then let them fly open as she ducked under Alec's arm. No longer under his domineering presence, she could think. She backed away a few steps down the barn aisle, eyeing him, then stood still.

"Surely one night is not enough," she said carefully.

Alec cocked his head, listening.

"My mother was the Lady of the Tournament in her day. Surely you've heard." Deftly she undid the pins holding her braid and let it unravel to her waist. The mild act of undressing served its purpose.

Alec had visibly tensed as he looked at her. "I had a feeling you could rival Lady Gwen in beauty when you stop hiding behind all that dirt. I already told you I want you."

"You expect me to set you free after one night, free to go back to my husband and tell him of my indiscretion? You as sure as kill me with this proposal. Lezay will be furious. Embarrassed yes, but he will hunt you. And me. Can you protect me? Are you ready to meet his wrath yourself?"

Alec studied her for a moment. "That would not be necessary if you were long gone before he found out about us."

She shook her head. "You threaten to expose me. You use one night to stir Lezay's jealousy, and it is the same as many. My secret is out. I again flee manor to manor, waiting for him to catch up to me. Yet if I do not agree to play this part, you take the reward and hand me over to my 'husband.' I can run, today or after the tourney, but then I am back to running. I have been running from Lezay for eight years. I am tired. To my greatest ability, I offer to help you seek your revenge for whatever Lezay has done to you if you can promise to protect me." She took a deep breath, wondering if she was about to make the biggest mistake of her life. "Take me with you, tourney to tourney. Back home with you if you have a place. I will play the role of your mistress."

"Mistress?" Alec said in amusement. "And I thought myself lucky to have you for a night."

"With two rules."

"Which are?" Alec asked impatiently.

"I stay 'Ella'. You say nothing of my true identity to anyone, or you will be publicly humiliated. Of this I assure you." She smiled. "And regardless of what we may lead the public to think, you will not . . . consummate . . . our relationship."

"What?"

"Every night they will think it. Every night!" Ella emphasized.

"You won't last. You can't play the part and not want it."

"If that becomes the case, *I* will come to *you*," Ella agreed, hoping to give him a glimmer of hope.

Alec crossed his arms and looked her up and down as if he was purchasing a horse. "I won't say I'm opposed, but how does this help either of us? I don't think it solves any of the problems you so carefully pointed out."

Ella sighed. "It buys me time."

"You would put yourself through public embarrassment, for you know how they'll treat you if I take a commoner as a mistress, just for time?"

"Time for my secret to remain intact."

"That seems a harsh trade just to avoid your husband."

"A knight that can afford a mistress is a rich man indeed."

"I offered to be discreet! This is the opposite! Why not just give me one night and trust that when I tell Lezay what we've done, I will not tell him where you are?"

"Because you know now, *Sir* Alec! You *know*!" Ella shook her head, her shoulders slumping in defeat. "I can never let you travel the kingdom with what you know. I *don't* trust you!" Her plan was the only way. She could act. He would not touch her. And she could watch him to be sure her identity was safe. Yes, that was certain. Alec would never be far from her so long as he held her secret. And maybe, just maybe, he really did hate Lezay as much as she and would help her to be free of him. "I will never lie with you. You think you know how I've survived the past years alone. It was not by selling myself!" Her voice had risen nearly to a shout, and her chest heaved as she struggled to regain her composure.

"I will be your maid and scrub your floors, polish your boots. I will be your mistress in name, that you can brag to all your friends that you conquered the 'English Winter.' I will dress up and smile and act the part. But I will not let you leave Sarum without me." Her eyes pleaded with him. "All I ask is that you do not seek out Lezay, and remember I will not – I will not . . ." She closed her eyes in frustration.

Alec stepped up to her until he was right in front of her. Proximity forced her to meet his gaze once again. "Every tournament you will act. And to my greatest ability I will protect you once Lezay discovers you." His eyes twinkled with something akin to mischief. "It shall not be long until you come to me, my lady," he whispered. He straightened. "We leave tomorrow. You should tell your lady."

Ella nodded agreement and hurried out of the stable to the manor. Once inside the kitchen, she closed the door behind her and leaned against it. Another stroke of fate for one cursed by her past. She could not cry nor scream, though she longed to do both. The years had trained her to withhold feeling. With a push of inner reserve, she strode through the kitchens and up to Gwen's chamber, where the lady would be dressing for dinner.

Ella dreaded the conversation ahead. Gwen had been nothing but kind to her this past year. Sarum was the closest thing to home she had had in years. Not to mention, her own shame for what she would be pretending to do made her a bit queasy. She almost couldn't open the door. She thought of going back to Alec, informing him that she had changed plans and would stay at Sarum. But then she remembered Lezay, and she reached for the door and pulled it open.

Gwen stood by the window, pensively watching the last remaining knights pack and leave Sarum for their homes across England. She was as gorgeous as ever, the train of her gown pooled around her bare feet and her golden hair twined about her like a halo. She was older than Ella, maybe even old enough to be her mother, but her features didn't bely it. Had they looked anything alike, one might have guessed them sisters. Gwen turned to Ella as she entered, her mood light and youthful.

Before Ella could speak, she asked, "So you like him?"

Ella opened and closed her mouth. "I . . .uh . . ."

Gwen smiled. "It's my own fault. I told you to talk to him yesterday. I didn't know then how . . . convincing . . . he could be. You poor thing, you didn't stand a chance against a man like that."

Ella figured it was best to get to the point before she lost her nerve. "He asked me to leave with him tomorrow."

Gwen nodded, the smiled flickering on her lips but holding. "I am sure he did." She turned back to the window. "You know, Ella, I did not choose my husband. He was chosen for me when I was young. There is a blessing and a curse for status. For beauty. I was fortunate. I am married to a good man. A man who cares for me, will do anything to protect me. He would never hurt me or let anyone hurt me." She paused, gathering her thoughts. "I may be the Beauty of the Tourney, but I am such with Gawain at my back. He gives me quite a bit of rein to enjoy; some say too much. But I have him to pull me back in if I get into a mess where I could be hurt. Not physically, I don't mean that. I mean my heart. I play my part, even enjoy it, but I never put my heart in play. You seem like a smart girl. I think you know this already. But a man like Alec, Ella . . .he could chew a woman up and spit her right back out." Gwen shuddered a little. Then she turned to look at Ella, her light girlish tone now serious. "Go with him, with all my blessing. But guard your heart, my dear. He is ambitious, and I'm not sure even he knows the full grasp of his power."

As Ella packed and readied for bed for the last time at Sarum manor, she was silent in her thoughts, tuning out most of Helin's constant babble that usually kept her mind off of her own world.

"Janece told the most fantastic story at dinner tonight, Ella," Helin said. "It was in in the time of King Arthur. There was a knight, much like your Sir Alec, named Tristen. He was nursed back to health by the Lady Isolde after a grievous wound. He should have died, but she healed it, and she fell in love with him. And he, her. Only she was promised to Tristen's lord, Sir Mark. They could not be together for years, and yet in the end, she finally broke away to be with Tristen. To hold a love so pure! They say there is a vine . . . two vines intertwined . . . that grows on their grave. To this day! It really was a wonderful story, Ella. I can't tell it to give it justice. You'll have to ask her to tell you."

Helin sighed. "One day my knight will come for me, Ella, just like yours! You just wait and see. He will see me at one of the tournaments, whisk me away, and make me his bride. We will live in a castle together by the sea, surrounded by our friends and fine things he has won in battle. The king will be our guest! Oh, Ella, those fairy tales have to come true at some point, for were they not once based on fact?"

"They were based on dreams."

"Tush. Even dreams come true. You saw how that Alec looked at you yourself. He will treat you like a princess."

"No, he won't."

"Yes, he will! I saw how he looked at you. He's madly in love with you."

"This is not one of your fairytales, Helin! It is life! Any knight that will carry us away on his horse will be twice our age: a stranger you will wish you had never met. He will lock you in his tower, not put you to peaceful rest there. There, for the rest of your days, you will slave away much as we do here, cleaning, cooking, and waiting for him to return from his battles. And when he does, you will receive a peck on the cheek in passing, until he calls you to his bed late that night, taking you as his wife, and perhaps, for that brief moment, he will treat you as if you are wanted. But he will be gone in the morning, long before you have risen, and he will again be off with the hounds, or the men, or to battles. Within a few short years, if you are lucky, you will conceive his child, laboring day and night to bring it into the world. If it is a son, you will find favor in your husband's eyes for a time. A daughter and he will ignore you, fuming that you have created a worthless extra mouth to feed. And the next time, and the next time, and the next it will all be the same. You will bear, praying for a son, his heir, hoping the child will live longer than a few years. And through it all, praying that your failing body can handle another, before you succumb to the one that is not normal, the one that takes your life." Ella gently cupped her friend's chin in her hand as she watched tears stream from her eyes. "There is no fairytale, Helin."

"You are not leaving because you love him then?"

"No. Not in the slightest."

Helin avoided Ella's eyes, then searched them. Receiving no respite, she fell into Ella's arms sobbing. Ella was shocked, but supported her friend, sorely wishing she could take back her words and say she had lied. She could not. She believed them herself, as much as she didn't want to. She had observed and experienced too much.

When Helin had turned away to her own bed, Ella laid awake for hours, the name she had never wanted to hear spoken again burning in her mind.

Lezay.

The images she had suppressed in the stable returned. Lezay's rough hands on her body. Lezay's foul tongue in her mouth. The stench that rolled off him, of sweat and body odor. Pain deep inside her as he took her maidenhead with brute force. Then the feel of his blood as it splattered across her naked body. She fingered the ugly scar on her abdomen through her shift, the stinging tear from her flesh he had taken in retribution reminding her of just how close she had come to death at his hand. Her legs ached again from running, running, running. For days, weeks, months. For eight whole years. Out of her homeland and across the sea. Now, just as she thought she had made a life for herself somewhere respectable and safe, he was on her trail again.

And Alec knew.

Chapter Three

When Ella awoke from her last night at Lady Gwen's manor, she roused Helin for a brief goodbye with a quick embrace as an apology for her hard words the night before. She really hoped Helin would find the love she sought, even if she herself could not. Then she set off with Alec and his squire into yet another life. Perhaps he had cornered her into this, but he had also promised to protect her. No one had done that for a long time.

It turned out that Alec was not just a knight-errant, but the steward of Castle Neroche to the west of Sarum. The journey was fairly easy. The trio remained on the wide and level main roads until they got closer to Neroche. There the rolling hills tightened into a dense forest of hilly ravines before suddenly opening into small fields edged in grey stone walls. Alec's manor stood against the skyline in the distance, toward the top of one of the hills. From what Ella could tell, it was quaint, quiet, and as far as she was concerned, a very remote prison.

Alec, his squire Lance, and Ella each rode in silence. Lance was about sixteen, an age where a boy eager to be a man felt himself invincible in many ways. He was lanky, with greasy hair and eyes that seemed too small for his face. There was something about him Ella didn't trust. Perhaps it was that leering smile. She felt bad for him; the poor man probably didn't even have control of it. He often glanced at her with the intent of conversation, but he was always silenced with a cold glare.

"Not much longer now," he finally dared. He was greeted with the same cold silence. "Sir," he said to Alec, "why did you pick such a mean one?"

"She'll be the most interesting in the end. Just watch," Alec replied, with a snide look at Ella. She caught it immediately and finally lost her composure.

"Did you talk to no one at the manor?" she demanded sharply.

"Of, course," replied Alec. "They all said you would be an excellent catch if you had but a bit of desire."

Lance snorted in laughter.

"No desire?" questioned Ella, amused. "Is that what they say? They are right. I could never desire a pig. I'd rather prefer a man."

Lance winced and Alec smiled.

"So what exactly qualifies a pig to be a man?" Alec asked.

"A brain, bravery, and sight beyond the eyes."

"How can one see other than with one's eyes?" inquired Lance.

Ella turned to him for the first time. "That, lad, is where the brain comes in and the bravery to look into the dark."

The two men were silent as they crested the last hill. There before them was Castle Neroche, Alec's very own, very small, very run-down fortress. They rode up through the first rampart around the castle, which was no more than an earthen wall that surrounded the seven acres of fields where the horses, cows, and sheep grazed on the fresh spring grass. Ahead was a massive stone wall that dropped sharply down into a twenty-foot-deep ditch. The moat. It was completely dry. A thick plank drawbridge lay across the ditch and looked like it hadn't been raised or lowered in over twenty years. They continued over it and into the walls, which protected the village of three wooden huts within. There was a blacksmith's forge to her right, and next to it a stable. The main keep sat on the very top of the hill, maybe another hundred yards from the last of the huts. The household of the manor stopped to stare at Ella, their eyes curious. The hair on Ella's neck prickled. Maybe she was the first woman Alec had brought back to Neroche? She dismissed the thought, watching his confident greeting to his tenants. *Impossible.*

The two field workers and the blacksmith, who were in the yard when they arrived, put down their work and gathered toward the travelers. A tall man, older than Lance but still with a youthful look about him, emerged from the stable, his stride long and confident. He took Alec's horse, murmuring to it, as Alec dismounted. An old man with a cane hobbled from a hut across the yard, and then two women, one old, one young, emerged from the manor keep itself.

"How was the tourney?" the tall stableman asked.

"Excellent," Alec replied, running a hand through his hair, glancing up at Ella with a half-smile. He raised his voice and addressed his village, "Everyone, I would like you to meet Ella. My new maid."

Ella waved a little nervously from atop her palfrey.

Alec assisted her in dismounting. The tall man gave her a curious smile and led the horses toward the stable. Lance followed. Alec put his arm around her, which made her cringe, but he held tight as he steered her toward the crowd. "You know Lance, and that stable lad Wilfred is my groom. This is Godfrey, my blacksmith. Henry and James, field workers. Old Guillaume here is the caretaker." Ella couldn't help but wonder just how much caretaking Guillaume was capable of. Alec continued smoothly, "Margarete, Godfrey's wife, is one of the best cooks of any manor, and this is her daughter, Marie." Margarete was a plump, middle aged woman who looked as if she could run the manor herself with an iron fist. Ella realized that she probably did. Her daughter was a gentle faced, full-figured girl with curly blond hair that looked to be about Lance's age. The two women looked at Ella with suspicion.

"Where would ye like me to set her up, Sir Alec? She staying with Marie and us?" Margarete asked. Ella realized that the one-room huts were likely already full with this small crowd of villagers. Godfrey's family obviously had one, and the other men must somehow share.

"She'll be up in the manor with me," Alec stated.

Margarete's eyes flicked at the arm that was still draped around Ella's shoulders, and she pursed her lips but stayed silent. She took her daughter by the arm. "We'll go add more to the stew pot then." She practically dragged Marie away as the young woman stared at Ella.

The other men of the manor looked uncomfortable. They nodded their heads politely to Ella, and a few muttered "Welcome" before they excused themselves back to their work. Ella looked up at Alec with exasperation as their backs faded. In one sentence he'd set her reputation with her new companions before she'd ever had a chance to introduce herself. Yes, she knew what she'd signed up for, but moving to a new place where she was now an instant scandal made her uneasy.

He'd made it no secret. She was Alec's femme.

The small keep was three stories high, a round tower. The lower level was storerooms and a kitchen, with a staircase that curved along the outer wall up to the second level, a main hall with a massive fireplace. That level was decorated with old pennants and shields, with some massive antlers as decoration all around. The tattered tapestries on the walls showed hunting scenes. Neroche had once been a hunting lodge, she realized. The stairs continued to curve up the wall into the upper floor, where there was a narrow landing and two doors. Alec opened the one to her right and gestured her into a wedge-shaped room whose outer wall curved with the stone of the tower. Another door was in the second wall of the wedge to her left. A full framed wooden bed was pushed against the curved wall, with a diamond-glass paned window to its right. There were no linens, and everything was dusty. Ella took a little comfort in the fact that at least Alec didn't do this often. She had a beautiful view of the surrounding countryside. And at least Alec wasn't expecting her to share a room with him.

"Will this do?" Alec asked.

"If you can lend me some sheets and a dust rag, of course," Ella replied. She hesitated. "If the manor folk live out in the cottages, where do you stay?" She had a suspicion of what was on the other side of that second door, but she was hoping she was wrong. Maybe there was another level still.

Sure enough, Alec smirked his lopsided grin and led her over to the door on the opposite wall. With a click of the latch he pushed it open and gestured toward a very lived-in room. It was laid out much the same as the room they now stood in, but with more furniture, including a table and chair, nightstands, and wardrobes all around. Not tidy, but not disgustingly dirty either. The cozy, comfortable feel was a complete contrast to the bareness of Ella's room. She swallowed.

"Any time you want to visit, you just come right on in," Alec said in a low voice.

She stepped away from him as he made as if he was going to brush her cheek with his hand. "I'm going to see if I can find those sheets," she said, and hastened down the stairs, leaving Alec smiling to himself behind her.

There was no way for anyone to tell if Alec visited her or not. And for the first few weeks of her stay, contrary to what most in the manor assumed, he did not. The other villagers were polite but kept their distance from her. Ella knew the men were afraid of Alec seeing them talk to her, and the women just didn't want to bother with her. It was lonely, but nothing Ella wasn't used to. She threw herself into her work as a maid and tried to prove her worth to the villagers, and slowly they noticed and respected her for it.

But in late May, on the first balmy, early summer night, Alec came to her room and said, "It's time."

Chapter Four

Ella lugged the huge wooden laundry tub in front of the kitchen fire in the middle of the night. The manor staff were in their cottages fast asleep. Ella swung the huge cooking cauldron, brimming with hot water, out of the fire and carefully tipped it into the tub. That pot was so big that it only took three small buckets of water to top off the tub and cool the water to a comfortable temperature. Steam curled up from the water as she peeled off her dirt and sweat encrusted clothes layer by layer. The pewter ring on its chain hung between her breasts, the metal cool against her fire warmed skin. She didn't linger nude. Ella stepped into the wooden tub, unbraiding her dark hair until it hung like a curtain around her.

The water came up to her waist as she sat, just deep enough for her to wiggle down and get her whole body wet. With careful thoroughness she scrubbed her body cleaner than she had been in years, working away what her daily rag bath in cold water was insufficient for. Her fingers lingered on the small scar on her abdomen, just below her navel. The physical pain had healed within days. The emotional pain still lingered. The water was already turning a dirt color as Ella moved to her hair, building suds with her hands then rubbing them up to her scalp. The grease and grime rinsed clean, leaving the knots behind. Ella stood and poured a pitcher of cold water over her head, gasping at the temperature and quickly completing her rinse.

Ella reached for the linen sheet on the chair and wrapped herself in it as she stepped out of the tub. Remaining on the chair was a tiny glass vial, a scented oil she had bought from an herbalist in the market back at Sarum. The sweet scent hit her nose as she unstopped the bottle. Amidst notes of lavender and mint she worked the oil into the ends of her knotted hair. She sat by the fire and took a comb to the mess, the sheet wrapped tightly around her and tucked in the front. As she combed her hair, she stretched out her toes and wiggled them in the warmth of the fire. Her brain was so numb with fatigue she could not think about why she went through this work. But it did feel surprisingly good to be clean.

She finished her hair and reached for her second shift. It was tattered, but clean.

"No," a voice said from the corner.

Ella whirled around to see Alec seated in the far corner of the kitchen. Ella instinctively crossed her arms over her chest, still barely covered by the thin white fabric of the linen sheet. "How long have you been there?"

Alec rose and came toward her. His unlaced shirt was open to reveal a solid chest spattered with dark hair. He held a bundle in his hand at his side. "Long enough," he said and handed Ella the bundle.

She eyed him warily, then untied the package to reveal a new gown and shift. It was a deep emerald green with embroidered trim and full skirts. Thick laces ran down the back. She was grateful to see the sleeves were the kind that would lace down her forearms, not flow with a volume of fabric like Lady Gwen's gown did.

"I think it will fit you. And be lovely. No chores anymore—not with that on. That wasn't your job in the first place."

Ella only stared from him to the fabric. She had never owned such a fine garment, but its purpose repulsed her still, so she didn't know how to react. "Thank you," she managed to get out.

"I'll help you," Alec said, reaching for the new shift. Ella didn't move. "Dawn will be here soon and the rest of the household with it. You don't want to be caught undressed with me just yet, do you? There's nothing I haven't seen."

Ella turned away from him and pulled the new shift over her shoulders, making sure it dropped around her before she let the sheet fall. She turned back to Alec, who already held the gown ready for her. She let him slip it over her head, pulling out her hair and wiggling the fabric into place. Alec's fingers worked from the base of her spine up to her neck in soft movements as he did the laces. The gentleness of his strong hands surprised her. She could not protest vocally, though every brush of his fingers caused the muscles of her back to tense. By the time he was done, she stood there as straight-backed as a princess, the skirts of the gown pooled around her ankles with a slight train intended only for those of nobility.

As Ella looked down at the garment, the finest she'd worn in her life, Alec caught his breath. He stared at her with wide-eyed appreciation, the lust again pooling in the depths of his eyes, the tension in his jaw.

Under that gaze, she felt more naked than when she had nothing but a sheet on.

She had often wondered what she would look like if she dressed the part her birth had granted her. She had tried to hide her feminine features, become invisible, and still it had taken many cold glares to keep men at bay. Alec's expression warned her that now, clean and appropriately dressed, there was no hiding. Despite the fact they were living together, used to each other, he was not immune.

She turned from him, reaching for the buckets to start dumping the wash water.

"Oh, no. I said no work," Alec said, gently taking them from her hands. The touch of his fingers, however brief, sent a shock through her.

"I can't leave this for Margarete and Marie," Ella insisted.

"I'll take care of it," Alec said quietly. "Go get some sleep while you can. We leave just after dawn."

Chapter Five

The first tourney was at Sarum, quite familiar territory for Ella to test out her new role. As the manor came into view on the raised motte across from them, pennants flying in the breeze, Ella's stomach clenched. What would her old peers think of her now? Her shining long hair was elegantly fastened back in a thick braid woven with green satin ribbons. It twisted softly from her temples back into the braid, exposing her blue eyes. The green gown hung almost to the ground as she rode her palfrey. She wondered if they would recognize her. She hardly recognized herself.

Sure enough, heads began to turn as they rode into the knights' encampment. Ella's back straightened with nervousness. At first she glared at the knights who dared to make eye contact with her, but after a few of them started leering instead of looking away, she focused forward, ignoring everyone.

She still heard the whispers.

"She left Sarum with him."

"His mistress?"

"His whore . . ."

The speakers kept their voices quiet, the murmurs like the gentle buzzing of bees. Ella inwardly cringed in shame but lifted her chin anyway. Shame she could handle.

Alec pressed his horse closer so that their legs touched and reached for her hand. She glanced at him in surprise but did not pull away from the heat that seemed to radiate from his touch like a burn. He smiled with a twinkle in his eye. "Your transformation has worked."

"Perhaps too well," Ella said through gritted teeth.

"Having second thoughts?" Alec smirked.

They halted their horses and dismounted in the center of the encampment. Wilfred and Lance got to work setting up their camp. Alec offered Eleanor his arm and guided her through the crowd. The whispers continued, from men and women alike.

"Looks like someone thawed Winter."

"Why is she dressed like a noble?"

"Stunning . . ."

"Can I win the tournament for a commoner? If he can, why can't I?" said a knight. When Ella looked at him with alarm, he broke into laughter.

Alec merely smiled and pulled her along.

Ella squeezed his arm and stopped in a break in the crowd.

Alec's gaze narrowed. "This was your idea, my lady," he said under his breath.

"I know. I just . . ."

"If you are to act the part of my mistress, you must sit and watch me compete. I will offer to win the tournament for you, and you will give me your token as any loyal lady would do."

Ella held her breath and closed her eyes. "And then it's over, right?"

Alec absently brushed a strand of her hair behind her ear. "After the evening festivities, it's over. We come back to the tent. We sleep." His eyes twinkled mischievously. "Then your secret will remain safe."

"You wouldn't tell . . . not now. I don't mind working the manor. Have I not proven myself to be a good maid?"

"We had an arrangement, my lady. Do you intend to rescind on your end of the agreement?"

Ella looked him hard in the eye, frowning. Her eyes narrowed in loathing. "No."

Alec smirked that accursed, lopsided grin. "Then come." He guided her forward to the nobles' platform.

The murmur in the crowd caught Lady Gwen's attention as she sat on her elaborate high-backed chair. She craned her head to look as faithful Helin at her side stood to get a view. Helin made a surprised face, then a little smile as she recognized her. She whispered into Gwen's ear something that made Gwen clap her hands in amusement.

With a tug on Alec's arm, Ella pulled him toward Gwen.

"My dear, what a transformation!" Gwen smiled as they approached.

"Thank you, my lady. It is good to see you again," Ella replied, and meant it.

"Will you join us while your dashing beau goes off to the tourney?" Gwen asked.

Ella smiled, relieved. She graciously accepted and took her place behind Gwen. With the Lady of the Tournament at her side, no one would pay further attention to her. Except Alec of course, but Gwen would expect that.

After nearly an hour of idle small talk with Gwen and Helin, in large part made up of Ella's usual silence, the first contestants began. The first event was sword fighting. Alec was first, and he pledged his win to her. She did her duty and made a show of giving Alec one of her green ribbons, which he tied around his upper arm, the ends trailing in the wind as his sword swung true. One by one the other knights pledged their hearts and victories to the beautiful Gwen, only to lose any chance of those victories to Alec. But then a bold young knight stepped forward before it was his turn to face Alec and pledged to win the fight for Ella.

All three ladies went wide-eyed in surprise, then Gwen and Helin slowly turned to Ella. Ella frowned at them, wishing her bench was set a mile further back from Gwen. Gwen looked slightly offended that she was upstaged, but she said nothing. What could she say? Ella looked back at the young knight's pleading gaze. He could not be much older than Lance, perhaps eighteen.

Gently, she said, "Sir, I am honored. But I am not the one you should pledge your victory to. I have pledged my support to another."

The young man's face turned bright red in shame. With a bit of anger, he quickly turned and strode to the competition circle where Alec waited. The expression of fury on Alec's face was visible even from the stands. The two men postured for a long minute, wolves with hackles raised. When Alec attacked, the younger man yelped at the immediate impact. He tried to fight back, striking in quick, solid blows, but he made little contact. At least not enough to sway the furious beast that hammered away until the man was in the dirt. Ella watched, for the first time appreciating the deadly skill Alec possessed with a sword and wondering what she had gotten herself involved with.

Gwen and Helin sat quietly, sharing an occasional glance. They were surprised at the young knight's brazen ignorance of Gwen, the traditional beauty of the tourney, not to mention the actual Lady of the Manor. Worse, that young man, defeated by Alec in the sword, would not be the last one that day to shirk Gwen and try to win Ella's affections. In the wrestling competition, a big ogre of a man bowed to Ella and pledged her his victory.

She impatiently told him off, even though Alec wasn't even competing in that event. Then in the joust, the most prestigious of all the events, not one but *three* other men pledged to win the event for her. She made a show of favoring Alec, even exaggerating it so far as to blow him a kiss, which made him smirk with thorough enjoyment, then impatiently refused each consecutive man.

Exhausted and embarrassed, Ella stood and took her leave of the platform, mortified to be upstaging her lady. "My Lady, I am so sorry. I should never have come." The other noble ladies whispered amongst themselves and glared at her.

Gwen forced a smile and patted her on the arm. "You've been bolder than I thought, Ella." With a wave of her hand, she dismissed her. Ella hastened down the stairs of the platform and into the crowd.

The commoners weren't much kinder than the noble women.

One of Lord Gawain's squires, who had tried seducing Ella when she'd first arrived over a year ago, approached. "So you were holding out for a knight after all," he scoffed. "You only needed to give me another year, Ella." She sidestepped around him, arms crossed to hide her trembling fingers.

A whore from a nearby brothel sidled up to her, looping her arm over Ella's shoulders. "Do you want me to tell you how he likes it, love?" Ella flinched, and the woman laughed loudly, shoving Ella that she almost fell.

Ella caught her footing and stood for a moment, steeling herself. She'd known this would happen. Surely today would be the worst, then it would get easier. She picked up her chin and squared her shoulders like she'd seen Lady Gwen do a hundred times. She may be Alec's mistress in name, but she wouldn't succumb to shame like she was his whore. She glided through the rest of the crowd like the lady she was, finally reaching the end of the list where the squires waited. She saw Wilfred and Lance and stood next to them.

Lance leered at her but quickly focused his attention back on the joust. Wilfred shifted his weight, biting his lip. "Tough day, huh?"

Ella nodded.

"Almost through." Wilfred motioned toward the list, where Alec was in a full gallop toward the smallest of the rings. It slid onto his lance easily, and the crowd roared its approval. For the second time already that spring, Alec was Tournament Champion. As soon as he was off his horse, Ella was glued to his side.

Alec whispered in her ear, grinning ear to ear, "Well done!" The knights glared at him in jealousy as he wrapped his arm around her and steered her toward the manor for the evening's festivities. "You had them so distracted, you made this victory easy."

With that revelation, Ella saw the situation differently. Everywhere she turned, someone was staring at her: Gwen and Helin in jealousy, the knights she had shut down in anger. Others were fascinated with her to say the least. She tried her best to smile at Alec's jokes as he boasted with his friends and relived the day. She sipped her ale, grazed at her food, and finally it was time to return to the tents. With Alec's arm around her, he steered her down the path to the temporary tent city that had popped up during the day. His tent, big enough for four people and all their gear, was green and black striped. It had been patched several times, but it was fine enough to hide just how poor Alec was back at his manor. Appearances for the tourneys were more important. Other drunken knights were also pulling their ladies down from the manor with them to their tents. As they walked through the makeshift city, occasional giggles and whispers could be heard. Ella steeled herself. She had to keep acting until they were in that tent. But would Alec hold his end of the deal at that point? Would he try to take things further? Did he remember she was only acting?

Pulled from her thoughts as they stopped outside the tent flap, Ella looked up to see Alec very close to her, his face a mere breath from hers. He cupped her face in his hands, gently. She felt the panic flash through her body but did not pull away. She closed her eyes, knowing what he wanted as the last part of their show, willing it to be over.

And she felt his lips on hers. Gently. Surprisingly so. Coaxing. Patient.

She softened the pursed lock of her mouth and it opened, so slightly. He stopped. She opened her eyes. His thumb stroked her cheek, then he leaned in again. She knew she should tell him to stop. That they had acted enough. But this time her lips followed his. A tremor shot through her, an ache deep in her belly. A feeling she had never felt.

Silently, without losing his grip on her or her lips, Alec pushed the tent flap back and pulled her inside. As the flap closed behind them, she pulled back and opened her eyes. A dim candle lantern shone in the darkness of the tent. On the far side, Wilfred quickly got up out of his pallet bed and exited through the opening in the back of the tent. They were alone.

"I knew you wouldn't resist me for long," Alec huskily whispered in her ear. His hand traced a stray piece of her dark hair and tucked it behind her ear.

Ella shivered. She took a step back. Then another. With a shaky breath, she stared at the ground as she answered, "We have put on a great show today, Sir Alec." Then she looked up into his eyes. "No more."

Alec simply stared at her for a long moment. Quietly, somewhat coldly, he said, "No one would stop me. No one will protect you."

Ella did not reply. She merely kept his gaze.

"I guess that's what Lezay thought too, isn't it?" he paused. Then to himself, he asked, "What did he do to you?"

With a sigh, Alec turned away from her. He pulled off his boots and tunic and flopped down on one of the pallets. There were four set up now that she looked around. He nodded toward a pallet across the tent from him. "Wilfred set you up over there."

And that was the end of it.

What had he done to her? Ella thought as she lay on her pallet. What could one man do to make her cower so, to be so needily reliant on Alec, a stranger? For true, as much as he had stirred feeling in her this night, she knew deep down he was only trying to seduce her. And she knew Alec would eventually tire of the games. What then? Would she run again? Hide? Change her identity and live in fear year after year? Alone? Why keep going through all this? What had he *done* to her?

Her mind had protected itself, hiding those horrible memories deep down that she did not have to replay them every hour of every day. It was how she survived, focusing on the day-to-day tasks at hand. When the past surfaced, she forced it down. Now, as she lay there sleepless, it all threatened to burst forth. Was it better to visit those memories at night or by day? With a friend or alone? In suppressing so much for so many years, Ella knew she was running from an unnamed monster. How could she move on, conquer her past, if she could not face it full on in all its ugliness? She had to. She had put it off long enough. But now was not the time, not in a tent full of men, surrounded by dozens more. *Soon*, she promised herself. As sleep finally claimed her, she wondered if by facing her past, she could one day pick up enough pieces to be happy, perhaps even to love.

Chapter Six

With the first tournament deemed a success, Alec brought her to every one he was invited to in the month that followed. He kept a full schedule through June, barely returning to the manor. They camped in the big tent in the yards of many manors and cities across England. Lance was Alec's main squire, with Wilfred trailing along tending to Alec's horse and setting up the tent. Lance and Wilfred knew that their master's relationship with "Ella" was complicated, and though they all shared the tent at night, they were careful to steer clear of her and to leave them alone together as often as they could. Particularly after Alec's victories.

And Ella was quite the actress.

Most places the scenes played out the same. She would give Alec her token, a few strangers would try to pledge their victories to her, and she would refuse to allow them. It had everyone talking. No unwed, low-born woman refused a knight's attention . . .especially the successful ones, of which there were a few. True, Alec was not completely undefeated in all his events, and when he lost, the victors took a sharp dislike to Ella following "the loser" back to his tent like a puppy.

The other women weren't quite sure what to think of her, so making friends was no easy feat. She didn't dare sit near Gwen again. Gwen and Helin were giving her a cold shoulder. At other manors, no matter where she sat, the ladies avoided her. She was not quite a whore, but certainly not a reputable woman, not a common village girl, not a noble lady. She was a unique class of her own, and with that she found herself lingering at the end of the list with the squires more than with the spectators.

"Bloody Hell!" Alec fumed and threw his cracked shield into the dirt at a manor outside London. A hot summer wind seemed to rise up from beneath their feet like a fire from Hades. Ella cautiously stooped to pick up the shield, studying the splintered wood beneath the battered, hard-boiled leather. She turned back to the devil before her, eyes wide.

"I'm not his bloody anvil!" Alec scowled and massaged his forearms as he paced restlessly on the edge of the tournament field.

"Who is he?" Wilfred asked.

"Bloody Lord something. Bloody tree for a crest. Who makes a tree their damn crest?" Alec spun to Ella. "You know crests. Who has a tree?"

"I . . . I didn't see his tunic or shield up close. A lot of men have blue and silver colors. And with the crowd cheering I couldn't hear the herald . . ."

"Damn bloody tournament champion he'll be, and we won't even know his name."

"He's good," Ella said absentmindedly, looking across the field to where the blue and silver tunicked knight was calmly consulting his squire. And he *was* good. The newcomer had put Alec in the dust of the sword arena faster than any other knight she'd seen yet. His style was familiar, but she couldn't place it. She'd probably seen him years ago at another tournament.

"Remember what knight you're cheering for today, *darling*," Alec growled.

"You'll get him in the joust," Lance encouraged, approaching with Alec's destrier Ches.

Alec frowned as he took the reins and vaulted into the saddle. He caught Ella's eye, and she wordlessly looked away. They all knew that Alec had finally met his equal. And the joust was not his best event.

A few hours later, Ella was seated beside a grim-faced Alec as he nursed his wounds with a tall mug of ale in the great hall. Ella sat straight-backed, her fingers near white as they clutched her mug.

Two noble ladies walked past their table, frowning down on her, noses pointed in the air. Ella looked away, only to fall into the intense gaze of an older knight as he stood among his friends. He made no move to look away, and she watched his bristled lips crack into a leer. She shifted uncomfortably and looked away. Lezay had a beard like that, long and unkempt.

"Alec," she whispered quietly. "How late are you going to stay tonight?"

Alec poured himself another mug of ale, his hands as steady as they'd been the first pour, now several hours past. He wordlessly toasted her, his face still gloomy, and turned back to his quiet conversation with the man next to him.

Ella glanced back to the man along the wall, who still stared. She glared at him, then abruptly stood. "I'm going to get some air." Alec caught her wrist, eyeing her speculatively. She met his eye, and he allowed her to pull away.

"Don't be long."

Ella gave him a single nod and quickly stepped out of the hall.

In the passage beyond, drunken men still lingered. Some had already claimed their amours for the evening. Ella gave them a wide berth. One squire was passed out on a bench, a bottle dangling from his fingertips, its contents mostly spreading across the floor. A solitary man stumbled toward her.

"Heeey, mi lady. You look so purdy 'night," he slurred.

She ignored him.

The man from the hall stepped in front of her, forcing her to catch his gaze. She tried to duck her head and step around him, but he cut her off. She held her ground and glared. It had been a long day, and she was in no mood for drunken knights.

"Why Alec?" he drawled, crossing his arms.

Ella wordlessly met his gaze, unwilling to give him even the satisfaction of conversation. After a long minute, the man softened his expression and laughed, stepping aside.

"English Winter . . ." he chuckled to himself. "I'm surprised Sir Alec doesn't have frostbite."

Ella pushed past him and up the stairwell to the battlement, pushing through the heavy door. She breathed a sigh of relief. The wall was empty but for the two solitary watchmen at the far corners. She walked to the edge and leaned on the corniced stonework, watching the stars twinkle as a distant storm flashed on the horizon. The breeze was a welcome reprieve from the hot day.

Ella's hands trembled as an unbidden wave of emotion washed over her. It had been an exhausting day. Between the stares of the knights, the whispers of the women, and Alec's sour mood, it had been more work than usual to hold her place at Alec's side. She'd distracted herself by watching the crowd, which had worked until she'd spotted one of the knights greet his wife and child between events. The girl was maybe four, dressed regally, her little hands clapping as she cheered for her father. Her beautiful mother, though not as fair as Lady Gwen, had beamed at her husband, occasionally leaning over to point something out to the little girl.

As happy as the scene was, it had yanked at Ella's heart harder than the whispers of her peers. She had once been like that little girl, standing at the rail at a tournament, cheering for her father on his big black horse. Her mother had stood tall at his side in a flowing, elaborate gown more detailed than the one she herself now wore, smiling at her husband with a love so bright Ella often thought she had imagined it. It was so long ago, she somehow had started letting herself forget. She was so young when they died. How different her life would have been had they lived. Not just a life away from the cruelties of her guardian Uncle Montag and Sir Lezay, but a life away from the peasant labor she had slaved away at since she was five years old.

Now, looking out across that empty field, she reminded herself of who she was. She was not a blacksmith's daughter. Nor just the runaway wife of a knight. She was a blood-born equal of the ladies like Gwen. She was the daughter of the great knight Sir Enric de Levan d'Aquitaine and Lady Igraine d'Alsace. She was nobility in her own right and the deeded heiress of an estate in Aquitaine she had not seen in more than a decade.

Faint sounds of merrymaking could still be heard from the hall. A man and drunk maid laughed off into the darkness. The warm summer breeze swept a wisp of hair across Ella's eyes, and she brushed it back behind her ear, resting her hand on her cheek, her other arm across her chest. Her hand closed around the pewter band on its chain around her neck. It was her father's. Emblazoned in the plain pewter was an elaborate design of three discs wreathed in tendrils of fire that danced along the band: the Levan crest. He had been a poor knight, trying to rise in station by valor to earn the respect of his wealthy-born wife's family. He had failed.

She put her head in her hands and took a steadying breath.

Emotionless. Cold. Like the English Winter. That was her. Not this trembling, embarrassing fool. Her mother would never have tolerated it.

Ella straightened instantly. Her mother had been a master of her emotions. Ella had seen many times over her first five years the mask the Lady Igraine could click over her countenance. There was the smiling face for tournaments, often real but not always. There was the ladylike face she wore when dealing with matters of the estate: regal, confident, even though Ella had seen her shaking with emotion after some meetings. Then there was the brave face she'd worn for Ella when she'd told Ella her father was dead. And the even braver face she'd worn as she died, ordering Ella to be brave and act like a lady and manage the estate like she'd been taught.

Ella shook her head. No five-year-old could manage an estate. No five-year-old could pretend to know better than a seasoned lord, a victorious battle-hardened grown man. She didn't stand a chance asserting herself to her Uncle Montag. And he'd made sure she knew her place quickly, as a servant.

Another laugh echoed up to her from the hall. Ella remembered how jovial her Uncle Montag had been as he returned from tournaments. If he won at least. In the weeks he lost, he became unbearable, terrorizing the household with demands and complaints no matter how hard they tried. As a child she had learned quickly to hide. She took her escapes with her older cousin Raoul and his friend as often as she could. Though itself forbidden, the comradery had given Ella the skills she'd later used to survive.

Footsteps approached from the wooden steps leading to the top of the stone battlement where Ella stood. She crossed her arms and continued to stare out into the countryside, still frowning slightly at the unbidden memory of her later childhood.

"Beautiful night, isn't it, miss?" a voice gently said next to her. She felt the heat from the man's body as he stood looking out over the wall beside her. His musky scent, intriguingly masked by notes of evergreen and spice, drifted faintly on the wind. Too close.

She glanced up. An arm's length away stood a knight dressed in a tunic with a silver tree with two rings entwined beneath: the tournament champion. "Yes, it is," she said as her eyes were drawn to his. She squinted a little; the feeling transmitted was not unfamiliar. His face was familiar somehow, too. His brow furrowed as he looked down into her eyes.

"What's your name?" he asked.

"Ella," she said without hesitation.

"Ah, Sir Alec's maid."

"Yes, sir," she said and broke the gaze at the tone of scorn in his voice. Whether it be for her or for Alec himself, she couldn't tell. She glanced again at his tunic, the crest jarring her memory but from where? She turned back to the courtyard and absently picked at the loose pieces of gravel in the stonework. He didn't leave, but stepped up to the wall beside her, still an armlength away. After a silence she said, "Grand win today, sir. In the tourney."

"Ah, thank you."

"Have you seen battle yet?"

"Yes."

"I thought as much. You don't fight like this is just a game."

"I was with King Richard during his last trip to the Holy Land. Thankfully I was not with them when he was captured. I'm in London for a few months helping him raise funds for Normandy, then I will return."

"Ah."

After another silence, Ella still avoiding his watchful eye, he spoke. "You are unlike the other maids." She stifled a laugh. "No, really. You show no interest in the knights, though they kneel before you. All but Sir Alec that is of course. I watched some great men pledge their victories and hearts to you today, and you stomped them into the mud."

Ella started to protest, but he cut her off.

"We aren't so different you know. I, too, think it's a bit of a ridiculous tradition, pledging your heart to someone different every event. I think it's better to just choose one and be faithful. From the talk I hear, it seems that's how you feel about Sir Alec."

Ella was silent.

"May I ask you a personal question, my lady?" the man inquired gently.

Ella started a little at the formal title. She looked at him carefully. "I will not promise to answer."

They caught each other's eyes again. "You are not Alec's mistress as he so says, are you?"

Ella stayed silent and looked away. He nodded at her silent answer.

"But you are from France, as he says?"

"He says that?"

"He says you are from Brittany, yes."

"Oh." She laughed. "Yes".

The knight raised an eyebrow. "You are not from Brittany."

"Yes, I am".

"No, you're not." Ella's heart skipped a beat. He leaned close enough that only she could hear, though there was no one around. "Your name is Lady Eleanor de Levan d'Aquitaine, but you are from Les Vosges in Alsace."

The scene before her blurred as her panic rose. "You know. He told you. It was for nothing . . . nothing!" She gripped the wall in front of her, fighting the blackness that encroached on her field of vision. She was suddenly hot and very nauseous.

"Eleanor, no. Listen. I know you. You know me. Elle, I was your friend once. And a friend of your cousin Raoul. You know me. Edmond de Fougères."

"*Elle,*" she mouthed as recognition fully sunk in. The dark-haired friend of her youth. *Edmond de Fougères.* But he had left her! *Elle.* He once called her "girl" as a way to mock; only years later had it turned into a term of endearment. *Edmond.* Here. Now. Unmistakable recognition now sunk in. The silver tree with rings. Oh, she had searched for that mark, near a decade ago. Had she blocked that much out from those years that she had not recognized it? Ella saw his eyes quite clearly once more before stars started flashing in her own eyes, blinding her, making the earth sway. And she fell. He caught her in mid-air.

The cold battlement wall behind her reminded Ella of where she was. The world was still spinning, and she felt sick. Her head felt numb and distant, as if it had flown away on the wings of birds. A hand touched her knee, which she pulled up to her chest, curled with her back to the wall in an upright ball.

"Edmond de Fougères," she breathed and squeezed her eyes shut tight. "Impossible. Simply impossible."

"No, Elle."

"Oh, God, that name!"

"I'm sorry, do you wish me to not use it?"

"No! I mean yes. It's fine," her eyes flew open. "It is what you've always called me."

The memories flooded her vision. She had begged her older cousin Raoul for years to let her tag along as he and Montag's squire, Edmond, rode and practiced and played. After many fights, the boys had finally been convinced she was tough enough, fun enough, to be included. Raoul and Edmond were her best friends. If they had not taught her to wield a knife, she'd be dead now. They'd called her "Girl" to make fun of her. Another memory burned of a quick kiss in the woods, two adolescents experimenting.

Did he remember? He'd called her Elle then too, but with a different meaning.

Ella stared into Edmond's eyes again, searching, as the two sat on that battlement wall, then abruptly forced herself to her feet, one arm over her stomach as it threatened to hurl.

"Your same determination, I see," he observed.

"You have no idea. What happened to you, Edmond?" she bombarded him. "C'est combien d'ans, Edmond? Neuf? Nine years!" She stared at him, her childhood friend turning into a man before her eyes as she carefully picked out the familiar features she of all people should have recognized sooner. "You have a beard," she stated bluntly, eyeing his short scruff.

He chuckled. "Yes, I have had a beard for some time now. And you know what happened. Crusades, war, diseases, and things no woman should have to hear about. I thought I was long forgotten, so forgive me for not hunting you out in my spare time. Last I heard you had married Sir Lezay."

"I did."

"You did? Eleanor, how could you agree to such a thing? Beyond appearances, have you any idea who he is?"

"Edmond, have you noticed who I am with? Have you noticed my reputation as a pretty little whore? Do I appear to you to be the wife of a lord?"

"No, Elle. At least not the wife of that one. And you're not a—what are you to Alec?"

"I did not realize I was that convincing of an actress. But then again I guess I'm not, since you figured me out by a ten-minute conversation." She scowled.

Quietly Edmond replied, "Actually, I recognized you this morning, before the tourney even started. You've grown up, but I could never forget your face. You were a pretty girl then, but now . . . Eleanor you truly are gorgeous."

Despite having heard that claim by several men throughout the day, something in how Edmond said it made her believe him. She blushed, glad he couldn't see it in the dark.

"I left him the night we were married," she blurted, watching Edmond's surprised expression. She asked cautiously, "Lezay. Have you seen him in recent years?"

"Yes."

She shuddered involuntarily.

When Edmond's eyebrows went up in surprise, she turned away. A flush of shame rose in her cheeks. She knew full well how it sounded when she told people she left her husband on her wedding night, which was why she didn't tell anyone. She should have been grateful for a wealthy husband, an opportunity to get away from Uncle Montag's enslavement and be a lady. There was so much more to her story.

A single finger on her arm brought Ella's attention back to Edmond. "What happened?" he ventured.

A slightly panicked look flitted across Ella's face. "I . . . I can't . . . not here . . . yet." Her mind raced again as she looked into his face. It really had been quite a long time. His strong features and deep brown eyes still commanded the same attention, but the sparkle that had once flashed from him, the willingness to jest, was hidden. The wars had taken their toll. And he was only halfway into his twenties. She imagined her own reflection looked similar in his eyes. She was far from the girl she had been those years ago.

The entrance of a knight to the courtyards below caught their attention. As Edmond turned back to her, she looked deep into his eyes as they danced with the fire of the torches lighting the courtyard. He did not avoid her gaze. He did not even ask her what she looked for. He gave it. "I am glad to see you," she whispered and smiled, the first real one in a long while.

With the scrape of a sword scabbard against the stone battlements, a young watchman climbed onto the wall, dutifully reporting for his shift. Ella stepped away silently, head bowed as was proper.

"Elle," she heard Edmond say, but his words trailed away when she did not slow. She couldn't. He was too familiar, evoked too many memories. True, it had been a long time and they both had changed, but something about him drew her like it had when she was a mere girl . . .when she was "Elle".

Chapter Seven

*G*o *back to being Ella,* she told herself as she entered
the hall, body and mind still reeling. Alec would
expect a final appearance with her. If it was not granted,
he would tell or in his drunken stupor, slip on the truth.

"Ella!" shouted Alec from far down the hall. "Come, my
darling, come! These fellows here tell of wives as wondrous
storytellers. You can best them all, I'm sure! Create a tale
for our a'listening ears."

Ella stiffened with worry but did not allow it to show on
her face. He was certainly in a better mood. Was he actually
drunk? "My lord, I fear you have had a bit too much ale
for the night. You should retire. A storyteller or wife I am
not."

"No, no, Ella. I'm fine. We have the whole night before
us! Tell us something of home."

Ella frowned. "Not much to tell about Neroche." The
men burst into laughter at her joke.

Alec laughed, too, but shot her an intense look of warning. He was not half as drunk as he appeared. He was using her as his puppet, thus she had no choice but to act.

"Surely my lord, why would you want a story from me?"

"Because you are my pretty little maid." He caught her around her waist and pulled her onto his lap. The men laughed again, but Alec maintained his mischievous gaze with Ella.

"Well, then, let me think," she said, glaring discreetly. "Really, I don't . . ." she paused as she noticed Edmond enter at the far end of the hall. "Sir, I do have the perfect story, but it is not of this country. May I tell it?"

Alec inclined his head in cautious agreement.

"Oh, my lords, you shall adore this tale. Where to start, oh, yes," Ella pulled away from Alec to stand behind him, grasping his chair. "In the far realm of Tuscany, maybe a century past now, there was a knight, much like yourselves, who struck fear into the hearts of all opponents in the tourneys. When a neighboring vassal challenged this knight's elderly father, what choice did she have but to take his place on the tilting field?" She paused to let her words sink in.

"Wait, *she*?" one man asked.

"No, you idiot, you're too drunk. Get your ears checked man! Let the lady tell the story," growled another.

Ella caught a warning glance from Alec but continued on. "*She* took up her father's spear, donned his armor, and met the challenger in a joust. And yes, sirs, I mean *she*. Her name was Adelaide of Tuscany."

"Some bloody story she tells, Alec!" the first man protested.

"Don't you at least want to know how the story ends?" Ella asked.

"She gets killed, of course," chimed in a third listener.

"No!" Ella exclaimed, not coming out of character. "Quite the contrary. Adelaide took up the lance, rode her stallion right against the challenger, whose name history does not even remember. Because *she won*. She laid that arrogant swine right into the dirt, ripped off her helm, revealing the long golden hair that hung to her waist. It swirled around her in the wind like a halo of golden fire as she, on her great horse, stood over the shamed man. After that, many more contested her father, and she met every one of them. She defended her family and her lands for decades to come, the chevaleresse."

The knights and lords looked silently at each other. Their drinking had made them dizzy and giddy. They could not think.

"Fame may be won by the strength of your arm, pleasure by the wit of your tongue, and favor by the number of men you kill in battle. But none of these things will ever put you into *legend*. Adelaide was a mere woman, and her name lives on in legend by her deeds, as she showed courage when many would expect her to cower. You laugh, sir." Ella glared at the man who had commented. "What have *you* done worthy of memory? What historian has taken note of you? Honor, my lords, is something we all should strive for. It is the one thing we can pass on to our children."

Alec reached up and clasped her hand, smiling wickedly. She ignored him, locking eyes with Edmond, who had seated himself with the others at the far end of the table. The questioning look he shot her made her skin burn. He remembered some things, too, then. She broke away from both men and went on. "I am not sure how much of a story that was, my lords. But it is a tale that I am sure will make its way into the annals centuries from now."

The knights were silent in thought, then one started laughing. "A female knight. What a sense of humor your girl has, Alec," He laughed. Then all the men started laughing at her, and the rowdiness resumed. Ella gritted her teeth in silence.

"Come," Alec whispered in her ear as he rose, leading her away, an arm around her thin waist. Ella didn't even risk a glance at Edmond, following without protest. Once they were out of sight of all, she pulled away from him.

"I did not agree to play the role of your joker," she fumed under her breath as they strode to the tent. She set a quick pace in her fury, but Alec's long stride kept up easily.

"It was a bit of a test. How much will you tolerate me doing before you decide your secret is not so important to you?" Alec asked. Within a few seconds Ella judged he was completely sober. He continued, "From what I gathered tonight, you'd do just about anything."

"What do you have left to do to me? What's next?" she seethed. "I have lost the few friends, nay, acquaintances I had for this . . . act! I have given up my reputation as an honorable woman. My pride. I have worked your manor like a slave. I have endured the jests of your friends, the sneers of my peers. You though, *you* have gained in popularity. Face it, you are invited to more tourneys now than you ever were, because people want to see *me*. Our reputation as a couple is spreading like wildfire. They invite *you* to see *us*, and yes, it is your own skill that lets you win the prize purses, but you are getting wealthy by *using me*. All I ask is your silence and to let my past be obscure for as long as it can. What more do you want from me?"

"It doesn't take much creativity to come up with something."

"I thought there was more to this arrangement than just me owing you for your silence. I thought you too were against Lezay. Why don't you tell me what your plan is? Or is it merely to bed me and hand me back to him?"

Alec tightened his jaw and remained silent.

She continued, her voice low and furious. "Sir, you of all those in that room should have listened to my story tonight. A woman with nothing to lose can do *anything*. I will see you in the morning." She turned and walked ahead of him, her head high.

"Think on my question, Ella. What is your secret worth to you? You know not when you will need an answer."

Chapter Eight

As Ella listened to the snores of Alec and Lance, she pulled the covers tighter under her chin. Her mind refused to quiet, her thoughts bouncing from anger at Alec to fear of his question, to joy that she had seen Edmond to sadness at all the long-forgotten memories that now surfaced. If Wilfred had been along, he intuitively would have distracted her with other conversation, but he was back at Neroche. She rolled again on the hard ground.

How could Edmond think she had willingly married Lezay? If only he knew what Lezay, and by default Montag, had done to her. Maybe he did need to know. If he had heard of Lezay's search for her, like Alec had, he should know her side of the story. Perhaps he could set it right.

She shivered. By night or by day? With a friend or alone?

It was time. If Edmond would listen, her story would be told. She had only to find him.

Quietly, she rose from her blankets and tiptoed out of the tent. It was the darkest hours of the night, with a half moon and stars to guide her. She lit no lamp. She did not want to be a solitary woman among this crowd tonight.

Luck was with her, and she found Edmond's tent quickly, just a few away from her own. It was unmistakable, with the silver tree and rings embroidered on the sides. Edmond was just now headed to it from the manor. His eyes widened in surprise.

"You all right?" he whispered.

"Can't sleep." She studied his reactions in the moonlight, doubting her decision.

"Me either." Edmond sighed, "I can't believe we finally meet again. I can't get our conversation off my mind. I wish you could explain more, but I understand if you can't."

"Come with me?" Her eyes pleaded. Edmond rested his hand on the hilt of his sword in thoughtful habit, questions in his eyes. With a glance around, he motioned for her to lead the way.

And lead she did. As yet another secret, this wasn't her first time to this manor. Years before she had been here and found her own quiet spot in the woods. And that is where she led him now. The path was still there, barely visible in the moonlight. The little clearing wasn't far in, but it was very secluded. A creek gurgled nearby, the water sparkling in the dim light. She motioned for Edmond to sit on a fallen log, and he did so. She started pacing in front of him.

She sat down next to him, then stood up and paced again. "I'm sorry. I'm a fool to keep you up. I'm sure you have to leave early in the morning."

"Eleanor, it's fine. What's wrong? Did something happen with you and Alec?" Edmond asked.

"No! Well, at least nothing beyond the usual." She paused. "I'm going to need to figure out how much my secret is worth."

Edmond waited for her to explain.

"Ugh, God, where do I start?" She pulled her hair back in frustration.

"How about you tell me what you are to Alec? You're not his mistress or his wife or his maid. What the hell are you doing with him?"

"He knows about Lezay," she started. "He threatened to turn me over to him. For his silence, I agreed to *pretend* to be his mistress as . . . a trophy. I work as a maid at the manor, too, when we're there. He has something against Lezay himself. He agreed to protect me once Lezay found out, which eventually I suppose he will. Especially since I'm apparently becoming famous. I didn't think this would ever happen! I thought this whole thing would buy me time until I could figure something else out. Maybe move again. I don't know."

"You are *quite* a big deal. I heard about you even in London. Not by name of course."

"I know, I know. But now I *can't* leave Alec, or he really will start talking. But I do think he feels . . . something . . . for me. I think he actually *would* try to protect me from Lezay."

"Eleanor, he's a man. Whatever game you are playing, whatever line you are walking, he's not one to be denied what he wants forever. He might protect you from Lezay. I know many men that would be that protective of someone they are very . . . *close* to."

"Are you telling me to sleep with him?" Her eyes went wide in the moonlight.

"No! I guess I'm implying you'd have to marry him to get that kind of dedi . . ." his voice trailed. "Wait, you aren't sleeping with him?" Edmond's eyebrows shot up and his eyes widened.

Ella's shoulders slumped as she sat on the log next to him again. She shook her head. "I can't. I just can't."

Edmond let out a low whistle. "Well woman, you have the whole world caught up in this charade. Alec most of all. You've got some powerful hold over him, that's for sure. And all this so Alec doesn't tell Lezay where you are?"

She nodded.

"So why are you so afraid of Lezay? Why did you marry him if you were so afraid of him?"

She took a deep breath. "I wasn't given a choice."

Edmond waited patiently.

"It was eight years ago. I was fourteen. Raoul tried to intervene when he heard but . . . he's no match against my uncle." Ella took another deep breath. "Montag knew the manor folk were starting to disobey him in favor of me. It started with you and Raoul. You know Montag hated that we spent any time together. You know he wanted me completely isolated. After others saw what we did though, hunting and playing like the children we were, they realized I wasn't a crazy invalid like Montag wanted people to believe. They started treating me like I was . . . normal. I made friends. Madame Brigitte the cook, Gustave the guard, Michel the horsemaster. When you and Raoul started to include me in those silly childhood adventures, it changed everything.

"Well, Montag hated it of course. I've been trying for years to understand him, and I think he felt that people being kind to me somehow undermined his own power. I was a child! But suddenly I was even more of a problem than just being an extra mouth to feed. What better way to get rid of me than to marry me off? You know him, couldn't just hand me off to some random peasant tradesman and get me out of sight. I needed someone *special*. Someone who was his ally to assure I would be controlled. And Lezay had just had another wife die."

"Another?" Edmond prompted.

"I am wife number six. The rest are dead."

"From?"

"Seems suspicious, doesn't it? I've been told childbirth, but Lezay has no children."

They were quiet a moment.

"Anyway," she continued, "I was pushed to the altar that day. They cleaned me up and everything. I refused to speak the vows, so the priest just skipped that part and pronounced us man and wife."

She hesitated, ready to answer another question that Edmond hadn't even asked. "No, I didn't kick and scream and fight. What was the point? No one would have defended me from the punishment *that* would have warranted, not in a room full of men that 'owned' me. So I stood there. I kept silent as my only protest. And then I obediently followed Lezay to our wedding bed."

A shudder ran through her, and suddenly she couldn't stand to be close to Edmond. She stood again and paced in front of him. With her eyes closed in the night, everything was black. But it didn't blur the images that burned her eyelids. She continued, determined to finish the tale in all its ugliness. "He barely had the door shut when he literally ripped off my gown. His hands were unwashed. He smelled almost unbearable. Body odor and onions and manure . . . I've never smelled another like him. He's probably never bathed in his life. So there I was, fourteen, barely a woman, fully a virgin, naked in front of the worst pig of a man you can imagine. You know he's over fifty?"

Edmond didn't respond.

"My *plan* had been to not let it get that far. My *plan* was to use my father's dagger and gut him like a pig with his pants down. I was bold in those days. And so ignorant. I thought it would be like when you and Raoul let me practice sword fighting with you. In reality, I didn't even have a chance to reach for the dagger, which was hidden in the folds of my gown. He was so fast, so strong . . ."

She was silent a moment, steadying herself. "I haven't told this to anyone. Not one other soul." She took a shaky breath. "I had imagined what would happen if it got that far. I knew about the birds and the bees; the older girls talked. They always giggled about it. I knew already that when he . . . that I wouldn't giggle about it. But I'd at least hoped that if it got to that point it wouldn't hurt too bad." A tear leaked from the corner of her eye unnoticed. But her voice was still steady. "I didn't fight him, not once he already had me on the bed. I didn't know what to do, not without the dagger. Still, he was not gentle." She paused in the telling, reliving what she could not put words to. The stabbing pain as his cock ripped her maidenhead and slammed against her womb. The ache in her arms as he pinned them to the bed. His leering taunts that she wasn't good enough, pretty enough, even as he grunted with pleasure while deep within her. "And it was not short." She clutched a fist to her womb. Frustrated that he did not have her squealing, Lezay had flipped her around and taken her in an even more sensitive place. That had done the trick all right. "He did things to me I didn't know could hurt like that without leaving scars. He reduced me to begging for him to stop, but of course he didn't. He loved my pain, my tears."

Ella let out a sob, catching herself and Edmond off guard. She crumbled to her knees in the forest earth, her head in her hands, her shoulders shaking. Edmond jumped to his feet and knelt beside her, pulling her into his chest as his strong arms held her. She melted into him and cried, letting the sobs shake her for the first time since the incident. She let the pain roll through her until she gagged and gasped for air, then slowly started to steady herself. She sat up again, pulling away from Edmond slightly and wiping her eyes. Then, still kneeling there with him in the middle of the forest, she continued.

"When he was finished, he just rolled off me and fell asleep. I couldn't move for the longest time. Every part of me ached. The door was right there, closed but unlocked, and I couldn't make myself move to it. I didn't know what to do. I was his wife. He had every right to do what he did. There was no one in the entire castle that had come to help me while I lay there screaming. None of my friends. Certainly not my uncle. And I know, it's stupid, everyone has sex, and I suppose I should be grateful it was only by him and not by five men after invaders won the manor. I know that's what they do to the women they find. Maybe I'm weak, maybe I'm making a big deal out of—"

"That is not what intercourse should be like. Even in arranged marriages, that is not what the marital bed should be like," Edmond interrupted. "Lezay is a complete pig."

Ella stared into his eyes. "I hope you're right." She suddenly rose back to her feet, and he rose with her. He watched as she started pacing again.

"Well, after I was done feeling sorry for myself, I realized that if I didn't do something, it was going to happen again, probably as soon as he woke up. And every night thereafter, till death do us part. I . . . I couldn't. So I slowly went to get out of bed. He woke and caught my arm. I made the excuse that I wanted to use the chamber pot, and he let me go and closed his eyes again. I got the dagger, but I knew he was paying attention to what I did, so I . . . like an idiot I laid back down next to him." She chuckled coldly. "I don't know what I thought I was going to do. Roll over and plunge the knife into his belly? Why didn't I just run then? He must have heard the fear and anticipation in my breathing, and he rolled back on top of me and pinned my wrists quicker than I could move. 'And here I thought Montag a fool to warn me about you,' he said.

"But I was braver this time. I flipped the blade in my hand and stabbed his wrist. We were covered in blood as he jumped off of me. I made a dash for the door but . . . as you know, Lezay is a lethal warrior. He had his sword by then and blocked me. Actually had me backed up to the door, the blade at my gut. I thought for sure he would kill me." Her voice trailed off.

"Remember that trick Raoul used to do when you cornered him? How he'd drop his hand, feign defeat, then with his hand down low he could knock a low sword away and slash in? He got cut so many times doing it. Montag always would tell him he'd be killed in real life if he did something so stupid with a real knight."

"That's what you did?" Edmond asked.

"Yes. And it worked about as well as it did for Raoul all those times." Her hand went instinctively to the scar on her abdomen. "I got cut, but obviously I survived. He was cut worse. Did it scar?" She motioned to her left cheekbone, indicating Lezay's cut.

"You did that?" Edmond asked, incredulous. "He looks like he almost lost an eye."

"I had hoped he did." She frowned. "It was enough that I got through the door at my back. I ran naked through the castle. I passed Raoul . . . I think he did something to stall Lezay because I had enough time to steal a shirt and breeches from the wash pile. Remember Old Michel, the stable boss? He threw a saddle on Montag's destrier faster than lightning and threw me up there. He's the real reason I got away. Of course, once *Lezay* started screaming, Montag came running. But by then I was on the fastest horse in the stable and riding for my life.

"I ran that poor horse into the ground. Stopped at a convent before dawn, where the nuns patched me up as best they could in an hour. Better clothes, bandages for the cut, water, food. They were so kind, so sympathetic. They told me I could stay and become one of them. Several among them were there because they had been in my same situation. But I've been cloistered enough in my life. It was time to be free, even if I was running. Even if I've been hiding since. At least it's by my choice! I left the destrier there and took the strongest little horse they could offer me. We cut up into the mountains, into the thick of the forests, heading west. The agony of that ride! I didn't stop until I was in Normandy. I would have looked for you, but . . ."

"But I was in England." Edmond finished for her, his brow furrowed. "You came to find me? Why?"

"Where else could I go? You were a good friend. I haven't had many of those in my life. It didn't matter since you weren't there. Probably better that way. Montag probably would have looked there for me."

"He did actually. My father said he visited not long after all this must have happened. He didn't say why though. Lezay has only been more vocal about your 'kidnap' the last year or two."

"So they are more actively looking for me now than then. That must be why after all these years of silence, suddenly Alec met Lezay. Why now?"

"I don't think they ever stopped looking, Eleanor." Her blood chilled. "He's just getting a bit more determined. And creative. I really thought you'd married willingly by how he talks." Edmond shook his head. "He had a troubadour write a song about your love, and it's spread across France."

"Bastard."

"I know that now," Edmond replied. He took a deep breath. "Eleanor, I am so sorry for all you have been through. I am sorry I believed Lezay. I am sorry I did not keep track of you after I returned home to Le Fougères."

"No, don't apologize. How could you possibly have known?" Ella answered. "I didn't tell you all this for sympathy. I just needed . . . I needed just one person to know. This has been eating at me for years. It has consumed me like a poison, ever more as I try to forget it."

"Well, let me warn you then. You are playing a very dangerous game with Alec. He doesn't know any of this?" Edmond asked.

"Only that Lezay is looking for me."

"You need to find out what Alec has against Lezay. It will solidify your partnership with him in this without putting the pressure on you . . . for other things. Because you *will* need him to protect you. Lezay is not going to find you years from now. With the talk you two have stirred up, I would say you have months before he gets curious and starts competing in English tourneys. Maybe

by next spring if things have quieted down in France."
Remorsefully he said, "I would take you with me if I
wouldn't be dropping you off at Lezay's doorstep and
leaving to fight with King Richard."

"You think he will come that soon?" she asked.

"I do. Elle, I wish I could do more for you. I will find
a way to do whatever I can. If I hear news about him,
particularly about him coming to England, I will send you
a warning. I hope to come back in spring myself. I will
bring you news."

"Thank you," Ella said softly. Then she threw her arms
around him and hugged him.

He held her tight and kissed her forehead, whispering in
her ear, "Just so you know, not all men are like that. Love
can be a beautiful thing. Maybe Alec isn't the one to show
you. Maybe he is. But you deserve to be shown love in all
the tenderness and pleasure it can be." He squeezed her a
little tighter and just held her there in the moonlit clearing
as long as she would let him.

"I feel like I'm holding fire," Edmond whispered into
her hair. "You always were like that, Elle. So brave. And
despite what you've been through, it's still there."

Ella kept her face against his chest, breathing him in. It
was the closest she had been to a man in years; close enough
to hear his heartbeat. For whatever reason, Edmond did
not scare her. He never had. But he had left once before, as
he admittedly would again. Slowly she pulled away.

Edmond's grip tightened a moment, then eased. He looked conflicted.

That gave her some comfort. It should be difficult for him to tell her to put her faith, maybe even her heart, in another man's hands.

Chapter Nine

Alec finally gave them all a break from tournaments. Maybe it was what Ella had said about him only being invited because of her. Maybe he just wanted a break himself. Or maybe he actually needed to manage the land he was steward of. But they were home, at Castle Neroche. Ella was back in her grunge clothes, working like a serf.

Hope had been renewed in Ella since she had met Edmond. Someone out there knew her story and was keeping an ear out for news of Lezay. Her conversation at the last tourney with Alec had made her snap to her senses, as did Edmond's warning that Lezay would come to England by spring. Alec was right. She had a decision to make. Just what was her secret worth? Better yet, what was this partnership against Lezay worth? It was obvious that Alec wanted her as his mistress in truth. Though she didn't want that, she also did not want to be sent back to Lezay.

She took Edmond's advice and attempted to find out more about Alec. She attempted to bring Lezay up in casual conversation when she could catch Alec alone. After all, there was no sense letting the rest of the manor staff hear that name. But Alec was an expert at changing the subject. Had she been right when she asked him if what he really wanted was to bed her and give her back to Lezay? Was this charade for nothing?

As the days wore on, she realized that she simply had to know. There was no point in waiting for another tourney, where he would pressure her again, nor waiting until Lezay himself knocked on the door to take her back. She waited until night. She laid in bed staring at the ceiling of the tower room, still fully dressed. Eventually she heard Alec come up the stairs and retire to his own room. He had always been respectful of her while they were at Neroche. Though there was only a door to separate them, he had not opened it but once, and that was in broad daylight. She hoped he would be just as respectful now.

She knocked on the thin wooden boards that separated them.

Alec did not come and open the door for her, merely said "come in." Ella unclicked the latch and pushed the door open. He had two candles lit on the table and was dressed in nothing but his breeches. He stood facing her, the candlelight shining on skin shadowed by hair and the contours of his wiry muscles. Faint, white lines of scars etched their trails across his arms and shoulders like constellations. He bunched his shirt into a ball and tossed it on a chair, putting his hands on his hips casually.

"Evening," was all he said, watching her.

She stood in the doorway, seriously considering just closing the door again and going back to bed.

He waited a full minute for her to say or do something, then with one hand picked up the chair and put it in the middle of the small room, gesturing to it.

Ella sighed and entered. She turned the chair to face him, standing behind it. When he sat down on the bed, she sat down on the chair, studying her nails. She couldn't look at him. He was the most handsome man she had ever seen when he was like this. She thought back to how he kissed her after the first tournament, and her stomach fluttered again. Her frown deepened as she cursed her body for its betrayal of good sense.

Another minute went by. Alec yawned and stretched out on his back across the bed, one leg still draped over the side. He rubbed his face with his hands. "You going to sit here all night or did you want something?"

Ella shifted in the chair then bravely looked at him, hoping to meet his eye. Quietly she said, "I want to know what you have against Lezay, if anything."

Alec sat up and spun around to face her again, planting his feet on the floor, his arms on either side of him, propping him against the bed. He eyed her for a moment. "Why do you want to know so badly?"

"I need to know if we are partners against him or if . . ." her voice trailed.

"Or if I made it up to get you to come with me," Alec finished. He sighed and leaned forward to put his elbows on his knees. "Both. If you want the truth."

Ella's eyes went wide, but she waited, hoping he'd continue.

"I like you, Ella . . . Eleanor. You're beautiful. You're hardworking. I'm hoping I can still get you to like me just the same."

He let that statement hang in the air for a while. But when she didn't move or say anything again, he knew she really did just want the answer to her question. She wasn't going to get it easily.

"Please," she said, "Just tell me if he did anything to you."

"He did."

She waited for him to continue, but Alec revealed nothing. Instead he patted the bed beside him. "There are ways to loosen a man's tongue you know."

Ella rolled her eyes and got up.

"Wait," Alec ordered, and she obeyed, turning back to him. Slowly he rose to her, stepping in close. He cupped the back of her head in his palm and pulled her lips to his. With his strong bare chest pressed against her it didn't take much for him to coax her lips apart in a deep kiss. The achingly pleasant knot in her gut settled in again, and she realized her own hands were making their way up Alec's back, across his bare shoulders. His hands ran down her back, settling on her hips, then lower as he pulled her close into him so she was hip to hip against him, lips still locked.

She gasped and her eyes fluttered open. Her heart pounded. He kissed her lightly on her lips, then her cheek, still holding her in tight against his body. She let her eyes close again, letting him hold her, resting her head against his solid shoulder.

It seemed like Alec would make it so easy if she gave in to him. He would tell her everything. Lord, if it felt like his kisses, maybe it would even be bearable. Maybe eventually she would give in to him. But first, she had to know if she still had other cards to play. Now was not yet the time.

She pulled away. Alec did not protest but smirked slightly. He knew he had her defenses breaking down. It wasn't until she had closed the door behind her, back in her own room, that she realized he still hadn't answered her question. What had Lezay done to *him*?

A few days later, Ella was given the opportunity to try out the last card she held in her hand. She and Marie were doing laundry outside in the sunny courtyard. Gradually a ruckus from the far side of the yard reached the women's ears, and they looked up.

"Will Wilfred never learn? He is no match at all for Lance," Marie said.

The women winced as the fight grew worse but kept to their washing. Ella watched the young men. It was rather comical how they scattered chickens and tripped over their own feet as they spun around. Neither was very good. As Wilfred pushed Lance into the manure pile Ella laughed out loud. Lance glared as he picked himself up and strutted over.

"You think it's funny, eh?" he demanded.

"Of course not, sir. It takes far too much skill to avoid the manure pile. And the chickens. And water troughs. It would not be funny at all if you were to encounter those things, as they are great challenges."

"You think you can do better?" he asked.

Marie stopped her scrubbing, watching Ella.

"I know I can," Ella said quietly, daring to look Lance right in the eye.

Lance moved to strike her, but she dodged him and slapped him back. As he stood in shock, she picked up two brooms and tossed one to him. "How far would you like to go?" she asked.

He clenched his broom and glared. "Till the end."

Ella made a cut for his stomach, catching him in the ribs. He stepped back, then ran toward her in blind rage, broom raised. She stepped to the side as she blocked his swing, rolling the broom in such a way as to fling his broom back toward her. She caught it in midair as he stood confused.

"Finished yet?" she asked playfully, then tossed it back to him.

He made a blow at her knee, which she again blocked. She hit his arm, then knee, then back. He made an angry and wild swing at her head, which she ducked to poke him in the stomach. Very soon he was on the ground, doubled over. Ella crouched beside him and asked if he was finished once again. He hissed "no" and took her hand as she helped him to his feet. He made a few hits at her, all blocked. Then she hit his leg again, and he fell.

"Who are you?" he panted through breaths of pain.

She picked up his broom and smiled as she stood over him. "I have far too many names for you to remember."

As she turned to put the brooms back, she noticed Alec standing in the doorway. He and half the manor staff had stopped their work to watch.

"Fighting with my squires, Ella?" he asked.

"Yes, sir," she answered him quietly.

"Let us see how you fare against a real knight." He handed her a sword. She felt the cold metal in her hand and stared at the blade. She had only meant to experiment a little with the squires, not take on an actual knight with an actual sword. It had been almost a decade since she had held a sword. Not counting the dagger she had used so poorly against Lezay . . ..

"Sir, I don't think—"

"Can't handle one, or scared to handle one?"

That irked her. "I don't feel the need to hurt you unnecessarily."

"Ella, if you cut me, you can keep the sword. And I promise I won't actually try to hurt you. You're too pretty." Alec swung his blade, and the metal hummed as it cut the air. His posture was relaxed, casual. His eyes twinkled, watching Ella to see if she flinched back from the song of the sharp blade. She did not.

Ella looked down at the carved handle and long, strong blade in her hand. It was smaller than a traditional long sword, lighter. Her size. "Do I have your word on that, sir?"

"Yes." Alec took a step forward and swung at her, missing as she quickly ducked and sidestepped away.

"Afraid?" he asked, just as she took two steps in and made an upward slice. He blocked it barely in time.

The fight went on as they swirled and sidestepped around the courtyard. The entire manor came out to watch, some in shock, some amused, all waiting. The fight lasted what seemed like hours, but perhaps was only minutes. Each movement became more desperate and daring. Yet neither Alec nor Ella lost their form. Every move was anticipated. Attacks were made while maintaining a defensive block. Their feet stayed firm, their eyes studying each other. As soon as Alec swung his sword, Ella was there to block it. But she did not have the strength to push past his blocks into a sufficient blow. Ella watched him as carefully as she could, looking for his one mistake that she could take advantage of, but fatigue was getting the best of her. Her eyes were blurred with sweat and effort, and her reactions were getting slower. He, too, was tiring, but his conditioned masculine strength allowed him to keep the fight going.

Finally, Alec made a cut at Ella's chest that she could not step back from in time. The blade grazed her, leaving a thin red line from the base of her neck to her shoulder. As Alec took a split second to stare in surprise that he'd hit her, she took a swing at his arm and nicked him. He fought back quickly and backed her into the stone manor wall, his blade at her neck. "Drop it," he said simply, and she obeyed, her sword clanging to the ground. He breathed hard as he stepped back from her and squinted at the cut that bled down his arm.

Ella glanced down at her own cut, which had already bled down her chest in a slick crimson trail. It stung but was mostly superficial. Her bodice was soaked with sweat. She too fought to catch her breath. Alec was good with a sword. Very good.

"Get cleaned up," he said quietly, still in surprise. "Meet me in the keep."

Ella stiffened and raised her chin as he turned. Then she looked down at her feet. The gilded sword was hers. She picked it up, the manor-folk still watching her. Ella's fingers closed on the sword's handle. Its familiarity still surprised her. Had it really been years already?

She flinched as Alec yelled from the doorway, "Back to work!" and the spectators hurried away.

Ella stared after them, not sure what to do. Lance kicked a bucket across the yard, muttering a string of curses as he shot Ella a glare. Wilfred stared at her, before slowly turning and heading back into the stables. Marie, who had never left her place at the wash tub, was the last one remaining.

"My, you're just full of surprises, aren't you?" she observed, almost to herself.

Ella stood there with the sword in her hand, bloody and sweaty, torn as to whether to help finish the washing or not.

"No," said Marie, reading her mind. "I'm not starting over to scrub bloodstains. Best you go do as Alec said and get yourself cleaned up. Bring your things down here, and I'll clean them before they stain."

Ella gave her a look of gratitude and hastened to the cistern to draw a bucket of water. The cut across her upper chest was long but not deep. A scratch really, but thank God it hadn't been higher, or it would have cut her throat. She cleaned it carefully and then hurried up into the tower to change into a clean shift and tunic. Already the faint line had stopped bleeding, though it was tender. She glanced nervously over at Alec's door, hearing him move around, and again picked up the sword, staring at her reflection in the polished blade. She had just fought the greatest swordsman in the country, perhaps all of Europe, and survived . . . and then some. She not only still had the skill she had developed as child's play in her youth, but she was stronger than she had been before and definitely improved. Perhaps all those years of watching tournaments with her ladies had taught her something after all.

She hadn't expected Alec to step in to their little fray. She just wanted to see how she would fair against Lance and Wilfred, to test if she was still capable of defending herself, or if she would be quickly cornered like she had been on her wedding night. But apparently Alec was too curious about her. He had tested her against the greatest swordsman in England: himself.

Ella's mind whirled. True, she had cut Alec. But he had also put her back against the wall and with a stroke could have killed her, had that been his intent. She wasn't ready to stand up to Lezay. But she hadn't cowered like she had years ago either.

At the very least, she wasn't scared of Alec anymore. And without fear of him, why should she fear her own identity? Why deny who she was? She was not born a commoner. She was of noble birth, the daughter of a warrior. She was Eleanor still, no matter how hard she tried to forget who she was and become someone else. Why fight it? "I am Eleanor de Levan d'Aquitaine," she whispered to herself. She rose and squared her shoulders. It wasn't time to show her true self yet, but time started counting down toward that moment. Somehow, she would find a way to be herself in name and action and stop living in fear of Montag, Lezay, and all the other men who had abused their power over her.

The next identity she took would be her own. Eleanor.

She sheathed and belted the sword to her side over her dress. Her hand instinctively grasped the hilt. How mad would Alec be? She heard him move on the other side of the door again and took a deep breath. She knocked once and pushed the door open, hesitant to cross that threshold. He was seated at his table, shirtless, working a bandage around the cut on his arm one handed.

"Attached to it already?" Alec asked, nodding to the sword on her hip.

"Yes, sir," Eleanor replied in a steady voice. She stayed on her own side of the doorway.

"Where did you learn to fight?"

"I've never had formal training."

"You lie," he stated without doubt, then looked away, struggling with the knot of the bandage. Eleanor did not argue; she didn't want to anger him further. He continued, "It does not matter. Ella, you have skill." He suddenly turned toward her. "I want to teach you how to fight."

"What?" Eleanor asked incredulously. "I am a woman, sir!"

Alec gave up on the bandage and let it unravel as he rose and came toward her, his face serious. "And you are a good fighter. Better than that lout I've been wasting my time with. I want you to compete in a smaller tourney, where we poor knights host to show off our protégés. Maybe it will force Lance to practice harder before his parents deem me a failure and send him somewhere else."

"Sir, how would you conceal—"

"It can be done when we get the mail on you. Will you agree? I can make you better. We both know it's only time before Lezay comes to visit. I promised to protect you, but even I have my limitations. When he shows up, I won't placate him. He will be an angry bear if there ever was one. I don't intend to let him get past me, but I'm a mere mortal. If you can defend yourself like you did today, just imagine what you will be able to do months from now. With *practice.* And the formal training that you claim to have never had."

Eleanor contemplated the idea. It was exactly what she needed to prepare herself to face Lezay. And maybe even Montag. But she still was just a woman. How could she ever face off with full grown men in a tournament setting, with crowds watching? "I don't know if I can carry the mail."

"We can use the lighter leather then. Pretend you're a poor country fellow. It will still be bulky enough. And we're just entering you in the sword. At least Lance redeems himself in the joust. I'm keeping him going there. Do you know the clearing where I practice with the squires?"

She nodded, still somewhat stunned.

"Meet me there at dawn tomorrow."

Eleanor hesitated, trying to gauge just how serious Alec was. From what she knew of him, he wasn't one to jest with something like this. Finally, she nodded her agreement and a smile flitted across Alec's lips. She glanced down at his arm. "How bad is it?"

"A scratch."

"Let me see." She motioned for him to sit at his table and followed him into his room. He leaned against the edge of the table and patiently let her undo the sloppy bandage. Her hands for once were steady around him as she gently probed the deep cut in his bicep. There was a sort of paste pressed into the wound with a sweet odor, though it looked disgusting.

Alec noted her curious expression. "My father's concoction. Works like a charm. Don't ask what's in it. You don't want to know."

Eleanor raised her eyebrows and carefully wrapped the bandage around the wound, settling it with a firm knot. "Sorry," she said quietly. She felt bad for hurting him, however much he infuriated her.

Alec shook his head and caught her fingers. "If you're going to be a warrior, you can't apologize like a woman.

You made a decision to fight me. I knew this could happen when I handed you the sword. You have nothing to be sorry for. You did your job. The rest is left to God." He released her and went back to moving around his room and dressing. Eleanor quietly exited, taking their bloody clothes down so they could be laundered. Her heart still raced as she silently rejoined Marie in the work. As if her situation with Alec wasn't confusing enough, now she was going to learn how to fight.

And Eleanor did. They met in the days after, without fail. In rain and blistering heat they fought, practiced. By the end of the first week her body began failing her, the constant physical exertion making each step an effort and a pain. She tried, and to some extent succeeded, in pushing it out of her mind, but there were physical limits nothing but bloodlust could overcome, and such is not in constant supply. By the beginning of the second week Alec became harsh and critical, constantly challenging her. Though she was completely furious with him and even her own weakness, she still could not do the things he so wished of her. She pushed herself as hard as her strength would allow. By the end of the third week, the workouts no longer pushed her to the brink of nausea, though they continued to make her sore enough to ensure that her muscle was developing.

Within a month Eleanor had transformed enough to hold her own against Alec. She never would quite catch up to him completely, as masculinity gave him too much of a physical advantage, but she was strong enough to perform the various new moves that her women's ingenuity could devise. Her size and agility allowed her to spin and move in ways the men would never expect. She gradually discovered every trick Alec knew and built up the strength to execute and block each. Had he been wise, he would have learned her moves as well, but his pride blinded him to the fact there could ever be more.

Even when she was not with Alec, Eleanor constantly thought of the sword. She theorized angles and blocks as she scrubbed. Her mop spun maneuvers on the wood floors. She rehearsed the things she had once known so well in childhood with Edmond and Raoul, remembering hints from not just sword, but lance, club, and dagger. A dangerous thought stirred in her mind as she eyed Alec, day after day. Eleanor realized that with his help she was now able to "answer his question". What would she do to protect her secret? She would stay on with Alec as long as he'd have her, helping him as much as she could. She would even continue to play the role of the Lady of the Tournament, as that was an opportunity to get out of the manor and find out what was happening in France, specifically news of Lezay, Montag, and Edmond. But no more than that. She would participate in his game of seduction on her own terms. And if he pressured her for *anything* she did not want to do, she would fight, she would run, and then she would continue to stand on her own feet, even if that meant she was going to tell the world her secret herself. Even if it meant that when she left Castle Neroche, she left as Eleanor de Levan.

Chapter Ten

Alec burst into her room through their shared door. Eleanor woke with a start and snatched the blankets up to her chest, sitting up.

"At least I knock!" she exclaimed.

"We're hosting a tournament. A small one. Just got a message from Lord Gawain with his permission. And his financing! Just for squires. Here at Neroche. You are competing. And Lance, of course. Neighboring knights will come for a hunt, and the squires compete." Alec beamed.

"Really? You actually want me to compete in sword fighting against a bunch of men. In front of an audience of men?"

"Why do you think we've been practicing so hard?" He sat next to her on the bed and slapped his hand down on the blankets next to her. "You are ready! You'll be brilliant. It's about time I had a squire with enough skill to actually win one of these things."

"And you woke me up to tell me this *now* because . . ."

"We have to get ready. They start arriving tomorrow!"

"Tomo—" she stuttered. "Alec, are you mad? Do you know how much work needs to be done before they get here? You don't even have a tournament ring."

"It's about time we made one. Always wanted one. Don't worry, Wilfred, Lance, and I will take care of that. You can take care of the rest."

The rest meaning where to get food to feed a few dozen people, where to tell them to set up their tents, where to put their horses, hay for their horses, water for everyone, ale for the men, getting the manor cleaned up, getting the animals put away before one of the visitors decided to snack on them . . . the list went on. Eleanor groaned.

"Well, get to it then," Alec said with sickening cheerfulness. He brazenly kissed her forehead and left as quickly as he had come.

Eleanor groaned again and pulled the covers up over her head. His madness was catching. What had she gotten herself into?

Alec boasted about his "great new squire", and the knights poured out. Soon the little manor at Neroche swarmed with knights, squires, and a massive pack of hunting dogs. Eleanor was sure it was the most people the plot of land and little stone keep had held since it was occupied in King Stephen's time, decades before. Never had Eleanor seen so many people gather for a simple squire fight. Her body tingled with the excitement that was in the air, and her adrenaline pumped just trying to keep everything organized behind the scenes. True to his word, Alec, Lance, and Wilfred had built a tournament ring in the practice field with astonishing speed. The manor looked the part.

Though it took some convincing, Alec had her cut her long hair to her shoulders, and she tied it back like she'd seen the other knights do. She kept her braid so she could still pin it into her existing hair when she played the "lady". Charcoal gave her the illusion of a five o'clock shadow. When she was dressed in her leather-pieced armor she could not be differentiated from the other men of the manor but for the fact that she was smaller in stature.

"What if they ask for me? For Ella?" she asked Alec in the midst of the preparations.

"Can you make an appearance in the middle of the tourney?"

"While I'm fighting? How on earth am I going to do that?"

"You are only in the sword event. While Lance and the others are jousting, make an appearance then."

"And if I actually do win the sword? You want me to change back into a squire again for awards? If we have awards. And what's my name, Sir Alec?"

"Alfred. I'm sure you can manage." He gave her a wink and went back to his tasks.

With the charcoal on her face, her shorter hair, and thick boiled-leather armor, no one gave "Alfred" a second glance. They thought she was a small pubescent boy, and she was grossly underestimated.

Eleanor started the day with a skinny, tall boy who she beat easily. The same with the next and the next. As the day progressed, they got harder for her to beat, but still she was fine. None of them fought anything like Alec. When the sword event finished late morning, she had beaten twenty squires, most of whom towered over her, without taking any serious hits.

Ella made an appearance during the joust that afternoon, faithfully standing at Alec's side as he cheered on Lance, who did terribly. Then she quickly scruffed up her face again, changed, and became Alfred so she could receive her prize, an intricate hauberk of small metal links. Eleanor held the mail shirt aloft, in awe of the workmanship. It was nothing fancy like the nobles wore, no gold wires or designs woven into the iron rings. This was purely functional, and for once, it was hers. She could even take it to an armorist and have it adjusted that it would fit her small stature. She smiled as Alec clapped her proudly on the back, boasting that he finally had made a champion squire. Lance glowered at her from a distance away. Wilfred congratulated her, then went back to taking care of the horses.

Sunset fell as the knights and squires readied themselves for the hunt that would set out in the light of a full moon. Dating from the time Castle Neroche's first stones had been laid, this hunt with a pack of raches, small hound dogs, was always intense. The leashed dogs would bay and lead them to a wild boar, then the raches would be set loose to chase it down and corner it so the knights could move in. It was extremely dangerous, particularly in the dark, and an ultimate test of manhood.

"Alfred" got to stay out after the awards, with the excuse that "Ella" wasn't feeling well. It gave her more freedom to move through the crowd than she usually had. Everyone was making last adjustments to their equipment. Most knights were taking one squire out that would hang back from the main pack a bit with spare weapons in case they were needed. Eleanor saw Wilfred and Alec arguing behind the barn and slowly headed over, curious.

"Just this once, Alec, let me go along," Wilfred was insisting.

"One squire." Alec looked impatient. "You aren't a squire, and you don't even have a horse. Are your jobs done? Where are our mounts?"

Wilfred seemed to yield. "They're ready." He motioned to the barn and his shoulders sagged.

Alec entered the stable and emerged a minute later with his horse Ches. Lance followed with his own horse. They mounted up, and then Alec spotted Eleanor and rode to her.

"God speed," she offered.

Alec winked. "Maybe next time you'll get to come along." He rode off, leading the knights and the braying dogs into the forest.

Wilfred still stood with his arms crossed, frowning. "And there go all the real men," he said to himself.

Eleanor approached him as the manor yard was suddenly empty and quiet but for the sound of the dogs barking in the distance. They watched into the darkness together, trying to envision what was happening.

"I don't know how you've done it, but you slip between all these roles quite well," Wilfred said, breaking the silence.

"You think anyone has caught on?" she asked.

"Nope. And certainly none of us are going to tell. Alec threatened to cut out our tongues himself if we told anyone that 'Alfred' was 'Ella.' Even poor Marie. Scared her so much she hasn't left the kitchen all day."

"So subtle, isn't he?" She smiled. "So what's your story anyway? You're older than Lance. Why is he a squire and you get all the grunt work?"

"He's nobility. I'm common." Wilfred didn't elaborate, and she didn't push him. "Lance pretty much hates you now, just so you know."

"Yeah, I got that impression."

"Watch out for him. I don't think he'll talk about you; he values his tongue like I do. But he very well might try to cause trouble for you some other way. I don't know how. I just have a feeling he's out for revenge. He's not one to take defeat quietly."

Chapter Eleven

The leaves were changing across England as Alec, his squire, his groom, and his trophy "Ella" headed to the last tourney of the season. Eleanor was confident on her palfrey as they rode into Sarum and the castle that was once her home. She was used to people staring at her now and did not try to shrink away anymore. She had an air of nobility about her, even though all the people knew she was as common as they were.

At least they thought she was common.

Sarum was as packed as ever as knights from the entire kingdom came together. Nobility packed the central observation stand, so Eleanor had to find a place along the rail with the other commoners. Somehow, though, perhaps by her reputation, she was gestured forward to receive a place at the rail where at least she could see.

"Ella!" She heard a woman's shout and turned to see Helin waving from behind a few other taller men. Eleanor pulled her friend through the crowd up to the rail with her.

"Whew!" Helin said. "This place is packed today. I'm glad I found you, or I would never get to see anything at all."

Eleanor smiled and put aside the desire to point out that Helin hadn't spoken to her since that tournament in May, her first as Lady of the Tournament.

Helin leaned over to whisper with a smile to Ella, "So after all this time, do you believe in love yet?"

Eleanor grimaced, caught off by the question. "I'll be honest, I'm struggling with it, Helin. But he is a good man. He is treating me well. He is brave and talented in what he does. I cannot complain."

"From what you say, it sounds like you *are* in love with him."

"It's more . . ." Eleanor started, but her voice trailed off. A shadow of a horse blocked their view of the list.

"M'lady," a familiar voice called from above the horse. Eleanor glanced up into Edmond's eyes, then over at Helin, who had blushed bright red and stared at him open mouthed. Maybe he was talking to Helin. "My Lady Ella." Eleanor's head jerked back to him, her eyes wide. "I shall win this tournament for you."

Never before had Edmond offered to win a tournament for anyone. It was Eleanor's turn to stare at him open mouthed. He held her gaze with a smile until she blushed. Even after so many months apart, watching Edmond looking down at her stirred something in her that even

Alec's kisses did not touch. With a quick glance at Helin she stepped forward to the very edge of the rail. Alec already had her ribbon. But there was one other token she had to give. With a slow, subtle movement she slipped the old chain with her father's ring over her head. She squeezed the ring tight in her palm for a moment.

"My lord, I would trust you with my life." She held out her token to him, waiting for his strong hand to take the only proof of her birthright.

"I will not break that trust, m'lady." He nodded, placed the chain around his own neck, and rode off.

Eleanor trembled as she watched him ride off down the list. Her heart pounded in her ears, deafening the whispers around her.

Helin elbowed her in the ribs, nervously glancing around at the staring faces. "Ella!" she hissed. "Do you know who that is? Do you know what you've done?" She pulled Eleanor back from the rail, through the crowd. Her vision of Edmond broken, Eleanor realized how the atmosphere around them had changed. Helin's discomfort was not unwarranted. Every man around them was staring.

"He called her a *lady*," one woman scoffed.

"I thought she was Alec's whore?"

"His *mistress*."

"What's the difference?"

"She's exclusive."

"Not anymore, she's not. Two tokens!"

They laughed.

Eleanor blushed furiously. Helin dragged her behind the stands, where the crowd thinned. Then she spun on Eleanor. "What game are you playing?!"

Eleanor shook her head, surprised at her normally jovial friend's tone.

"You just gave Lord Edmond your token of affection. Playing games with a poor knight like Alec is one thing but getting involved with a noble? What are you thinking?!"

"They always offer. Why can't I accept for once?"

"It's a show, Ella! A show!" She pulled Eleanor to where they could see between the spectators' feet across the tilting yard to Lady Gwen. Even then a knight was pledging his victory, and she was flirting and jesting with him. Then he rode off. "See? No token."

"Of course. She's married. Like you pointed out last spring."

"And unless you want to be the newest village whore, so are you. To Alec."

"But we aren't—"

Helin shook her head. "Doesn't matter." She sighed. "Ella, you know I'm no saint. I've had my share of fun. But we have to stay within our class. Cook boys, stable lads, the like. Not . . ." She gestured wildly in the air, searching for words. "*Upper* nobility. Not in public."

"They already call me a whore. What does it change if I give two tokens? If I pit two men against each other to truly compete for me in the way this tradition started in the first place?"

Helin studied Eleanor, frowning. "Do you know this Lord Edmond?"

Eleanor stiffened. "We met at a tournament outside London."

"You let him win that one for you?"

"No! He didn't offer."

"Are you a whore?"

"Helin! No!" Eleanor belted out a tense laugh.

"A woman traveling alone to Sarum. Then Alec, now Lord Edmond. If I didn't know your views on love, I'd say it all makes sense that way."

"If I was a whore would I still be scrubbing laundry and emptying chamber pots? That is my glamourous life at Castle Neroche."

Helin sighed and took Eleanor's hand. "I know you've seen so much more of the world than me. You're older, but I worry about you, Ella. You've changed so much these past months. I don't know you at all."

"Oh, Helin . . ."

"Look, what's done is done. People are talking. Watch your back today, lest any of the crude men around here think you're for hire. I'm sorry. I can't . . .I have to go."

"I understand." Eleanor frowned and rubbed her forehead. What had she gotten herself into?

"Who do you want to win?"

"I don't know," Eleanor realized.

"I will cheer for both then." Helin paused, gave Eleanor a gentle smile, and re-entered the crowd.

Any more knights that dared to vie for a lady's attention directed it at Lady Gwen after that. Those that had witnessed the exchange between Edmond and Ella had passed it around like wildfire. Never had anyone known of either of them participating in the volley for attention, at least not beyond Ella's predictable blessing for Alec. Those watching did not know *what* Eleanor had given Edmond, but they knew, like Helin, that any gift of a token allowed compensation for the knight's victory.

Eleanor took Helin's advice to heart and moved to stand near Wilfred and Lance, away from the majority of spectators but still in view of the competition. Alec rode up to her in a fury as the joust commenced.

"I feed you, clothe you, and yet it is not enough. Still you hide here with *my men* for protection from your scandal?" Alec spit in the dust at her feet. Eleanor backed away from him, heart pounding. "And *him* of all men? Who is he to you?" Eleanor stared at Ches' hooves, unable to meet Alec's frightful expression.

"Men still die in tournaments you know. I hope he doesn't mean much to you." Alec whipped his horse back toward the list. "Lance! Get her a seat with the other peasants. I don't need a distraction."

Lance guided her to a place near the stinking privy, and there she remained motionless through the tournament.

Alec and Edmond competed neck and neck. They each entered two events. Alec won at sword. Edmond won wrestling. That left the joust to settle the score and, as it counted double, tournament champion. Round after round, they snagged each of the rings in increasing difficulty. In the end, Alec and Edmond were the only two knights left. After *fifteen* rounds of snagging the smallest ring available with the lance, the other knights were amazed. The crowd rumbled with murmurs of anticipation, excited at the anomaly, yet they all wanted the long day to be over. Even the horses were exhausted.

Lord Gawain rose above the crowd and ordered silence to those protesting. "My lords and ladies, please. I do so assume you want a winner of this tournament?" The crowd cheered below. "Then I find but one resort. A contact joust!" The crowd broke out in a chorus of breathless whispers. Eleanor paled. A contact joust was not far from battle. It was rare, as mail was weak when placed on a point with the force of a galloping horse behind it. It was dangerous but also a supreme test of bravery and skill. The two men agreed. They were each given padded gambesons with hauberks buckled over them, and helmets, and their horses armored as if for battle. The heavier lances were brought out, their sharp battle tips removed with some hope of protection. As the two men took their places at opposing ends of the field, the crowd went silent.

Eleanor felt sick, remembering Alec's words. What had she done?

Lord Gawain's herald called out, "The first man to break a lance on the other shall be the victor. However, if one man should unseat the other, that man should win above the broken lance. Any blow to the horse is a loss, and you will never be invited back here again. My knights, are you ready?" They nodded. "Then joust!"

The crowd was silent as the two men thundered toward each other. There was no sound but the horse's footfalls. For Eleanor, they moved in slow motion. "He's weighted in the left hip, Edmond. Blow to the right," she whispered to herself.

Suddenly there was a loud crack as the two collided. Edmond's lance hit Alec's side and his uneven weight unsettled him and almost pushed him off. Alec doubled over but held on. The crowd went wild! The herald announced Edmond had won. Many people went up to congratulate Lord Edmond, but he looked only at Eleanor. She nodded her congratulations and smiled as he turned toward his crowd of well-wishers with an answering smile.

By the time Eleanor made it out of the stands, most of the crowd was already heading toward the manor. The autumn sun was setting, and it had been a long day. Across the tilting field, she saw the only two knights still on their horses deep in discussion: the last two knights of the day, Alec and Edmond. Her heart sank. After a day of fighting, could they really be fighting more? She stood in the open across from them, watching.

Whatever was being said, they were both adamant, gesturing wildly. When they saw her, Edmond turned his horse and walked away, while Alec walked his horse to her.

He halted in front of her and looked down at her coldly. "If you want a place to live after tonight, you stay with me," he said.

Eleanor looked back to Edmond as he continued walking away. She nodded at Alec, confused and hurt. Why did Edmond offer to win the tourney for her if he didn't even want to talk to her?

Obediently she stayed at Alec's side throughout the banquet. Gwen and Helin gave her curious glances. The knights wondered where their champion was, murmuring amongst themselves and shooting Alec and Eleanor curious looks. Edmond never appeared. Eleanor tried to assuage Alec's stormy mood. He was short with her, and she withdrew to silence.

As they headed back to Alec's tent after the festivities had died down, she questioned him, "What did you say to him?"

"I think I have a right to ask questions first," Alec insisted.

"Fair enough."

"How do you know him?"

"Childhood friend."

"So he knows who you are?"

"Yes."

Alec sucked in a breath. "And you do realize that by pledging your tokens to two men you promised to give yourself to the winner. Or are you just pretending with him as you are with me?"

She didn't answer.

"If I had won, would you finally yield to me?" Alec asked, stopping to look her in the eye.

She kept her silence but met his eyes. He closed the space between them in a footstep and kissed her, pulling her into him as he always did. She looked down after he stopped, trembling slightly.

"Do you love him?" Alec asked quietly.

She didn't look at Alec. She didn't know the answer to that herself.

He took her by the shoulders and looked her in the eye, asking again, "Do you love him?"

"I don't know," she managed to whisper. "I don't know."

She continued walking miserably toward Alec's tent. He followed in silence. She pulled aside the tent flap and entered. Edmond looked up from a stool in the corner.

Eleanor gasped and looked at Alec. His face was expressionless.

"What is going on?" she asked, looking from one to the other.

Edmond rose.

Alec crossed his arms and nodded to Edmond. "Go on. This was your plan. Not mine."

"Eleanor—" Edmond started, but she cut him off.

"Why did you offer to win the tournament in my name? You never do that . . . for anyone. Nor do I . . . participate." Her words started to rush, a blush climbing her cheeks as she glanced at Alec.

"I'm sorry to say I used you as a bargaining tool."

"Excuse me?" Eleanor asked in shock.

"Works in my favor," Alec said under his breath.

Edmond looked at Alec sternly. "In exchange for Alec getting to 'keep' you, despite *losing*, he agreed to give us something of his own in return. You going back on your word to me tonight has solidified the story that you two are lovers, not that you needed much help in that area. People are going to talk about you even more. Which means sooner than later Lezay is going to hear about the romance, get curious, and show up at a tourney. I want you protected," Edmond said sincerely. Then he looked meaningfully at Alec and said, "At all costs. She has been through enough." Looking back to Eleanor he continued. "I wanted to know for myself why Alec really wants you, and in exchange for everything I just said, he has told me. I get the impression you have not told *her* any of this yet?" he asked Alec.

"I'm better at keeping my secrets than you two appear to be," he said, still standing with his arms crossed before him.

"Why didn't you just ask him, Edmond?" Eleanor said in exasperation. "Why go through the whole tournament drama? For goodness sake, you two took it to a contact joust! One of you could have been hurt."

Alec held up the corner of his shirt to reveal a purple bruise the size of a melon on his side. "I agree." He raised his eyebrows at Edmond.

Edmond replied quietly, "I have reasons of my own for that." In a normal tone, back to Eleanor he said, "I've heard rumors of his story, which he confirmed when I confronted him on the tourney field. But I didn't have time to get the details. So I offered this . . .arrangement. Alec, you swore to tell her everything."

"You should also hear what he threatened to do to me if he found out I lied," Alec injected.

"Enough!" Eleanor broke in again. "What's the big story?"

Edmond waited patiently for Alec to start.

"Lezay is a foul ogre of a man," Alec began. "I still don't know what he did to you; you two are keeping that secret well enough. But I can imagine it was selfish, cruel, brutal, dishonest. Need I add more?" Alec paused, watching their faces. "As you probably know, my father passed a few years ago. The Lord of Homme Castle in Worcestershire. Loyal vassal of King Richard. What you probably don't know is how. The story *I* was told originally is that he deserted his company in the Holy Land. Labeled as a deserter, he was disavowed his lands here in England. This cost me, as heir, everything I have. Would have cost me my own title, too, if I had not gone across Europe myself to search for him. Thankfully I didn't have to go that far.

"The best place to hear things is at taverns and tourneys, so there I frequented as I traveled through France. I was approached by a farmer outside of Reims that recognized my crest, and we struck up a conversation. He'd buried a corpse he'd found dumped in his field about the time my father went missing. A knight, with a ring like my crest, and a bloody mess of stab wounds. My father didn't desert. He was murdered. The farmer had alerted the sheriff and had merely been told to bury the man. That sheriff and I later had a good long conversation as to proper procedures when knights randomly show up dead. He won't be neglecting to find the family of the next victim. The farmer was an honest man, and he had kept the ring, which he kindly returned to me. It was the proof I needed to retain my title, though it was too late for Castle Homme, which has been granted to another lord. Castle Neroche was a weak consolation if you ask me.

"I still needed to know who killed him and why. By tournaments and taverns, I finally got part of my answer. I still don't know the why, but I know who. Lezay. His tongue gets loose as he drinks. He told his . . . comrades . . . how they were picking off Crusaders one by one. Only if they got too close to Alsace, of course. Well, my father was never much of one for the sea, and the continental road to the Holy Land swings right through Alsace, through the mountains with castles on every hilltop. How Lezay described how they killed them . . . it was exactly as the farmer described his body. I have no doubt it was Lezay and his men that separated him from his company and murdered him.

"He couldn't just leave it at murder, either. He spread the rumors that my father was a deserter when people asked. It was he who paid off the sheriff of Reims to forget about the body." He frowned even deeper as he finished, "So yes, I want my revenge. I want that bastard to lose everything. His wife. His land. His honor. Then I want him to curl in a ball and rot out a nice long life with nothing. Death is too kind for his sort."

Eleanor and Edmond were silent. There was no tear in Alec's eye, only hatred of a kind Eleanor had never seen in him. It was fearsome. She didn't dare be the first to break the silence and speak.

Edmond broke in with a cautious, "So now we know why you have use for Eleanor. You are a third of the way into your plan."

"Almost a third. Almost two thirds. A lot of almosts with this one. Perhaps she could be easier to persuade if you'd stop meddling and leave us to our own revenge," Alec growled.

Eleanor cut in, "Almost *two* thirds?"

"You want to trade something else for *that* information?" Alec asked, his glare deepening in challenge.

They noted that Alec was finished. The deal was done. They would get no more from him that night. Edmond tilted his head to Alec. "Thank you for holding to our agreement." With a glance to Eleanor he added, "Take care of her." Alec said nothing, did nothing, so Edmond headed out the tent door.

Just as the flap was about to close Alec said, "Take her with you." He kept his back to Edmond. "She is your prize tonight after all."

Eleanor's eyes went wide, looking from one man to the other.

Alec nodded for her to follow Edmond. Coldly he said, "Go. Do your duty." The tone of his voice warned her not to argue. She was being dismissed. Quickly she followed Edmond out of the tent like a scolded dog.

Edmond led her quickly to his own tent and shut the flap. He lit a candle, the contours of his strong jaw glowing in the light. He was a different kind of handsome from Alec. Alec was solid, strong jawed, and athletically built. Edmond was gentler featured but no less solid in musculature. Maybe it was the rounder curve of his face, the curl to his hair.

Eleanor took a shaky breath and looked around her. The tent was much like Alec's inside. Equipment easily accessible by the entrance. Two bedrolls rolled out in the center, one for Edmond, one for his squire Gregory. A small trunk that the lantern sat on was set along the left wall. And then there was the man in front of her, tournament champion. The man who had promised to win the tournament for her, done so, then somehow traded her back to Alec for information that would help her. But Alec didn't want her tonight. Did Edmond?

"I . . ." she started, but the words caught in her throat. She had been prepared to be the Lady of the Tournament earlier, but with everything that had happened, she had lost her resolve. Yet if Edmond wanted it, she could not refuse. She did not want to refuse. Her stomach did a backflip in anticipation. Would he be gentle, the way Alec kissed her? Or would he just jump on her like Lezay? She shuddered. She had liked Edmond when they were children, but he was so much older that she'd always assumed he was unattainable. She was just a silly child in his eyes, his "Elle." How little she knew then! Lezay was some thirty years her senior when they were wed. Edmond's few extra years of age were nothing.

Lezay, Lezay. Why did her thoughts always go back to him?

She jumped as Edmond said her name. "I don't know what to do!" she awkwardly burst out.

Edmond just smiled at her gently. "You don't know how to sit down?"

She focused on him, realizing he was gesturing toward the pallets. *Oh no, no no no no no.* Her eyes went wide. Should she run back to Alec?

"Eleanor," Edmond said sternly. Her look of panic stilled him. He called to her again, "Eleanor . . ." until he got her attention again with a little less wild-rabbit of a look. "Stop. I expect nothing. I won't touch you." She focused on him a little more. "I won't touch you." Finally, she took a deep breath and her shoulders relaxed. Edmond motioned again to the bedroll on the floor of the tent. "You can sleep here. Gregory will be up in the manor until dawn with his friends."

She nodded and stepped toward him. He pulled his own bedroll a little bit further from the one he had given her, just to reassure her, and sat down on it. She sat across from him, cross-legged. He unbelted his sword and laid it between them, then stretched out on his side, watching her. She fidgeted with her clothes, the blankets . . . anything to avoid his gaze.

"I thought . . . since you are tournament champion and you chose me . . . I thought . . ." she stammered.

"You thought I'd expect you to lie with me," Edmond finished for her. She nodded. He chuckled quietly. "Trust me, Elle, it's not that I don't want to. But you are nowhere near ready."

Eleanor pulled her knees up to her chest, wrapping her arms around herself with her head on her knees. "I'm broken."

"You are healing. You are much stronger now than when I last saw you in that little wooded clearing. You were afraid of Alec then, afraid of me. I do not sense that kind of fear in you anymore. I don't know where the confidence is coming from, but without it I know you would not have given me your favor at the tourney today. Speaking of which, here is your ring." He lifted the chain from around his neck and handed her the ring. She took it gladly and squeezed the metal, warmed by Edmond's body, in her palm.

"I want to be healed." Even quieter she said, "I want you to be able to touch me."

A pained look crossed Edmond's face, and he looked away from her.

"While you still have this remarkable guise as Ella and the protection of Alec, I am trying to stay on the sidelines. And yes, he will protect you from everyone but himself; I see it when he looks at you. But Elle . . . I—" he stammered. "Have you ever heard anyone define love?"

Eleanor watched him tentatively and was silent, remembering her rant to Helin.

He continued, "I dread any farewell to you. The thought of never seeing you again, the thought of you becoming another's, as you surely one day will, even if Lezay never discovers you. It is, my lady, the hardest blow I may ever receive. You are exceptional in so many ways. I have been thinking of you constantly since we met on that battlement wall. Yet it makes me even more sick to think I am not in a position to protect you. Perhaps that is what love is. The tear between knowing that to protect someone you must send them away and knowing that to send them away would be intolerable. Am I selfish to keep interfering between you and Alec? To do what I did today?"

"No."

"No? Elle, I think you know better than that."

"Non, Edmond. I am here. I want to be with you!"

"Pourquoi? Why would you possibly want to stay with me?"

"Je ne sais pas." She shrugged. "You make me feel safe."

She turned her head from him, and he gently turned her face back to his with a single finger. "Elle, do you remember when we were children? Or at least close enough, in our innocence at least."

She swallowed and nodded. She remembered exactly the moment he spoke of, had relived it a thousand times.

"Raoul had left us. It was just you and me there in the woods." Edmond smiled, remembering. "The way the sun shone on your hair, you looked to me to be a fairy of the wood." His fingers caressed her jaw as they had years ago, before he had claimed her first innocent kiss. He hadn't been very good at it, and they'd run back to the manor and never said another word about it. Still, all these years later, it burned in their minds.

Edmond suddenly rose up to his knees and kissed her, and a tremor ran throughout their bodies. She opened her eyes to glance at him, then let herself melt. There was a completely different spark in Edmond's kiss than Alec's. Edmond's lips were gentle yet urgent. The scruff of his beard rubbed her face, and she felt the hard muscles of his body beneath his shirt. He was a man now. This was not the mere boy she had known. Her lips were on fire as a tingle shot down her spine to her toes. She put her hands on either side of his face and pulled his lips even more into hers. A tremor ran through him and for a moment, she wondered if he would go back on his word. He took his lips from hers to kiss the curve of her neck. She tried to catch her breath.

"Edmond," Eleanor whispered, pulling away from him as he cupped the side of her face in his hand.

"That is all I will ask of you, Elle," Edmond replied, releasing her. "It will be your choice even when I return."

Eleanor smiled faintly. "I'm sorry."

"For what?"

"My weakness. That I cannot just leave with you in the morning. That I must fear those who would love nothing more than to ruin what little happiness I have found."

"You, Elle, are far from weak. If it is to be, we will see each other again. Soon."

As dawn broke and Gregory returned, Eleanor readied herself to return back to Alec. She was too tired, too confused, to care who watched her. She brushed Edmond's face with the back of her hand and kissed him a final time. The few knights awake in the camp stopped and stared. Alec fumed in the distance as he sat outside his own tent, where he had probably waited all night. When she stepped away, Eleanor brushed a single tear from her cheek. She did not let go of Edmond's hands until her feet had carried her beyond their reach; their fingertips locked, ever so reluctant to part.

Eleanor was distracted as she returned back to Neroche with Alec. Edmond made her head swim. She relived her kiss with him over and over. The feel of him next to her sleeping, afraid to kick him during the night. His order to Alec to take care of her while he promised to send her word from France of any news he could. No other man had gone out of his way to help her like he was. Who else would win a contact joust just for information for *her*? Alec had made it pretty clear that there would only be one way for her to get that information out of him. Edmond had sidestepped that for her.

And Alec had also made it clear what her value was to him. He wanted Lezay to know he had his wife. And to just pretend didn't really count in his mind. She could tell by how his hand lingered on her as he helped her on her palfrey and how the muscle of his jaw twitched as he glanced back at her as they rode that he wanted her now more than ever. Her stomach clenched. How long could she walk the ridge between the two men before one of them pulled her clear over the cliff?

Chapter Twelve

November 1196
Petite Andelys, Normandy

A snowflake floated through the air, catching Eleanor's eye. She pulled her cloak tighter around her, glancing heavenward where dozens more of the tiny flakes drifted lazily to the ground. French ground.

Her heart had been pounding for weeks in anticipation of this arrival, and now that she was there, it was too tired to flutter anymore. As if in a daze, she stood in the path, watching the snowflakes, frozen not by cold or fear but her own thoughts. Eight years it had been since she'd left, and she'd never anticipated coming back. Slowly she turned to look behind her, noting how the morning sun sparkled on the River Seine. Bursts of orange-gold light framed the clouds as the last remnants of the sunrise faded. She'd never spent much time in Normandy, but here and now, the place was gorgeous.

Hoofbeats sounded a few steps behind her, and she automatically stepped to the side of the narrow dirt path and glanced up.

"I think you've been spared. None of them are here," Alec said to her from atop his horse.

"Thank God," Eleanor replied quietly. She fell into stride with Ches and followed Alec toward the tournament field. They'd known it was a risk for her to return, but with no word from Edmond on Lezay's whereabouts, Alec had been itching to cross the channel for a little reconnaissance of his own. An invitation to tournament from King Richard himself solidified his journey, and Eleanor would not let him travel so close to Alsace without her. Fortunately, or perhaps unfortunately, they had not had any news of Lezay thus far, though they'd been in Normandy for several days and the tournament was to start in only a few minutes.

"Just remember your promise, Eleanor," Alec warned.

"I remember." She frowned. "Since he's not here, it shouldn't be an issue." As they neared the field, she couldn't help but glance around for Edmond's crest. He wasn't there.

She sighed, following as Alec veered off the path toward the open field. It was a small tourney, with the most informal of benches surrounding the bare field. The great, newly begun fortress of Chateau Gaillard was on the hill above them, currently a mass of stone and scaffolding;

the tourney field tucked between the river and the newly constructed village that primarily housed the workers. The pungent smell of fresh wood drifted on the breeze. Absently Eleanor pulled her ribbon from her braid and tied it to Alec's left arm. This was habit for them now, automatic. He still would smirk at her with a suggestive smile, but she didn't let it bother her. She sent him off with a half-smile of her own and a roll of her eyes, giving Ches one last pat on his sleek brown neck. For these seven months, Alec had asked nothing more of her than an obligatory kiss for show every now and then at a tournament. He was respecting their arrangement. What more could she want?

Silently she found a place in the small yet boisterous crowd where she could see the tournament unfold. It would be a small, short one today. It had been called as a bit of a celebratory reprieve for the construction workers. They would continue to work through the winter, but King Richard was already pleased with their progress on his stronghold. The worker's joy at a day of rest was as electric as if there was a crowd of hundreds more.

Her gaze froze and her peaceful heart roared into a pounding rush. She saw Edmond from across the field as he trotted into view, the blue and silver colors of his horse's caparison blowing in the breeze. He looked so safe; the kind of strong man that could protect anyone. He looked like someone to spend your life with. Their kiss flashed through her mind, and she looked away, willing the color in her cheeks back down before someone could notice.

He trotted right to her seat in the crowd. She wanted to melt as she looked into his warm smiling eyes. *Please don't say anything*, she prayed in her head. But Edmond held out his lance in salute. "My Lady Ella, I will win this tournament for you."

Everyone was watching her now. It would be so public, so rude of her, but the words came quietly. "I'm sorry, Lord Edmond. I have chosen another knight for this tourney."

Edmond said nothing. His face was expressionless. He shifted his lance, nodded, and loped his horse away. Eleanor saw Alec choose that moment to trot past him, her green ribbon in obvious view. She cursed him and the promise she'd made him: to not let any other man pledge his victory to her. It was the deal she'd had to make to convince him to bring her along to Normandy. As the crowd tittered around her and she watched Edmond's stiff posture, she cursed again. A deal with the Devil it was.

She watched Edmond stop next to his squire and dismount. Gregory ran over to the herald to say something, then the two of them headed in the direction of the stables on foot. As the tourney began, the herald announced Lord Edmond's horse had gone lame, and he would not be competing. The competition was open for Alec to win everything.

Eleanor sat numb as the events were run, one by one. It was a quick day, and as expected in Edmond's absence, Alec was the victor. He came to get her from the empty arena, where she still sat long after the day was over. She didn't say anything to him as they passed food around the common room of the large wooden guardhouse where the visiting knights had been offered board. She herself barely ate. When she could stand his boastful stories no longer, she took her goblet and walked to one of the windows of the hall. The stars shown bright, the moon's reflection bright on the dusting of snow left earlier in the day.

"Take the flight of steps down to the cellars. Take as long as you need." The voice came from over her shoulder and before she could turn to look at him, Edmond's back was already fading into the crowd.

She looked back at Alec. He was still laughing with his friends. But he glanced at her even then, and she knew he was paying attention to her. Could she get away? As she sipped the last of her sweet wine a thought came to her. Could she get Alec drunk enough to put him to sleep early? She'd never seen him truly drunk. He was pretty tolerant of his alcohol even though he sometimes chose not to act like it. Perhaps with something stronger than wine? Or in a drinking competition? She tried to spot a man who would be a match for Alec's bottomless pit of tolerance. She saw one, a goliath of a man who she had seen before but didn't know, not far from where Alec sat.

He towered over the other men even sitting. His head was twice as big as a normal man's, and his shoulders were as wide as two of her. If anyone could get Alec drunk, he could.

She walked back over to Alec's table, reclaiming her seat. She waited a moment, then said casually, just loud enough that his friends could hear, "That man down there is massive. I thought you were a bottomless pit for ale, but he's been drinking tankards all night." She pointed.

Alec followed her finger to the big man and shrugged, then tried to go back to his conversation.

But his friends had overheard. "That's Gregor. He has drinking competitions at the pub in London every time he's in town. Wins every time. I once saw him sit down and go through a whole barrel of ale."

"A barrel?" Alec raised his eyebrows.

"No joke, Alec. She's right, you down it all just fine but not in comparison to Gregor." He chuckled. "I'd love to see you try though."

"I don't think you can," another friend chimed in.

Alec stole a glance at Eleanor, who kept her face innocent. "You realize I've never been drunk in my life?" He was looking at her, but he spoke more to his friends.

"We know!" they shouted in unison, laughing.

"And a great waste it is! We want to see you drunk, Alec." He banged on the table gleefully. "Or at least as drunk as us for a change. You're tournament champion for goodness sake! Enjoy it!"

Alec pulled his eyes from Eleanor and yielded to his peers. "Gregor!" he boomed. "A fresh barrel and a few toasts until it's empty!"

Gregor chuckled, accepting the subtle challenge.

The men seated themselves across from each other as their comrades cheered them both on. Cup after cup of ale went down, the first few pretty quickly. As the pace slowed yet persisted, Eleanor wondered if her plan would backfire. Gregor was starting to look a little tipsy, but Alec was as steady as ever. A few hours later, after a few dozen toasts to everyone in the room and at least twenty to the regrettably absent King Richard, and nearly a whole barrel of ale in, Gregor burped and said, "I have to piss." As he stood, he swayed for a moment, caught himself on the table and then was steady. "Be right back, Sir Alec!" he slurred. He took a few steps, then went down with a thud that shook the table.

Alec's friends cheered and patted him on the back. Eleanor clapped as well but frowned. She was running out of time.

"I think I'm ready for bed, my dear," Alec said to her and pulled her to his lap. He pulled her green ribbon from his hip-pouch and waved it through the air. "I have won the Lady of the Tourney twice over!" He planted a sloppy wet kiss on her lips before she could pull away. "G'night, boys!"

he called as he rose, an arm still tight around Eleanor's waist. He was fairly steady on his feet, but Eleanor noticed he used her for support to a degree. They climbed up the short wooden stairwell on the east side of the hall, toward the big open sleeping quarters that would one day soon house the castle's permanent garrison. Everyone already up there was fast asleep, their snores nearly matching the din below. Eleanor thought of who waited just a few floors down. Would he still be waiting for her?

She led Alec to their area and let him sit down on the narrow bunk. The alcohol had had an odd effect on him. He was acting sober, and yet he acted tired. She helped him pull off his boots and put his sword next to the bed. As she turned back to him, he pulled her onto his lap again, burying his face in her hair, which was starting to fall out of its elegant knot at the base of her neck. "I told you I knew you would come to me."

Eleanor felt a moment of panic. "That's not why—"

He brought her down with him onto the bed, pulling her to his chest with his strong arms.

"My Ella," he whispered. But not long after his head hit the pillow, he started snoring. His arms still tight around her, he was asleep.

Carefully Eleanor pulled herself from his grasp. It had worked! He was out cold, and hopefully would be for hours. That man truly was a bottomless pit for alcohol. She looked around the sleeping quarters. Everyone was still asleep. Now she just had to get down the stairs without anyone else seeing her. With one more glance at Alec, she tiptoed to the staircase. It was only wide enough for a barrel of wine to fit through. Anyone she passed would be close enough to see exactly who she was. She listened carefully. Silence. She quickly went down to the first doorway which led to the common room. She peeked around the corner; no one was nearby. She went down the next flight, which ended the staircase in a vast underground room with barrels and barrels of wine from ceiling to floor.

It was like a maze. Wine everywhere. The dark rows of different varieties were illuminated only by two torches at the door. She quickly moved down the rows, looking for Edmond. But it was too dark to see.

Suddenly someone pulled her from behind. Before she could call out, Edmond's voice shushed her. "Come this way." He took her hand and pulled her behind the barrels, weaving into the darkness. Just as she was sure it was too impossibly dark to see anything, she saw the glow of a single candle around a corner. It sat on the floor, next to it a flask of wine and a blanket.

"I figured this would be safe enough to meet, as long as we're quiet. I think they're about done drinking up there and won't be down for the rest of the night."

Eleanor turned to him and wrapped her arms around him. With only a moment's hesitation she kissed him with full force. It only took Edmond a moment to get over the shock and kiss her back with a passion so fierce they both had to stop for air. They each panted slightly as Edmond kissed her forehead, resting with his lips there.

"I'm so sorry about the tourney." Eleanor looked up at him. "I had a deal with Alec."

"It's alright. I understand you're in a delicate situation. And like I said before, I am grateful of Alec's protection of you. It's better than I can offer you right now. Do what you have to do. Within reason." He smiled knowingly. "I just didn't have the heart to compete today after that. Didn't want to give him the satisfaction of winning you from me a second time."

Eleanor nodded, and leaned against him, her head on his chest. "It wasn't as easy to get away from him tonight."

"I heard the drinking competition. You know that was a foolish idea, right? That man has never been drunk."

"He fell asleep quickly enough."

"Don't try it again, okay?" Edmond implored, pulling her face up to look into her eyes, the faint candlelight making them sparkle.

Eleanor changed the subject, "I was worried about you. The siege obviously was a success."

"Yes. I am to return back to England in a few weeks. At least for a while. I hope I can see you then."

Eleanor still clung to him.

"Here, have a seat," he led her to the blanket. They sat and leaned back against the wine barrels behind them.

"Any news of Lezay or Montag?" she asked.

"No, they're back in Alsace. For now. I'm sure they'll look for you again once all this fighting calms down." He uncorked the bottle of wine and tilted it in the candlelight so she could see it was only a third full. He handed it to her. "Sorry, not much left since I've been waiting hours for you to get Alec drunk. But you can have it."

Eleanor took a big swallow and leaned against Edmond. He put his arm around her. "You're not sleeping down here are you?" she asked.

"I'm staying as long as you want."

She curled against him more. "Then talk to me. Tell me everything that's happened since Lord Gawain's tourney."

So they talked for hours like friends that had never been apart. The good stories and bad. Of the battles across Normandy and sights of the ancient Holy Land. Eleanor's dream of freedom from her past. Edmond's upcoming orders from King Richard. But in all their talk, Eleanor yet again excluded her adventures as a squire at Neroche. Part of her just wanted to feel like a woman when she was with Edmond. The other part feared he would consider the risks Alec had put her up against to train and compete too dangerous for her, which they probably were. Either way, it was in the past. Alec had not brought up "Alfred" again now that his point had been made. His attention was refocused on Lance, whose noble parents had been none too impressed with Alec's preparation of him. For a brief moment Wilfred's warning rung in her head from those months ago.

There was not much left of night when Eleanor could no longer keep her eyes open. After a long kiss the two finally made their way from the cellars back to the sleeping area and their respective places. Eleanor curled into the bunk next to Alec. He still slept like a rock. And in the morning, he woke with Eleanor beside him.

Eleanor herself slept late the next day. As she woke, she heard two men talking quietly not far from her bed. She listened, still feigning sleep. The sleeping hall sounded quiet other than the two men, most of the knights already at breakfast down below, their muffled voices rising up from the wooden floor.

"I already said I will do what I can to protect her," Alec was insisting.

"You are baiting not just Lezay, but Montag! You need to understand that." Edmond hissed.

"I know, you have said. But that doesn't explain why he wants her. He gave her to Lezay, so she's Lezay's problem . . . and property."

"But Montag is the main head of the monster. He's the one that has it out for her. Lezay was always just the means by which to torture her."

"Torture her?" Alec asked. "She bears no marks of torture, Edmond. I've seen her naked."

Eleanor bit her lip to keep from saying anything. She heard Edmond suck in his breath. When he spoke again his voice was colder. "There are ways to torture that do not leave marks, Alec. I mean only to warn you, it is not just Lezay you need to be wary of."

Eleanor heard boots thud past her toward the stairs to the hall. Edmond paused just inside the view of her narrowed eyes, where the mid-morning sunlight glinted off his dark curly hair. "This arrangement will not last forever. I am using you to protect her as you are using her to get your revenge. Know, Sir Alec, that one day I will have her, and it will not be by threat or by price. I will have her heart to bind her to me always, and even better yet, it will be by her own free will. And even if I do not win her heart, I will forever be true to her, as a man should be. She is not just the Lady of the Tournament; she is so much more. It would do you well to recognize that." Edmond thumped down the rest of the room and down the stairs.

Eleanor lay quietly for a moment. *I will have her heart,* Edmond had said. Eleanor's very heart pounded. She sat up. Right into Alec's hard gaze.

He studied her, searching. Eleanor shifted under his gaze, standing and straightening her gown awkwardly. He said nothing. She glanced at him again as she turned for the stairs, noting how his hand hovered by his sword. Then she had turned the corner, and he was out of sight. She could still feel his attention on her. There could be no denying the truth to the threat Edmond had made, to steal her heart as his own. Neither man knew he had already won it.

Chapter Thirteen

December 1196
Castle Neroche, England

Alec could not get Eleanor away from Edmond fast enough. He had heard the truth not only in his claim toward Eleanor but also in his warning regarding Montag. As soon as they were back in Neroche, he started training her again. Their feet danced through the dusting of snow as they practiced with the sword. Eleanor became so good with it that she and Alec started to consistently stalemate. Desperate to learn something new, she asked, "What if I don't have a sword?"

Alec raised his eyebrows. "Grab something and club him with it."

"And if there's nothing to grab?"

"Are you asking me to teach you hand to hand combat?"

"I don't want to be completely vulnerable with no weapon." Her mind drifted back to the night her dagger on the floor had done nothing to protect her.

"You are no match for a grown man," Alec said, but he was thinking out loud, not saying there was no solution.

"I know," Eleanor said quietly.

Alec sighed and set his sword aside. She did the same. "I may regret showing you this. And you'll never be able to fight in a tourney with these skills. Wrestling is a different matter altogether that you are far too small for. But . . ." he sighed again. "So if he comes at you from the front, take the heel of your hand and shove it up straight and fast, into his nose. We are not doing this for real!" he added quickly, but he took her hand in his, lingering on her thin but callused fingers as he demonstrated the movement. "It will break the nose bone and shove it up into his brain."

Eleanor's eyes went wide as she inhaled sharply and nodded. "What else?"

"I'm sure you know by now that a kick to the groin pretty much disables a man. At least temporarily. We aren't doing that either." Alec thought for a minute. He grabbed her wrist suddenly and she tried to jerk it back in surprise. Alec held tight. "Can't get away like that, huh?" He let go and took her hand and had her clasp his own wrist. She held tight, then he twisted his arm outwards in a circle, forcing her to break the connection. "Out, fast, and down. Knock their wrist away." He grabbed her arm again. She tried it but wasn't fast enough. He jerked her into him, inches away. As he leaned in to kiss her she tried again, faster and harder, and succeeded in not only knocking his wrist away but shoving him back a step.

Alec's teasing smile was cut short as he noted the mild fear in her eyes and shook his head. "You going to tell me what the deal is with you, Lezay, Montag?" She stayed silent and he shook his head again. "I told you my reasons for hating Lezay. Yours can't be worse than that." Still she was quiet. He sighed, continuing, "So other sensitive places for a hit are much the same as with sword. In real life all is fair. Throat, gut, knees . . . any joint really. Stay on your feet like you do with sword and be quick."

She still stayed silent, watching him. It was so unlike her that Alec stopped demonstrating and looked at her with his brows furrowed.

"He raped me," she blurted.

Alec paused and slowly began, "A marriage bed is hardly—"

"No." Eleanor cut in. "He raped me. Brutally. Purposefully. He did things civil men just don't do. Things the church forbids. He took joy in my pain. And I was barely a woman. It was not a mere consummation of the marriage."

Alec softly echoed Edmond's words, "There are ways to torture that don't leave marks." Eleanor just watched him, her face still mildly pained, emotions still conflicting behind her eyes. "Edmond knows all this, doesn't he?" Alec asked.

"He was the first soul I ever told," Eleanor replied.

Alec nodded. He turned from her and picked up his sword, re-sheathing it at his side. He looked at her sideways and asked, "The scar on your abdomen . . .he cut you too, didn't he? I know I didn't mention that to Edmond. He doesn't even know about it, does he? Which means you haven't—"

"The one physical mark Lezay left me with." She ignored his second question.

Alec slowly came up to her and put his hands on her shoulders, looking her in the eye. "I hope one day you will let a man show you that is not how it is supposed to be. Until then, we are against Lezay together."

He released her, and the tension in her left her like an arrow from a bow. She fetched her sword and strapped it back to her side, not saying another word as she turned her back to him and headed to the manor. Just as she was about to step over the threshold, a loud thud behind her snapped her attention back to Alec once more. He stood with his hands braced against the wood of the ring, the muscles of his forearms visibly taut even from a distance as his hands gripped the wood. In a huff, he straightened and yanked his sword from where it was sunk into the rail beside him. That was what she had heard. As Alec stormed towards the barn, Eleanor ducked inside the manor and ran into her room, barring the door behind her.

She leaned on the frame a moment, heaving air into her lungs. Emotions rushed through her, no solitary one taking charge. At the sound of hooves, she stepped to the window, watching as Alec vaulted onto his destrier's back with graceful ease. Snow was falling again, the fine steady kind that alluded to heavier snow to come. Alec didn't notice. The horse reared in protest from a sharp kick, then bolted out the gate.

It was then that the wet tears fell down Eleanor's face. For a second time she had told someone about that night, and it had not gone like it had with Edmond. She did not feel relieved to have shared it. She felt damaged, and she wasn't sure how. She watched Alec fade into the burgeoning snowstorm, feeling his anger as she watched his horse pick up speed. Was he angry at Lezay or at her? Perhaps both? A figure emerged from the stable and caught her eye. Wilfred had a saddle on the wild coal-black colt she knew everyone was forbidden to touch. Her eyes narrowed as he headed toward the back field and out of view. Grabbing her cloak again, she hurried down the stairs, eager to see what he was up to. No sense pining away in the tower like a hopeless maiden.

Chapter Fourteen

Noir, he was called. At a height of seventeen hands of a man, and the true build of a warhorse, he was a magnificent spectacle. Rumor had it that he was the fieriest horse Alec had ever acquired. He had tried everything to break the horse's spirit and ride him but failed. Completely and utterly failed. It had gotten to the point where no bit could be placed in the stallion's mouth, no saddle on his back, and Alec could not even enter the stall. Alec had shut the door on the beast and left him. Aware of his reputation, he did not sell the animal. Wilfred was given sole care of the beast with orders to do no more than feed him and put him to pasture.

So when she saw Wilfred and Noir through the falling snow, Eleanor was spellbound. She could not take her eyes from the horse. He looked down at her, glared at her for even looking at him. The steam of his nostrils looked like smoke in the cold. His presence was pure nobility, and he had the body to match. His coat shined; his long mane hung down past his neck. The long feathers of hair around his ankles framed giant, strong hooves. His body was rippled with muscle, each taut with anticipation of Wilfred's next move. Even as Wilfred vaulted onto his back, the horse did not object. Eleanor proceeded to watch the pair as they performed a variety of maneuvers. They trotted, they cantered, and yet it all held a certain grace to it. Suddenly the horse reared, and Eleanor started in fear for Wilfred, but as they came down she realized Wilfred was perfectly calm. When it happened again, she realized that this too was being commanded by Wilfred. Everything the horse did was being asked of him. Even when he leaped into the air and kicked out, Wilfred was ready, asking for it. As the sun broke through the clouds to signal the end of the day, Wilfred dismounted and rubbed the horse's neck, whispering as always.

It was only then that he noticed Eleanor and paled.

"Ella, do not tell Alec what you have seen."

"Why? Wilfred, that was beautiful. Should he not know that his horse can now be ridden?" she stepped to his side, then edged a few more feet away as Noir snorted at her.

"No. Alec would be furious that I have even touched this horse beyond feeding him, let alone that I did something he cannot do. He must not know, or Noir and I will be cast away. Separately."

"So you taught Noir everything? Even the aires above the ground?"

"He is amazing for his age. I just needed to guide him. You've never seen these things before?"

Eleanor shook her head.

"Battle tactics, m'lady. Ches over there," he motioned to Alec's destrier, still tethered in the stable, "can do them too, but Noir is more balanced. He has a short body. Very compact to get the power from the hindquarters."

"Can he joust?"

"Of course. Any horse can run a straight line," Wilfred replied. Then he looked down into Eleanor's thoughtful face. "No, you can't ride him."

"Could you teach me? Please, Wilfred."

"It's bad enough that I'm riding him. Alec would kill us both if he caught you on him. No. Not to mention he is far too much horse for a woman, yes even you, to handle. No."

"Wilfred, I will do anything." Eleanor pleaded, glancing back and forth between Wilfred and Noir. "I will show you it is possible."

"I know it is possible. It would not surprise me at all. But why should I sacrifice my horse to your glory?"

Eleanor's eyes lit up as he said it. "Why not sacrifice your horse to *your* glory?"

Wilfred was silent as he furrowed his brow in contemplation. "How so?"

"You are old for a squire, much less a groom. You should be made a knight. I will teach you the sword techniques.

You teach me to ride like that. Then one day you will fight a great knight and prove your worth and be made a knight yourself. Just like all the others."

He ignored her fantastical vision. He was, after all, a commoner. "You think you're good enough to joust?"

"I know."

Wilfred watched Noir for a moment. The great horse seemed to nod as he watched back. "You can try. We begin tomorrow, dawn. You will teach me to fight, and I will teach you to ride. Under two conditions."

"Yes?" she asked eagerly.

"You do not speak of this to anyone, and you do not question anything I tell you to do. *Anything*. I tell you to jump off, you jump off. Understood?"

"Yes, sir." Eleanor smiled and they shook hands. With a last glance at Noir, she walked back toward the manor as Wilfred headed to the stable. The falling snow covered the footprints and erased the fact that the horse had ever been out of the barn.

When Alec returned late that night, his cloak soaked with snow, his mount sweated to a foam, it was Eleanor who met him in the main hall. She handed him a hot mug of cider, her hands for once steady as she faced him. He gave her a strange look, though his usually intense gaze avoided hers. With a yawn he turned away from her and up the stairs, the door to his room thudding a bit harder than usual behind him. Eleanor stood alone in the hall a long while, watching after him. Her mind told her she didn't care where he had been or what he had done to so exhaust himself. Yet if that was true, why did she feel so . . . alone?

Eleanor met Wilfred just as dawn broke. He was there with Noir already, bridle in hand. As he led the great horse outside and into the pasture, where his snowy footprints would be expected when Alec woke, he eyed her for any sign of fear. He found none. Eleanor stood next to the great beast and stretched out a hand to stroke his black neck. He was not the first destrier she had ridden. She had ridden since she could walk and her equestrian education had not ceased at Montag's manor. Still, her escape on Montag's destrier had been her greatest challenge. That horse had had fire in his soul, but she had known then that if she did not ride him, she was dead anyway. This horse seemed to burn with the same fire. As she felt the power of the muscle beneath her hand, she looked into Noir's eye. He stared back at her with that same presence, waiting. With a whisper, she swung herself onto his back and took up the reins Wilfred held ready.

Noir lifted his head, the tension in his back balling up like a fist, ready to punch her into the air. She patted his neck and whispered to him.

"Just let him walk," Wilfred commanded. "He'll walk it out. Don't make him stand still too long."

Eleanor obeyed and the pair walked forward. The horse's back still tensed with a dragon's fury, but he obeyed her. She laid a hand on his neck and felt the tension ebb. Wilfred was silent. Eleanor began walking Noir in circles, focusing him, feeling how he responded to her aids. She pushed him to each side with her legs, feeling how he reacted quickly. Within a few moments she felt the light weight of his head in her hands as he searched for a command from that plain bit.

"Trot him." Wilfred said. He folded his arms as the pair glided around the open field in the dawn light, performing the same maneuvers at this faster gait. "Canter", he said, and they stepped into a floating rocking horse rhythm. Noir's energy was completely controlled, his mind willing, his body functioning as if there were no rider at all. They halted in front of Wilfred, completely immobile.

"He is like Pegasus," Eleanor breathed.

"Who taught you to ride?" Wilfred asked.

"My father originally put me on a horse." She bit her tongue as the words spilled out, reminding herself that she was supposed to be keeping her past a secret.

"You learned well."

"I am out of practice. I will be sore tomorrow."

They knew they were running out of time before Alec rose, so Eleanor untacked Noir as Wilfred practiced a few of his sword moves in the barn aisle. He showed better form than he had with Lance, but already she could see his footwork was a mess and he kept leaving himself open for blows. She picked up a wooden sword to join him, and they entered a mini-battle. It wasn't hard to touch him with her sword, but when she did have to block his blows, the force reverberated all the way up her arms and across her back. He hit hard.

"You'd be incredible if you had form," she said when they finished. "Has Alec *ever* worked with you at all?"

"No, I've never been exactly a priority. I don't know who my parents are. No noble lines that could one day be useful. I'm just supposed to work. I'm a groom just because I'm useful with the horses, and that's all I'll likely be. Lance is destined to be a knight by blood. Good, old family."

"Well, that's what our deal's for. First thing is your feet and balance. It's just like riding."

Wilfred paid apt attention as Eleanor explained his mistakes. They worked in the barn as long as they dared, finishing as the cook called the household for breakfast.

A few more months went by in which Eleanor learned Noir's talents inside and out, always careful to work only when Alec was away from the manor, which tended to be more often than usual. Wilfred taught her the technical movements used on battlefields, and they practiced for the joust, galloping toward the rings set in the practice area. She was exceptionally steady and snagged them consistently. In return, she helped Wilfred finesse his swordsmanship, learning things about her own technique as she taught. By early spring, she was ready. Ready for another tourney, ready for Lezay, ready to face her uncle. The combination of training had put her in peak condition, and Noir was as finely tuned as ever.

Chapter Fifteen

May 1197

England

Alec had been absent for much of those winter months. He frequented Sarum and the village there nearby. Politics, he claimed, but the rumors were flying that he had tired of the Lady of the Tournament and was frequenting the taverns . . .and their whores. When he was at the manor, he kept his distance from Eleanor. She could not tell if he was disgusted with her or if he no longer trusted himself to be alone with her.

At dinner in the manor one night in early May, Eleanor casually asked Alec, "When are you going to do another tourney, sir?"

"There is one in Chester in a few days. We'd have to leave tomorrow. Would you like to go?" Alec looked indifferent. He didn't even look up from his plate.

"If you wish me to, sir," Eleanor replied.

"There's a gift for you in my room. I'll give it to you tonight."

When they retired later, Alec knocked on the door between them, not waiting for her answer before he opened it. In his hand was a plain canvas bundle wrapped in twine about the size of a jousting helmet. He tossed it to her as she sat crossed legged on her bed and came to sit beside her. She undid the twine to reveal a gorgeous new gown in a deep berry red.

"It's beautiful," she said in awe and thanked him.

"Try it before the tourney this weekend. Should fit like the green one did. Figured it was time to give you enough of a wardrobe to pretend you have some value to me." Eleanor did not mistake the bite in his words.

"Alec, I—" she started.

"This will likely be the last tourney you have to put up with me at. They are calling most of us to France, to battle, not the luxurious tourneys you are accustomed to. You will not come with me."

"Alec . . ."

He ignored her and continued, somewhat to himself, "Really, quite frankly I don't know why I even have you here anymore. I realize now that you will never give yourself to me, and I am not like Lezay, however you despise me. Thus despite all appearances, I did not truly steal Lezay's wife. With this tension between England and France, I cannot meet him and thus shame him in tournament. And how else can I take all he has? Without revenge, you are just a mouth to feed. So again, why are you here?"

Eleanor was quiet for a moment, feeling devalued and burdensome. "Where else would I go?"

Alec looked at her like he wanted to accuse her of something, then sighed and ran his fingers through his hair. He suddenly rose and slapped the bed post. Eleanor jumped a little, her eyes wide.

"Alec, I am still on your side," she began carefully. "We both want Lezay to suffer. And I know it is frustrating that a whole year has gone by and we are no closer, but think of how much more prepared we are to face him now. You have trained me to protect myself. You have bolstered our 'love story' at the tourneys. All that is left is to face him. And I know him enough that he will not stop looking for me. It is only a matter of time. We need to come up with a plan for that moment."

"I have tried to think of a plan for months. What are we supposed to do? Just show up at the same tourney as him and say, 'Look here, I have your wife. Now come and try to kill me!' No! It's not even cowardice, it's idiocy." Alec fumed in frustration. "It's been three years since he killed my father, and I haven't even told him I know the truth of what he did."

"We just need time—" Eleanor started again.

"Time! How much time? Time enough that he dies peacefully as an old man? He's what now, nearly fifty? Still fights like a bull, I'm told."

Eleanor shook her head. She knew too well that Lezay had an unnatural ability to preserve the finer qualities of youth despite his age. "Just remember, I am on your side."

"Eleanor, all you ever wanted from me was my silence. I understand why now, and yet I've watched you work like a serf all winter. You aren't, though. If you're staying for revenge, the point is mute – you can't help me. If you're staying for my protection, I'm afraid that's more dangerous than your previous obscurity. Perhaps it's best if you just change your name and disappear into the crowd tomorrow. I won't say a word." Alec turned his back to her and slammed the door between them.

When the shock of his words wore off, Eleanor curled up in a ball and cried quietly. If she had lost her value to Alec, where would she go then? She could not go to Edmond, not while he was on the battlefields. And alone, with the rumors she now had going about her . . .. She shuddered.

When they left for the tourney, Eleanor tucked her sword in amongst the bags.

"Probably not a bad idea," Wilfred said as he piled the last of the gear on the wagon. "He's been in a rare mood all week. He's been downright nasty to Lance. The pressure is always on him to win and win. He puts that pressure on

Lance, too. And he can't even test him in another squire tourney because there are none. Wilfred shook his head, "This event at Chester might be the first tourney of the season in all of England, even for the knights. And it's a small one."

Alec and Lance joined them.

"Are we ready?" Alec asked.

He gave Eleanor a boost onto her usual palfrey where she sat aside. Wilfred rode the draft with the little cart harnessed behind it, and Lance and Alec rode their destriers. Within no time, the four were off to Chester.

The usual bustle of the tourney was reassuring in a way. They settled in among the tents surrounding the castle, few though they were compared to other locations the previous summer. As the squires set up camp, Alec took Eleanor on his arm and made the usual rounds to meet up with his friends. Eleanor was glad to see Edmond's tent among the rest, and later they passed him. Her heart swelled to see him. He gave her a smile and a nod, but he looked as stressed as Alec. Something was on his mind as well. She grew cold just to see it. She was sure he would tell her if they could find time together.

Alec left her in a seat amongst the other peasantry. No familiar faces this time. She pulled the green ribbon from her hair and gave it to Alec as always, even managing to smile.

It wasn't long before Edmond rode up to the stands. Eleanor heard one girl near to her whisper, "He must be coming for one of us this time. I heard Ella turned him down in France. In front of everyone!" He stopped in front of Eleanor but said nothing. She smiled this time and slipped the chain from her neck. She kissed her father's ring as she handed it to Edmond. He smiled and some of his usual warmth returned to his eyes. She knew he had something on his mind.

The events went smoothly with average excitement. As Eleanor watched, she wondered what was wrong with Edmond . . . and Alec, too, for that matter. They both were just slightly off in form. Alec won the sword competition; Edmond won the joust. The big man Gregor that Alec had drunk with in Normandy won the wrestling. A northerner won the archery, and so it went throughout the remainder of the weapons events. No overall tournament champion, which left Eleanor to her own choosing. Eleanor obligingly waited for Alec before they headed up to the castle for dinner. He gave her half of a smile but then avoided her gaze. She wondered if he had really believed she would disappear into the crowd.

Through dinner they both sat tensely, formally. Alec bantered with his friends as always, practically ignoring Eleanor unless the others drew her into the conversation. She was quick to smile and play her part but when she could, she shot glances at Edmond, who remained with his own squire and friends. The tension between her and Alec was reaching a palpable strain. Eleanor wondered how the others could ignore it. With trembling fingers she pushed away from the table and excused herself to use the necessary. Instead of returning to the table, she turned further down the hall.

The solitude was like a breath of fresh air. She paced for a moment, shaking out her fingers, which still prickled with sweaty tension. She smoothed back her hair, pressing the wisps that had escaped throughout the day into some semblance of order. Finally, she stopped at the narrow window and pressed her hands to the cool stones. She drew a deep breath, exhaling slowly.

It should not matter how he treated her. It should not matter if he wanted her to leave. She had made it clear they were together only for revenge, and he was respecting exactly that. And now that revenge was looking impossible, he was right to separate from her. She would be alright on her own. She always had been. She didn't need Alec.

Eleanor took another deep breath, closing her eyes as she let it out into the cool spring night.

She smelled him, felt him, before she heard him. She kept her eyes squeezed shut, her palms sweating anew for another reason. "Edmond," she acknowledged quietly.

"Eleanor," he said as softly as a breath as he stepped beside her. He was so close to her that her skirts brushed his leg. She could feel him, yet he held back from touching her, as if she was a phantom that would vanish if he reached for it.

Eyes still shut, Eleanor said quietly, "I missed you, Edmond."

"I missed you. You have no idea." Edmond chewed his tongue, considering his words. "It tortures me to think of you with him. Has he been good to you?"

She sighed, and finally turned to him, blinking as she studied every line of his jaw anew. "I can't complain. And you? How are things in France?"

"Much the same. Wish I had more time to spend here." The pained look returned to his eyes. "I had hoped you would be here today. I will not be back for a long time. I was finally chosen as an advisor. I will be in Normandy for a long while."

"How long exactly?"

"Possibly years." He avoided her gaze.

Eleanor squeezed her eyes shut and turned back to the cool breeze of the window again. "God, I wish I could go with you. Would you allow me to?"

"You know it's not safe for you in France right now. But I hope one day you can meet me." He leaned against the wall next to her, brushing a piece of hair from her cheek. In a whisper he breathed in her ear, "I would make you my wife."

Her eyes flew open into his steady gaze. "Don't tease me," she scolded. As his steady gaze held hers, he smiled gently. He was serious. "But Lezay . . ."

"I know, I know," Edmond allowed. "Thus not yet. But I am patient." He kissed her forehead. "Do you want to go back to the hall?"

Eleanor shook her head.

"A walk then?"

Silently Eleanor turned from her window and led the way down the stairs and out of the castle into the courtyard below. Their pace was easy, absentminded even. Eleanor unconsciously led them to the encampment of tents next to the tournament ground. She hesitated when she realized this, then suddenly plunged forward. "Edmond, come with me. I want to show you something." She led him to Alec's tent, and as he waited by the opening she quickly went inside and retrieved her sword. His eyes widened at the sight of her with the weapon, and even more so when she belted it on over her dress. "Come," she urged, and they made their way through the moonlight to the sword ring that was still set with pennants from the tourney.

"Elle, what are you doing?" Edmond asked.

She unsheathed her blade and stepped back from him. "There are still some things you don't know about me. Let's figure out our dilemma. With *all* the facts." She motioned with her sword for him to unsheathe his.

"Elle . . ." he said as he obeyed cautiously.

"No one can see us down here. We have an hour or so yet before they head to bed."

"This isn't a game," he insisted. But already she was on the advance; he had no choice but to block her blow. The strength she came with startled him. He was almost too slow to block the next flurry of strikes she aimed at him. He tested her with a mild advance of his own, but she only pushed him back further. He tested her a little more. Same result. Soon he was locked in full battle with her, just as if he was against a real knight. But she was quicker than the knights he normally fought.

She made another advance at Edmond that he blocked a little easier than she'd hoped. Edmond knocked her sword arm away, spun in close to her, and pinned her against the rail with his sword at her neck. But Eleanor flicked her sword up in a quick movement that knocked his sword back enough that she could duck free and give him a little push from behind.

Edmond gritted his teeth in frustration. "Who are you, woman?"

She took a couple quick swings to him, backing him into the same rail he had just pinned her to. "I am Eleanor de Levan d'Aquitaine," she said. She held her sword at his throat for a second, just to show that she had him, then dropped it and smiled, stepping back. He dropped his sword and covered the distance to her in a step to kiss her passionately, both his hands pulling her face to his.

They were both sweaty and out of breath despite the cool evening.

"Where on earth did you learn all that? You just made me work harder than I had to the whole tournament. Except for that round with Alec," he grimaced.

"It started with you and Raoul. But Alec's been teaching me all winter. I actually won a tourney at Neroche last year. Against all the other squires. Figured I should finally tell you about that. Well, show you."

"A squire tourney?" His mind smoked to keep up. "This is how Alec intends to destroy Lezay's honor? By facing you off against him? I don't like it," he said and furrowed his brow.

"No!" she exclaimed. "This was just so I can protect myself."

Edmond breathed a sigh of relief.

"Do you think that would work?" she asked, his false assumption inspiring her.

"Would what work?"

"Me fighting Lezay."

Edmond drew a sharp breath. "I did like Alec's plan of dishonoring Lezay and taking everything he has. But not by putting *you* up against him to fight to the death."

"What if it's not a fight to the death? What if it's a controlled fight, rules . . . like a tourney? What if it *is* at a tourney?" Her mind was spinning.

"Eleanor . . ."

"No, listen. You are right. If I fight him and win, then reveal who I am, it will shame and dishonor him in front of all the other knights. No man wants to lose to a woman, Lezay above all others. And if I reveal myself in a big crowd, he and Montag will not dare try anything in front of everyone else. The aftermath will be dangerous of course, but everyone will know. Everyone will be watching out for me; they will not be able to make me disappear like they did Alec's father."

"The *other* knights you best at the tourney will also not take kindly to losing to a woman."

"Unless you and Alec stand by my side in a show of chivalry." She frowned, "Worst case, I tell everyone what Lezay did to me as a warning against those who—"

Edmond cut her off. "No, that is personal and needs never be told to anyone other than me. I will stand by your side. I think Alec will too."

"Things are not going well with Alec," she said, looking away. "I told him, Edmond. I thought he would react . . . I don't know. Differently. He can barely be in the same room as me anymore. He thinks I have too much of a past and realizes now that I meant it when I said ours was to be a chaste relationship. I deny him the first of his trio of revenge. So in his words, 'why am I here?' And I must say, he has a point. Something needs to happen. Then I can be free of Lezay, Alec can be free of me, and you . . . do you really want to marry me?"

"Yes, Eleanor. As soon as we can do it safely." He took her hand and squeezed it gently. "I have your ring by the way." He took her chain with the pewter ring from around his neck and hung it back around hers. She fingered it a moment with one hand, her other hand finding Edmond's again. She needed to feel him, to anchor her as her mind swam with the idea blooming there.

"Edmond, in all seriousness, what if I reveal myself as a chevaleresse? You were there when I told the story of Lady Adelaide. I wouldn't be the first. Even Queen Eleanor used to ride into battle with her husband! I would be free. I could reclaim my lands and titles. It would be a life of war, but if you truly mean to marry me, it would mean I'd have a place at your side."

"So dangerous, Eleanor . . ."

"No less than now. At least it would be a danger that I could face. Edmond, every day I worry they will find me. At any one of these tourneys they could show up, kidnap me 'home'. Montag is probably livid enough at this point that he'd just kill me and be done with it. Lezay would say I died in childbirth like all his other wives. But you know they won't make it a simple death. They catch me here, or at Alec's manor unaware, and I am done. I cannot go back to them. I would rather die." Her hand shook with the thought. She went to pull it away, but Edmond held it fast.

"If that is what you choose, then this is the way to do it. You proved to me that you have the skill to match the knights in self-defense. But to finish them you will have to learn to joust and—"

"I can joust."

"What? You need a destrier. How can you possibly joust?"

"It's taken care of." She kept quiet about Wilfred's help.

Edmond looked at her in awe. "Well, then that settles that. If you can win a tourney, you will have them where you want them."

"I will use my father's crest."

Edmond nodded, "They know the crest. It will allow you to compete. Pretend you are a nephew of the Levans."

She shook her head. "My uncle on my father's side died young." She hesitated. "I can say I am Enric de Levan's son."

"Won't they know he had no son?"

Eleanor looked down. "He did. My brother would be seventeen now, had he lived more than a day. It wasn't long after that when I went into Montag's care, so people may believe he stayed hidden like I was. If they remember my father at all, they'll remember my mother's two pregnancies." Eleanor thought back to the songs the troubadours had sung about the Fair Igraine. Some of them she'd sung in the halls at home, her mother laughing after her. Others her pink-cheeked mother had scolded never to repeat. "Things happened so fast when they died, I don't think anyone except Montag knew my brother passed."

Edmond nodded solemnly. "After the tourney, I will help you get out of there. I'm still hoping Alec comes around and will help you, too."

Eleanor frowned. "The marriage is still a problem, though. Lezay will say I have to return with him because I am his wife. Do you still have contacts in the church? Can they petition the pope, tell him what Lezay did to me? I swear, I did not say my oaths. Do you think he would grant an annulment?"

"I will write my contacts and try. But the pope is not an easy man to reach."

"Imagine the blow to them if I not only beat them in the tourney but show a writ proving my freedom from Lezay." Eleanor beamed at Edmond for the first time, then threw her arms around his neck. Hope was such a powerful force.

Edmond held her tight but cautioned in her ear, "Promise me, don't plan any great revealing until we have all the players in attendance. Me of course. Alec, Lezay, Montag . . . they all have to be there. This can't get to one or the other by word of mouth or they will have time to raise forces against you. And Elle, you have to win. Do you understand? If you lose, we don't reveal you as you. We find another way. If you lose but reveal you're a woman they'll still be insulted that you even competed, but you won't be enough of a threat to keep them away from you, to make them respect you as a knightess. They will still see you as a foolish, disobedient woman and treat you as such. You hear me? You lose, they never know it was you."

She looked into his eyes and saw the genuine concern there. She nodded.

Voices from across the field interrupted them, and they quickly retrieved their swords and ran to Edmond's tent. After checking to make sure no one had seen them, Edmond came in after her, running into her in the dark. He reached to light a candle as her arms encircled him once again, pulling him away from the task. She kissed him lightly, nervously, as her heart pounded. He stood frozen as her fingers traced his chest down to his belt buckle. He caught her fingers in his own.

"Don't tease me," he said roughly. He squeezed her fingertips lightly and brought them to his lips, kissing them with a delicacy that made Eleanor shiver.

She knew he was right. The decent thing would be to leave now and go back to the party. The chivalric thing would be for him to protect her virtues as a damsel and send her back to her own lonely bed. Yet Eleanor was no damsel, and all decency had been lost months ago during her charade with Alec. With that negated, there was only what she felt in this moment, and right now, that was a need to be with Edmond. Her gut ached for him. Her heart pounded. Her palms sweated in a rush of emotion she had not felt, had not allowed herself to feel, in years.

Gently he tried to push her away.

"I need to know," she said simply.

He froze again, her fingertips still in his own.

She reached for the shadow of his face, tracing his jaw with a languid caress. "I need to know what it should be like." She blinked away a tear, grateful for the darkness.

Edmond didn't move, couldn't speak. But he did not stop her as her hands nervously traced his body. She unbuckled his sword in the darkness, then her own, letting them both fall to the ground with muffled thuds. Her hands reached for him and worked the toggles of his tunic by feel. Just enough moonlight shown through the tent fabric for them to see the shadows of each other.

Edmond looked into her eyes in the dim light and pushed a piece of her hair out of her face. Even in the moonlight he could see the sparkle in her eye, pleading. "You're sure? You're ready?"

She nodded, fearing for a moment that he would reject her. "You are the tournament champion, Lord Edmond."

But he did not reject her. He could not help himself, whether you call it love or lust or simply a man's passion, he did not need to be given permission a second time. When his lips touched hers, she melted. She leaned against his solid frame and his arms wrapped around her. When he pulled away from the kiss she didn't move, just stood with her eyes closed, lips parted. When she let those blue eyes flutter open she met Edmond's intense gaze. They pulled back into each other simultaneously, something more urgent in their touch.

Eleanor's fingertips pulsed as she traced his back, her hands finally curling around his shoulders to pull him to her. His hands caressed her back, then cupped her face. His breathing picked up as she felt a hard bulge through their clothes, clothes they pulled from each other, layer by layer. He spun her around to do the laces at the back of her gown, and she caught her breath at the memory of how roughly she had lost her dress before. Edmond slowed, kissing her neck as he pulled each lace gently free.

"Just me, Elle. Just me."

Eleanor took a few deep breaths as he carefully pulled the gown down her shoulders so it fell in a puddle of fabric at her feet. She covered her chest with her arms, even though she still had on her shift. But this, too, Edmond coaxed down her shoulders, kissing her neck, her shoulder, her back as the fabric fell away. She was naked before him in the veiled moonlight.

She turned back to him, suddenly shy, but he wasn't having it. He pulled her hand to the bulge in his breeches. "You finish it," he said, putting his hands on his head and letting her explore his body. Her fingers traced the muscles of his abs, the line of his hips. She freed his belt buckle, tracing the anatomy beneath it with her fingertips, torturing him. He reached for her and pulled her into a deep kiss, letting his naked body press against hers. Then he laid down on his bed of blankets on the floor of the tent. Layers of warm wool blankets formed a nest that he opened to her, and she joined him. Hip to hip they laid as their breath mingled.

"I love you," he whispered, a bit in awe as if the words were a revelation.

Eleanor smiled and pulled him down to a kiss. Maybe, just maybe, this is what love really was. She let herself get lost in the kiss and said nothing.

If Edmond noticed her lack of reply, he didn't react to it. He pulled her on top of him and guided himself into her. She whimpered at first, curling against his chest. There was no pain, only fear. He just laid there locked with her, caressing her until she relaxed, then he let her lead. Gradually the tension between them rose until their hearts pounded as one, taking them to another place, another world where problems could be forgotten. Eleanor did not pull away, and he could not let her go. The two lines became one very poignant combination, setting in motion the events that would eventually change everything they knew. As their breath returned to a normal pace, they curled together beneath the blankets. There in the crook of Edmond's arm Eleanor felt safe and content for the first time in many years. She felt like she was home.

Chapter Sixteen

He knew. As soon as he saw her, he knew.

Edmond had insisted when dawn broke that she go back to Alec so they could keep him both apprised of their plan and on their team. And she had. But he *knew*.

She stood awkwardly outside the tent in the early light, blushing furiously as Alec stood before her with his arms crossed, barring her entrance to his tent. He was silent, but the fury on his face was obvious. He did not need words, and the look he gave screamed everything. *Where were you? Why him? How dare you come back here? Why are you back here?*

So she stood there in front of him, willing herself to meet his glare without turning away, dressed in the gown he had bought her but Edmond had taken off of her the night before. The minutes dragged on, both of them locked in a showdown. Her blush faded and turned to her own glare. She did not belong to him. Why should she feel shame?

The tension was only heightened when Lance stepped out of the tent yawning, saw the showdown and guessed what it meant. He started laughing. Wilfred came out behind him and started passing worried glances back and forth between the two of them. His hands clenched and unclenched at his sides, and Eleanor knew he would defend her if Alec turned physical on her. But Lance would be right at Alec's side.

She sighed. "Sir Alec, I am still on your side," she reminded him.

The four of them still stood frozen outside the tent. Wilfred and Lance kept looking back and forth between them, one with anticipation and one with fear, while Eleanor and Alec held their stare-down.

Finally, Alec conceded. "I hope you have a good reason for showing up here. Get in." He nodded to the tent. To his squires he said, "Get the horses ready. We leave now."

Wilfred hesitated as Eleanor entered the tent with Alec behind her. Alec turned back to him and glared. Wilfred tilted his head, took a deep breath, and headed to the stable.

Inside, Alec still had not softened toward Eleanor. "You better have a good reason for being here after what you've done."

"I told you, I'm still on your side," she insisted. "And we have a plan for revenge. Your revenge. In full."

Alec raised his eyebrows.

She continued, "We've always liked your idea to take everything that Lezay has . . . but his life. Part one, me. Edmond is helping me seek an annulment through his contacts in the holy land. I intend to wave it in Lezay's face that he has no claim on me. Part two, his land, is contingent on the success of part three, his honor." She took a deep breath. "I want to fight in a real tournament. When the moment is right, I will fight, and I will win. And Lezay and Montag will be shamed by losing to a woman. I want to be recognized as the heir I am, that I can rightfully get my lands and titles back. But I need your help. I need you to support me on that day, even if I beat you, in true form of chivalry so the other knights follow suit. And I need you to let me stay with you." She finally broke from his gaze and looked down. "Edmond returns to France. It is not safe for me there until this plan is complete."

Alec looked her up and down, his anger softening somewhat. At least she had decent reason for returning. Her plan for revenge was exactly what he wanted, though unlikely to succeed as it was. "And if you lose?"

"I don't reveal my true self, and we come up with some other arrangement."

Alec nodded. "And when do you two plan to have this big reveal? And where? There are hardly any tourneys this season. At least in England. Do you hope friendship is rekindled in France where they will once again invite knights of multiple nationalities to the same tourneys?"

"Yes," she said with certainty. "We wait until then."

She was optimistic, Alec would give her that. If she could wait for that plan, so could he. "And after we finish with Lezay, you go with Edmond?"

Eleanor blushed and nodded. "When the annulment comes, we will be married."

Alec crossed his arms. "I see. So how exactly do you picture our arrangement working until then? Am I to lock you in the tower at Neroche and avoid you?"

Eleanor fidgeted with the stitching of her gown. "Nothing needs to change yet," she mumbled.

"What?"

"Nothing . . ." She sighed and forced herself to look into Alec's eyes. "I told Edmond that if you'd let me stay, I would continue this charade. How else will I get to scout out the tourneys without a dozen other men stalking me?"

Alec furrowed his brow, studying her. "He agreed?"

"He's about as happy about it as you are." She frowned.

Alec shook his head at her, eyes wide with incredulity. "Well then, my lady, I suppose our arrangement continues. Until then." He held out his hand to her. "Should we head to breakfast?"

Eleanor looked at him cautiously and took his hand as he led her back out of the tent. A few yards away she saw Edmond, sword belted to his side, arms crossed over his chest, watching them carefully, and realized he had stayed within earshot of them the entire time. If Alec had acted on his anger and she had screamed, Edmond would have been right there. Alec noticed him too. As Eleanor went to pull her fingers from Alec's grip, he squeezed them tighter and pulled her into him. He gave Edmond a look that was half sneer, half glare, and clearly showed that his protection of Eleanor wouldn't come without his continual efforts to change her affections. Edmond stormed over to Alec, who pulled Eleanor behind him and popped him a heavy punch on his jaw. Edmond gritted his teeth and straightened back up. He came no closer. Silence echoed across the sleepy field of tents.

"Take care of her," Edmond conceded, knowing that it was the only way to keep Eleanor safe for now.

Alec put his arm around Eleanor's shoulders and sneered. He steered her toward the manor once again. She hung back as best as she could.

"Just let me say goodbye," she pleaded.

Alec leaned to her that his lips brushed her ear and hissed, "You had all night to say goodbye."

Chapter Seventeen

May, 1197

Castle Neroche, England

"You need to come in hard, hard enough to knock me back!" Alec shouted at her in frustration as they practiced back at Neroche later that week.

"You know I'm not strong enough for that. I'll never be. But if I step wide—" Eleanor protested.

"No knight is going to make that mistake."

Eleanor swung at him again with all her strength, only to hit metal to metal with their blunted practice swords. The force reverberated down her arms and she cried out in pain, barely stepping back in time as Alec swung at her again.

His onslaught was unending. Ever since she had told him of her and Edmond's plan he had been forcing her to practice with him daily just like he had the past fall, and he was more ferocious than ever. She was sore, bruised, and straight up exhausted.

Eleanor gritted her teeth. It was time to end the practice. If she was going to do this, she was going to win her way, not how Alec thought she should. As he swung at her again, she sidestepped around him, whacking his hauberk on his open side. The blunted blade would not cut the metal, but he'd have a bruise. He started yelling at her again about how that move was stupid, so she cut in again, toward his knee. Just enough of a whack to make him limp a stride. As he back-swung in fury, sword raised, she nimbly ducked and charged toward him, letting the blade slice along the front of the hauberk this time, just enough force to knock the breath out of him. Before he could regain it, her blade rested along his neck.

"No knight will make that mistake, eh?" she chided, then stepped back and sheathed her sword.

Alec straightened, fury in his eyes.

"I'm done," she told him, signaling with her hands toward him, palms out. "This is going too far."

"You're the one who wants to compete against the fiercest warriors in the land! Don't you want to know what you are up against?"

"Not like this, Alec."

"Not like what? Like the brutal reality it's going to be?"

"I know what it's going to be! I've been around tournaments my whole life. I appreciate you trying to help me get stronger, but this . . . this is something else. You are relentless Alec. This doesn't do us any good if one of us – either one of us – gets hurt."

He was silent in his anger as her words hit home, so she turned and headed back to the manor. He called after her, "You can't do it if you can't joust! It's a bit different than riding that little palfrey!"

She didn't acknowledge him. She knew *that* part of her training was going solidly well with Wilfred. She also knew that when Alec found out what horse she was using to prepare, all hope of jousting would be lost and possibly all of Alec's support of her plan. It was a detail she was still trying to work out.

Eleanor reached up and held the ring around her neck tight in her fist. As much as it reminded her of her father, it now reminded her of Edmond as well. To bind herself to someone only to be immediately separated . . . it was a new kind of torture. She knew Alec was right in part to yell at her. She was making mistakes. She was distracted. Her daydreams strayed all too often to the precious night she had had with Edmond. She had to find a way to make this plan work, that she could be with him for good. The first thing she would do when she saw him again would be to tell him she loved him. She was a fool for not having told him already.

Between the emotions with Edmond and her frustrations with Alec, Eleanor felt overwhelmed by the time she had made the short walk back to the manor. She swung by Wilfred's cottage just off the manor courtyard, which he shared with the old caretaker Guillaume. Eleanor had watched him enter and leave the building many times, and yet she had never dared go near it. Something about the way the caretaker watched everyone at the manor unnerved her. It was as if he knew far more than he let on. She approached the worn oak door and knocked.

"Hi," Wilfred said when he opened it, his eyebrows raised in mild surprise.

"Hi," Eleanor said cautiously. "Would you mind going for a ride with me?"

Wilfred blinked at her, then silently followed her, shutting the door behind him. In silence they tacked up the draft and the palfrey, and Eleanor led the way away from the manor. A few minutes into the ride, when they were out of sight from the manor, Wilfred spoke, "What's on your mind?"

Eleanor let the silence go on a minute longer, half listening to him, half listening to the sound of the horses' hooves. "Fight with Alec."

"That all?"

"Course not." She hesitated. "I miss Edmond. But you probably know that." She hesitated. "Thank you for coming out with me."

"Any time. Not like I've got a lot of friends around here either. Alec is Alec and Lance is . . . Lance. Marie is nice enough." Wilfred cleared his throat. "She doesn't talk much. As you know, the rest of our lovely manor staff are nice folk but it's nice to know someone your own age. I can't say much to your Edmond situation, but Alec . . . he may have a temper, but he has pretty good control of it."

"He didn't have a lot of control left today. It turned from instruction to self-defense. Does he say why he's so mad?"

"Edmond, Ella. Everyone knows about you two. When the greatest knight in the kingdom, the knight who will have no woman, finally chooses one, who just so happens to be the most desired woman at every tourney – and hardest to win over – everyone talks. And they talk about how you were so devoted to Alec before that . . . and after. It's confusing, even for those of us watching it in front of our eyes. It has Alec in an odd spot among his peers; they ask him things I don't think he himself knows how to explain. Of course, he has always wanted you for himself. It is only natural for him to loathe the fact that you gave yourself to Edmond, and there is nothing he can do about it. And still, you won't yield to *him*. I don't know how you do it."

Eleanor shrugged. "It's not always easy. But now since Edmond . . ." She blushed. "I'm not sure how the conversation got here, but I'm sure you don't want to hear about all this."

Wilfred shrugged. "Would you rather talk about sword fighting some more? Jousting? The war in France? More manly topics?"

Eleanor smiled. It was ironic, this line she walked between the men's world and the women's. If she was with Helin back at Lady Gwen's they would be talking for hours about Alec and Edmond and love. Yet instead her life was secrets, swordplay, horses, sweat, and blood.

"Men can fall in love too, you know. It's not just a woman's fantasy," Wilfred said.

"I've only met one that talked about it. Making love, yes. But actual love, not so much."

"Not all men can be taken at face value. Just like you women, we hide things until we let someone in. Feelings. Strengths. Secrets." Wilfred glanced over at her as they rode side by side. "The sun falls, leaving grey. No power of black night; no daylight to yield clear sight. The grey gloom reveals the truth between, lies and cruel intentions seen. We draw too close, kiss the stars, by half-light be burned."

Eleanor looked hard at Wilfred, surprised by his poetic moment.

"Kiss the stars in their half-light, and you will be burned," Wilfred whispered to himself. He shot an apologetic glance at Eleanor. "Sorry, it's just something Old Guillaume always used to say. Usually when I was asking too many questions."

"Am I asking too many questions?" She narrowed her eyes at him, offense bubbling in her already sour mood.

"Not exactly," Wilfred said carefully. "I think . . . I think Old Guillaume's point was just that we should pay attention to the answers we already have, while being aware what we think is right is only part of the truth."

Eleanor frowned. "What am I not seeing, Wilfred?"

Wilfred twisted the reins in his hands absently. He was silent a long moment. "You have allies, Ella. That's all."

Ella closed her eyes a moment, readying to fend off yet another young amour, disappointment washing over her that it was her only friend at Neroche. "Wilfred, you and I . . ."

He chuckled. "We are friends, Ella. That is plenty."

"Oh good, it's just you said . . ."

"Thank the good Lord, you are not my type, Ella. Perhaps every other man in the world's."

She wasn't sure if she should be offended or not, but she smiled, in part with relief.

"I am one of those allies though." He reached toward her and gave her shoulder a gentle push. "I promise you won't get burned around me."

Eleanor studied him carefully, her lips turning to a smile with the realization that he meant it.

"Hey, we should head back."

Eleanor nodded, her mood lightened somehow, and turned to follow Wilfred as they headed back toward Neroche.

When they got to the stable, still in twilight, there were five extra horses in the barn.

Wilfred inhaled with trepidation. "His friends. Can't say I'm surprised, being as they haven't had tourneys to get drunk together. You better get cleaned up before they see you. I've got your horse. Go."

Eleanor thanked him and hurried up to the manor. As she made her way up to the hall, where Alec and his friends were sitting around the hearth, she overheard their hushed conversation.

One man was saying, "Alec, we knew you had to be told. We've all known for months that being called over there was imminent. But after the men that have been butchered, it makes you wonder if King Richard's aspirations are too high."

"And you're sure it was him?" Alec asked.

"You can't mistake that crest, Alec. Tournament champion! I must admit I was getting tired of seeing it placed above mine at the tourneys," the first man said.

A second man interjected, "Not like there's to be tourneys until all this quiets down."

Alec answered, "I think there will be. Soon. King Richard has made his point. The blood was on both sides. This should give us a short truce."

"But he will still call us over there," said the third man in a gruffer voice.

Alec questioned, "You said his group was outnumbered. Ambushed. Are you sure it was the French? The French under the order of the king, or others working alone like they did with my father?"

"I didn't hear," said the first man. "They say his squire Gregory survived and was en route to Richard with the news."

Eleanor froze in place. She already felt the blood running from her face, yet she was breaking a sweat. France. Tournament champion. A squire named Gregory. She must have misheard. Or it was a coincidence.

"He has no heir?" Alec asked.

"No. You know his reputation. None like ours, that's for certain," said a fourth voice with a slight chuckle.

The first voice cut back in, his tone somber, "He was a nice enough man. Shame to end the way he did."

Eleanor came around the corner of the staircase into the room and stood with her hand still trailing the wall. All six faces looked up at her in synchrony, then looked to Alec. They were not the haughty looks they usually gave him when they dined together at the tourney feasts. They were solemn for the first she'd ever seen them.

She knew. But she asked anyway.

"Lord Edmond?"

No one answered her for a long moment. Finally, Alec nodded.

Eleanor's eyes went wide. She didn't know how much Alec's friends knew about her and Edmond, so she tried to check herself. But as her knees started to shake, she knew she would lose the fight to quell the pain within her.

She uttered, "Excuse me," barely intelligibly and ran up the second stone staircase to the top of the tower.

With the door to her room shut tight behind her, she could hold back the flood no more. She gasped as sobs shook her shoulders. Suddenly her stomach flipped and a wave of nausea drained her until her stomach was empty. She opened the window and leaned with her hands against the sill, heaving air into her lungs. But she couldn't breathe.

Edmond was dead.

She heard the door open and tried to slow her breathing, wiping the tears from her face with her sleeve.

"Just breathe," she heard Wilfred's voice from the doorway. "Count to three with each breath. Let it out slow."

She turned to face him, leaning back against the wall, her shaking fingers covering her mouth, her eyes wide. Wilfred had not left the doorway, merely held the heavy door open with his hand, the toes of his boots firmly on the other side of the threshold as if he was afraid to cross it.

Alec suddenly appeared at the top of the stairs, giving Wilfred a hard look.

He pushed Wilfred to the side as he brushed into Eleanor's room, "What brings you here, my little *groom*?"

Wilfred didn't bat an eye at the insult, particularly since ironically enough he was taller than Alec, though younger and leaner. "I merely am concerned for her. Edmond's death is a great shock," Wilfred said calmly.

"Go! Leave us!" Alec ordered.

Wilfred was ready to protest when Eleanor took a deep shaky breath and again stood straight before them. She wiped her eyes with the edge of her sleeve and brushed past both of them to lead the way back into the hall without a word. Wilfred and Alec exchanged glances and followed. She sat quietly at Alec's side the rest of the night. His friends were tactful enough not to bring up Edmond or France. Alec mercifully called it an early night, and guided Eleanor to the stairs with a gentle hand on her elbow. Alone at last, she curled in a ball on her bed and let her shoulders heave again with silent sobs, tears streaming down her face, until she slept a restless sleep of living nightmares.

Edmond was dead. She was again alone.

Chapter Eighteen

June 1197

Castle Neroche, England

Eleanor was never one to mope, but in the days that followed the loss of Edmond, she was lost. She didn't leave her room but to refill her water pitcher and use the privy. The warm breeze that blew in through her window made the tears that stained her face burn cold as she lay in her bed, staring at the beamed ceiling. It was not just the loss of the man she had given herself to and was so close to admitting she loved, but it was the loss of her future. Love or no, she liked being with Edmond and pictured her life with him. She trusted him, a thing which in her life was a stark rarity. The future she foresaw was one without fake identities, without fear of her past. She was happy at his side, his partner even in battle. She pictured that she would protect him as he protected her.

But she had not protected him.

Here she was, hidden away in another man's home, while Edmond had been fighting for his life. And he had failed. And she had not been there to help him.

Eleanor buried her face in her pillow for the hundredth time, willing her mind numb. Maybe wine would work? But that would involve getting up and going down to the kitchens, and the kitchens would smell of food, and just the thought of food repulsed her. Her stomach had never quite settled since she got the news. It didn't matter, she had no desire to eat. She had no desire for anything but to turn invisible like the wind and drift far, far away from Neroche, from England and France.

Nothing could hurt the wind.

What was she to do now that her plan was upended? Without Edmond's support, how could she rally the other knights to her when Lezay and Montag turned on her? Alec seemed unreliable at best. Without them, win or lose at the tourney, she was alone. Her own charms would be all she had to rely on, and she had never been the most eloquent orator.

She heard voices on the stairs.

Alec's voice rang clear as he stomped up the stairs, "I've had enough of her tears! I gave her time. More than I should have."

"It was a blow to her. You understand that," Wilfred pled, his voice more distant than Alec's.

They paused, just outside her door.

"Aye, I understand that. And what do you know of it?" Alec snapped.

"She loved him."

"She told you this?"

"Not in so many words, but one can tell."

"Is she the one you've been sneaking off to see? Have you two been *talking*?" Something in Wilfred's expression must have triggered Alec, for his tone grew darker. "You thought I didn't notice? You've been looking like a stag in the rut for months. I swear, Edmond is one thing, but if you've been . . ."

Wilfred cut him off quickly, "I swear to you, Alec, I've never touched her. We are only friends."

There was silence a moment, then Eleanor's door banged open with enough force to shake the roof. Any normal person would have started, but she still laid there, face in her pillow, numb and wishing to be invisible.

But she was not invisible to Alec.

He made it to her in two long strides and ripped the pillow from her hands, shoving her onto her back. She looked at him emotionlessly, her wrists caught in his strong hands while he stood over her, anger flashing in his eyes.

"It's been too long that you've been locked away, *Ella*." He stressed her plain name for Wilfred's sake, and she could tell he was tired of it. "Time to get up, move on. But I need to know some things first." He let go of her and stood, and though she should have stood up herself, she didn't care enough to, and just laid there like he'd shoved her, her eyes looking out the window to her left, seeing nothing. She heard Wilfred shift his weight awkwardly in the doorway.

Alec asked her coldly, quiet as a breath, "Is Edmond the only one?"

The question surprised her, despite what she had overheard between him and Wilfred. She turned to face him again, blinking.

"Is he?" Alec asked again.

She shook her head, in part from confusion, in part to answer him. But he already knew the answer was no.

His temper flared again, and he leaned over her, his arms supporting his weight on either side of her head. He wanted her to look him in the eye when she told him how she'd been playing him with not only Edmond but Wilfred and who knows how many other men. Then she and perhaps half his staff would suffer. He pulled her close and hissed in her ear, "Who have you spread your pretty little legs for other than your precious Edmond?"

She blinked, looking him in his sharp brown eyes. Then she said firmly, "Sir Rothulfus Lezay de Leuwenstein d'Alsace."

Alec studied her, perhaps finally deciding she and Wilfred were telling the truth. Without taking the pressure off her, he asked, "Are you still willing to be the Lady of the

Tournament, as we originally agreed before Edmond put all these silly ideas in your head about fighting?"

Eleanor wanted to argue that it was *Alec* who had first pushed the idea of her fighting and had instructed her but didn't. "If that is what you wish, sir."

Suddenly his lips were on hers, his hands tightening on her wrists like vices. Just as she was about to fight and pull away in panic, Wilfred cleared his throat and Alec let her go and rose to his full height again. She didn't dare stay laying there now. She rose to her feet, her fists clenched at her sides, furious.

Alec half-smiled. "That's more like you, Ella."

She reveled in the spark that emanated from her, the thrum of blood in her veins. The breeze from the window stirred her hair in a wild halo, and Alec's gaze held on her. She could only imagine how the rest-deprived circles under her eyes clashed against the flush of her fury.

He cleared his throat. "Finally, a tourney again. In three days, at Lord Gawain's. It will be a week-long affair this time. You should get cleaned up. And for God's sake, eat something." Alec turned his back to her and all but pushed Wilfred back out the door and down the steps.

Eleanor grabbed the nearest thing she could find and threw it hard against the door. It just so happened to be her mug, which shattered to pieces.

That man had some nerve, to come in here, accuse her of being a loose woman, then kiss her himself. *While she was grieving.*

Or did he simply know that fury could quench misery?

Chapter Nineteen

Eleanor's face was set as she entered into the carnival-like atmosphere. She looked at no one, nothing. Her eyes were blurred as she walked next to Alec through the crowd. With such a delay to the start of the season, this week would be one of pure revelry and socialization. The events would start the next day, broken up over the course of the week with the joust as the finale. Eleanor was in no mood for it. If spoken to, she nodded or answered as briefly as possible. Her cold glare at anyone who approached her ensured that no one would attempt to win the tournament for her. Even Alec did not talk to her but in politeness.

Wilfred spoke to her when Alec walked away, "Ella, people will soon notice if you do not relax a bit."

She looked at him, but he was staring straight ahead. "Notice what?"

Wilfred still did not look at her. "You need to mingle with the others more, or at least look around. There are events unfolding that would do you well to note."

"Events such as what?" For the first time that day she noticed the crowds and the knights and the competition. Her eyes caught the red and black crest as Wilfred spoke the name.

"Sir Raoul de Montag."

"Raoul," she breathed.

Wilfred touched her elbow and nodded in another direction. "And . . ."

Eleanor's eyes widened at none other than her uncle himself. He was surrounded by a group of knights a way down the field from where she and Wilfred stood, asking questions about her. Eleanor, even from the distance she was away, could hear every word her uncle shouted.

"Lady Eleanor was kidnapped, but we still have faith she is alive. Our sources indicate she is in this country. The award to be given for her return to us is one-hundred pieces of gold. That's a pretty penny, boys. You can treat your own ladies fine with that."

Without realizing it, Eleanor clenched Wilfred's arm.

"M'lady," he said softly, and she glanced quickly down and let go.

But her eyes went wide. "Wilfred, you know who I am," she breathed. He gave a single nod to confirm. "How long have you known?"

"I've suspected you had noble blood for some time. You carry yourself like it when you play the part at the tourneys. So when you gave Lezay's name yesterday . . . not hard to figure it out after that. I've got good ears. I know the stories."

"You overheard." She quieted. That had been her own mistake, forgetting in that moment with Alec's pressure on her that Wilfred was within earshot. "Have you told any of this to another?"

"No."

"Let's keep it that way." Her eyes went back to her uncle, who thankfully was working his way in the opposite direction. She glanced around, unsure of where to go.

Alec returned, clasping her hand as he pulled her arm into his own, casually strolling in the opposite direction of Montag. For once she didn't pull away. His strength grounded her in that moment.

Alec needed no explanation. He had seen and overheard Montag himself. "One hundred pounds could buy me a new sword. More horses. Serfs. Pay taxes for months," he whispered to her.

"Please, let's go home now," she pleaded in a whisper so those around them wouldn't hear. "I'm not ready to face him. Not now." Her hands shook. Alec must have seen the desperation in her eyes, for she saw the concern in his own. It was an expression akin to pity, yet Eleanor was too terrified to care.

From what they had overheard, Edmond had been right to warn that Montag was the greater threat. The man was a talented charmer, and there was no softness in his words for Eleanor though he made it clear he wanted his "favorite niece" back. Without ado, Alec agreed to take her home. He left Lance to watch their tent, intent on competing against his rivals later in the week.

The thought crossed Eleanor's mind that they had traveled for days for nothing, and Alec would have to travel even more to return, but she did not apologize. A numbness she had not felt in years overcame her, a longing to hide in a deep dark cave away from the world. How could something from so long ago still awaken such emotion?

When they got back to Neroche, Eleanor went straight up to her room, miserable. The only words spoken on the ride had been between Alec and Wilfred, and they were only instructions on what needed to be done now that Alec had to make the long journey to Sarum again in the morning. In her tower, she sat with her back to the door, her face to the window where the stars shown in the warm early-summer night. Twilight fell unnoticed, at least until Alec silently lit the torches of the room, breaking the dim light but not chasing the shadows. Only her hair moved, dancing in the gentle breeze from the window. For once she had let it hang loose in its long dark waves. She still was fully dressed in the burgundy gown, the laces drawn tight up her back. They kept her upright, her vision focused on the far horizon.

The voice that came from her didn't sound like her own. It held so much pain, yet the monotone of it showed a numbness only a mind trying to protect itself can create. "I know what you want," she said. "Just take it. I will go back to him soon anyway. He has almost found me."

The sound of Alec moving around the room behind her stopped, and he seemed to hold his breath. After a long moment, he sat on the bed next to her. She didn't move. They sat like that for a long while, staring at the stars. On the distant horizon, lightning flashed, lighting up the far hills. The distant sound of thunder echoed toward the tower.

"When I was a boy there was a storm like this," Alec said quietly. "My grandfather always said this kind of storm, when the stars fire bolts at each other, is a battle storm." As if on cue the wind picked up outside, the hot breeze blowing across their faces through the open window. The stars sparkled as another bolt of lightning flashed across the horizon. "He said when this storm comes, the charge in the air will set fire in the hearts of all who see it. The fire will burn their deepest desires brighter, and when among warriors, it can ignite war. But the stars, the stars arrest that fire and hold it until it need be released. Just like a warrior can hold strength until he needs it most."

"It is the second one of its kind I have seen this year," Eleanor said, her tone still stiff, but less pained as she remembered the night she first met Edmond on the battlement wall outside London.

Alec continued. "Maybe you still have a great battle coming. It is building up your stores." She caught his glance at her. There could be so many meanings to his words. Which had he intended? He changed the subject. "I won't throw you out, Eleanor."

"Then take what you want from me," she again said coldly. "Make it 'worth your while'."

Alec didn't move, his silence belying his concern for her indifferent tone. "I'm not Lezay."

Suddenly, he stood in front of her, blocking her view of the window as the distant boom of the thunder could be heard again. Her eyes snapped up to his, and before she could react, he shoved her back on the bed and was on top of her. "If you don't want this, fight back," he hissed. She didn't fight. His lips found hers, and he roughly coaxed them apart with his kiss. His hand ran up her thigh, beneath her skirt. She squirmed beneath him. "Shh. You said I could," he reminded her. She quieted and stilled. She opened her legs to him, the decidedly careless way she did it creating a flash of pain in Alec's eyes. She looked away as his hands retreated from her thighs, only for his lips to catch hers with greater passion, desperately asking for something more than just the kiss.

He let the length of his body rest on top of her, catching her wrists in his hands, keeping his lips locked to hers. Suddenly her lips were responding to his. He released her wrists to caress her cheek and eased off of her slightly. When she twined her hands into his hair to pull him in closer to her, Alec's pulse quickened, the drum in his neck visible in the torchlight. "Eleanor," he breathed, the lust in his voice as he kissed her with a new passion.

Yet the sound of his voice was like a whip across her face. Eleanor suddenly realized where she was and who she was with and squirmed away, a hot flush in her face that the dim light veiled. For a moment, just a moment, she had forgotten everything that had happened that week. The guilt at betraying Edmond in this way stabbed her anew.

"I can't," she said, resting on her elbows, still beneath him but ready to pull away.

"I can," Alec said slyly. The storm outside was almost there, the stars now gone. A bright flash and a loud boom shook the tower windows. He moved to kiss her again.

"No!" she shouted, and pulled herself away from him, kicking him square in the chest with both of her bare feet. He reeled back a few paces to the wall. She quickly spun off the other side of the bed and fetched her sword from its scabbard at the bed's head, aiming at Alec, ready for him to fight.

But Alec had no sword. She looked; it wasn't even in the room. She looked back to Alec, still holding her sword at the ready, and was shocked to see the smile on his face. Confusion flitted across her face.

"Welcome back, Eleanor." Alec chuckled. "Didn't take as much as I thought to bring you back to life."

Eleanor frowned, then realizing he was no threat, lowered the sword. Her anger turned inward to herself. "I would have let you!"

Alec laughed even harder. "No, you wouldn't have. You didn't! You have a sword pointed at me. And you kicked me! A weaker man could have broken a rib with that one." He rubbed his chest. "I almost thought for a minute that I had convinced you, but I guess I'll have to keep trying." Then he stilled himself, looking her in the eye through the torchlight as the storm flashed outside again, on top of them now, the rain starting. "You are stronger than you think, Eleanor." He walked around the bed to her, wary still of her sword arm. "And not just physically, Eleanor." He tapped her heart with his index finger. "Here. You can overcome this, and whatever else is coming your way. *You are strong.*"

Eleanor's lip quivered as the rain blew in the open window, sending a spray of water across the small room to them. She went to it, the sword still in her right hand. The wind blew her hair back from her face as the rain spattered her dress to an even darker red. Her tears were washed by the storm. When she turned back to face Alec, framed by the open window behind her and the flashes of lightning, the torchlight from the far wall glowing on her sharp features, she was a fearsome sight to behold. Battle Storm indeed.

Lady Eleanor de Levan was born anew.

Chapter Twenty

"What are you doing?" Wilfred asked as Eleanor packed saddlebags with provisions, her sword, the hauberk she had won, and blankets. She wore the same clothes she had worn at the squire tourney months before: breeches, tall leather boots, and the bulky leather jacket Alec had scavenged as "armor." She threw a filthy old gambeson over her arm, brushing bits of straw off of the thick quilted padding.

"Going to a tourney," she answered. She grabbed an apple and bit it halfway, holding it in her teeth as she continued to gather supplies. Wilfred caught a flash of a blue and yellow tunic in her saddlebag.

Wilfred looked confused, "But we just came back from Lord Gawain's."

Eleanor took a bite of the apple and spoke with her mouth full, "I'm going back." She paused and looked hard at Wilfred. "Why aren't you there? Alec left before dawn this morning."

"I'm a mere groom, remember? Can't go along to every tourney." He followed her as she went back to gathering things, his long legs stretching to meet her purposeful strides as she headed to the barn. "And I'm supposed to be keeping an eye on you. He told me you wouldn't want to go today. Why are you going back there? Yesterday you were hiding from Montag."

She stopped outside the barn door, smiling mischievously before wrenching it aside. "Now I fight him."

Wilfred stood in shock for a moment. He had known she was preparing for something, but this? She was hiding from Montag, and it didn't take much imagination to wonder why, but there was no way she intended to actually fight in a knight's tournament. Who would allow it?

"Ella . . ."

"Eleanor," she corrected him.

Wilfred rolled his eyes in frustration. He couldn't keep up with who she was, moment by moment. "Just because you won a squire tourney or are the Lady of the Tournament does not mean you are a knight. Only ordained knights may compete, and you know it."

She held her father's ring in front of Wilfred's nose. "You know who I am. You know this crest. So does everyone else. I will enter under my father's name, claiming to be his long-lost son. With my helmet on and hair up, no one will know the difference. And they won't know if I am or am not officially knighted."

"If they catch you—"

Eleanor hesitated, Noir's saddle on her hip. Softly she said, "I know". Then she pushed past Wilfred. "But I'm done hiding. My past is dark, and I've been afraid of it too long. But I'm going to throw the windows wide open on it now and let the sun burn every last shadow away. Fear of the future is at least . . . different." Wordlessly Wilfred watched as she tossed the saddle up on Noir. The big horse pawed the ground impatiently. With a deft movement Eleanor had the horse's bridle on and turned him toward Wilfred. He stepped aside to let her pass, following a few feet behind them.

She mounted Noir in the courtyard, her hair blowing wildly in the wind around her. The great stallion tensed, but her hand on his neck kept him in check. "You've been a good friend, Wilfred," she said with sincerity.

"There's nothing I can say to stop you, is there?" Wilfred asked, looking up at her, his hand on her rein.

"I've never been so certain of something in my life," she said solemnly. Wilfred released the rein, and with a cluck to Noir she was on her way.

Chapter Twenty-One

When she reached Sarum, she tied Noir in the familiar stables, hoping to delay Alec noticing him until it was too late. She strode the crowd with confidence, which helped her overcome her shorter stature. The men made way for her as she boldly marched toward the registrar with her hand casually on her sword, hair tucked under her helm, padding it to help it fit better. With the tourney already in progress, men were everywhere, already in their armor, so her helmed head was inconspicuous. Gauntlets laced tight around her forearms, almost reaching the demi-length sleeves of the hauberk. The bulk of the armor alone lent her the figure of a man. Her blue tunic had three yellow disks sewn across her crest and was belted tight around her middle. Her calloused working woman's hands would wear no gloves, all the better to grip her sword.

"Sir Enric de Levan d'Aquitaine," she stated gruffly to the registrar.

The registrar looked up at her in surprise. "He's been dead for years." His eyes lingered on the crest of her tunic just the same.

"I am his son, given his name," Eleanor replied steadily, swallowing the twist of nervousness in her stomach without flinching.

"He had no son."

"Ah, so you are a master of genealogy, too, then?" She leaned toward him, fire sparking in her eyes. "I am the child of Sir Enric de Levan. I swear such on my father's grave." She noted the registrar's skepticism so she added, "Sir Enric, son of Sir Enrique de Levan, Son of Sir Enrique the Fierce, son of Lord Guillaume Fitzguillaume, son of Guillaume le Barbare. Would you like me to continue?"

The registrar balked, more gently asking, "You have proof of bloodline?" His eyes widened when Eleanor showed him the ring, which she now wore on her thumb. The famous engraving of flames surrounding three disks flashed up at the man. "I did not know any were left in that family, son or otherwise. But nonetheless, I wish you luck, sir." He whispered quietly, "May you bring the Levan name to the lips of the people again."

Eleanor nodded and walked back into the crowd, finding a spot where she could see. She had struck the badges of the sword and lance, entering herself in both the joust and sword competitions, the last events of the week.

"Ella," someone said behind her quietly.

She jumped and turned with her hand on her sword to see Wilfred. "You came?" she questioned, her eyebrows raised.

Wilfred remained expressionless, watching the events, pretending he wasn't talking directly to her. "Figured you could use some help. But I give Alec about five minutes before he notices me, so I need to head over to him and pretend I came to help *him*. Unless he knows about this plan of yours?" He glanced at her, but she remained silent. "Thought so. Anyway, you may be interested in who is here," said Wilfred softly. "Sir Lezay d'Alsace, Lord Montag, Sir Raoul la fil de Montag, Sir Alec of course, and . . . Lord Edmond's squire".

Eleanor's eyes went wide, "Gregory?"

"Aye. And he recognized me. He wants to talk to you." Wilfred pointed toward the trees at the back of the tilting yard.

Eleanor gave him a wide-eyed glance and walked over to where Edmond's teenage squire Gregory stood, just on the edges of the crowd. He wore a leather brigandine open in the summer heat, sword belted to his side, his horse in hand with a habergeon tied to the back of the saddle. He looked exhausted. He must have traveled constantly since Edmond's death to get back to England so soon. She stood before him a moment, checking her emotions, then asked, "Is it true?"

Gregory nodded solemnly. The survivor's guilt was on his face. "It was an ambush. He–"

Eleanor cut him off. "I can't handle the details right now. Eventually I may want to know but not today." She added gently, "I am glad you are safe."

Gregory nodded with understanding. "He gave me this for you." He held out a leather pouch about the size of Eleanor's hand.

Eleanor accepted it with shaking hands, hesitating before pulling the string. Inside was Edmond's gold crested ring. She held it for a moment and stared. There it was, the two rings twined beneath the tree. Though she appreciated the finality, she wondered why he had given it to her. It was generally scorned, even dangerous, to entrust a family crest to someone not of the blood. She blinked back emotion. No time.

As she tucked the ring back into the pouch her fingers brushed the folded parchment inside. Her heart skipped a beat. Had he succeeded in the short amount of time he had? Carefully she pulled it out, her fingers shaking. She glanced at Gregory, who smiled slightly. As she unfolded it, there in a monk's neat black script was a certificate with her name on it. An annulment. Signed by the pope.

"Good Lord . . . Gregory." Her eyes widened at the squire before her. "How did he—?"

Gregory dropped his voice to a whisper. "Forged, m'lady. But it should be enough. You'd have to take it to the pope himself to verify its accuracy. He paid a monk friend that he trusts a pretty sum to make it up and keep quiet. He had a papal seal on hand that we could copy. If you look closely you'll see it's backwards from a true papal seal. But who's going to look that close?"

Eleanor let out her breath in a low whistle. She studied the scripted letter, the signature and crossed key seal at the bottom. It looked real.

Wilfred appeared before them. "They are calling for you." he said, jolting Eleanor back to the real world, and the tourney at hand.

"Thank you Gregory. So much. And take care of yourself," she said, and then hurriedly refolded the parchment into the pouch and tucked the pouch deep into her jacket.

Within moments Ella was heralded into the sword ring. When her name was announced only a few of the older knights shared looks and paid attention to her. The rest watched as if she was just another knight. The bets were certainly not in her favor. She was so small! How could such a scrawny boy succeed against these big warriors?

She fought with all the skill of her training: weaving, ducking, and getting hits in on her opponent before he could react. She exited unscathed. Three more knights went down flawlessly in the following rounds, securing her place in the final.

She watched from a spot along the rail as the other men fought. Lezay and Montag had not entered the sword competition, but Raoul had done reasonably well up until this last round, where a brute of a man had dealt him a blow that made all the spectators wince. He yielded and was out. In the ring now were the big man, Sir Geoffrey of Cheshire, and Sir Alec.

No matter who won, Eleanor would have her hands full in the final round.

Wilfred appeared by her side, silently watching as Alec's skill was slowly eating away at the big man's brute strength. "You've done well," he said quietly, not looking at her.

"It's about to get much harder," Eleanor said through gritted teeth as the crowd gasped as the big man dealt Alec a blow that left him staggering backwards.

Wilfred discreetly handed her a flask of water. "Drink up."

Eleanor gratefully took the flask and drank deeply, watching the men over the rim. Alec had regained his footing, and with a sly twist and a duck hammered Sir Geoffrey in the knee. The man bellowed in pain, clutching his leg with his free hand. Before his sword hand could come up to block Alec's next blow, Sir Geoffrey had a broken nose and was on his back in the dirt, Alec's sword blade at his neck. He yielded.

Wilfred gave Eleanor the briefest look and an encouraging nod, then walked over to his knight. Alec took his helmet off and wiped sweat from his brow, smiling as his men congratulated him, still oblivious of her. Eleanor drank a little more, then checked her armor and stepped into the ring, ready.

Alec stretched his arms, eyeing her as she waited for him to take his well-earned break before the final. His eyes narrowed at the familiarity. Then he saw the crest. In a fury he grabbed his sword and headed toward her, unhelmed and unheralded. Wilfred got in front of him, his strong arm across his chest, for once getting in Alec's face. The words he said were calm, too quiet for Eleanor to hear, just like how he talked to Noir when he seemed ready to breathe fire. Alec stopped. Whatever Wilfred had said, Alec was listening. Wilfred released him, and Alec put on his helmet.

Eleanor spun her sword in her hand, the leather straps she had woven around the handle keeping the grip from slipping with sweat.

The herald was announcing them.

Alec's fury was unmistakable, but he was cool. He spoke that only she could hear over the noise of the crowd, "I wish you had told me this was your plan last night. I would have withdrawn. I cannot let you win, Eleanor, not here in the final. And you will get hurt. I'm not holding back in front of all these people. Withdraw now, go home."

She shook her head, "You know I can't. And I know you can't. Do your best."

In answer Alec took the first swing, and it reverberated down her arm as her sword instinctively raised to block the hit. It was the only hit Alec would get on her.

Soon the two were locked in a dance of swinging swords and footwork the crowd had never seen. Never had two so well-matched fighters met in the sword ring and evaded each's other's blows for so long. Alec began his tricks, yet she caught and blocked each before he could fully execute. He seemed surprised that his attacks were so easily thwarted, and it threw him off. Eleanor swung hard and hit him across the shoulders. His mail protected him, but it would leave a bruise. His shock turned to anger, and they continued on. He spun and swung, but instead of his sword hitting the knight that had stood there moments before, he sliced air. Eleanor got a second hit in, to his chest, pushing him back a step. Steel clashed on steel for a while as the crowd around them grew. Both their names rang on the people's lips, but they were deaf to it, focusing solely on each other. Eleanor feigned a swing to Alec's knees and as he jumped back to avoid it, he tripped. His heavy mail made him stagger, and he lost the opportunity to hit Eleanor's stomach at the vulnerable moment in between. She made contact with his right shoulder and Alec gave a yelp of pain. His arm failed him, and he dropped his sword to clutch his arm. Eleanor had her blade at his neck in an instant. The herald called it her victory, and with a polite, chivalrous nod to the stunned Alec, she turned and walked away, into the crowd that patted her on the back. She did not smile, though inwardly she breathed a sigh of relief. One event down.

In the field nearby the joust had started. Five rings hung from a pole, with knights gallantly trying to stick them with their lance. The very smallest ring was the size of a thumb, just wide enough for the very tip of the lance to run through. No one had yet attempted to get it. As knight by knight dropped out by missing the second smallest, or continued on by ringing it, Eleanor prepared Noir for her turn, listening to the crowd and the heralds. Lezay, her uncle, all were there. They too competed, and they had all continued on up to the second smallest ring.

Alec took his turn just before her, his great chestnut destrier carrying him true to all the rings, down to that second smallest. She took a deep breath, pushing her helmet down a little lower as she rode Noir past him toward the field.

"What the—!" she heard Alec exclaim when he recognized Noir. He rode up next to her, and she felt Noir tense. She laid her hand on Noir's neck, not slowing her approach to the tilting field. "You're going to get killed on that horse," he said to her, obviously angry now. "Go home before this goes to Hell!"

But then she was in the tilting field, and he was behind her, and there were four rings that she needed to catch in order to move on to the next round. She rode Noir forward with a steady arm, catching each ring until finally she was aiming for the second smallest. Easily the lance slid into the ring, pulling it free from the string as they galloped past. She was in.

She trotted over to the sidelines, sweat dripping down her back. It had warmed up and she was sweating, but she dared not take off her helmet or any of her layers. Wilfred discreetly handed her another flask of water then disappeared back into the crowd. As she drank from atop Noir, she watched.

Alec was clearly a favorite. The ladies called to him whenever he trotted past the stands. They were thrilled that Ella, the Lady of the Tournament, was nowhere to be seen. But Alec, who had been playing to them before he recognized her, was now venting to Wilfred about her and her use of his horse, which he didn't dare bring up publicly in the middle of the tourney. At least he cared for her enough to not make the whole thing blow up at that moment. Wilfred was trying to calm him down and having some small success, as Alec kept telling the glowering Lance to shut up and insisting they all be quiet. Her cousin, Sir Raoul, was also popular with the ladies, but he wasn't doing as well in the tournament. He was out, having missed that second smallest ring. And there, on the opposite end of the field, she saw her uncle's colors: a bright red flag with black stripes. Next to it, the black and white pennant of Sir Lezay himself. So they really were both there after all. Eleanor watched them awhile, but their attention was focused solely on the joust still going on. There were seven more men to go, and none of them seemed to be succeeding.

Eleanor eyed the crowd for Lady Gwen. She was seated with Lord Gawain at her side for a change. She had heard rumor he was injured, and the cane he had tried to hide behind his chair proved it. Gwen looked as beautiful as ever, with Helin obediently at her side.

Eleanor's attention was caught by a conversation between two merchants next to her.

"Many men did well today. If everyone gets that smallest ring they will go to full combat."

"Full combat? I thought they stopped that after Prince Geoffrey was killed?"

"Last year Lord Edmond of Fougères and Sir Alec Earnblaec did a round. They were riding tie for tie for what seemed hours. This is pretty close. If things continue like this, what else can they do? Some of these knights will be lancing rings all day if they don't think of something."

"I think Lord Montag will win. I doubt anyone can maintain the power he does to finish the competition strong."

"I agree," the second merchant said.

As the last knight finished, people around her spoke of a contact joust. Too many made it to the next round. Even if they only took those who had looped that second smallest ring, there were still five: Lezay, Montag, Eleanor, Alec, and a Sir Jacques de Gascon.

A herald rose, and said, "Those who rung the second smallest ring will have another go. You must ring the smallest to continue."

The knights reorganized and prepared once again for the contest. One by one they went forward. Alec and Jacques both missed it, cursing as they left the field. Eleanor followed, and to the roar of the crowd and by the steadiness of Noir, got it. Lezay followed her and missed, brushing the ring that it merely swayed on its ribbon. Eleanor allowed herself a smile. Even if she did not win, she had beaten her husband. That was all that mattered. Last was Sir Montag. When he too succeeded there was a deafening cheer. Two finishers! Eleanor shifted in the saddle, refocusing.

The herald ordered the two to ride again, and both succeeded. When they did it yet a third time, with both succeeding again, there was a murmur through the crowd. A contact joust was expected, and by Lord Gawain's order, a contact joust was to be had. The knights were sent to opposite sides of the field and armor checked. Wilfred appeared at her side and took hold of Noir's bridle. "Please don't do this," he pleaded.

Alec rode up, halting next to her. "El—" He stopped himself, eyeing the crowd, "You can ride in a straight line, but you've never been hit with a lance. The force is like the kick of a horse. He will *kill* you."

Eleanor patiently held out her hand toward Wilfred for the new lance. He and Alec exchanged worried looks, but then he handed it to her. While Wilfred held Noir's reins, she did a final check of her mail. Alec was right, her small frame would have little protection from the blow of a lance running at full gallop. But she couldn't think about that now. The rush of victory, not just over Montag and Lezay but as Tournament Champion among all the man, was so close she could taste it.

Alec shook his head. "This is suicide," he whispered under his breath. "Think of Edmond! Would he have approved of this plan?"

Eleanor frowned, the bite of those words hitting true. "What choice do I have now? I am this close. This close! This opportunity will not rise again. This is not suicide. I am going to win." She looked past Alec toward the list, her hands steady as she held lance in one and reins in the other. Noir snorted, and she didn't flinch.

"I won't watch you kill yourself." With a last long look at her, Alec turned his horse and headed back into the crowd, out of sight.

The announcer called.

Montag looked well, now that she saw him directly across the field from her. He was as huge of a man as the mountains he was named from, solid bulk but not fat.

His trimmed grey beard stuck out from under his helmet, which was little more than a metal cap with a nosepiece, just like hers. The destrier he sat on was even taller than Noir. Eleanor smiled inwardly for a moment, wondering if that horse was as fast as the destrier she had stolen.

"Ella," Wilfred said quietly from her side as she turned Noir toward Montag. "He looks away a stride before he hits. I saw him in a melee once before, years ago. This time around make the horse step sideways at that moment and avoid the blow, throw him off. I need a round to watch his form. You won't get him off by sheer strength."

Eleanor nodded just as the announcer called for the two knights to charge. With a solid kick Noir leaped forward with Eleanor perfectly in tune with him. She leveled her lance but did not aim; she watched Montag's head. They were six strides, four strides, two strides apart when she prepared Noir to sidestep. Just as Montag looked away and thrust with his lance, Noir glided sideways and the knights passed each other with no contact. Montag's lance thrust into air, and the empty impact nearly made Montag drop it. Before the crowd could notice, Noir was back on the same line he had been. They circled back to their squires, the crowd murmuring in wonder. The battle-hardened Montag never missed, particularly when his target was much larger than a tiny ring.

Wilfred was ready for her when she returned. "It's his left hip. He weights himself in it to brace, but in doing so his upper body turns, just slightly. Hit him on that left side, as hard as you can. Use Noir's force. It will push him off balance and he will fall toward you. Be wary of his lance in the process. In theory it should swing to the outside, but if he holds onto it as he falls it could hit you in the back, long sided."

"And if he hits me first?"

"Don't let him. Thrust into it in that stride before."

The announcer called again and Eleanor spun Noir around once more. She felt the energy of the crowd transfer to him and his temper flare.

"Not now, ma chère," she whispered and laid a hand on his neck.

He settled enough for her to ask him to gallop, and he bolted forward. The two steeds rushed toward each other, and the crowd roared, but Eleanor heard nothing in her concentration. Just before the last stride she thrust with all of her and Noir's power. She hit Montag hard on the left side, the uneven distribution of his weight in his hips throwing his outside shoulder around. His balance lost beneath his heavy mail, he fell, his lance hitting the back of Noir's hindquarters. The black horse bolted, and Eleanor dropped what was left of her lance to grab both reins as hard as she could. She got him under control at the edge of the tilting field, circling back to face the long stretch where she halted and stroked the horse's neck, his whole body still shaking. The crowd stared at her in shock, silent. Montag was picking himself back up to his feet.

"Mon Dieu," Eleanor breathed. Then the world around them exploded.

The crowd roared its approval at the defeat of Lord Montag of Alsace. Montag took off his helmet and glared at her. Raoul was making his way to him somewhat in shock at the defeat. Wilfred was running the edge of the crowd toward her. Lezay, too, was approaching on his grey stallion, and he had the look Eleanor feared more than all the rest. He was beginning to figure out the puzzle. She glanced around for Alec, hoping that he would give her a sign that he would still stand up for her . . . or even a sign that she should cut her losses and keep her mouth shut, but she didn't see him.

And it was too late for that.

Lezay rode up to her. The sight of his scarred face sent a shiver down her spine and made her stomach flip. He stood his horse nose to tail directly next to her and smirked as he looked into her eyes. "Hello wife," he said, then to the crowd shouted, "Sir Enric de Levan is dead. He had no living son. Only a *daughter*, who would be the only one still in possession of the Levan family crest."

Noir sidestepped away from Lezay's big horse, but he followed. Eleanor spun Noir so he was facing the grey horse head on, pivoting as the grey circled them.

"What's wrong, wife?" Lezay teased in a voice only she would hear, again pushing his horse toward her so that Noir had to back up.

"I am not your wife," Eleanor said, keeping him in front of Noir. She noted that he was pushing her toward Montag, who still watched them in the center of the ring.

"But it *is* you. Show them, Eleanor, show them who their tournament champion is!" He pushed her back a few more steps.

On cue, Noir rose into the air and struck out with his front feet. Lezay's grey skirted sideways. Noir came back down, his nostrils flaring, his eyes wide. Lezay kept his distance and halted, the two horses and riders staring each other down.

Eleanor reached up with one hand and pushed her helmet and the padded cap beneath it off her head. She tossed them into the dust at Lezay's feet as her long hair tumbled down. She knew that without the helmet or her hair cut short, she could not fake her gender. The crowd made a collective gasp and went silent, watching the scene play out in front of them in awe and confusion.

Knights could not flee. She would not flee. So she stood before them on her black dragon of a horse, her hands full of Noir's reins. Sweat dripped down her back and between her breasts. Her long, dark hair framed her face, and what wisps weren't damp with exertion blew gently in the breeze. Even in armor, everyone could tell she was the Lady of the Tournament.

Lezay took all this in, his leer chilling Eleanor as it had when she was a mere girl. It was the look of a man who wholeheartedly believed he owned her. To the crowd Lezay shouted, "Ladies and Gentlemen, I give you Lady Eleanor de Lezay . . . my wife." He gestured toward her and started laughing, as if he had made a grand joke. But the crowd to its credit did not laugh. They were still confused.

"Sir Alec of Neroche! Where are you? Sir Alec!" Lezay shouted, his eyes searching the crowd. Alec stepped forward, the crowd parting to allow him through, still mounted on his destrier, his reins lazily in one hand as he let the horse walk in slow motion to the center of the field. His face was unreadable. Lezay continued, "Really, Sir Alec, it is you I am surprised with. I would have figured you to be one to report her. Yet I must admit, she's matured to be quite lovely. Was the sum not as high as the services provided? For yes, I gather it was you who sheltered and trained this dame; she fights with your style. And your love story has reached us all the way in Alsace. That is why we are here!"

Alec said nothing.

Lezay continued, "What was your deal? Did my little *wife* let you take her to bed every night as your reward? I see you didn't manage to pound any obedience into her, or I daresay she would not have humiliated you as she has today." Lezay persisted, his anger to Alec openly burning. "You know what the punishment for adultery is?"

Before Alec could answer, Montag closed the gap between the knights and walked straight up to Eleanor. He was met by a glare of pure loathing, and the eyes that gave that glare were none other than his niece's.

"It has been a long time, Uncle," she said, keeping him in front of Noir. She would not let him get close enough to pull her off the horse, nor to grab Noir's reins. She saw the fury in his eyes, worse than ever before.

"Too long perhaps. It seems you have forgotten your place, child."

"Child I am no longer. Under your control I am no longer."

Montag stepped toward her but was stopped by a snort from Noir. "Wrong, girl. You have played in front of the wrong crowd. Get off that horse before they realize what you've done. I will be reasonable. I doubt the other knights will be now they know a scullery maid thought she could play knight."

"Reasonable! What is reasonable to you, Uncle? Was it reasonable to deny me my birthright? Was it reasonable to marry me to a man *thrice* my age?"

"You know I married you so that you could keep your inheritance; it was your dowry. And yes, there are certain . . . *obligations* that go with Lezay *protecting* you. But I'm sure you don't want everyone hearing about such private matters. So let's go talk somewhere else."

Montag held out his hand to her, willing her off the horse so she would go with him. His words were quiet, so the crowd would not hear him. Judging by the dull hum, they still weren't quite sure what was going on, and Eleanor knew if she dismounted that it would look like she was yielding to Montag. She knew that was his goal, and that in so negating her victory he would silence her, then deal with her in private. Smart man. No wonder no one had ever thought to remove her from his care. He was such a gentleman; no public scenes.

But Eleanor knew better now.

She yelled so the crowd could hear her, "You will not silence me, Uncle. I am your equal now. I defeated you in your best event, in front of all these witnesses!" She gestured to the crowd. "You cannot hide me in your dungeon or pass me to your friends any more. I will fight you. And I will not back down."

As they spoke, a merchant shouted from the edge of the tilting field, where Eleanor was surrounded by the group of knights, "I recognize that hauberk! I made it for the squire tourney at Neroche last year! Sir Alec's squire Alfred won it! She's Alfred! Remember how small statured he was? It was her all along! Alec trained her!"

"You're right!" said another. "Same build as that young boy that won at sword!"

"Yes, yes," the crowd shouted, realization setting in.

"It all makes sense now!"

"Alec trained her."

"But she's the Lady of the Tournament! It's Ella!"

"Silence!" bellowed Lord Gawain from the stands. He and Lady Gwen both were on their feet, her hand on his arm, alarm on her face. "What is going on here? This whole place is in an uproar and no one can get their story straight," he shouted across the field. "My wife seems to think this knight," he gestured to Eleanor, "Is her former maid Ella. But I hear the name, Enric, Eleanor, Alfred . . . can't hear over all this noise! So who the hell are you?"

Eleanor took a deep breath and rode up to him so they wouldn't have to shout. "Lord Gawain, I am all of those names. I was your Lady's maid for a time, under the name of Ella. But my real name is Lady Eleanor de Levan, and I am the daughter of the late tourney champion Sir Enric de Levan. I fought today in his name, to bring my true identity out of the shadows."

Gawain gave her a hard look, sizing her up. "If I hadn't watched you all day, I would say this is some joke. But Gwen recognized you when you took off your helm. I watched you in the sword event and remarked on your small stature . . . but fearsome with a blade! Why on Earth are you competing in a man's tournament?"

"It's a long story, sir, but know this, I am not safe until you acknowledge my victory here today. I pray you say I won today with all the fairness that the code of chivalry defines."

Gwen whispered something urgently in Gawain's ear.

"She is my wife!" Lezay cut in, snarling. "Let me take her from here. She has embarrassed enough men today."

"Actually, no." Eleanor reached into her pocket. She held the parchment up so that Lezay could see. He couldn't read, but he could see her crest and the seal of the pope at the bottom of the parchment.

"What is that?" he growled. She pulled it out of his reach as he tried to grab it.

Eleanor turned the parchment toward Gawain. "An annulment," he said.

"I'm not his wife. And I never was," Eleanor declared. The blow was struck.

Lezay tried to turn against Alec. Turning his horse back to him he shouted, "You! You poisoned her mind to me!"

Alec chuckled but without amusement. "Not I. You did that all on your own. I just trained her enough that she may rise in defiance of the treatment she receives at the hands of less chivalrous men than I." Alec shifted his gaze to Gawain. "My lord, regardless of title or history, I believe she has proven her abilities as our champion today."

The crowd was still listening and watching intently, their voices a buzz as they spoke amongst each other. They were starting to pull for Eleanor's side.

"Why did you fight here today?" Gawain questioned her.

"For my honor, my lord," she answered, and bowed her head. "Just like any other man here. I want my name, my honor, and my lands back."

Lord Gawain's voice boomed above the crowd again. "My lords and ladies, I would like to introduce you to our new tournament champion, Lady Eleanor de Levan!"

The crowd roared its approval. She was their friend the maid, she was their Lady of the Tournament, and she was a fighter! The other knights she had competed with acknowledged her by tipping their helms. After all, if Sir Alec supported her and he was the usual tourney champion, who were they to argue? Montag and Lezay glared at Gawain, Eleanor, Alec, the entire assembly. There was nothing they could do. The people loved her.

They could not touch her today.

The cheers went on as relief registered on Eleanor's face. Wilfred came up to her and congratulated her, patting Noir on the neck. Alec rode up alongside her, cutting his horse between her and Lezay, his face still expressionless. The trio made for the arena exit, but Montag blocked them. His words barely audible over the crowd's cheers, he coldly said, "You ever come to France again, niece, and I will kill you myself." Then he smiled and graciously stepped aside to let them pass.

He would wait in France.

"Should we go home?" Wilfred asked once they were out of the crowd.

Alec answered, "And have two knights and whatever allies they can scrape together attack us in the middle of the night? No. We are safer here with Lord Gawain and the rest of his vassals. At least until Montag leaves." He gave an involuntary shudder. "That man could charm a snake. I thought you were going to accept his offer to 'go talk' there for a minute. And Lezay! If I'm alone with him I swear I'll slit his fat belly open just like he did my father's. Where is Lance?" he glanced around the crowd.

"Probably pouting somewhere," Wilfred mumbled.

"Go find him," Alec ordered. "The two of you have horses to tend to." He and Eleanor were still mounted on the destriers. They stopped under the shade of a tree, finally relief from the hot afternoon sun.

Eleanor looped her reins over her arm and quickly braided her hair back so it was off her neck. She knotted the end of the braid since she had no string. Alec watched her in silence. She knew part of him wanted to scream at her. Her plan was so brazen, so risky. And she'd dragged him into it. But on the other hand, she had succeeded. She beat Lezay. And her uncle. And him, but that was another matter. She beat Lezay *in an all-out tournament*. Lezay was furious, but there was nothing he could do about it. She'd won Lord Gawain's protection for the night. Even Montag wouldn't challenge that, at least not with Gawain's entire assembly of knights in attendance. Every reason Alec had for being mad at her, she had remedied already, all on her own. Judging by his silence, he knew it, too.

Eleanor sighed and started fussing with her gauntlets, working the laces free. Noir stood with a hind leg cocked, his eyes closing, enjoying his break. Suddenly Eleanor went still in her saddle, her face in her hand. Her hand shook.

"I'm sorry I pulled you into this," she said quietly.

Alec stayed silent.

"This was all for nothing. They will keep hunting me. Only now they know where I am. Who I'm with."

"You are safe in England," Alec replied carefully.

"And am I to hide in England forever?"

"We still have phase two, Eleanor. I'm not done with Lezay yet, and you shouldn't be either."

Chapter Twenty-Two

Lord Gawain allowed them to sleep in the castle that night, sharing Alec's philosophy that they were safer with the rest of the vassals than they were back at Neroche, at least for now. Alec insisted that they stay among the guests in the great hall as long as possible. Eleanor was the center of attention, receiving both a mix of congratulations and glares from the ladies and men alike. It seemed no one really knew what to think of her. She was exhausted from the day, and grateful when Alec let them sit at a table in a far corner of the hall, out of the main flurry of drinking and entertainment. Eleanor had stayed in her breeches, not having thought to bring her dress. She was grateful too that they could sit, just so she wouldn't have to feel everyone stare at the hips that the full skirts of her gowns usually masked.

Wilfred joined the two in the corner. "I found Lance," he said. "And you aren't going to like it." He nodded toward the end of the hall. "Toward the left, at the long table." And sure enough, there they saw Lance, deep in conversation with Montag and Lezay. "He's probably telling them everything he knows, which isn't much."

"Filthy rat," Alec snorted. "Looks like I'm down to one squire now."

Wilfred raised his eyebrows at being called a squire but said nothing.

"Have you seen Raoul?" Eleanor asked.

"He wants to speak with you," Wilfred said quietly. "I told him I could get you toward the north battlement wall, midnight, after the crowd dies down. If you want to meet him of course. I got the impression you and he are on better terms than the other two?"

Eleanor nodded. "I'll meet him."

Alec and Wilfred said simultaneously, "I'm going with you." They glanced at each other in surprise, then Wilfred looked down and away as Alec again insisted, "*I'm* going with you."

Eleanor ignored them both. "What time is it now?"

"Judging by the moon's height, likely close to midnight," Wilfred replied.

Eleanor sighed. Never a moment's rest. Then she rose, Alec with her.

She laid a hand on Wilfred's shoulder as she walked past him. "Thank you."

Up on the north battlement wall, Raoul already waited. He strode eagerly toward them when he saw them, stopping in front of her, his face bright. "Cousin!" he smiled, and the two of them embraced. He held her at arm's length and studied her. "Well, you've grown a bit, eh?"

"It's good to see you too, Raoul," she said, smiling. Turning to Alec she said, "We have things to catch up on and not much time. Can you wait here for me?"

Alec crossed his arms and leaned back against the wall.

Eleanor took Raoul's elbow to guide him down the battlement a bit, out of Alec's earshot.

"Forgive me for skipping the pleasantries, but I know we don't have much time. I don't want to face off with your father again today. So what *really* happened after I left? I have heard every rumor."

Raoul sighed, "I knew you would ask, and you will not like what you hear."

"Go on," Eleanor prodded.

"Lezay came tearing out of your room with a gash on his face. He said right from the start that someone had kidnapped you, and he had tried to fight them off. I knew, of course, you had done the damage and run. You saw me heading toward him. I only managed to distract him a few minutes, saying you hadn't passed me so you must be hidden in the hall somewhere with the 'kidnapper.' We searched room by room, until we heard the hoofprints galloping in the courtyard. Lezay took one look out the window and turned on me. Still have the scar from that blow. By that time, Father was up and screaming at the grooms to get his destrier ready. You should have seen the look on his face when the grooms came running back to tell him the destrier was gone. Old man Michel...he didn't make it. I'm sorry Eleanor, there's no way to put it gently. He knew what he was doing and did it willingly. We all did and accepted the consequences." A visible shudder ran down Raoul's back.

She blinked tears from her eyes, thinking of the kind horse-master that had saved her. In a whisper she asked, "He flogged you?"

"Oui. Still have those scars too." Raoul avoided her eyes.

"I'm so sorry, Raoul—"

Raoul pressed on, "Your father's manor was burned, Eleanor, to ensure you would have no refuge and there would be no land disputes. It's a pile of rubble now."

She took a deep breath. "I heard that rumor."

"After my father made it clear what the further consequences for my disobedience would be, I was sent to Edmond here in England to see if you would search for him. We didn't know what other friends you could run to. My father himself went to Normandy and met with Lord Fougères. Edmond had not even heard of your wedding. I truly thought he was going to kill me when I told him you had been married. I believe he blamed me for not stopping my father. For not stopping you. But there was nothing I could do. We did not part on good terms, try as I did to explain to him that I could not *do* anything. I tried. Eleanor, you know that, don't you?"

"Yes, Raoul. And I told Edmond."

"You met Edmond?"

"Yes. Go on."

"Well, my father could think of no further hiding places, but we all knew you wouldn't be able to stay away from manors and tournaments for long. It's in your blood. So we searched for you wherever we competed. Spread the word to every knight we met. We offered a reward for mere information on you, Eleanor. Beaucoup d'argent. However, the world was silent of news of you. Until now. And Eleanor, though tournaments were our top place to find you, never did we expect you to compete in them. How have you learned? I know I never taught you that much. How—? No, explain everything."

Eleanor took a deep breath, deciding brevity was safest, just in case her uncle questioned Raoul. "I worked as a maid until I met Alec. You've heard the rest."

"Eleanor, you said you met Edmond. When?"

"I first met him last year. At a tourney." She did not elaborate.

Raoul frowned. "Have you heard what happened to him?"

"I know he's dead. Can you tell me . . . was it by Lezay's hand?"

Raoul took a sharp breath. "Worse. By Montag's."

Eleanor's eyebrows went up. "For all the bastard he is, I didn't think he was one for pure murder." The blood drained from her face and her pulse quickened.

"I don't think he would call it murder. He'd call it tying up loose ends." Raoul avoided her gaze. "Montag knew we were getting closer to locating you. The stories had reached us of Alec and his lady, and Montag had suspicions from the start. Alec's still single so why wouldn't he just marry the lady he fancied instead of parading her around like a whore?" Raoul flinched. "Sorry. Anyway, it made no sense unless *she* wasn't actually single. So we suspected. And Montag wanted to be sure that once we had you back, no one could claim that the marriage to Lezay was invalid." Raoul hesitated as if deciding whether to disclose something or not, then seemed to decide it was best to get it out. "I only recently learned that the whole reason Edmond apprenticed under my father, the reason we searched for you so much amongst the Fougères family, was because you were betrothed to *Edmond* as a child by *your father*."

Eleanor gasped loud enough to catch Alec's attention. She covered her lips with her hand, staring wide-eyed at Raoul.

"I thought you knew," Raoul said in surprise. Seeing Alec heading closer, he talked faster. "My father was originally going to ransom Edmond. He's resourceful like that. Lord Fougères would have paid. But

Edmond wouldn't tell us anything about you without encouragement." Eleanor paled a little. "Maybe he didn't know anything in the first place. But if you met him as you say, he did know something. But since we couldn't return him back to Lord Fougères, or King Richard, in that state, Montag decided it was best to silence him completely. You see, without another fiancé, Lezay has full claim to you." Raoul glanced toward Alec. "Montag made it look like an ambush. Then we started making plans to come to England and meet Sir Alec and his lady for ourselves."

Eleanor took this news calmly, but she was distrustful of her own loyal cousin. "You say 'we' a lot." She was actually grateful Alec had stopped only a few yards away.

"Eleanor, I've stalled what I could. I have not passed information on, not that I knew much. But I'm not in a position to challenge my father. If he says go, I go. If he says fight, I fight." He caught the shock in her eye at that. "No, I was not there when Edmond was killed. Even Montag knew it was too much to ask for me to kill a former friend."

Eleanor let out the breath she held. Then she asked, "Raoul, are you married yet?"

"No," he said. She raised an eyebrow at him, and he continued somberly, "I do not trust my father, Eleanor. Any woman married to me would face his wrath if I were to die or displease him. I do not want my wife or my daughters to suffer under him as you did. If that should mean that I have no heir, so be it. His is not a line that should be continued."

They both looked away, thinking.

Eleanor glanced up as Alec briskly took the last steps toward them. "Footsteps, east stair," he whispered, grabbing her hand and pulling her down the wall to the west stair. Eleanor gave a short wave to Raoul and ran. As they ducked out of sight, she heard Raoul speaking with her uncle, his deep voice unmistakable.

"Come," Alec pulled her on, running through the passageways they knew so well into the room they had been assigned for the night in the garrison tower. Wilfred waited up, nursing a mug of ale at a little table by the light of a single candle.

"Well?" he asked. "Did you learn what you wanted to?"

Eleanor took a deep breath and looked at their expectant faces. "I know who killed Edmond."

The men waited, eyebrows raised expectantly.

She turned to Alec, "I will still help you ruin Lezay. But Montag . . . Montag I am going to kill myself."

Chapter Twenty-Three

S he dreamed of charging, black hooves flying, a heavy lance in her hand, tipped with an iron spike tapered to dagger sharpness. The exhilaration pumped in her veins, the wind against her skin a caress. It grew red. The horse to the left of her faltered and went down, rider flailing. Edmond. The horse to her right charged on, foam flying from its mouth, nostrils red and eyes wide, wild. That rider stayed true, pointing ahead, telling her to focus on the enemy they were about to collide with. Stride for stride they hammered on, then there was the awful collision, the sound of metal on metal, the suck of flesh as it was cut with steel. She looked around, alone on the battlefield. Edmond was dead, sprawled in the grass below her horse's feet. She had failed to protect him. The knight that was on her right, where was he? She searched and searched. She wanted to thank him. Or had her folly killed him, too? She searched the dead, their vacant eyes staring up at her, Old Michel among them. But the second knight was not there. Who was he? She searched. . . . Hands began to grab at her arms, the hands of the dead, the hands of those who had died to protect her. She tried to pull away, her eyes still searching for the knight.

"Shhh! You're fine. Eleanor, you're fine." Gentle hands held her to quiet her thrashing.

She screamed, the dead in her dream pulling her toward them.

A candle flickered to light. "Shhh! You're going to wake the whole castle. It's only a dream. A dream. Wilfred, bring that over here."

Slowly Eleanor woke and gained her senses again. Caught in the delirium between the horror of the nightmare and her own brutal reality, she started to cry, curling against Alec's chest. He wrapped his arms around her, soothing her as he breathed a sigh of relief of his own. Wilfred squatted on the ground next to them, himself shaken as he held the candle.

"Good God, I thought someone was murdering her," Wilfred said in a whisper.

"I know," Alec said softly, arms still locked around Eleanor. She still trembled against his chest, whimpering. To Wilfred he admitted, "This week has taken everything out of her. We never should have let her come here."

Wilfred's shoulders slumped, and he shook his head. "We didn't. She wouldn't listen to you. She wouldn't listen to me."

"We could have locked her up."

"Alec, you know she'd never let you do that."

Alec sighed. Slowly Eleanor pulled away from him, wiping her eyes.

"I'm so sorry," she whispered.

"You just woke us and half the manor screaming bloody murder," Wilfred scolded. "What on Earth were you dreaming about?"

Eleanor shook her head, not wanting to relive the still very vivid dream. "Edmond."

The two men shot a glance at each other. Slowly Wilfred rose to his feet. "I'm going back to bed," he said quietly. He blew out the candle and padded back to his bunk. Faint moonlight broke the darkness, outlining Alec and Eleanor's figures in shadow.

"Do you want to talk about him?" Alec ventured, hoping she didn't.

Eleanor shook her head, pulling away a bit more. "I'm sorry I woke you."

Alec brushed her cheek with his calloused fingers, then rose abruptly.

"Good night."

Chapter Twenty-Four

The days that followed were like a chess match. Alec and Eleanor knew that if they left the protection of Lord Gawain's manor, Montag would hunt them down to Neroche. And Montag knew that his generous host would not ask his party to leave after such a long journey from Alsace, so he took his good old time, enjoying Gawain's hospitality, which came more begrudgingly each day, and watching Eleanor's anxiety. She dared not make a move against him while he was so on guard, surrounded by his burly squires and friends, including Lezay. She kept her own friends close.

After about five days, she and Alec rode around the estate to exercise the horses, who were tense after so many days of confinement. Alec had given up on warning her about Noir. The black horse pranced beside Alec's wide-eyed but stoic Ches. Eleanor absently checked her reins for the hundredth time, willing the fireball back to attention. The summer sun was warm but not sweltering. A perfect cloudless day.

"He's just waiting to get you alone," Alec said absently, watching the manor off to their left, far off across the plains.

"I know," Eleanor admitted. "You think he'll try to kill me here in front of Lord Gawain? Tournament champion or not, there's only so much Lord Gawain can do for me. Montag is not his tenant, nor is even King Richard his king."

"I think at this point your death would cause more harm than good to Montag. He's a practical man. He doesn't want you dead."

Eleanor snorted, checking back on Noir's reins yet again as he resumed prancing.

Alec continued, "The best thing for Montag would be to kidnap you, take you back home, remarry you to Lezay and make sure *everyone* knew the marriage was legitimate." He glanced sideways at her. "I don't think he intends to let you go again."

"I've always wondered why he hates me so much." She pursed her lips in thought. Noir tossed his head, and Eleanor sighed in exasperation. "Can we let these beasts run a bit before this dragon explodes?"

Alec gave her a sanctimonious look and led the way into a canter, then a gallop, up a slight incline in the road. They pulled up the horses at the very top of the low hill, the animals slightly more patient but still barely breathing hard and looked down at the plains below.

Eleanor turned to study Alec. His sternly handsome features furrowed as he frowned, deep in thought. "Why are you still with me?" she asked. It was a question that had bothered her since the tourney.

Alec looked at her in surprise, then turned back to the valley. "I guess I'm just used to you at this point." He was quiet for a moment, then instead turned his horse back down the path and started making their decent.

Eleanor followed in silence for a while, then tried again. "You don't need me anymore. You succeeded in taking Lezay's wife from him. I cannot help you with taking the lands or honor more than I already have."

Alec didn't turn back to her as he answered, his words reaching her on the breeze, "You've never been a captive, Eleanor. You're free to go."

Eleanor trotted Noir up next to him as the path widened. "Do you want me to go?"

Alec stared straight ahead and Eleanor and Noir were forced back behind him as the path narrowed again. Eleanor's mind whirled. What did *she* want? She had no land or titles of her own, except the ruins in Aquitaine that she would likely have to go to war with her uncle to reclaim. Alec had given her security this last year; despite his threats he had been a gracious host to her. But was it worth staying on with him longer? He had no need for her now. Would he turn on her? She doubted it. That moment would have been during the tourney some five days ago.

Instead, he had done nothing but stick up for her and stay by her side since. The men that weren't intimidated by Eleanor herself wouldn't dare confront her with Alec next to her. Two champion knights? No chance. But beyond that, did she even want to leave? Here she was, lingering with Alec as he was her.

"Alec?" she ventured. He ignored her, but she knew he heard. "Alec . . ."

He kicked Ches up into a canter, down the hill. Eleanor had no choice but to follow as Noir tossed his head and took off after Ches. The horses scrambled for their footing on the rocky path, both riders leaning back to help them balance. On the flat of the plain, Alec leaned forward in his saddle and took off toward the manor. Noir took the challenge and kept up with Ches, stride for stride. Eleanor glanced over at Alec, wisps of Noir's black mane flying in her face, but his face was unreadable.

They brought the horses to a walk a few yards from the barn. The horses still barely sweated or breathed hard, a testament to their excellent conditioning. Wordlessly they dismounted and entered the barn, tying the horses in their stalls, pulling off saddles. The barn was quiet but for the sound of the horses munching hay. The grooms had done their morning chores and left it empty.

Eleanor heaved her saddle onto its rack and froze as she felt Alec behind her, the hilt of a sword away. He breathed heavily on her neck, placing his hands on the stall wall along either side of her head. She was penned in. But this time she wasn't scared. She was not a maiden that didn't know what he wanted. She knew. There was an ache in her own gut, a need to relieve the pent-up stress of the past week. There was a reason men celebrated victories by taking women to their beds. It eased the tension of what it took to get there. An evolutionary trait to ensure the strongest spread their seed perhaps? Or a psychological need to lose control for just a moment with another human being and escape one's reality, to give the mind a chance to reset itself? It took trust to work right . . .thus why Lezay had scarred her so deeply. But with trust both parties could find the escape they needed. Edmond had taught her that much. She was ready to gamble that she could at least trust Alec enough to not hurt her physically. She didn't need to love him. Desire was a whole other game, and she had never been blind to her desire of him. Slowly she turned to face him, leaning back against the wall. The lust was vivid in his eyes. A challenge was in her own. The muscle on his jaw worked as he debated what to say.

As he opened his mouth to speak, Eleanor cupped the back of his neck in her hand and pulled his lips to hers.

She felt the control in him snap.

Alec pressed his body into her, pinning her against the wall as his lips roughly kissed her. As he pulled back just long enough to kiss her neck she gasped, trying to catch her breath. But his hands were on her breasts. His hips pressed hers against the wall. Then his mouth was back on hers, his hands now cupping her bottom as he lifted her up the wall, her legs wrapped around his. Eleanor's hands pulled his lips tighter to her own, all inhibitions gone. *Alec Alec Alec* her mind chanted, her lips too busy to make a sound.

Alec stopped, just long enough to look at her and catch his breath. He planted a soft, short kiss on her brow, as her lungs heaved between him and the wall. His hips kept her locked there, her legs wrapped around him, as his fingers brushed the warm place between her legs. "Damn the britches . . . of all the days not to have you in a dress." He let her slide back to her feet, then worked the buckle at her waist. He spun her to the right, intent on bending her over a large feed bin next to them. But as his hands went to slide her breeches down over her hips, Eleanor straightened and spun back to face him, fear in her eyes.

"Not that way." She breathed. Lezay's face swam in the back of her mind.

Alec took a step back in frustration. He didn't want to spook her now. But she could not deny him. Not after that kiss. He motioned toward her belt, not trusting himself to step closer to her again. "Buckle that back up." The bulge in his pants was painfully obvious to them both. With a last glance at the horses, he took her hand, glanced out the barn to see that their path was clear, and strode quickly into the manor, entering by the kitchen door the same way

Eleanor had the first night they had met. Thankfully the kitchens were quiet, not yet readying for dinner. Eleanor knew the back staircase he took, racing along with him, her hand as tight on his as his grip was on her own. They emerged on the landing of their loaned room, where Alec paused, and without taking his eyes off her, pressed the heavy oak door open. Eleanor froze.

And there at the table, as usual, was Wilfred. He rose to his feet. "Back already?"

Alec started at this realization and quickly entered the room, leaving Eleanor in the doorway. "Out!" he hissed, grabbing Wilfred by the shoulder and steering him out of the room.

Wilfred stopped in front of Eleanor, his eyes imploring if she was okay. She gave him an embarrassed smile and a nod. Wilfred shook off Alec's hand and backed away. The look on his face made the warning clear: whatever was going on, no one would hurt Eleanor, not even Alec.

Alec spun Eleanor through the door and slammed it behind him, sliding the bolt home to lock it securely. No one was getting in. His shoulders rose and fell as he breathed, the heat of desire rolling off him in waves.

"If you have any more protests or ideas about changing your mind, now would be the time. I have waited too long. I'm not a brute but once we start—" He sighed in frustration. "Are you sure?"

Eleanor's knees went a little weak, and she leaned back against the table. Was she sure? Alec breathed a whole different passion than Edmond's tender caresses. She felt like she did before she entered the sword arena with him. Energy pumped through her veins. If she stayed ahead of him, met his challenge, she would emerge unscathed. She didn't want him to stop, at least now, but what kind of beast still raged in him?

Alec ran a shaking hand through his hair and approached her, quietly now. "Just tell me what your rules are."

Eleanor took a shaky breath. "I need to be facing you. Always."

"Anything else?"

Eleanor bit her lip. She could ask for it to be like it was with Edmond, but that wasn't fair. Nor did she think she could handle the emotions it would wake in her. She could ask him to be gentle, but nothing about that last kiss had been gentle, and she hadn't wanted it to stop. So she shook her head.

Alec pressed his lips into hers again, softer this time, less urgent. He coaxed them apart, flitting his tongue against the tip of hers. She reached for his hips, pulling him into her. He pulled back for a moment and lifted her onto the table, kneeing her legs apart. He reached for her belt buckle, pulling it free. He undid the toggles of his leather vest while he kissed her, then smoothly undid hers. Their vests off, he pulled off her shirt, smiling as she nervously tried to cover herself. Her hand brushed the gold ring that hung on the chain around her neck and a shiver ran down her back. *But he isn't here*, she told herself. *He isn't coming back*.

Alec hesitated as she shivered, his eyes lingering on the gold ring around her neck. Without comment, his eyes locked back onto hers. "M'lady, you were brave enough to fight the hardest knights in England a few days ago. Do you really mean to tell me you're afraid to show yourself?"

Eleanor sighed and placed her hands on either side of her on the table, leaning back, full chest exposed. For a moment she regretted it, as Alec took that moment to pull off her boots and her breeches, and suddenly she was stark naked, sitting on the table. She resisted the instinct to cover herself again. But Alec covered her body for her, pulling her into him again, his lips exploring her. The buckle of his belt pressed into her navel. With one finger she pushed him away, sliding her hands up his muscular torso to grasp his loose linen shirt and pull it over his head. Her fingers lingered in the thick dark hair of his head, teasing. For a moment she just looked at him. She'd seen him shirtless before, but not this close. If Edmond had been the physical ideal of a warrior, Alec was something more. His chest was chiseled with defined muscle, his shoulders broad, his jaw strong. There was not a soft place to him, and yet none of this muscle seemed to be excess bulk. How had she ever fought him, sword in hand, and survived? Her other hand pulled him back to her by his belt, then worked it free.

She hesitated a mere second before pushing his breeches down over his hips.

She could feel it pressed against her, but his lips were more demanding. And with a slight touch of his hand, he had guided himself into her. She gasped at the feel of him. Not painful, but full. Alec pulled her hips to him, rocking against the table she sat on. She opened for him, arms twining around his neck, pulling him deeper while her breasts pressed into his hard chest. His lips sought hers again, demanding more as their passion unfurled.

A warm pleasure grew in Eleanor's belly until she gasped, every nerve alive as her body quivered in waves around Alec. Her nails clawed into his back and she felt him wince, thrusting himself deep into her before giving to his own pleasure, flooding her depths with warmth. They leaned into each other, still locked, sides heaving.

Eleanor was the first to speak. Quietly she asked into Alec's shoulder, "What was that?"

Alec gave a short chuckle. "I've heard that women can feel the same pleasure as a man. I believe you just did." He straightened, and pushed her hair out of her eyes, looking at her gently, serious now. "I can't believe you've kept that from me this long."

"I wasn't ready."

Alec nodded slightly. "I know." He touched the ring that hung around her neck, frowning. "How many men have there been? Other than Lezay and Edmond?"

Eleanor just shook her head, looking away.

Alec pulled out of her, reaching down for his breeches around his ankles and pulling them on. "Really?"

She stayed silent, suddenly embarrassed, and reached for her shirt, which was tossed over a chair. He pulled it away from her, pulling her to him again, his lips finding hers again. "I believe you, Eleanor," he whispered against her lips. A long kiss later he pulled back to look her in the eye. "Is it wrong of me to ask you to deny the others? Until we part ways at least?"

"Do you mean as Lady of the Tournament? Or this?"

"Both."

"Alec, contrary to what you've made my reputation out to be, I am not a whore. There is no one else." She hesitated. "I'm curious though, would you agree to the same?"

"Until we part ways." The muscle in his jaw twitched like he had more to say.

"And when do we part ways?" Eleanor asked, reminding herself to keep her emotions under control this time. She could not allow herself to care again like she had for Edmond.

Alec avoided the question by kissing her again. In one movement he scooped her in his arms, her eyes wide in surprise, arms quickly twined around his neck. He carried her to his bed, and then pulled off his boots and lay pressed tight to her.

Alec propped his head on his elbow, the fingers of his other hand tracing her bare arm as they studied each other. His thumb lingered on a tiny white scar. "What's this from?"

"Edmond," she whispered quietly, not even having to look. Sword practice with boys older and bigger than you hadn't always ended well. He'd been sorry; she'd made sure of that a few days later with a little help from Raoul. Eleanor blinked quickly and studied Alec's face, which had gone somber. She was a fool, a bloody fool, to play this game. Now she had lost so badly she didn't even mind. She sighed and curled herself in tighter to him.

She fingered a scar on Alec's shoulder, still bright from new healing. "I did this one, didn't I?"

"Yes, you did." He moved so she could see his back, where a colorful bruise ran between his shoulder blades. "And this one, just a few days ago."

"I'm sorry."

"Never be sorry. You made the decision to fight. Unless you regret that, never apologize for what happens in that fight. Strength lies in decisiveness. And you can't be sorry for that. It's what keeps you alive." He ran his hand to her abdomen, touching for the first time the scar Lezay had left her. The white jagged line had once been an ugly wound. "Does this one ever hurt?"

"Not there," Eleanor said quietly.

Alec pulled her into his chest again, laying there hip to hip with her. After a few minutes he said quietly, "I thought once would be enough, Eleanor, but it's not. We have nothing to do today but hide from your relatives. And worry Wilfred. Let's let them all wait a little more, shall we?" he coaxed.

Eleanor, pleasantly satiated, met his next parry, twining her fingers into his, letting his body enfold her and his kisses soothe her mind. It was one afternoon of pleasure.

That was all.

They still lay curled with each other at sunset when a loud banging at the door interrupted them.

"Alec!" shouted Wilfred, still hammering. "Alec, open up! Alec!"

Alec groaned and pulled on his breeches as he made his way to the door. Eleanor buried deep into the blankets, trying to disappear. Only her eyes and the top of her head showed from the tiny bed.

"Alec!" the call came again from the door, more urgently.

Alec glanced back at Eleanor, then opened the door so widely that Wilfred almost fell into the room. He composed himself quickly, ignoring Eleanor after a quick glance around the room located her.

"They are leaving," Wilfred rushed. "Lance saw you two in the barn this afternoon. They know you're up here. Montag protested to Lord Gawain that this was adultery and you should be punished. Quite the confrontation. But Lord Gawain insisted the papal edict was legitimate, he saw it with his own eyes, and thus there is no adultery and that Lezay should get his fat ass back to France and get a proper wife as Eleanor is free to do what she pleases here in England. Montag drew his sword, which made Lord Gawain draw his, even with his injury, but Lady Gwen screamed, and Lord Gawain's squires ran in just in time to join the fight, got Montag out the door with Lord Gawain still shaking in rage at him, threatening to call all the vassals back to tourney to teach him a lesson." Wilfred gasped for breath before charging ahead. "They saddled up and looked like they were headed to the coast. Do you want me to follow? They've only been gone maybe ten minutes. If I take Noir . . ." His voice trailed off, likely remembering he wasn't supposed to touch Noir.

"Take Noir," Alec said firmly. "Stay out of sight, make sure they get on a boat, then meet us back at Neroche." He sighed, "I'll go make amends with Lord Gawain. Lord knows he's done enough on our behalf, he didn't need to defend himself too." Alec picked the last of his clothes up off the floor, pulling them on as he did. "Eleanor, I'll see if I can talk Helin or Lady Gwen into lending you a gown until we get you home. I'm sick of the other men staring at your backside." To Wilfred he nodded, "Get going," and a moment later he had pulled the door shut behind them.

Eleanor tossed the covers off of herself, keeping only the sheet wrapped tight around her as she ran to the window. She could see the band of knights in the fading light in the distance, quickly covering ground in the direction of the coast, which was still a day's ride away. As they faded out of sight there was another knock at the door. Eleanor answered it and found Helin, a gown tossed over her arm. She smiled, motioning her in.

"I was hoping to see you before we left," Eleanor said warmly.

Helin gave a weak smile. "Well, it's hard to chat with you when you're surrounded by men all the time. Or *fighting in tourneys*." There was a mix of jest and bitterness in her tone. But her face softened to a smile. "I am happy for you, Ella. We all cheered for you in the tourney, not even knowing it was you. You should have seen Lady Gwen's face when you revealed yourself. She nearly swooned!" She laughed and held up the dress. "Here, let's get this on you."

Eleanor turned her back to Helin for just a moment as she pulled on a clean shift. Then she raised her arms, and Helin slipped the gown over her head. It was a pale blue linen. A little big for Eleanor, but clean. Gently Helin did the laces up her back.

"So do you think you'll marry him now?" Helin questioned quietly. "I've always said you'd fall for him eventually. Didn't know you were already married. Or not married? I get confused about that part."

Eleanor was quiet. Helin continued, "You know, there are far worse things than marrying a handsome knight, Ella."

"I know."

"Yeah, I've been realizing you do," Helin paused, tying the laces in the back of the dress in a neat bow. She stepped back. "But you, Ella, you deserve an actual love. Don't let him get away. He's crazy about you. We all could see it at the tourney. For real this time. I could see how you felt about your Edmond . . .but Ella, you've had Alec by your side this long. That means something." She took Eleanor's hand and gave it a reassuring squeeze, then turned to go. She paused with her hand on the door. "Good luck to you, Lady Eleanor."

Eleanor smiled. "And you, Helin."

Chapter Twenty-Five

"He's back!" Eleanor exclaimed and ran from the kitchen at Neroche. It had been a whole week since she and Alec had returned. Wilfred was long overdue. As he dismounted from Noir, she rushed to his side. "We thought for sure something happened to you. I was going to go looking for you if we didn't hear anything by tomorrow."

Wilfred looked travel weary. There were circles under his eyes and dust coated him, his clothes, and Noir. Even Noir's sides were panting, and he already had one foot lazily cocked in rest. "It was a long ride." He looked up to the doorway of the manor, where Alec had just exited and was making his way over. He moved to meet him, Noir begrudgingly following the loose rein. "They're on a ship now at least," he said.

"Took their time, did they?" Alec asked.

Wilfred snorted. "Spent a few days in London in the company of Prince John. I couldn't follow them into the castle, so I don't know what happened in there. But

Montag looked awfully smug when they left the castle. They were on a ship headed for Aquitaine that afternoon. I rode west as soon as it crested the horizon."

"Aquitaine?" Eleanor asked.

"Aye," Wilfred nodded toward her, but didn't look her in the eye.

"You think they have edicts from Prince John to reclaim Eleanor's lands?" Alec asked.

"That would make sense, wouldn't it?" Wilfred replied.

"Is Raoul with them?" Alec asked.

"No," said Wilfred. "He sailed two days ago for Normandy. I assume he's going back to manage Chateau Brunstein. And Leuwenstein."

Alec gave Eleanor a hesitant smile. "Well, you're safe for now I suppose." He turned away and headed back to the manor.

"Alec, we need to talk," Wilfred called after him.

Alec waved him off. "Later."

Wilfred frowned, watching after Alec with a complex look that mirrored his thoughts.

Eleanor clasped Wilfred's elbow and looked him in the eye. "Thank you."

He broke her gaze and studied the dust on his boots. "You okay?"

"Yeah," she answered honestly. "I am."

"Good," he said, and led Noir toward the barn without another word.

Eleanor frowned. He was mad at her, that much was certain. For sleeping with Alec maybe? Was he jealous, or was he just being overprotective as a friend? She wiped her palms on her skirts. She should feel shame for her week of adulterous relations with Alec, but she couldn't. They had been quiet about it, but they had put the door between their rooms to good use. She did not regret her actions. Yet the last thing she needed was to complicate her friendship with Wilfred. She likely would need them both before this was over.

Eleanor worked her way back to the manor, almost getting knocked over by Marie, who rushed full speed down the path. She watched her in surprise as she ran into the stable. Eleanor shook her head, then entered the manor to find Alec in his room, shuffling through papers on his desk.

"Where is that annulment you got from the Pope?" Alec asked.

Eleanor turned back into her room and retrieved it from its hiding spot. She hesitated, then handed it to Alec. He read through it quickly, then held up the seal close to his face, studying it.

"This is a fake," he said in surprise, looking at her incredulously.

"Yes," she answered.

"How?"

"Edmond."

"I see." Alec drew a sharp breath. "So you actually *were* married to Lezay, and you *don't* actually have an annulment?"

"Yes."

"Which means, technically, you are still Lezay's wife."

"I never said any vows, but I'm a woman, and no one ever seemed to think my agreement was of any importance. You know all this. Why are you surprised?"

"Well, a real annulment would have been nice."

"I doubt anyone needs to look at this close enough to find out it's a fake."

"The monks at the cathedral where we could be married would."

Eleanor's eyebrows arched toward her hairline. "Really now. And what makes you think we'd be getting married?"

Alec drew a deep breath. "Well, for starters, like I said last week, I've grown used to having you around. But since you're a strategist, how about this? We marry." He smirked. "As the wife of his loyal vassal, you may persuade Lord Gawain to send assistance in our efforts to regain your lands. We sail to Aquitaine with a small army, enough to claim the ruined manor as your own. We work to establish enough influence to ensure that Lezay loses all claim to that property." He leaned toward her. "Then we work our way north. To Leuwenstein."

"You'd need a huge army to get into Alsace. Those are Germanic lands. They answer to whatever king they choose, relying more on their princes for local affairs, which my uncle basically is. They have resources, money . . . you'd need—"

"The king's army," Alec said simply.

"King. Richard's. Army." Eleanor looked at him incredulously. "Are you mad?"

"If we bring an army against Lezay for his crimes against us, that would cost him everything."

"And the lives of hundreds of men that have nothing to do with this."

"Better than the thousands King Richard would send to the Holy Land for another crusade. He enjoys new conquests. And he's got a strong sense of chivalry when it comes to women." Alec sighed. "One flaw to the plan though. You actually were married. Thus Lezay was not at fault, no matter what he did to you. And you have no annulment, so I *cannot* marry you."

Eleanor leaned back against the wall. She was frustrated. All week they had been bashing plans like this back and forth. If only she wasn't married to Lezay. If only she had an army. If only she wasn't a woman. With Edmond alive, at least they could have argued that the marriage wasn't legitimate because of her childhood betrothal, but Montag had already ensured that claim could never come to fruition.

She kicked the wall behind her, crossing her arms and starting to pace. "Has all this training been for nothing?

Has winning a tourney and bringing my name to light been for nothing?" Her voice rose. "I should just go to France and join King Richard's army myself! At least then I could help accomplish something! I am so sick of waiting for Montag or Lezay to make the next move! I need to do *something*."

"Let's go to France." Alec and Eleanor looked up at each other in surprise, then to the man in the doorway that had spoken. Wilfred stood there on the stairwell, arms crossed in front of him. He shrugged. "You can't get married, not without a real annulment. Any priest will see right through it if Alec could. Which means you are Lezay's spouse. If you don't want to live with him, no one can argue that. Spouses live apart all the time. But if you want revenge and more importantly to move on with your life, you need to either kill him or raise an army large enough to enter Alsace and ruin him there. The only army of that size is the king's, so you better go start proving your worth to him. Earn his trust, his ear. Maybe after a few years he'll care enough about your cause to help you."

"Send her to war?" Alec asked incredulously.

Wilfred shrugged again. "She wanted to be a knight."

The three of them stood in silence.

"No," Alec said at the same time Eleanor said, "Let's do it". Wilfred just stood there indifferently.

"It's suicide," Alec insisted.

"You said that about the tourney, and I'm still here," Eleanor insisted.

"War is different. War is . . ."

"War?" Wilfred offered.

Alec glowered at him. Wilfred didn't look like it bothered him a bit. "Lance sent his regards by the way. He's working for Montag now."

The muscle on Alec's jaw worked as he thought.

Eleanor broke the tension. "I'm going. Wilfred's right. I wanted to be a knight. What does a knight with no land do? Go to war and earn some." She held up her hand as Alec started to protest. "I have nothing more to lose. If I was a man, we wouldn't be having this conversation. I'd already be over there fighting. And you do not have to come along. Really, you shouldn't. You have too much to do here."

"Have you ever killed a man, Eleanor?" Alec asked quietly.

She was quiet a moment. "I tried. I know what it takes."

Wilfred cut in again, "Great! So when are we leaving? Because every day we wait Montag is sailing toward accomplishing whatever it is he's doing in Aquitaine."

"Tomorrow," Eleanor answered, her eyes locked with Alec's. "And I go alone."

Both men snorted in laughter.

"Wilfred, don't you have work to do?" Alec asked, glowering again.

Wilfred still smiled as he turned and headed back down the stairs.

Alec closed the door behind him and turned to face Eleanor. "It isn't like the tourneys, there on the battlefields."

"I know."

"The men . . . they won't all *understand* why you're there."

"I know."

He stepped close to her again, brushing her cheek with his thumb. "I can only do so much to protect you."

"You don't need to protect me."

He kissed her, but she pulled away. "Alec, this is going to change things."

He froze. "What?"

"I can't be *this* to you if we're going to fight with the other men of England. No one will take me seriously if I'm with you."

Alec took a deep breath. "Are you really going to do this to me again? There are ways to be discreet. Of course I'm not going to take you on the field of battle or in a camp surrounded by passion-starved men. But are you really going to pull away from me again? Eleanor, you don't have to fall in love with me. I won't claim to be in love with you. But you cannot expect me to forget everything that's transpired. I didn't force you any more than you forced me. So you can't tell me you didn't enjoy it."

"I did, it's just—"

"You just want control, is that it? I can only touch you when *you* want?"

She looked away, and Alec realized that was *exactly* what she wanted. He groaned and paced and slammed his fist down on his desk. Then he walked up to her with a flash in his eyes, the same flash he had when he had tried to kiss her when they first met. She didn't pull away as he pulled her into him and kissed her until her lips softened to his own. "One more time then," he breathed. "Until we are back in England. God willing we survive that long." Then, then she would have no more excuses, and he could make her his own.

She hesitated, but his hands were already working the laces of her gown, his lips hot against her neck, working their way to her bosom. She gritted her teeth and grasped the buckle of his belt, whipping it loose. She pushed him back toward his bed and pulled his breeches down around his ankles before pushing him onto it. His erection stood up hard against her thigh as she straddled him, one hand on his chest. Her gown flowed around her, covering them both. She impatiently dug beneath the skirts to grasp hold of him, guiding him into her. He gasped, laying back on the bed. Gradually she built the pressure until Alec couldn't stand it anymore. Still locked deep inside her, he rolled her over to her back and took up his own rhythm. Eleanor bit into his shoulder, hard enough to leave a bruise. As he hit the back of her womb, she clawed him involuntarily in pain, which only made him buck harder. It was like a battle of the flesh as they rode the line between pleasure and pain, forcing the passion out of each other. She curled herself into his strong arms, willing him into her, and finally he came.

They panted together, locked as one. Alec rolled off of her and she hastily rose to her feet and straightened her gown. "Not again," she reminded him. "Not until we are back in England."

"Strictly professional," Alec echoed, still stretched out half naked on his bed.

Eleanor gave him a sideways smile, and turned to her own room, closing the door behind her. It was time to pack for France.

Chapter Twenty-Six

"That beast is going to kick this ship apart," Alec lamented as they stood on the deck of the small sail ship, listening to Noir express his fury at being confined on the rocking boat.

Wilfred sighed. "I'll go back down with him again. Maybe he ate all his hay."

Alec snorted, "He was kicking the walls when he had hay."

Wilfred shrugged and headed down the ladder to the belly of the ship.

"At least we're almost there," Eleanor offered.

The coastline of France was visible on the distant horizon. Eleanor, Alec, and Wilfred had managed to secure passage for themselves and the two destriers on a ship bound for Normandy two days after Wilfred had returned to the manor. It was summer, but the sun was behind cloud cover and the day had a grey, damp feel to it.

"I hope he's still at Chateau Gaillard," Eleanor said. That was where they heard the king was stationed last. If he had already moved on, they would have a big country to search.

The salty wind swirled Eleanor's skirts, and she put her hand on the hilt of the sword she had belted over them. She'd opted for a mixed wardrobe. Just like her mixed role. She could be a warrior and a lady, at least for now. She glanced over at the maid Marie, who stood a distance off from them, her arms crossed as she stared out at the sea.

"She claims she's getting married?" Eleanor asked Alec quietly.

"A friend of her father's. Widower. I met him once. Fantastic blacksmith."

"And the family didn't want to come for the wedding?"

Alec shook his head. "I offered to pay for their passage, but they say they have too much work to do now that we're all gone. Which is true. I am blessed with a good household."

Wilfred returned to Eleanor's side at the rail, Noir's racket considerably quieter from beneath their feet. "Told you he was just out of hay. If he's going to be your horse, you need to understand him."

"Thank you, Wilfred. I'll get him next time."

Alec grumbled, "Or Wilfred, you remember your place is to serve your knight—"

Wilfred interrupted. "'And part of service to a knight is to his horse'. You've told me. And you know I'll always serve the horses better than you. They're more deserving."

"Watch your tongue," Alec growled, glaring at Wilfred.

"Or what?" Wilfred snapped. "You'll be hard off without a *squire, Sir* Alec."

Eleanor looked at him in alarm. She'd never seen him say a word against Alec. Judging by his expression, Alec was taken aback as well.

"Look, if this is about me lending Noir to Eleanor, you know full well any other knight would have had you flogged till you never wanted to sit on a horse again. I've chosen to ignore your disobedience in light of the circumstances, but don't push me."

Wilfred glowered, staring at the waves. He looked like he wanted to shout a thousand things at Alec, but he didn't. He hadn't said much to Eleanor since he'd returned from London either. He grasped the railing with both hands, his knuckles white. Eleanor gently laid a hand on his shoulder, but he shrugged her off.

A few hours later and they disembarked in the Norman port of Harfleur. Marie thanked Alec for all his generosity toward her family and took her leave without a glance toward Wilfred or Eleanor. They watched her approach a middle-aged man with the burly arms of a blacksmith. Wilfred abruptly turned away and headed for the livery, where he would try to purchase a mount. He didn't need a highly trained destrier like Alec and Eleanor, so they had opted to save the hassle of transporting a horse by boat and let him buy his horse there in France. Alec gave him just enough money to buy a cheap rouncey, a plain riding horse. By the time Alec and Eleanor had their horses unloaded and saddled, Wilfred emerged from the livery with a big smile and a bigger horse.

"Got him for a bargain!" he exclaimed, his mood markedly improved. And it wasn't hard to tell why. The big chestnut stallion made Noir look like a placid pony. Even then, he was trying to bite Wilfred, his eyes wide and rimmed in white. Wilfred absently kept pushing the horse's nose away, pulling slightly on the reins to keep it from dragging him into the crowd.

"Wilfred, what is that?" Alec asked skeptically.

"Meet Harlequin!" he beamed. "He's perfect." As he put his foot in the stirrup, the horse reared up. Wilfred kicked his foot back out and patted the horse's neck, soothing him. He looked up at Alec and Eleanor. "Uh, you might want to get on your horses first. Once I'm on, we're going, and probably fast." Eleanor chuckled to herself, and mounted Noir, who was fidgeting impatiently himself.

"Which way are we going?" she asked Alec.

He nodded down a side street from on Ches. "Down to Rue la Main and out of town. We'll stop in Rouen for the night. It's about fifty miles from here. Long ride."

They started as the sound of clattering hooves thundered next to them.

"Let's go!" Wilfred shouted from half-way down the alley, his hands tight in the big chestnut's mane as it cantered sideways down the street, kicking out occasionally and giving them a wide path through the frightened pedestrians.

Alec rolled his eyes and Eleanor smiled. They followed, trying to keep up with the fiery chestnut.

Chapter Twenty-Seven

Two days later, they arrived at Petite Andelys, the little town that had sprung up in the shadow of Chateau Gaillard. A steady curtain of rain had escorted them as they splashed through muddy wagon-tracked roads. Harlequin already looked like a different horse. Keeping up with the big destriers had already taught him that he should save his energy for productive matters. Like going forward. So as they stood at the gate to the town, he kept his head down and stood still like a perfect gentleman. Eleanor pulled her sodden cloak tighter around herself as Alec knocked hard on the big gate. A face appeared through the small sliver of glassless window.

"Yes?" the old guard asked.

"We are here to meet with the king!" Alec had to shout over the pouring rain.

"He expecting you?" the old man shouted back.

"No. We have information for him. Sir Alec Earnblaec of Neroche and Lady Eleanor de Levan d'Aquitaine."

"Levan d'Aquitaine you say? He's likely eager to see anyone loyal to him from Aquitaine these days. Ye *are* loyal to King Richard, aye?"

"Oc!" Eleanor shouted in her native Lange d'Oc, proving her nationality.

The old man squinted at her, then shouted something over his shoulder. Turning back to them he said, "Forgive me for the wait, but I'm going to have the steward meet you before I let you in. We've had a lot of conflicting stories lately. Those are my orders." And he disappeared.

Eleanor sighed and shrugged. "I can't blame him." She tucked her numb fingers in her armpits, slumping in the saddle against the deluge. The roads they had traveled told the story of the situation in France. Cottages burned, crops destroyed. Most of the villages they had passed were locked up with suspicion like this one. No one was certain who to trust, or even who their loyalties should lie with. The new castle on the ridge was yet another testament to the unrest. It apparently was going up in record time, as already the white stones towered over the river and town below. Scaffolding still could be seen on the upper towers, but judging from the light streaming from the windows, it was now occupied.

The steward appeared at the gate, eyed them, and then it creaked open and he came out to them. "May I see your crests please?" he asked. The man looked exhausted, but he still carried a professional mannerism and was neatly dressed in the colors of the king. Eleanor and Alec both held out their ring hands, and the steward nodded his approval. He eyed Eleanor's sword, still strapped to her hip. "I heard that Levan's daughter had returned. The king will want to meet you."

Eleanor exchanged a surprised glance with Alec. They had hoped to meet the king after a few weeks, certainly not right away. If her name already could gain them an audience, that was certainly to their benefit.

"And you are?" the steward directed at Wilfred.

"Just Wilfred," he answered, smiling as he leaned forward on the pommel of his saddle, Harlequin's reins loose as the horse napped.

"My squire," Alec added.

"I see," the steward said, then opened the gate wide enough for them to enter. "Where will you be staying?"

"Any recommendations?" Alec asked.

"The Black Crow Inn may have a few rooms left. I will send a messenger for you there in the morning once I have told the king of your arrival. Welcome to Petite Andelys, the best mud hole in France." He gestured with sarcasm to the grey, sodden village. After latching the big gate behind them, he turned back into a nearby house, leaving them in the street.

"If I remember right, the Black Crow is on the left side of town," Eleanor said softly.

"You've been here?" Wilfred asked, surprised.

"Tournament last year, Wilfred. Lance came along, not you," Alec said bluntly.

Sure enough, they found the inn on a back street in the left, western quarter of town. And they did have one room left, with four beds. Eleanor wondered for a moment if she would start a scandal by sharing a room with two men, but the gruff innkeeper ignored her. Must be as common an occurrence here as it was at the tourneys. With the horses tucked in the stable, they were pleased to find the small room was equipped with a fireplace and plenty of hooks to hang their sodden garments.

Alec stripped down to his breeches and started the fire as Wilfred and Eleanor pulled off their own sodden outer layers and unpacked the wet provisions. Eleanor faced the corner and quickly slipped her spare shift over her head and let the wet one fall to the ground. Her spare gown had a few damp patches but was mostly dry thanks to the well-oiled saddlebag and the protection of the oilskin she had wrapped it in. She slipped it on. She glanced over her shoulder at the men as she picked up her wet shift and hung it on one of the many pegs. They were both down to their breeches and bare feet, trying to dry themselves by the fire, which now roared with warmth. She noted how the firelight made every muscle even more defined on their chiseled bodies. Wilfred was leaner than Alec, but taller. And Alec . . . her face got red as she remembered what it was like to feel those solid arms around her. She rung out her hair, ran her fingers through it, and tied it in a bun on top of her head. She joined them by the fire, warming her hands.

They were quiet for a while, slowly rotating themselves to soak in the warmth and to dry their clothes. Eleanor's damp spots on the gown dried well before the men's sodden breeches did, so she offered to go down for food. When she returned with a plate of stale bread, salt pork, and apples, they were still by the fire, talking quietly.

"Don't you think it seems odd, though, that they even knew her name?" Wilfred asked Alec.

"It's been almost two weeks since the tourney. Those champion rosters go out to every corner of the kingdom. Of course they've heard what happened."

"But it's almost like the king is *expecting* her," Wilfred insisted.

Eleanor cleared her throat. "Dinner."

The men shared a look and left the warmth of the fire. Alec frowned as he took a bite of the stale bread. They finished it all though, eating quietly.

"I think he wants to know how to get over the mountains. Les Vosges," Eleanor said quietly. Wilfred and Alec looked up at her, then exchanged a look. She continued, "As far as I know, I'm the only one that's managed to take a horse over that range without taking the normal roads. They are densely forested, rocky hills. And there's a castle on every hilltop once you reach Alsace. If

King Richard can establish an unknown route to the East, to Rome and to the trade routes even further east, it could supply him with the goods and funds he needs to re-secure France. Maybe even enough left over to launch yet another crusade. As it is now, all the known routes are constantly plagued by bandits, mercenaries. It is expensive to protect the goods. And that's how he was captured a few years ago."

"But how does he know you've gone that route?" Wilfred asked.

"I emerged from the wilderness near Gisors, just a few miles from here. King Richard has had his eye on that fortress for years and is constantly searching for information from his spies. He must have heard rumors about me." Eleanor paused. "Wilfred, what *do* you know about me? You've followed me all the way to France, and you know my real name, but what else do you know?"

"I know you were forcibly married to Lezay. And tried to have the marriage annulled, but it isn't really. And your Uncle Montag hates you for some reason. And now you want your family lands back."

"So you don't know how I escaped to England? Or why?"

Wilfred shook his head.

She looked at Alec. "Do you know?"

"I know you were raped. That's all," Alec said.

"Raped?" Wilfred questioned. "A marriage bed is hardly—"

Eleanor cut him off. "When I escaped, I galloped the roads west to the Nunnery of St. Catherine. Made those seventy miles before daybreak. The horse was horribly lame, and I thought about staying there, but I just couldn't picture that life for myself. I wanted to continue on, try to find Edmond. He was my only acquaintance outside of Chateau Montagne. But by the time I was rested enough, even though it was only a few hours, word had already reached the nuns that Montag had his army out in full force looking for me. Which means they were already ahead of me on the roads to the west. The nuns could give me a palfrey, but there was no way I could outrun Montag's men. So I took to the mountains. *Deep* in the mountains." She took a sip of ale. "I came upon so many ravines, cliffs, briar patches. I wasn't sure I would ever get out of there. But I came far enough west that eventually I broke out of the woods over to the east of here, near a little village called Chancily. I stayed there a day to heal. It seemed like a quiet enough town. My knees were blistered. I was exhausted, half starved. I was dressed like a boy, so no one paid me too much mind for being alone, but they could tell I'd been in those mountains at least a week and running from something. Once I got my bearings and could think straight, I wanted to go south to Edmond's manor in Fougères. But by the time I rode to Gisors, which is just east of here, word again reached me that my uncle was looking for his kidnapped niece. I knew the villagers at Chancily could put that together and figure out it was me. About the same time, I saw a tourney announcement with Edmond's crest on the top. He was in England. There was no protection for me here in France. I had to get on a ship to England.

"You can figure out the rest of the story. My point is, the people in Chancily likely figured out who I was not long after I was gone. And they knew I had been over the mountains, off the main roads. From what I know of King Richard, he makes it his business to find out strategical routes like that. If there was ever a rumor of it, he will have heard. And he will have heard that it was the Levan daughter that made the trip."

"So can you tell him the route?" Alec asked.

"Of course not." Eleanor laughed without mirth. "I was half-starved and barely conscious. Not to mention injured," she added quietly. "I should have died in there. I have no idea how I got out."

The men were quiet. "Let's not tell the king that just yet," Alec cautioned.

Eleanor got up and went back to the fire, adding a few logs and then standing there watching it burn.

She heard them whisper together on the other side of the room.

"Rape? Really?" Wilfred asked skeptically below his breath.

"I think so. I don't know the details, but I know it's affected her," Alec replied.

Wilfred let out a huff. "And you'd know now, wouldn't you?"

Alec leaned toward him across the little table. "Why the . . . do you care?" he hissed through gritted teeth. "You've known I've been with her for over a year. Why are you so protective of her? Jealous of me maybe? But why now after you've stayed out of our business all this time?"

Wilfred leaned forward too, dropping his voice even lower. "Because I'm the only one left to protect her, that's why. Edmond at least loved her. I don't know what you want from her yet. But she's been through enough loss. Don't you mess with her heart."

"I told her I don't love her; she had no preconceptions there."

Wilfred sucked in a breath through his teeth. "You bastard—"

"Hey," Alec cut in. "*She's* the one that ended it. And I said I would respect that. So don't start telling me I should be in love with her because we had a moment together."

Wilfred stood up, scraping the bench away from the table as he did so. He looked mad enough to punch Alec, but all he said was "I'm going to feed the horses." And he pulled his wet boots and damp shirt back on and stalked out.

Eleanor didn't look up from the fire. "He's right you know."

"Excuse me?"

"We never should have done it if we weren't in love."

Alec rose and strode over to her, leaning against the warm stone of the fireplace so he could see her face. "And why is that?"

Eleanor looked him in the eye calmly. "Because we are bound to each other now. Same as I am bound to Lezay. And Edmond." She looked back into the fire. "The priest said at my wedding, 'And the two shall become one.' It's true. Even without love." She shrugged. "I don't mind, but you should at least admit it to yourself. I don't want you to realize it when we're in the middle of a battle or something."

Alec watched her closely. "Bound, huh?"

Eleanor smiled faintly at him. "Like it or not. Our futures are now linked, for better or worse."

Chapter Twenty-Eight

Alec and Eleanor entered the throne room side by side, with Wilfred only a few steps behind. The three of them stopped a few yards before King Richard, Coeur de Leon, and bowed deeply. Eleanor clasped her trembling hands together. Though she was nobility herself, this was her first time meeting a king face to face. Here was a man with the wealth of all of England and half of France, an army strong enough to crusade into the Holy Land, and the power to determine if men – and women – could live or die. She swallowed and raised her gaze to take in the man before her. Richard was middle-aged but still ruggedly handsome. He wore his simple gold crown over a head of dirty-blond hair streaked with gray. His sword rested against the throne beside him. His riding boots were dirty, and he looked as if any moment he could walk back out onto the battlefield.

Eleanor straightened as she caught Richard's intense gaze. He casually slouched on his throne with an amused expression, observing her as intently as she observed him.

Richard's lips curved into a wry grin as he spoke. "I am pleased to meet you at last, Lady Eleanor de Levan. I have heard many stories about you and am anxious to hear which ones are true. And my loyal Sir Alec Earnblaec. So kind of you to travel to offer your services. We have need of a knight of your skill here. How do things fare in my beloved England?"

"England is well, Your Majesty. Of course, your subjects are always eager for your return, but things are well handled while you attend to the rest of your kingdom." Alec's voice was steady, as if he regularly met with kings. Eleanor inhaled and tried to mimic his confidence.

Richard turned to Wilfred. "And you, sir, are?"

Wilfred bowed deeply again. "Not a sir, Your Majesty. Just Wilfred."

"My squire," Alec explained.

"Ah." Richard nodded, still eyeing Wilfred. His eyes flicked back to Alec for a moment, and he frowned. "A commoner?"

Alec shrugged. "I had a noble-born squire, but he recently deserted me for Lord Montag of Alsace. Or so we believe."

"And Lord Montag is why you are here." Richard leaned back again, tapping long fingers against the arm of his chair. "I have heard a great deal about the Alsatian lord as of late. I believe we should start at the beginning." He turned to Eleanor, clearly fascinated by the woman with a sword belted over her dress. His eyes sparkled. "Are you truly Sir Enric de Levan's daughter?"

Eleanor stepped forward to show him her father's ring, the famous design plain on her finger.

"He was a good knight. I had the pleasure to joust with him several times. How did you come to be married to Sir Rothulfus Lezay?"

Eleanor took a deep breath. "My uncle, Lord Montag de Brunstein d'Alsace, arranged it."

"Not an uncommon practice. My own marriage was arranged by my mother. As you may have heard, I do not see much of my wife, lovely lady though she is. But she is still my wife. How did you end up in England with Sir Alec? I'm getting ahead of myself, but are the stories of the two of you true?" His eyes flicked between the two of them.

Eleanor's face flushed, and for once Alec remained silent. She felt him shift next to her.

"Ah, I see," the king continued, amused. "So how did that happen?"

Eleanor bit her lip, aware the question was directed at her. She steadied her voice then replied, "I knew my marriage would not be a happy one. I was fourteen. I panicked. I ran. And I do not regret it though it has caused me to live in fear of the consequences. England seemed to be far enough away to be out of Uncle Montag and Sir Lezay's reach, but apparently even that was not far enough. You heard what happened at the tourney in Sarum?"

"I received a letter from Lord Gawain directly. He says Lord Montag threatened him, claiming you were legitimately married to Sir Lezay and thus committing adultery, yet Lord Gawain swears you showed him an annulment, and that you are not married. He asked me to advise him on what to do, since as an Aquitanian noble you are not his subject to protect but rather mine." Richard narrowed his gaze at Alec, considering his words, but then turned back to Eleanor. "Do you still have this annulment?"

Eleanor paled. This meeting was far beyond what they'd expected. She felt powerless, even embarrassed, like a scolded child. Still, she nodded and withdrew the folded parchment from a pouch tucked into her skirts. She couldn't hide the tremble in her hands as she handed the fake document to the king.

Richard read through it carefully, frowning. His eyes lingered on the seal at the bottom of the page. Slowly he raised his eyes to Eleanor's. "This is a rather convincing forgery."

Alec exhaled through his nose, tension building, but Eleanor was surprised to feel relief that she would not have to lie. "Yes," she simply said.

Richard did not smile. "How?"

"My friend . . ." She inhaled. "Lord Edmond de Fougères had it made up for me." Suddenly the words came out in a rush. "I didn't know how else to be rid of him, Your Majesty! I tried running away. I tried to seek an annulment and could not. So Edmond tried to help me fake an annulment. Tell me . . . tell me how I can be free of Sir Rothulfus Lezay, Your Majesty, and I am at your service!" She brazenly looked the king in the eye, praying he would give her a task that would absolve her past. "I will fight for you. I will work for you. I will—"

"Shush. Calm, woman." Richard held up a hand to her. Eleanor instantly bit her tongue. Richard turned to Alec. "This is why you have not married her?"

"Yes, Your Majesty." Alec replied.

Eleanor could not tell if they spoke of her annulment or her hysterical behavior. She took the insult and dropped her gaze, hoping to hide her furious glare.

"I heard Lord Edmond de Fougères is dead under suspicious circumstances," Richard said.

"He is." Alec nodded.

"My cousin Sir Raoul d'Alsace admitted it was at my uncle's hand," Eleanor said, exhaling the anger that bubbled in her chest.

Richard thought for a moment. "I've also heard that rumor. Much like your father, was it not, Sir Alec?"

Eleanor raised her eyes to look between the two men.

"Yes, it sounds very similar to what I've been told." Alec shrugged. "Similar stab wounds, and both along forest roads. And I know my father was killed by Sir Lezay. I heard that from his own lips."

"Really?" Richard's eyebrows went up. "If you knew, why did you not come forward before now?"

Alec shook his head, smirking slightly. "I have no proof by my word against his. What would your courts do with that? A poor knight-errant against a lordling prince of Alsace?"

Richard nodded. "Well observed, Sir Alec. Though I don't like it when my knights are killed by foreigners without penalty. Particularly when they are on pilgrimage, which was the case with your father?"

"Yes, Your Majesty."

Richard tapped a finger against the throne. His three subjects shifted uncomfortably before him. "Lord Gawain was not the only one to contact me regarding you two." His eyes again drifted from Alec to Eleanor. "My nephew Lord Otto, Duke of Aquitaine, was visited by Lord Montag just a few days past, and sent me an urgent warning that you, Lady Eleanor, would be arriving to try to reclaim your father's manor, a place which I was convinced about ten years ago, while I was still Duke of Aquitaine, should be burned to the ground to still a rebellion." He looked pointedly at Eleanor. "I fear now there never was a rebellion, was there?"

Eleanor looked bewildered. "Not that I was ever aware of, Your Majesty. That is when I ran. I was in hiding all these years, certainly never moving against you. My family – my father's family – was always loyal to you."

Richard slapped his throne and stood, beginning to pace before them on the dais. "Two of my knights dead, both under suspicious circumstances involving Alsatian lords. One of my manors destroyed by faulty information. And you, Lady Eleanor, somehow in the middle of all of it, appearing after a decade of masquerading as a commoner. With a sword in hand no less!" He chuckled and glanced at the blade at her side.

He whirled to face the three of them. "They want to challenge you, Lady Eleanor, to a trial by combat. Only they want to do it in the form of a melee, three riders to three." He gave them a moment to process the information. Eleanor felt her heart quicken. "For your crime of adultery, he challenges you. I was going to refuse it. You are a woman. And I believed, hoped, in your annulment much like Lord Gawain. But from what the three of you have just told me, I now want to challenge him."

"A melee?" Alec asked as the silence of the room echoed..

Richard nodded. "Complete with the possibility for ransoms."

Wilfred cleared his throat. "Forgive me, I thought melees were considered too dangerous?"

"This is not for sport," Alec said calmly. "It is a trial by combat before God, who will decide the victors."

Richard threw his hands up. "With what you've told me, it is the easiest way to settle this. All of this. The way I see it, we enter one rider for every charge. Alec, you ride for your father. Eleanor, you ride for your independence from your husband and in defense of their charges of adultery. Then we just need a third man to ride for Lord Edmond. Perhaps one of his brothers?"

"When do they expect this challenge?" Eleanor asked.

"Your arrival here in Normandy was most opportune. I have word that Lord Montag and Sir Lezay are to meet in Paris within a fortnight. They will choose their third. And I suspect them to ally with King Philip of France, so they have a powerful witness behind them as this score is settled."

"A fortnight doesn't give us time to send word to the Fougères family," Alec pointed out. "And honestly, I would rather not fight with one of them."

Eleanor shared his sentiment. Edmond had been the tournament champion of the Fougères family. None of his brothers had ever competed successfully if they competed at all.

"I'm not sure who else I would volunteer for this melee, Sir Alec." Richard shot a glance to Eleanor, revealing his fear that his three knights may not hold with Eleanor as their weak link. "We need someone strong."

Wilfred cleared his throat. "I am not yet knighted, but I would ride with them."

Every eye in the room locked on the tall, young man.

"Wilfred—" Alec began but hesitated when Eleanor laid a hand on his arm and shook her head.

The king considered the commoner. "You have a horse? Can you fight?"

"I have a great horse." Wilfred smiled confidently. "And yes, I am ready to fight."

"This fight will be intense. And if you lose, you will be their prisoner. For you, with no family to charge a ransom to, it will likely mean you will be a serf for life."

"If you survive," Alec muttered.

"None of us have family that would ransom us," Eleanor quietly pointed out. That sentiment quieted the room. "We are the perfect trio." The three of them met each other's eyes.

Alec smiled. "Those with nothing to lose are the most dangerous, right?"

The three of them turned to the king, who threw up his hands.

"If that is how you three want it, who am I to argue? But bring me my victory. I want justice for the men they've killed!"

"Yes, Majesty," the three of them echoed.

Richard sighed and waved them off. "I will ride with you to witness, with a small entourage. I suggest we move early, surprise them before they have too much time to pick their third. I would like to travel off the main roads. Lady Eleanor, you have traveled through the Vexin off the main paths in the past?"

"I did, though I don't remember much of how."

"Secrecy would be in our favor," Alec pointed out.

Richard smiled. "My men have made great progress on a secret route through the Vexin. We will travel that way, and if you have any suggestions along the way, if anything looks familiar, be sure to inform me."

"Yes, Majesty," Eleanor agreed.

"Well, it's settled then." Richard resumed his seat on his throne. "Take the next two days to prepare, and then we will ride."

Chapter Twenty-Nine

T hey traveled single-file through the forest, on paths barely wide enough for a horse to trod. Eleanor was impressed by the king's route. They had entered the woods in Chancily, and just like she had years ago, they cut into the creek beds whenever possible to conceal their tracks. Thus far she had given no direction, and the terrain was only vaguely familiar. While Alec had worked his way up to a place near the scouts and king, Eleanor and Wilfred had fallen toward the back of the entourage of a dozen horsemen.

They rode in silence.

A large monolith caught Eleanor's eye, and she halted her horse, staring at it. This place she recognized. She had rested here, under its great, upright shadow. Moreover, the strange lines cut on the rock were unmistakable. The line of horses wove past the rock, straight ahead, but Eleanor remembered coming in from the south. There was a river ahead, and she had ridden far along its eastern bank before finding an easy crossing to the south.

"What is it?" Wilfred asked.

"I wonder where they're going to cross."

"There's a river ahead?"

She nodded. "About a mile yet."

"If you know a better path, say so. King Richard said he was open to it."

Eleanor cut her horse around the line, weaving in between the trees. "Alec!"

Alec turned toward her, and the line of riders pulled up with him, including the king.

Eleanor addressed the king's scout, who led the line. "Where do you cross the river?"

The grizzled knight shrugged. "It's not an easy crossing, but there's a place a bit north of here."

"But we want to cut south." She shook her head and looked to the king. "There's an easy, sandy crossing south of that monolith." She pointed.

"How far?" Richard asked.

"Not much. But from there the forest thins and allows for faster travel."

"We'll be lost in the forest for days," the scout said.

Richard weighed things. "Are you positive, Lady Eleanor?"

"It's been ten years. What if the river has washed things away?" Alec asked, his words gentle despite his dubious frown and furrowed brow.

Eleanor blinked at Alec, surprised at his dissent, as rational as it was. "All I am certain of is that there was once an easy crossing south of here."

Richard frowned, then looked to his scout. "Better continue the way you know. Check out her claim on our return. We need to be in Paris quickly." The scout shot Eleanor a smug look and once again led the way.

Eleanor sat on her horse and let the line weave by, Alec with it, until she was back with Wilfred. "We just added hours of riding to our day," she grumbled.

He shrugged. "What did you expect?"

They rode in silence again, falling further behind when they reached the river, where each knight had to fight his horse across the rocky, rushing water. It was a horrible crossing, and they took it one by one, anxiously watching each other and cursing under their breath. It took a bit of coaxing to get the fiery Noir and Harlequin across, and when they did they were now at the end of the line, the other riders just out of earshot. Alec was completely out of sight at the front of the line.

"You want to know what bothers me most?" Wilfred asked as they picked their way back to the other riders. "You were so determined you weren't going to yield to Alec. For so long. You hated him even. I don't think you were scared of him exactly, but you stood your ground against him so fiercely, I thought for sure he would never break you down." He hesitated, flicking away a fly. "But then he did. And I don't know what changed. In you, in him, between the two of you. You finally had a chance to be independent of him, but now I don't think you ever really will be."

Eleanor frowned, letting her horse slow so she was next to Wilfred on the narrow path.

"You're a grown woman. You can do whatever you want. I didn't say a word when you were with Edmond. But you and Alec together scare me, Eleanor. Just tell me you aren't losing yourself. I know the shock of losing Edmond, the grief, the fear of Lezay coming back . . . that's all a lot to take in. Tell me you're with him because you want to be, not because he broke you."

Eleanor sighed. "Wilfred, I'm fine. Really."

"Then be careful, Eleanor. Alec is not going to let you free easily. He might keep his distance for now, obey your wishes, but whether he admits it even to himself or not, he thinks he owns you now." He shifted in his saddle. "I've known Alec a long time. Just be careful he doesn't become your next Lezay."

"Wilfred, how did you end up at Alec's manor in the first place?"

"I've been trying to figure that out for the last few months. It's not as simple of a story as I once was led to believe."

"Care to share?"

"Let's just say I took a little detour to Castle Homme on my way back to Neroche last week. It was rather enlightening."

"Castle Homme? Where Alec was raised?"

"Where I was raised."

Eleanor squinted ahead. They had almost caught up to the other riders. "Is that what's been bothering you?"

"Part of it."

Eleanor thought for a moment. "Are you sure you want to fight this melee? You of all people don't have a stake in this."

"I do though." They were in earshot of the others now. "I'll explain afterwards. I promise not to let you down." He winked at her, a twinkle in his eye.

Eleanor turned to him, the pine needles rustling beneath her. "Just so you know, I am grateful you're here."

"Where else would I be?" Wilfred replied.

Chapter Thirty

July 1197

Paris, France

The last few miles seemed to fly by as the forest opened into nearly flat, rolling farmland. In pairs, the horsemen emerged and fell into formation. Birthed from the king's secret path, this was the first they were seen by civilization in days. They cantered in unison as the sun rose in the eastern sky, rays of pink and gold light painting the billowy clouds. The weather was going to be perfect, temperate and sunny. Tournament weather. They saw Chateau de Louvre in the distance, its stone walls rising out of the farmland around it, while the Ville de Paris could be seen beyond it.

Eleanor's heart pounded as King Richard took the lead, his standard now unfurled and held by the knight behind him. She, Wilfred, and Alec fell in line behind his entourage, which now formed a square of men four across and five deep. The synchronized thunder of hooves mingled with the clang of mail, an unmistakable sound that would inevitably alert the garrison in Chateau Louvre.

Richard drew his men to a halt in the field outside the bailey. They watched as men ran back and forth along the walls, shouting the alert that the King of England had arrived. "Now they come out to us," Richard said, watching expectantly. "Alec, I hope you have given me reliable intelligence, and this is not an ambush. I've been taken prisoner enough times in my life. I'm not keen to do it again."

Alec rode past the ranks of horses to halt just behind the king's standard. "Your Majesty, I only give reliable intelligence." He waited expectantly behind the king just the same.

As if on cue, a rider rode out from the gate, a young squire in the colors of King Philip. He halted before the party, nodding politely to King Richard. "My lords, we did not expect you to make it. My king and his men will be out in short order."

"We were told to meet them at dawn, were we not? Why does he keep us waiting? We traveled all the way from Normandy!" Richard's anger made the squire swallow hard. "He better get his chosen knights out here now, or it will be Paris under siege, not Andelys!"

"Just a few minutes, Your Majesty," the boy stammered and quickly turned his horse to ride back to the safety of the fortress.

Richard smiled. "Well done, Alec. They must have been relying on their spies."

Alec smiled back, as self-assured as ever. "I hope they got good and drunk last night."

In only half an hour, the gates let out a stream of men, standards waiving. The King of France was at their head. Eleanor swallowed hard. Like Richard, Philip led his men in formation, all his pageantry waving. Behind the entourage were three knights, their colors not yet visible from behind the rest of the party. Slowly she exhaled, willing her nerves to settle. The two kings rode up to each other in the center of the field and spoke, but they were too far from her to be understood. Alec rode back to Eleanor's left side.

"Still want to do this?" he asked quietly, watching the negotiations on the field.

She nodded, not trusting her voice.

"Remember then, Eleanor, all you have to do is stay on your horse. If you're on your horse you aren't dead. And so long as you're up there, you are in the fight. Don't yield." He shot her a sideways glance, noting the thin line of her mouth. "Stay on your horse."

She nodded again, swallowing hard. "Alec, be careful."

"This will be fun." He smiled and gave her a pat on the back.

She snorted a laugh, which helped ease some of her tension.

"You alright over there, Wilfred?" Alec leaned back to see around Eleanor.

Wilfred sat stoically on Harlequin, his reins loose. The fiery horse tossed his head at a fly, and Wilfred absently flicked it away with his rein. He pursed his lips, considering. "Which hand do I hold my sword in?"

Alec looked at him in alarm, and Wilfred burst out laughing. Eleanor couldn't help but join him.

"You bastard," Alec said under his breath, but smiled.

Still chuckling, Wilfred leaned forward, peering at Eleanor and Alec both. "Let's just see who gets the most ransom money today."

"Who's worth the most?" Alec pondered.

"Who's fighting?" Eleanor rose in her stirrups to try to see over the heads of Richard's knights. They all grew quiet at that overshadowing question, watching as the two kings finished their negotiations.

Richard cantered back, calling the three melee participants forward. "Are you all ready *now*? Philip claims his men are."

The three looked at each other and nodded.

Richard took a deep breath. "Check your armor. You'll fight right here in this field. Our knights will spread out along the edges to form your perimeter. You surrender by raising your right arm, disarmed. Remember, by yielding you give yourself to the other knight, along with all your armor and your horse. Your families will pay your ransom." Richard grimaced. "Which you don't have."

The three riders before him shook their heads.

"My only family is those who wish me to yield," Eleanor said quietly.

Richard stared at the three of them as if wondering if he should call off the melee. These three riders were obviously prepared to fight to the death, not merely until they were forced to yield.

"Who are we fighting?" Wilfred asked, breaking the tension.

"Lord Montag, Sir Lezay, and Sir Jean the Young."

"Ugh," Eleanor groaned.

"You know him?" Alec asked.

"Ruthless jerk. Son of another of Montag's close friends. He'll fight dirty. And he's strong. Fantastic potential for a ransom though."

"Let's take him down first," Wilfred smirked, licking his lips.

Richard looked at Wilfred in surprise. "On that note, I'll tell my men to line up. Best of luck to all of you. May God be on our side and deem our enemies unworthy."

On cue, the knights spread out around the field, leaving the three of them alone with their lances in hand, swords belted to their hips. King Philip's men also scattered, leaving the three opposing knights framed against the backdrop of Castle Louvre.

Eleanor checked her armor one last time with her left hand, slapping any piece of leather or mail that could possibly come loose.

"You'll have to shout your charges against Montag before we start, and he yours."

Eleanor looked at Alec in surprise.

"Ceremony." He shrugged. "Let him go first."

The knights finished fidgeting with their armor and stared at each other across the field. Finally, Montag bellowed, "I, Lord Montag d'Alsace, do hereby challenge Lady Eleanor de Levan d'Aquitaine, to this combat before God by reason of a vicious attack and disfigurement of a knight, for abandonment of familial duty, and gravest of all, blatant and most shameful *adultery*! Ye shall pay for your sins!" A loud cheer went up from the two men beside him and from the half of the field Philip's knights circled.

Eleanor pursed her lips, fury burning bright within her. Her voice rang out strong and clear, "I, Lady Eleanor de Levan d'Aquitaine, do challenge you, Lord Montag d'Alsace to a Trial by Combat for the unwarranted torture and *murder* of Lord Edmond de Fougères and for aiding and abetting Sir Rothulfus Lezay de Leuwenstein in the murder of *Sir Alfred of Homme*! You shall pay for your sins!" As she shrieked the last words, she raised her lance, and her half of the field roared its own cheer. She glowered as she watched Montag and Lezay exchange a glance. They hadn't suspected their secret was known, and now Eleanor had made their darkest crimes public.

Her attention snapped to the present as Alec let out a roar and his horse lurched forward. Eleanor and Wilfred were a stride behind him. They leveled their lances at the trio opposite, who were now organized in a tight line, with Montag at their center. Lezay was at Montag's right hand, in line with Alec, and Jean was across from Wilfred on Montag's left. Hooves pounded as Eleanor counted strides to the collision, aiming her lance square at her uncle's chest. Three strides, two strides! It took her a fraction of a second to notice how the three knights galloping toward her had changed the aim of their lances. All three were now pointed directly at her. Before she could react, her legs knocked into the horses beside her as Alec and Ches slammed into Noir, throwing their entire line to the right. The crack of wood and iron rang in her ears as her and Wilfred's lances both splintered against Jean, throwing him clear off his horse. She heard Alec grunt as he took someone's hit, but the three were still locked in line.

"Turn, turn!" Alec shouted, pirouetting Ches back into line.

Eleanor turned without thinking, Wilfred still tight on her right. In unison they charged again, two knights opposing now. The two broke off, each taking aim at the two men at her sides. Eleanor could not level what was left of her lance at anyone and was funneled down the center toward Sir Jean, who though unhorsed, was leveling a massive pike right at her. She aimed her lance at him a second time, but the splintered length hit him just as he hit her thigh. She screamed in pain as Noir charged past. Dropping what was left of the lance, she put pressure on the gaping wound.

"Again! Quickly!" Alec shouted, and Eleanor loped back to his side, knee to knee with him, sword now in hand. Wilfred galloped past them with a look of blood-rage, his sword drawn. Eleanor flinched and looked behind her as he hammered Sir Jean to the ground for the third time. The man had been only feet away from Eleanor, pike again leveled. After Jean rolled back to his feet, he and Wilfred locked in combat, one on horseback with a sword, the other on foot with long deadly pike. She could not assist, as the other two knights were already charging directly at her and Alec.

"Go!" Alec screamed, kicking his mount forward. He still had a portion of his lance left and held it ready. Eleanor gritted her teeth and choked up on her reins, riding up to Alec's right knee. He stole only a glance at her as they kicked their horses in unison toward the two older, more experienced knights who were still armed with splintered lances. Alec aimed for Lezay on the left as Eleanor held her sword firm as she charged toward Montag on the right. There was a sickening crunch as they collided.

Eleanor felt the contact of her sword on solid mail and leather reverberate up her arm merely seconds before she felt a crack and a shooting pain across her own ribs. The force of the blow threw her back in the saddle, but the high cantle held her in place. She doubled over and pulled Noir to a walk, her eyes momentarily blurred, gasping.

"You're alright!" Alec yelled beside her. It wasn't a question, but an order. She blinked and straightened, reining back in unison with him to ready for the next charge.

But a new charge didn't come.

Alec was now fighting sword to sword with Montag, both of them still mounted. Wilfred dealt the last blows to Sir Jean, who finally fell to the ground without rising. As Wilfred cantered past Eleanor toward Montag, she couldn't mistake his mad grin. He and his wild-eyed horse had found their calling. The three horses locked into a swirling dance of sideways steps, rears, kicks, and spins, their riders fighting in an intense frenzy of sword work.

Adrenaline soared through Eleanor's veins, but she could feel herself weakening through it. Hunched in her saddle with a hand on her ribs, she willed herself to canter off toward the fight. Instantly she gasped in pain, waves of nausea rolling over her. She drew Noir to a halt. To fight more would be the death of her. She cursed in frustration, blinking back hot tears of anger and pain, watching the melee continue to unfurl. Perhaps she was a coward, to not die fighting.

She wasn't a knight.

She screamed as Noir suddenly bucked. Hastily she choked up on her reins and looked behind her for the cause of the sudden movement. There stood Lezay, sword in hand, tip red with Noir's blood as evident by the stain rapidly spreading through the fabric of the horse's caparison. Lezay moved to grab the horse's reins, and she jerked Noir away, backing him across the field. Lezay pursued, one arm pressed against his side, where a splinter of Alec's lance was lodged in his ribs. His eyes were bloodshot and wild. He'd lost his helmet in the fall, showcasing his hideous scar. He lurched to grab Noir's reins again, this time succeeding. The big horse pulled back but would not pull enough to break the hold of the big man controlling his face. Eleanor leaned forward, hacking with her sword, but was unable to reach the man she was now tethered to, her horse spinning in a circle around him, tearing up the turf of the field.

Lezay jerked Noir to a halt, and the horse obeyed, shaking in pain and fear. Lezay used that second to step into Eleanor's left side, grabbing her injured leg while defending himself from her blows with his sword in the same hand that held Noir's rein. Eleanor's blood pumped furiously again as she felt herself lose her stirrup and slide in the saddle toward Lezay. He was trying to unhorse her. Not kill her . . . unhorse her. Again and again she hammered her sword desperately at him, but her movement was limited by the searing pain in her side, and he was blocking every blow.

She gave Noir a sharp kick with her right leg, sending him sideways over Lezay. He kept his feet and held on, but it was enough to loosen his grip that she could center herself in the saddle and nail Noir with both her legs. The big horse reared in fury, ripping out of Lezay's grasp and striking out with his front feet. On landing he bolted forward a few steps, barely under Eleanor's control. Again the world blurred with her pain, and it took all she had to rein him in again. She blinked rapidly, working to gain her bearings again.

She heard a chuckle behind her.

She walked her horse to him and stared down. The sounds of the melee faded against the background of her thumping heartbeat. Sprawled on his back on the blood-spattered grass, Lezay pressed a hand into the hole in his mail, the broken point of Alec's lance now edged with a large red stain. Two muddy hoofprints marked the places where Noir had struck him: one on his chest, the other on the top of his head, where a large lump was forming. He chuckled again when he saw her, coughing on blood as he did.

"Wife," she thought she heard him rasp. It was not a plea. He sounded almost amused.

She thought about how she'd hoped for a moment like this, where she could take her revenge, where she could kill him. But in the back of her mind she knew if she dismounted now, she would join him in the grave. Her mind swirled as she replayed all the plans she'd dreamed of for this moment, each of them impractical for the reality at hand. For a long time they watched each other, Eleanor noting how his face grew paler and his breathing more labored. She should end his misery. But she wanted him to suffer as he had made her suffer. Should she treat him, help him? Perhaps the wound was not that bad, and he would survive. Perhaps she could forgive the old wrongs. Perhaps he would be her ally in France. Perhaps if Noir took one more step forward, Lezay would be dead.

Even as she thought these things, she realized she was losing sense. She shook her head to clear the fog and remembered her leg. One glance down at her red pant leg and the blood dripping down her boot was enough to make her dizzy. She used what strength she had left in her to twine her fingers tighter in her horse's mane. He stood patiently as the melee between Alec, Wilfred, and Montag went on. Such a good horse. Her heart beat louder. The edges of her vision greyed. Someone was riding toward them. She should ready her sword. But her arm would not obey. Her eyes blurred a little as she looked down at Lezay again. He was no longer focused on her but stared into the sky. His chest still rose and fell in awkward rhythm.

His hand shakily tried to reach for the dagger belted at his side. The rider that approached said something to her. She couldn't hear. She couldn't see. She gripped the horse's mane tighter; it was the only thing routing her to the present. The rider dismounted and leaned over Lezay, taking the dagger from his hip, staring at the hilt. Eleanor closed her eyes. She flinched as she heard Lezay grunt, then heard the quiet. The quiet of the field around them. The quiet lack of Lezay's labored breathing.

Alec's face swam in front of her for a moment. "You're going to be ok. We're going back to the castle. It's over." She felt his hands slide something around her wounded thigh and flinched as he pulled it tight. The pain momentarily alerted her again. She took a sip of the water he offered her and sat up a little more in the saddle. He held up a hilt of a dagger toward her. "You did well." Eleanor squinted at the Levan crest. It was her own, the one she had abandoned in her wedding chamber. Too weak to think more, she felt Alec belt the sheathed dagger around her waist, his hand staying on the belt to hold her steady in the saddle as he rode leg to leg next to her.

Chapter Thirty-One

Eleanor blinked in confusion at the ceiling. Rough boards. With heavy beams. A damp breeze blew in from a window somewhere, and she shifted her gaze. Wooden walls. Blinking quickly, the pains throughout her body returned. The worst was the throbbing in her ribs. Every time she took a breath, a hot skewer ran up her side. Next was the stinging in her thigh. Her muscles groaned in protest. Her head ached. Water. She needed water. She tried to sit up.

"Oh no you don't." Alec came into view.

Eleanor laid back down. What kind of Hell was this?

But he had water. Fresh sweet water, probably from an actual well. Gently she felt the cup against her dry lips and drank. She coughed slightly, which made her cringe and grasp her side. She promptly nestled back into the pillows.

"Yeah, broken ribs will do that," Alec said. "But they haven't moved, so as long as you stay put for a few days you'll be okay. Cut is bandaged too. You were lucky with that one." Eleanor reached down to her thigh, which was bound tight with linen.

Slowly it was coming back to her. "How long have I been out? How did you get me back here? Where *is* here?"

"We're back in Petite Andelys, in the inn. You rode most of the way back yourself, but I'll admit, it took Wilfred and me both to keep you in the saddle. You lost a lot of blood."

"Did we win?"

Alec chuckled. "The king is most pleased."

Suddenly Eleanor remembered Lezay. "Is Lezay dead?"

Alec nodded.

"You're certain?"

"I promise you. You are safe from him forever. We both are."

Eleanor looked back up to the ceiling, then back at Alec. "Wilfred?" she asked with a tinge of alarm in her voice.

"Just fine. Did pretty well for a mere squire boy." Sensing she was going to keep drilling him name by name, he added, "Sir Jean is in rough shape but alive. He is now Wilfred's prisoner, though they say his family is already en route with the ransom. Wilfred is going to be a wealthy man. Montag was a stubborn coward and surrendered to King Richard instead of Wilfred and I. King Richard allowed it, but he set the ransom for him so high, I doubt even King Philip wants to pay it. King Richard will be keeping him as a pet for a good long time. Quite frankly, I'm glad he's being kept on the king's coin and not mine."

"Where is he?"

"A comfortable room in the top of the keep here at Gaillard. Under guard of course."

Suddenly Eleanor was exhausted. She closed her eyes. "Am I absolved, Alec? I did not take prisoners. I could not fight in the end. Was it enough?"

"Aye, Eleanor," he said gently.

Eventually she felt Alec's lips brush her forehead, and the bed shifted as he rose and quietly left the room. She let a deep, sound sleep take her.

By the next day she was feeling significantly stronger. She gingerly sat up, a hand clamped against her ribs. She rubbed her eyes and looked around. Wilfred sat at the little table with a plate full of pork and beans. Just the sight of it made her mouth water. Wilfred chuckled a little and pushed the plate toward her.

"I feel like all I've done is eat and sleep since we got back," he said. "You've been even more productive. Your body has been trying to heal, too."

Eleanor gave him a weak smile, not daring to laugh, and tested her shaky feet. Thankfully they worked. Self-consciously she pulled at her baggy linen shirt, glancing around for her gown or at least a tunic. She opted for the blanket off the bed instead, pulling it around her as she shuffled toward the table. She sat across from Wilfred, and they shared the plate of food.

"King Richard wants to speak with us again, once you're up to it," Wilfred said.

"Any idea why?" Eleanor asked, her mouth full.

"Nope."

"Alec too?"

"No actually. But King Richard's been keeping him plenty busy. I don't know if you noticed, but he has a knack for getting information out of people."

She nodded her head. That he certainly did. She shifted and the bandage around her left thigh brushed her opposite leg. "How bad was I cut?"

"Don't know. Alec treated it. Patched me up a little, too." He motioned to his arm, where the bulk of a bandage was just visible under his shirt. "Brought you back up here and got you stabilized. Made some kind of ointment for it that he put on yesterday. We were pretty worried about you that first day." Wilfred looked like he wanted to say something else but held back.

Her belly satiated, Eleanor tentatively stretched, testing her aching muscles. "How soon can we see King Richard? I don't want to keep him waiting. Particularly if it has anything to do with my uncle."

"Probably now. But, uh . . . you should clean up a bit first."

Eleanor self-consciously touched her hair, greasy strands tangled into a massive knot. The movement gave her a whiff of herself. She winced.

"I'll give you a few minutes," Wilfred offered politely and left her, taking the empty plate they'd shared.

There was a basin and water across the room. Eleanor carefully washed herself from face to toes with a wet cloth. She blushed a little as she realized Alec must have cleaned the worst of the battle grime off of her. The bruise over her ribs was an impressive blue-black, but Alec was right, she could still feel the straight lines of each one. She would just have to move carefully for a while. She ran her hand over the slight bump of her belly, full from a real meal.

She sucked her breath in. After a day without food, there should be no bump at all on her slender frame.

She didn't let her hand linger. After a moment's hesitation she carefully unknotted the bandage around her leg. The slimy ointment Alec had put on it made the deep palm-wide slice look gruesome, but it wasn't red or swollen around the edges. She carefully re-wrapped the bandage and knotted it, hoping it would hold as good as Alec's had. With a comb she untangled and braided her hair, pinching her cheeks to fake color like she'd seen Lady Gwen do. She mustn't look like she'd been wounded, however much she hurt. Slipping into a clean shift and her dress was the hardest part. She bit her lip to hold back tears as she gingerly wiggled her way into the clothes. Finally, she could tie the laces of the gown, leaving the bottoms just a tad loose to hide her figure. She took a practice lap around the room, standing tall and avoiding holding her side. It hurt, but she would do well enough.

When she and Wilfred reached the throne room in the castle, Richard was already waiting. His face lit up when he saw them.

"My two loyal subjects!" he beamed.

Wilfred and Eleanor nodded politely. With a wave of his hand, Richard sent out the few servants left in the room and strode to his throne. At first he sat with relaxed posture, but quickly leaned forward toward them, energy lighting his features like a man decades younger. "Eleanor, you are everything that Lord Gawain described to me. I am impressed you rose to the challenge, and you never faltered, even when wounded. The true character of a knight. And Wilfred, you surprised me greatly. I questioned to the last moment if it was right to let you fight. I never in all my years at tourneys and battles have seen a squire show as much courage and skill as you did in that melee. You matched some of the most hardened knights I've met . . . and won."

Wilfred swallowed and lifted his chin. Eleanor couldn't help but smile with a little pride for her friend.

Richard continued, "Both of you, two of our unlikeliest warriors, victors in one of the most desperate melees I have seen in years. God has chosen our case, chosen you, over the petty claims of Sir Lezay and Lord Montag. Murder has been avenged." He turned to Eleanor, his expression falling to a frown. "Eleanor, I would offer my condolences for the death of your husband, but I know they are not necessary. No true husband would put his wife to the tip of his lance, nor voluntarily put her in such peril, as he did. I understand now why you have done what you have to avoid him, and I forgive you for it. There will be no further charges of adultery against you."

Eleanor clutched a fist to her stomach, emotion rolling over her. Years of tension dissipated, leaving her breathless.

"You have worked hard to regain your freedom, and I will not pressure you to remarry. I do ask one thing of you though."

"Yes, Majesty?" Eleanor asked breathlessly.

"Do not flaunt your freedom. The troubadours sing true. You are the Lady of the Tournament, like your mother before you."

Eleanor blushed.

"I ask that you either marry one you chose or be an example of chastity for the other nobility. You know the church's beliefs in these matters. It is not only to appease the clergy, but I will not tolerate my best knights dividing the kingdom over you."

"I hardly have that power—" Eleanor blurted in surprise.

"Ah, you do. There are two men dead over you already."

Eleanor swallowed. Edmond and Lezay. She could add more names to that list, but Richard didn't need to know that. She nodded quickly. "Perfect chastity. I can do that."

"Or marry . . ." the king prompted, raising an eyebrow.

Eleanor nodded again.

Richard smiled, turning back to Wilfred and again addressing them both. "Your willingness to rise above your stations and defend what is right has set a great example for all men in my kingdom. And for that I am very grateful." Richard hesitated, smiling. "I wish to ordain you as knights, if you are willing."

They glanced at each other, questioning how serious the king really was.

"It will be a process. It is a long ceremony. How long do you need to heal? Is a week enough? There will be day spent in prayer and fasting, followed by mass, with the ordination at the conclusion. Then we will celebrate!"

Eleanor closed her mouth, suddenly aware it had gone slack. Wilfred had already recovered.

"I would be most honored, Your Majesty," Wilfred said with low bow.

Eleanor quickly echoed, "Most honored," and bent her knee low.

Richard smiled again, with more seriousness. "I have plans for the two of you." He looked Eleanor in the eye, studying her reactions. She was looking at him only with surprise and excitement, albeit tinged with bemusement.

There was a not a hint of protest in her expression, nor her mind, though the thought entered that perhaps Richard had expected it. His smile broadened. "Among said plans are for you to return to Aquitaine and rebuild your father's manor as soon as possible."

Eleanor's eyes widened. "I would absolutely love to, Your Majesty."

Richard glanced at Wilfred. "I hope you will help her, at least for a time. Then we will see what else you are capable of, *sir*."

Wilfred's cheeks turned pink. A smile cracked through his lips, the eagerness evident.

"Congratulations to the two of you. Lady Eleanor. Wilfred. I will keep you apprised of the plans for the ordination." He stood in signal that they were to be dismissed.

"Your Majesty, what of my uncle?" Eleanor asked.

"Your uncle will be my prisoner for a long time to come, it seems. I'm not too keen to release him, and I set the ransom accordingly. He asked to see you. I made no promises. It's up to you."

Eleanor gritted her teeth and pursed her lips. "Can I think about it?"

"Of course." The king nodded to Eleanor and Wilfred both. "I will see you next week at the ceremony. Make sure you are well cleansed . . . body and soul."

Still stunned, Wilfred and Eleanor bowed and exited the throne room. As the door closed behind them, they exhaled, wide-eyed. They were going to be knights! They smiled and embraced each other in their joy. Eleanor winced at her side and gingerly pulled away. Alec approached them from the hall, a smile on his face, too.

"I take it he told you?" he asked.

"You knew?!" Eleanor exclaimed breathlessly.

Alec chuckled. "He only told me this morning. I am proud of you. Both of you." For the first time Eleanor had ever seen, Alec looked at Wilfred with respect. It spoke volumes for what had transpired during the melee.

"Without you both I would not be here now," Eleanor said somberly. She took each of them by a hand and squeezed. "Thank you." She quickly released them. "Alec, would you join us for a drink?"

"Momentarily." He nodded to her. "The Inn?"

Wilfred and Eleanor left Alec to his business with the king. He joined them a few short minutes later in the common area of the Black Crow, which was deserted at this time in the afternoon.

Wilfred pushed Alec a mug of ale as he sat down. "On me this time." He smiled. "Sir Jean's family paid his ransom today."

"Did the armor fit?" Alec asked as he grinned in reply.

"Like it was made for me. Only took the armorist a few tweaks to make it perfect."

"Excellent. And how do you like his horse?"

"Lazy. Sold him for a huge sum though. I might get myself a charger instead."

"Easier to travel without a spare right now anyway. At least until you get yourself a squire to help you."

Wilfred let out his breath in a whoosh and glanced at Eleanor. She quietly observed them.

"What exactly happened between you on that field?" She glanced from one to the other.

Alec kept his gaze on Wilfred but spoke to Eleanor. "Your friend here surprised us all. I've always known he was an expert horseman, but I didn't know he had the skills for battle that he does. He tells me that's in part thanks to you?" Alec raised his eyebrows at Eleanor. "Well, Wilfred is one of the few men I've known who has a gift for battle. He can be a bloodthirsty fiend, or he can arrest his tempers in mercy. It was no easy feat during the heat of the moment, but he did it. He helped me unhorse Montag, who is one of the strongest knights I've ever fought. And when Montag surrendered to not us, but King Richard, it was Wilfred who checked us both back and allowed it."

"Did you convince King Richard to knight me?" Wilfred asked.

"No, but I agreed that you deserve it."

"To be knighted by the king himself is such an honor," Eleanor whispered. "It is the only way it could be done for people like us, a commoner and a woman."

"Aye, it is." Alec looked like he was about to tell her something, but Wilfred interrupted his thoughts.

"Sir Alec, there is something I need to ask you." Wilfred fidgeted with his cup. "I went back to Castle Homme."

Alec's eyebrows went up. "When?"

"On my way home from London, a few weeks ago."

The muscle in Alec's jaw worked.

"Alec, I have known you since I was a small child, followed you around Castle Homme. My mother always refused to speak of my father, and you know I was very young when she passed and I moved in with Old Guillaume. When Sir Alfred died – after you came back– Guillaume would not tell me why you asked us to come with you to Neroche and not the others. But I think you had a reason." Wilfred sweated out the words, now more anxious than he had been before the melee. "There were a few people at Castle Homme that had been there from the old days. They told me stories. Now I need to know as I choose a name . . . is there any chance . . . Alec, was Sir Alfred my father too?" The earnestness in Wilfred's eyes was electrifying. Eleanor stared at him in shock. Alec was unshaken.

After a moment's hesitation, he sighed. "Yes, Wilfred. I've had mixed feelings about you my whole life. My father's affair devastated my mother. But yes, you are my half-brother."

Eleanor's mouth fell open. One had to stretch for a resemblance between the two men, but there was something in that jawline, in the way they carried themselves. The ten-year age difference didn't help. Brothers?

Wilfred nodded. "It makes so much more sense." Wilfred ran a hand through his hair. "Have you always known?"

Alec nodded. "I knew about the affair before you were even conceived."

Eleanor regained her voice and cut in, "What don't you know, Alec?"

Alec looked steadily at her, the gaze silencing her as a familiar, pleasant burning settled in the pit of her stomach. She had to look away.

Wilfred continued, "I need to take a name tomorrow. I can't be just Sir Wilfred of Nothing. May I take the name Fitzalfred? I know being a Fitz is nothing to brag about, but for the first time in my life I have a father. Would he have cared if I took his name? Or did he refuse to acknowledge me . . ."

Alec thought for a moment, sizing up the man before him. "My mother swore to kill my father if he ever acknowledged you as his son. She thought you would grow to challenge me. You've lived under my roof these years. You know I don't have much to challenge. The manor we live in is not even mine. My title is nothing stronger than the one you are about to be awarded next week by the king himself. We have fought side by side in melee. Is my mother right? Have you grown to be my enemy? Or are we to be allies? Brothers?"

Wilfred's face lit up in a smile. "I'll not swear fealty to you if that's what you're insinuating."

Alec's crooked smirk returned. "Wilfred, I would say take the name, but being a Fitz is no easy claim. And you have never been known as such. I think you can think of something more fearsome than that. Something that will make your enemies quiver, not snicker. Use this ordination as a rebirth."

Eleanor looked from one to the other as they bounced names back and forth, amazed at the change between them. It wasn't just this new revelation of brotherhood. They were now brothers in arms. They had fought together, bled together, and survived together. That was a bond between men that even heredity could not forge. She had the feeling they would be utilizing that connection in the future. For that she breathed a sigh of relief, relaxed back into her chair, and took in the moment for the strength it would feed her in the days to come.

Eventually Wilfred left her and Alec alone, and she eyed him expectantly. He leaned back in his own chair and watched her, his lips twitching into a mischievous smile.

"So what about you?" she ventured.

"What about me?"

"Wilfred won a ransom, armor, a horse, a title, and now even a name from all this. I am to be knighted and have finally won my freedom, even my father's estates depending on how things go when I get to Aquitaine. You cannot tell me that you, the true, valiant knight of this great ordeal, have gained nothing."

Alec's crooked smile lit his face again. "I've been granted estates of my own not far from Sarum. My liege lord will be Lord Cenric, the man who knighted me."

Eleanor's eyes went wide. "Alec, that is fantastic! Your own manor!"

"King Richard has been most generous."

"But don't you have to return to England then? Manage the property? Will the household at Neroche move with you?"

Alec shook his head. "I don't need to go yet. I'll stay for your ordination, then make plans from there." He hesitated. "Eleanor, I tried to convince King Richard not to knight you." He looked down at the table.

Her smile faltered. "Why?"

"Do you think you'll be strong enough? You almost died during the melee."

She blinked. "I'm always almost dying."

"You have my respect. You do! I've never seen anyone fight like you did that day: through the pain, overmatched in strength, determined as any warrior. I just . . . I fear to watch you do it again and again, which a knight has to do."

"You think I don't have that same fear for you? Alec, my father was killed in combat. I know the risks. You taught me these skills. This was your idea. I've worked so hard. Don't take it from me now."

Alec leaned forward across the table and took her hands in his own. "King Richard argued the same point, and I shut my mouth. If you want this, I will not stop you. It is a life I love, I just . . ."

"I'll be all right, Alec." Eleanor softly squeezed his fingers.

He sighed. "I hope so." He rose and muttered to himself, "Lord knows, whatever happens after this, you'll be taking me down with you."

Chapter Thirty-Two

"You don't have long before you go into seclusion. Are you sure you want to do this now?" Alec asked as they strode through the castle passageways toward the tower where Montag was held prisoner. Alec held a large keyring in his hand, the heavy iron key to the tower jail dangling.

"I will have twelve hours to think, and I don't want to think about *him*. I want this behind me for good, so I can move forward with my life," Eleanor responded. She picked up the skirts of her white gown, part of her attire for the knighting ceremony, as she hastily climbed the spiral stairs up the tower. A red cloak trailed behind her, clasped at her shoulders and thrown back against the summer heat. Her sword was belted to her hip as always, now joined by her father's dagger on its own belt. Her hair was braided into a halo around the top of her head.

Alec paused outside the door at the top of the tower, showing the key to the two guards stationed there. They stepped aside to let him access the door, and Eleanor squared her shoulders, her mouth in a stern line. The lock clicked, and the guards entered the room, hands on their swords. They looked around, noting Montag sitting casually at a small table, then stepped aside for Eleanor to enter. Alec waited outside.

Montag didn't look much worse for his imprisonment. The room was small and plainly furnished, but clean and dry. His beard wasn't as neatly trimmed as usual, but he had on clean clothes and certainly was as towering of a man as ever. He was still eating well. He smirked as Eleanor entered, looking her up and down.

"My, my . . . an angel in white," he mused.

"Uncle," Eleanor acknowledged, her face stern. She turned to the guards and asked, "He's unarmed?"

They nodded.

"Give us a moment, please," she said, her eyes returning to her uncle as the men stepped beyond the door and closed it behind them. The latch clicked, but there was no grind of the lock. Eleanor narrowed her eyes at her Uncle Montag. "Why?"

Montag smiled at her, his face showing traces of the handsome man he had been in youth yet hardened by a dark glint in his eyes. "I'm afraid you'll have to be more specific, niece. There have been a lot of whys during the past twenty years."

"Why a melee?"

"They're fun. And since you think you're a knight now, why not?"

Eleanor shook her head. She could think of a lot of reasons why not.

"You killed my friend, Eleanor. *Your husband*! That is the why I would love to hear."

"I didn't kill him."

"No? I heard it was a dagger that dealt him the last blow. And Lezay's dagger was missing. Perhaps he was trying to yield, to be taken prisoner as I, and someone murdered him instead?"

Eleanor swallowed, doubting herself. "I was standing right there. He died from his injuries." Her hand involuntarily closed on the hilt of the dagger at her hip.

Montag noticed and smiled. "Ah, but no blade touched him during the melee. At least not until his back was on the ground."

Eleanor paled. Then suddenly she shook her head. Montag lied. "You could not have seen. You were busy yielding to King Richard. You were at the opposite end of the field." These were the games Montag played with people. Eleanor grew bolder, angrier. She stepped up to his table, leaning over it toward him. "Can you explain to me what happened to Lord Edmond de Fougères?"

Montag's eyes narrowed.

She continued, "Tortured, then stabbed, and left to die along the roadside like a common victim of a petty crime."

"Perhaps it was." Montag held her gaze.

"I hear it was murder. And there was certainly no battlefield to confuse his wounds with."

Montag's lips snarled. "What is it you want from me, niece? You want to list my every sin? It is *you* who are entering into the cleansing portion of the ordination I hear. What of your own? Adultery, murder, arrogance . . ."

Eleanor smiled and straightened. She could see how it was done now. Her uncle could twist anything, talk circles around a person so they couldn't remember what it was they were supposed to believe, what they were supposed to believe *in*. Years ago it had reduced her to tears. It had belittled her until she thought she was no better than the maid she was forced to work as. But now that she saw Montag for what he was, she did not feel fear nor weakness. She felt strong.

A dozen more questions whirled in her mind, but she bit them back. He would never answer her. "Enjoy your stay here with King Richard, Uncle. At least they gave you a room with a view." She glanced around, taking in the unfinished walls and empty hearth, masonry incomplete. "Looks like you're going to have a long winter."

Without another word she stepped out of the room, pulling the great door open to the awaiting guards. Montag still sat at the table, a furious look on his face, as the guards shut and locked the door between them once again. Alec took back the key and followed Eleanor down the stairs.

At the foot of the tower, she paused.

"Did he answer your questions?" Alec asked.

"No," she said. "But he made them not matter." She drew a deep breath, feeling her tender ribs stretch, grateful that they had nearly healed since the week before. She squeezed Alec's arm briefly. "I'll see you tomorrow."

He watched after her as she took long strides down the corridor toward the chapel, her skirts and cloak billowing behind her.

Chapter Thirty-Three

Eleanor's knees ached from the cold stone of the chapel floor. She was only four hours into the twelve hours of prayer she needed to complete before the knighting ceremony the next day. She shifted her weight ever so slightly. It wasn't pain so much that bothered her. That momentary discomfort was nothing compared to what she'd been through in the past, even in the past week alone. It was being alone with her thoughts . . . with God . . . that was starting to get to her. She looked up at the flickering candle next to the crucifix. She caught the movement of Wilfred as he crossed himself, still mouthing a prayer, his hands folded earnestly as he knelt at the opposite end of the altar. He was having no trouble with this part of the cleansing ceremony.

God.

What did He think of her now?

First there was the sin question. It burned in her mind. "Thou shalt not commit adultery." She had not slept with a married man. But she had slept with other men while she was married. Did God care about the circumstances? King Richard said she was forgiven, but Eleanor doubted even the king had the power to say what God forgave. Worse was that she knew she should apologize for her sins. But she wasn't sorry. She wasn't sorry for loving Edmond. She wasn't sorry she dressed like a man and learned to fight. She wasn't sorry she fought for her king and her life. She wasn't sorry for whatever role she had played in Lezay's death. And she wasn't sorry for Alec either, whatever that even was. So how could she seek atonement if she didn't want it?

Her thoughts wandered to what Wilfred could be over there so reverently asking for forgiveness from. For hurting Sir Jean? For not obeying his lord? What?

Eleanor gritted her teeth, her fingers going white as she pressed them together.

What had Montag prayed for when he underwent his ordination? Ha, the man was the most unchristian knight she had ever known. He didn't even try to pretend anymore. Raoul said he once had gone to services, but that had stopped before Eleanor had come to live with them. Maybe she should have questioned him about that. Maybe that would have gotten him thinking in his tower room. What was he doing up there now? Probably sleeping.

Pray, pray, pray. She tried to refocus her thoughts.

Would God protect her in this venture? She supposed it depended on if He agreed with what she had become.

She'd almost died in the melee. But that was her own mistake. She should have seen Sir Jean coming. Should have moved faster. She had survived. Was that God's hand?

How long had it been since they entered the chapel? It was too dark to tell. The altar candles burned bright, maybe a few fingers shorter than they had been. Oh, it would be a long night if they had to burn to the end. How long had they been in Normandy? A month? Two? Almost two now, she decided.

Suddenly her blood went cold, colder than the stone floor.

In all that time, she had not bled . . . at least not as a woman. How long had it been? Certainly not since the melee or even since they were in France. Not at the tournament, or what had happened with Alec certainly would not have happened. Not in the weeks she was pining for Edmond. She kept thinking back, the panic rising. She must be forgetting something. She must! She had had a cycle the week before Lord Chester's tournament, as she'd gotten a bit of blood on her gown and been relieved for the new one. None since then? That would mean it had been months . . .

Nausea and dizziness overcame her, and she pressed her forehead into the cool stone floor. She absolutely could not be with child. And months along?

She remembered that little bump of fat that had appeared on her slender frame. Perhaps it was not fat after all.

A wave of fear washed over her as she thought about what it would mean. She was a fool to be undergoing a knighting ceremony in this state. She would not be able to hide it much longer, and then her fragile reputation would be ruined. She had promised King Richard chastity! Ha! An unwed, pregnant, knight? She sat up, forcing herself to breathe deeply and slowly, willing the nausea away. She would rather face Lezay and Montag on the field of battle again than what was growing in her womb. *Lord, let me survive this*, she thought.

But she would not face Lezay on the field of battle. He was dead. She blinked into the flame of the candle again.

A shudder ran through her. She pondered why she did not feel more liberated, now that the man who had hurt her the most was dead. He may be gone, but he had not taken her memories with him. The old scar on her abdomen twinged with sharp pain, as if to remind her.

She shifted on the hard stone. She would have to survive again.

Cleanse your body and soul, King Richard had said. Her body was as clean as it had been in years. Her soul . . . how could God cleanse such a soul? She was nothing she was supposed to be. Women were supposed to be chaste, silent, obedient.

Were there rules about pacing during the cleansing? She crossed herself and stood. Wilfred opened his eyes to look at her, his expression quizzical, but he was not allowed to speak to her. Eleanor tried to hide the panic on her face, knowing that she was failing and distracting her friend. She forced herself back to her knees, her hands clasped with new vigor.

She hoped God was listening because she needed help. There was no way out of this now. The wheels were set in motion, with no way to get off the running cart unscathed. Eleanor let a tear run down her cheek as she pleaded with God, explaining everything. When the words ran out, she was left with only calm. Peace.

Hours flew by as Eleanor prayed, the calm that overcame her lending to a mediative state. She was surprised when the door creaked open and the friar waddled in. She squinted at the pink rays of dawn that cut through the windows.

"Well done!" the friar said joyfully. "Now we ready you for the ceremony."

Eleanor and Wilfred rose on stiff legs.

As they fell behind the friar, exiting the chapel, Wilfred touched her elbow lightly. "Is everything all right?"

Eleanor nodded. "It is for now." She gave him a brave smile. "A few more hours, and we'll be knights."

Wilfred gave a half-smile back. "I hope the rest of this is easier than that was." He let out a long breath.

Eleanor again wondered what men had to talk to God about.

Side by side they sat through Mass, reverently taking communion with the assembly of their peers behind them. By mid-day, the "cleansing" portions of the ordeal were over, and the ordination ceremony was about to begin.

The tapestried throne room was magnificent in all its finery. It smelled fresh, the windows wide open to let in the late summer air and sunshine. Still the room was a little warm from all the people crammed inside, their excitement palpable.

The two of them knelt side by side before the altar and the bishop who crossed them. On cue, they rose to place their swords at the very base of the altar where the bishop blessed them with an extensive prayer. The swords were gently handed back to Eleanor and Wilfred, who then brandished them through the air three times, the blades whistling. They then knelt again, arms raised as they offered their swords to their liege, King Richard himself.

Richard took Wilfred's sword from him first. He laid the flat of the blade against his neck as Wilfred unflinchingly swore allegiance to God, to England, and to King Richard. Richard returned the sword to its sheath and slapped Wilfred with the flat of his hand: the last blow Wilfred would receive without retaliation. Then he handed the sword to Wilfred and offered his hand, raising him to his feet. The crowd clapped its approval as Wilfred turned to face them, his new peers, raising a hand in humble salute. His face remained serious, the weight of his new responsibilities settling on his shoulders.

"I give you Sir Wilfred . . . the Fyr Hors!" the king boomed. Wilfred's eyes went wide at the added determiner. *Fire Horse*.

The crowd loved it. "Fyr Hors! Fyr Hors!" they chanted and cheered.

Eleanor's arms trembled with the weight of her sword, still held aloft. A test it was, to be sure she could handle the weight of the responsibility she would now take on. Her heart pounded. Richard's attention turned to her, and he took her sword, repeating the ceremonial swearing. She agreed to serve God, England, and King. The cold blade was removed from her neck. She waited for the blow, staring ahead at the altar. None came.

She glanced up at the king's hesitation. His eyes looked conflicted, so she turned her right cheek ever so slightly toward him. The blow came swift and hard. He did not hold back, just as he had not with Wilfred. Eleanor did not flinch but stretched her jaw into a smile as the king offered her a hand to her feet. The crowd again roared their approval. She had earned their favor as well. She was a knightess.

Lady Eleanor de Levan d'Aquitaine was the name Richard called her. He had validated her birthright to the family lands of her father. For once, a surge of pure happiness rolled through Eleanor. She did not try to hide the beaming emotion. She had done it. She had come out of the shadows to become her true self. The world was wide open once again.

Chapter Thirty-Four

Temperance. One of the great virtues of a knight and a part of the code of chivalry. It was also absent that evening as King Richard ordered a third barrel of wine opened. Delicious, sweet, Bordeaux-made wine filled the cups of noble and peasant alike from a barrel five feet long and three feet wide. Needless to say, there was not a body in the crowded hall of Gaillard that wasn't some form of drunk.

Eleanor had resisted at first, but after cup after cup had been pressed into her hands by her new peers, eager to share in her celebration, she had relented to more than she was accustomed to. Wilfred was in much the same situation, and the knights in the hall were as fascinated by him as they were her. At first, they were impressed that as a commoner he had learned how to fight, as word of his performance in the melee had gotten around like fire to dozens of curious ears. He was interrogated on how he had learned to fight, and particularly his horsemanship. Eleanor heard more than one man considering making an offer on his horse. Wilfred took it all in stride, as if he had been one of them his whole life, not just common "Wilfred".

Eleanor watched him from across the room, fascinated by his confident transformation. The candles and torches around the room sparkled a little brighter than usual. She took one last sip of her wine and set the cup down. She needed to stop.

"M'lady, are you actually getting into your cups tonight?" Alec teased, appearing at her elbow. He was well into his own but controlled as ever.

She smiled at him and shook her head. The world might be rosy, but she felt pretty well in control of her mind and body. "I'm much like you, Alec. I don't show it like most."

"Ohhh," he chuckled. "Would you care to have a little competition to prove it?"

She rolled her eyes at him. "I didn't say I could handle *as much* as you."

A random squire danced by and forced another cup of wine into Eleanor's hand, bowing with words of congratulations, then dancing off again.

"I feel like I'm the lady of the tournament again," Eleanor said under her breath. She took a longing look at the wine then decidedly took a swallow. "Oh, fresh barrel. Very good." Hastily she held out the cup for Alec. "Here, I can't possibly drink any more." A pleasant shiver ran through her as his calloused fingers grazed hers. She definitely needed to stop drinking.

Their attention shifted to Wilfred, as he approached from across the room. Something had clouded his celebratory mood.

"What's wrong?" Eleanor asked.

"I'm going to ride over to Grande Andelys, across the river."

"Wilfred, it's the dead of night, after your ordination."

"I just heard . . ." he hesitated. "Someone I used to know is there. She—*they* may be gone by morning. I need to see—"

"She, huh?" Alec smirked.

"Alec, you wouldn't understand."

"It's a long ride in the dark. Can't you go at dawn?" Eleanor asked.

Wilfred shook his head, looking even more distracted and agitated. "I just need to go. They may not even be there still. I'll be back in the morning regardless." Without another word, he turned and left the hall, leaving Alec and Eleanor staring after him in surprise.

"I've never seen him like that," Alec mused. He took another drink of wine and handed the cup back to Eleanor. She absently took it from him and drank another swallow. Alec brushed her arm with his fingertips, studying her. "Eleanor," he leaned toward her and whispered in her ear. "May I have you this night?"

She hesitated with the cup of wine halfway to her lips. Her eyes locked into his hungry gaze. He was handsome. And strong. And he'd saved her. She took another long sip of her wine.

Another pair of knights approached them, asking more details about the melee in Paris. Alec and Eleanor answered them enthusiastically, reliving the excitement. All the while they stole glances at each other. When the duo finally moved on, Eleanor made her decision.

Silently she took him by the hand. She guided him out of the great room and down the winding stair out of the keep, staggering against him on the bottom step in her mild state of intoxication, cursing at herself. His solid arm wrapped around her, supporting her. Her eyes sparkled in the torchlight, and she kissed him among the other couples milling around the outer walls. The warm summer air felt like an embrace to them all. Her lips burned as she pressed into him, pulling his face to her own like a woman deprived. Then the torchlight faded to moonlight as they walked further into town and into their little room at the inn.

Safely bolted in their room, they stripped down as quickly as Eleanor's tender ribs would allow. Naked in the candlelight, Alec took a step back to study her more carefully than he ever had. The curves of her breasts were full, and just beneath them was the splotched bruise that now faded more each day. The thin line of Lezay's scar swirled across her abdomen, which bulged slightly. Across the top of her strong thigh was the bandage he knew hid a fresher, redder line that seemed to be healing nicely. His eyes went back to the bulge of her stomach.

She reached her fingers to him, and pulled him to her, tracing the lines of his muscles with her fingertips as her lips begged for his own. Alec's body pressed into her, hard with passion. He felt her need but willed himself to be gentle. He was achingly tender with her, teasing her mind and body away from all conscious thought.

As he lay locked with her, he grew bold. "Is it mine?" he asked, pausing their motion to look her in the eye.

Eleanor cupped his face in her hands and pulled him harder into her kiss. He thought he felt her nod. With joy and renewed passion, he kissed her as he set a higher tempo, still as gentle as a caress, making her gasp, until they both lay exhausted, locked together. As their heat cooled, Alec rolled off of her, spooning her with his body, his hand on her womb. She felt his hot tears on her shoulder, though he didn't make a sound. Suddenly sober, she felt one of her own leak from her eye.

Maybe it was true. Maybe the child was Alec's. But it could also be Edmond's.

She didn't know which to wish for.

Chapter Thirty-Five

There was a reason Eleanor never let herself overindulge on the wine. Waves of nausea washed over her as she sat up in bed. *Temperance, you idiot*, she thought to herself. The wine was never worth it in the end. She stood and cracked the window, allowing the cool night breeze to ease her. Maybe Alec had drunk more than his share tonight too, as he was still snoring. She'd shared a room or a tent with him at enough tourneys to know how he normally slept lightly.

God, she'd made a fool of herself tonight. What was she thinking, leaving with Alec? She couldn't *do* that anymore. She sighed. The nausea returned, and she heaved into a basin, then wiped her sweaty brow with the back of her shaking hand. She needed to get some air. Quickly she dressed, belting her father's dagger to her side in habit. She glanced over at Alec, who lay sprawled across the bed they'd shared.

What was I thinking? she asked herself again.

The cool evening embraced her as she walked across the road to the inn's livery stable. Noir nickered to her, his eyes half closed. She gently stroked his forehead, then again had to swallow down the bile as her stomach threatened to retch again. She closed her eyes and inhaled and exhaled slowly. Perhaps this was more than just being drunk. Perhaps this was the child. Perhaps it didn't like the wine.

She was still trying to admit to herself she was pregnant. She'd done the math a dozen times and kept pinning her last cycle to the weeks before the Tournament at Chester. That was months ago, at the beginning of the summer. That was when she and Edmond first had . . .

Oh, Edmond.

Finally, she could stand it no longer and slid down the wall of the horse's stall and let the tears flow. Noir watched her with the same quiet observance but did not interfere. For the second time that night, she let herself go, and this time it was completely different. All of the fear, adrenaline, joy, stress, and pain of the last few weeks overwhelmed her. She cried like that for hours, her sides throbbing, her eyes red. Weakly she curled up against the pile of hay outside Noir's stall and tried to sleep. The draft through the cracks of the stable brushed her hair across her face, cooling her burning eyes. But sleep did not come. Even when the sky began to lighten, she did not move. She let a few more tears run down her face and leaned her head back against the stall.

"Eleanor!" Alec said in surprise from the barn door.

She quickly wiped her eyes and struggled to her feet.

"Are you alright? Did the horse hurt you?"

"No, no," she said hoarsely, turning her back to him to pet Noir and keep him from seeing the tears that stained her cheeks.

"Ella," he whispered. He came to her and put an arm around her. "Eleanor, look at me." He turned her face to his with a finger. Their eyes connected and Alec held her gaze with his ever-present intensity.

Eleanor's chin trembled, and she turned her head away from him. He pulled her into his chest. "Eleanor . . ."

She spoke into his shoulder yet her voice was somehow steady. "I have gained everything, and now I will lose it all." She pulled back to look at him. "And I've done it to myself with my . . .*carelessness*." She pulled away from him. Under her breath she muttered, "And last night was a mistake."

She felt Alec stiffen at that, but he did not turn away from her. "What do you fear the loss of most?"

"Honor," Eleanor said without hesitation. "I've been dragged through the dirt my whole life, and now I finally have something to be proud of, something to contribute going forward. But soon they will find I'm no better than any other common maid." She scoffed.

"Marriage is honorable. Bearing children within a marriage is honorable," Alec pointed out.

"Who would want a woman that has done what I have done?"

"Me."

She stilled.

He continued, "If your greatest fear is what you will lose if you bear my bastard, then let me make the child my legitimate son. You aren't far enough along that people could prove otherwise."

"Alec, you wish to marry me?" she stalled. There was no legal reason she couldn't marry him now. Lezay was dead. But he was still Alec. She'd been conflicted about him so much of the time she'd known him. Things had changed, but she knew their relationship wasn't the steady, tender partnership she'd been forging with Edmond. He'd said he didn't love her. She doubted that had changed, though she knew he did care for her in his own way. The passion between them burned bright, there was no doubt about that, but Eleanor wondered if that was enough for a marriage to survive. She couldn't run away a second time. Emotionally, physically, logistically it was not an option.

Alec pulled her chin to face him, looking her in the eye. "There is no one else I have to ask permission from, do I? Would you like me to ask your uncle? I'm afraid he won't agree if that's the case."

"No, sir." She hesitated. As a widow and a titled knight, she had the right to choose her own husband now. Her heart pounded. She hadn't considered remarrying. She had barely accepted that she was now free. Of all the men in the world, Alec? She looked into his dark eyes, which searched her own with curious hope. He had been at her side for years now, even when there was nothing in it for him. There was no other option, and if this had to be the one, it wasn't a bad one. She took a deep breath, hoping to steady her heart, then said firmly, "I accept your offer. How soon?"

He smiled. "How about tomorrow?"

"Fine," she said flatly, still somewhat in shock. She searched his eyes, then whispered sincerely, "Thank you."

Alec bent down and kissed her. When he pulled away, he was smiling, and she allowed herself to smile as well.

Chapter Thirty-Six

"You're *what*?" Wilfred exclaimed as they trotted down the road that afternoon, getting the horses out for the first real exercise they'd had since the melee. Alec had wisely made sure Wilfred's hands were full of the fiery Harlequin before he brought up the subject of his and Eleanor's coming marriage. Eleanor's hands were full with Noir, who kept tossing his head and pulling on her still-healing body. She kept quiet and let the men have it out.

"Really Wilfred, you act like I'm some barbarian," Alec replied calmly, Ches keeping a steady pace as Harlequin pranced and bucked alongside him. "Marriage is a perfectly natural, honorable—"

"You don't love her!" Wilfred still raged.

Alec glanced back at Eleanor at that. She pretended she hadn't heard. "Since when is that a prerequisite to marriage?"

"It should be," Wilfred said stubbornly. "Eleanor, did you agree to this?"

"Yes," she said simply.

"You're barely widowed," Wilfred maliciously pointed out. "Oh, wait, that never mattered before either, did it?"

Wilfred bit his tongue and looked away as Eleanor and Alec shot cold glares his direction. He sighed, and his tone softened. "I'm sorry. Eleanor, you're my best friend. We've spoken before about my feelings about you and Alec. You can do whatever you want, but again, this seems so *soon!* Why don't you just wait a few weeks, let things settle? Let your emotions settle? Then if you still want to marry, I'll even be a witness at your ceremony. Wouldn't that appear to *everyone* to be more natural?"

Eleanor stared down at Noir's neck.

"Don't, Eleanor," Alec cautioned, reading her face.

"He'll know soon enough anyway. Wilfred, I don't have months to wait. I'm with child."

Wilfred opened and closed his mouth like a fish, then settled into a silent stare down the road. "You don't love her," he said quietly.

Now it was Alec's turn to raise his voice. "Only a lazy fool would shirk from his responsibilities and leave a lady to fend for herself in this situation."

Eleanor watched the emotions fly across Wilfred's face, settling on some kind of anguish she'd never seen in him. "Wilfred, did you find who you were looking for last night?"

"No." The question seemed to sink his mood even darker. "Argh!" Wilfred shouted and kicked Harlequin up to a gallop. The horse happily obliged and took off down the road ahead of them, leaving Alec and Eleanor fighting with their own mounts for control.

Once they settled back to a steady trot, Alec said, "I wish I could say he's wrong, but I want to be fully honest—"

Eleanor cut him off, "It's fine. What we have is . . . different. I know that. I'm alright with it if you are." She looked away as the intensity of Alec's gaze became overwhelming.

"Stop a second." They reined up. "Eleanor, I am not an eloquent poet. I can not sing you ballads of my love for you. You're gorgeous. But there have been many women before you . . . many just as gorgeous—"

"Alec, I don't need to hear this—" Eleanor protested.

"Please. Hear me out. There have been others. But from the moment I met you I knew you were different. You have a fire in you. Being with you lights a fire in me. You don't know how I've wanted to make you my own. I thought that it was just a physical desire, like all the others. I thought I would be satiated by now and set you free. But now that I've had the physical . . ."

Eleanor blushed.

"You're like rare wine, Eleanor. I want you for myself. I don't think that's quite love. Maybe just jealously, greed, possession—"

"Lust?" she offered.

"Lust for sure," Alec accepted. "But I do want this. I do want you to be my wife. Forever. Maybe this can become more, can become love." He bit his tongue, shifting slightly in the saddle as his eyes followed the way her hips moved with the horse's stride. Eleanor noticed, and he had to look away. She smiled to herself, fully cognizant that Alec's gaze was and had always been a world different from Edmond's.

She could live with that, given the circumstances. She had to.

Eleanor stepped Noir up next to him and took his hand. "It will be enough." Then she turned and headed back toward the castle.

Chapter Thirty-Seven

E leanor stood staring at the empty stalls in the livery, stalls that should have been occupied by the horses of her bridegroom and her best friend. A rooster crowed, and she flinched. With a last pat to Noir's nose, she spun on her heel and took the stairs of the inn two at a time back to their empty room, where she bolted the door behind her. Holding her arms around herself, she paced before the cold hearth.

"You don't have to do this, Eleanor," she said to herself. "You're a knight now. You don't have to marry. Just accept the shame and the consequences with it. They will go away before a husband will." She chewed her knuckle, panic rising. She could still run. Or could she? She was the famous Knightess now. Every time she went out people called her by name. And the glares and stares from scorned men were just as plentiful. No, her days of running were over.

A knock at the door made her jump. Sword in hand, she cautiously answered it. "Marie!" she exclaimed and welcomed her former coworker into the room. "How are you here? I thought you were married!" she took a step back and took in Marie's smiling face. And large stomach. "And you're . . ."

Marie smiled, but it didn't quite reach her eyes. "Yes, married. We're expecting already. Such a blessing. My husband Jorge and I were in the area, and I insisted we stop for a while. I heard you were knighted. I wish we could have attended the ceremony. But, you know, we're simple folk. Then I heard you were staying here, and I couldn't miss the opportunity to see you." She glanced around the room. "Is Wilfred with you? Sir Alec?"

"They're out," Eleanor explained. She bit her lip. "I'm getting married today."

Marie looked like she forced a smile. "Oh, lovely! Ah, so which one did you finally fall for?"

"Alec . . . who else?" Eleanor thought she saw relief flit across Marie's face, then a genuine smile took over the maid's countenances.

"Finally! Well, when? Shouldn't you be getting ready?"

"A few hours. Alec told me he arranged it in the village chapel at high noon. We opted to keep it quiet." Eleanor hesitated. "Marie, I know you have to get back to your husband, but would you like to attend? I could use a friend. You may bring him if you'd like."

"Of course!" Marie said quickly. "And Jorge is working. He won't miss me."

The two ladies clasped hands. "It is so good to see you, Marie," Eleanor said genuinely. They hadn't been close back at Neroche, but Eleanor realized how much she needed to see a familiar female face, today of all days.

Marie smiled, "Let's make you the Lady of the Tournament once again."

With Marie's help Eleanor twisted her hair into an elegant weave of braids at the base of her neck. Along the crown of her head Marie wove delicate white flowers. She would wear the white gown from the knighting ceremony. As she pulled it over her head she glanced at the slight bulge of her stomach and inhaled sharply. Her hand lingered there a mere moment. When Marie wasn't looking, she loosened the laces on the sides of gown so it hung loose enough to cover it. Eleanor gave the maid a sideways glance. She'd seen Marie two months ago. Despite the fact that Marie had never been as lean as Eleanor, there was no way Marie was only a few months along in her own pregnancy, especially not with a brand-new husband.

"Marie, have you heard Wilfred was knighted as well?" Eleanor ventured.

Marie answered quietly, "I did hear that. Who would have thought?"

"He so deserved it. We fought a melee outside of Paris. He was brilliant. I hope he gets a chance to compete in the lists now."

"There. All finished." Marie changed the subject, tucking a final flower into Eleanor's hair.

With a shaky breath, Eleanor stood and slowly twirled in the middle of the room, skirts flowing around her. Marie wiped a tear from the corner of her eye and smiled. "You're lovely, Ella."

A knock came from the door, and Eleanor opened it a crack.

"Raoul!" Eleanor exclaimed. She resisted the urge to embrace her cousin and glanced toward her sword, which rested only a few feet away.

Raoul caught the glance and held up his hands in peace. "I come with congratulations, cousin. Nothing more." His face was thinner than usual, lined and travel-weary.

Eleanor allowed him into the room. "Congratulations? How did you hear?" Her face paled. "Are you going to free your father?"

Marie looked at them both with curiosity.

Raoul sighed. "Yes. I have the ransom. It is my duty to deliver it." He saw her tense. "But I only just arrived. No one knows I am here. Word of your wedding is all over the town, so I had to come see you."

"He almost killed me, Raoul. How can you set him free?"

"I have to."

"Have to? Or are you too cowardly not to?" Her fists clenched at her sides.

"You know it's more complicated than that, Eleanor. But this is not the time to argue. I promise you, Montag will not be free before tomorrow. Go enjoy your wedding. Celebrate. I will warn you when the ransom has been delivered."

"Raoul," Eleanor protested. "You know I will not sleep now until there are many miles between me and Montag. There will be no peace. Not so long as he keeps you on your leash, which apparently extends from his prison on the top of the Gaillard keep all the way to Alsace! Cousin," she pleaded, "One day I beg you to choose your own side. Or I will surely be facing you across a field of battle."

Raoul was quiet. Finally, he said, "I wish you the best, cousin," and backed out of the room, pulling the door shut behind him.

Eleanor stared at the closed door for a moment, shaken. With a sudden decisive movement, she belted her father's dagger over her gown. Its ratty leather belt, cleaned but bloodstained, clashed with the elegant ensemble horribly, but even Marie didn't protest. "Will you stand as my witness?" Eleanor asked.

Marie brightened at that. "I would be honored." Instead of handing Marie a bouquet, she handed her the sword. The maid's eyes went wide. "Just in case," Eleanor whispered.

Alec came to the chapel dressed in his finest tunic, his coat of arms embroidered across his chest. Eleanor caught her breath. She'd known when she first met him that he was attractive, but clean and dressed in full regalia, without the sweat and dust of tournaments or travel or battle, he was impressive to say the least. He too was armed to the teeth. He smiled when he saw her. Her heart pounded. He offered her his arm and whispered in her ear, "You are stunning." Eleanor smiled back, but her distraction was evident in her eyes.

"I take it you've heard," Alec stated.

She nodded and patted the dagger on her belt.

"We will leave tonight," Alec whispered in her ear, giving her arm a reassuring squeeze. "We'll talk later, after I've made you my wife."

Eleanor felt a little dizzy as Alec opened the chapel door with one arm, allowing her to slip inside, followed by Marie to whom he gave a courteous nod of recognition. A rotund friar stood at the altar, smiling.

The priest that had married her to Lezay had smiled too.

Behind her the chapel door opened again, and Eleanor pulled away from Alec. Her breath picked up; her hand quivered over her dagger. Everyone glanced toward the door, but it was only Wilfred, with his hands up, placating the alarm he had caused.

"I'm sorry I'm late," Wilfred said in a rush. "But I wanted to offer my blessing . . ." For a moment he was distracted, staring at Marie. He stopped to clear his throat, tearing his eyes away from her. "And my apologies to you,

Sir Alec, for my words yesterday. I sincerely wish you both a long happy life together."

Alec's hand twitched on her arm, and Eleanor spun to face him. She looked into his eyes, delving as deep as she could go. He met her gaze and nodded. She exhaled.

"Okay?" he questioned.

She nodded and looked ahead again. Being in this chapel brought back such a mix of memories. The nerves were raging in full force, more so even than before a tournament. But then again, there were many tournaments. There was only one time when you chose the person to bind yourself to forever . . . or maybe two.

Alec shook Wilfred's hand and said something to him that Eleanor didn't hear, then took her arm to begin the procession down the short chapel aisle. They missed the glance between Wilfred and Marie as they filed behind them and took their places as witnesses.

The friar beamed as they proceeded with the ceremony. They'd warned him to keep it brief, so after a prayer and a scripture reading in Latin, he asked, "Do you, Sir Alec Earnblaec of Neroche, son of Sir Alfred of Homme, son of Lord Alfrec the Brave, take Lady Eleanor nee Levan d'Aquitaine to be your lawfully wedded wife, to protect, honor and cherish, forsaking all others so long as you both live?"

Alec looked into her eyes and without hesitation said, "I do."

"My Lady Eleanor nee Levan d'Aquitaine, daughter of Sir Enric de Levan, do you take Sir Alec Earnblaec of Neroche to be your lawfully wedded husband, to obey, honor, and cherish, forsaking all others so long as you both live?" They looked at her expectantly.

Eleanor hesitated. Her first wedding had glossed over her vows. There could be no denying the validity this time. There could be no escape. Her hands shook a little bit. Obey? She'd been disobeying Alec since she'd met him. She opened her mouth to speak.

Wilfred cleared his throat. "Friar, with all due respect, given the extraordinary circumstances that Lady Eleanor is a knight as well as Sir Alec, shouldn't her vows read the same as his?"

The friar looked baffled. "Who is running this service here? Would you like to just have it amongst yourselves and leave me out of it?" He grumbled to himself, then turned to Eleanor again, "Do you promise to *protect*, honor, and cherish this man forsaking all others?"

"I do," she said quickly.

"Wonderful," the friar said with relief. "Now, if you sir, can actually put that ring on her finger, then you are man and wife and the rest is up to you."

Alec slid the ring gently onto Eleanor's left ring finger, settling it with a gentle kiss to her hand. Then he pulled her fully into him and kissed her full on the mouth. Wilfred and Marie chuckled. The friar rolled his eyes and stalked out of the chapel, muttering about sacred ceremonies being wasted on the young.

Alec kept his arm around her waist, pulling her tight to him as they turned to face their witnesses. "*Sir* Wilfred . . . I am glad you could make it. But was that little interjection necessary? It would have been nice to finally have this wild one's obedience." The amusement lightened his voice as he smirked.

Wilfred smiled, albeit weakly, at Eleanor. "Wouldn't miss it."

"I am glad you came." Eleanor squeezed his elbow.

Alec cleared his throat, and Eleanor stepped back. She noted the muscle in his jaw twitched. "Have you heard Raoul is in town?" he asked Wilfred.

Wilfred stiffened. "No. Is he going to ransom Montag?"

"Yes," Eleanor answered. Alec raised his eyebrows at her. Apparently, she knew more than he did. "I saw him," she explained. "He came to the inn. He said he'd wait until the morning, but he is here to ransom Montag."

Wilfred let out a low whistle. "So I guess we aren't staying then."

"We?" Alec questioned. "You're a knight now. You aren't my little squire boy anymore. You're on your own."

"We. I go where she goes. I'd rather not have to complicate things by swearing fealty to her, but until I have a manor of my own to maintain, Lady Eleanor, I am at your service. If you'll have me."

"You are free to come and go as you please, Wilfred, but I would be grateful to have you around." She gave Alec's arm a squeeze to settle him. "I am under order to retake the Levan properties in Aquitaine." She sighed. "I always hoped to go back, but so soon? Winter is coming and there is no manor, no village, no supplies! And what of your new estate?"

"We will go to Aquitaine. What choice do we have?" Alec pointed out. "We cannot wait here in Petite Andelys and let your uncle get a head start. That would make it impossible to retake the property without an army. As far as my estates go, Lord Cenric said I can return in spring."

"You have word from him so soon?" Eleanor's eyebrows shot up.

"He is in Normandy, headed to a tournament in Poitiers. It was he I met with this morning."

"So you will go with me to Aquitaine?"

"Of course, my darling wife." Alec smirked and kissed her on the cheek. "But we have a bigger problem than Montag. I've received word from numerous sources that Lord Otto wants proof of your valor. He wants us all to compete in the tournament. You too, Wilfred."

"When is it?" Wilfred asked.

"Two weeks.

"How is that worse than Montag?" Eleanor asked.

"You can't compete," Alec looked at her pointedly.

Eleanor shot him a warning look, understanding his hesitations and not wishing to discuss them in front of Marie. "My ribs are healing nicely. By then I should be all right."

Marie suddenly held the sword out to Eleanor. She nodded with confidence. "Go, m'lady."

Eleanor nodded and took the weapon from the maid's hand. "Thank you, Marie. For everything." She embraced her gently.

The maid smiled. "Good luck, m'lady."

With his arm around her waist, Alec pulled Eleanor toward him again. "Well, two hours should do it. Then we'll pack up." He gave Wilfred a warning look that emphasized they were not to be disturbed.

Wilfred rolled his eyes. "Just don't touch my things. I'll pack myself when your time is up." He waved them off and turned to Marie. Eleanor had just a fleeting glimpse of Wilfred's look of concern for her friend. She could swear she saw him touch Marie's stomach before the chapel door closed behind them, and Alec steered her down the street back to the inn.

Eleanor's heart pounded furiously as they approached the inn. Alec's tightening grip on her arm made it worse. She was fourteen again, being "guided" through the castle by a man triple her age and twice her size. She stopped in the road, planting her feet. They were in front of a tavern. One fellow knight came out and shoved a mug of ale in

Alec's hand, slapping him on the back. "Good luck taming that one!" he jested. Eleanor blushed and pulled away from Alec.

Alec's eyes locked with Eleanor's, and he slowly handed the untouched ale back to the man. "I think I better keep my wits about me today, but I thank you for the offer, sir."

The well-wisher chuckled and downed the brew himself, retreating into the tavern.

Alec offered Eleanor his arm. She waited a long moment, then lightly hooked her hand over it, avoiding Alec's gaze. He guided her more gently to the inn and up to their room. Inside, Alec released her and bolted the door, leaning back against it with his arms crossed.

They stared at each other, both a little breathless for different reasons.

"You're stunning." Alec let his eyes linger over her every curve.

He approached her, his fingers gently tracing her hip, then her cheek, as he kissed her lightly. His lips locked on hers, pleading, coaxing, but not quite gentle in their need. He backed her into the small table they'd dined at these past nights and picked up her hips to set her on it, his lips never leaving hers.

She trembled.

"Why are you afraid of me today?" he asked, brushing the hair from her face gently. "This is nothing we haven't done before."

Eleanor shook her head. "Weddings change everything."

"This time the wedding doesn't change *anything*." His hands worked up her legs, up her thighs, pulling her skirts higher and higher until she was exposed to him. Lightly he caressed the bulge of her abdomen. Eleanor trembled, conflicted between her desire and fear.

"Eleanor, I'm not him." His fingers now intertwined with her own. "Do not let him rule our bedroom." He released her hands to gently pull her face up into his intense gaze. Reluctantly her eyes met his and then settled.

"Eleanor, can you try something for me?"

She merely blinked back at him.

"When you ride a new horse, each one is a little different, no?"

She nodded.

"You take it slow, show them what the rules are, while at the same time challenging them to see just how good they can be. And each horse responds in turn. A destrier will never carry an old woman. There is too much fire for her to handle. Likewise, a palfrey will never carry a knight to battle. It would die of fright before its little legs ever reached the enemy. Once you know how that horse responds, its strengths and weaknesses, that is when you can build the relationship with it. You know how to get the most from each ride without asking too much. Without hurting it. You and I, we've never taken the time to learn what each other are. To build the deeper relationship that would allow horse and rider to charge toward an enemy in unison."

"You're a destrier," Eleanor said quietly.

Alec pushed a stray hair from her face, smiling to himself. "Maybe so, but what are you, my lady?"

Eleanor leaned her cheek into his hand and sighed. "Do you promise not to hurt me?"

"Eleanor, you know I would never hurt you."

"Then you may ride me and find out what I am."

He came over her with a wave of passion so intense it threatened to drown her. She clung to him, gasping, worried, and struggling, then breaking free that she could ride it with a confidence beyond her experience. Her heartbeat synced with his own, the two souls swirling in a whirlpool of physical touch and emotional battle. Alec pressed the limits of her tolerance, and she met his advances with a passion of her own, a welling from a depth no soul had tapped. The waters of their souls finally crested and broke, sending them both gasping into a pool of emotion so deep it took long moments for them to break the surface once again.

Locked together, sides heaving, still partially clothed, their sweat was the proof of their tempest.

Legs shaking, Alec slowly pulled out of her, his fingers caressing her as he gently lowered her skirts and pulled her from the table and into his arms.

He pushed the hair out of her eyes, searching her face, imploring. Tears leaked from her eyes. "Damn. I did hurt you, didn't I?" he panicked.

Eleanor shook her head. "Only a little," she admitted.

He pulled her into his shoulder, kissing the top of her head. "I'm sorry. I'm sorry." He hastily wiped a tear from his own cheek. Eleanor pulled back to look at him.

She touched the tear stain on his cheek but did not meet his eye. "That's not why I'm crying. I'm glad it was you," she whispered. "It . . . helps that it can be . . .different . . .with you." She shrugged. "You're right, that's all I thought about all morning. Being dragged to the altar. Lezay. We've done the rest before, but I think you're right. He would have kept dictating what happened in our bedroom. Like a ghost." She curled into his chest again, burying her head in his shoulder. "You've shown me there is no comparison now. There is only you."

His fingers brushed the dagger on her hip, and he realized he'd never disarmed her. Her sword stood mere feet away. This had been more of a lesson in trust for both of them than he'd expected.

Alec pulled her chin up and kissed her. He looked into her face, studying every line. His eyes told her something he was not voicing, and it made her exhausted heart pick up pace again. "I promise I'll do it like a proper husband, too. Just give me a few minutes, okay?" He grinned his half smile.

Eleanor cupped his face and kissed him again, smiling with sleepy eyes. "Good. I need a nap anyway. After the next few hours who knows when we will ever get to sleep again."

True to his word, Alec let Eleanor sleep for a while, then took her again, slowly and with more tenderness than he had ever shown before, for any woman. It left her feeling satiated and warm inside. The two became one flesh, if not in mind, at least in body. They did not think about how this had changed them. They did not think about the challenges that awaited them in mere days. For the rest of those two hours, they were only themselves.

Chapter Thirty-Eight

Poitiers, in County Poitou, was the northernmost city in Aquitaine. It bustled with people, carts, and horses. In the center of the city was the first true castle they had encountered in France, with massive stone walls, towers, and a stone bailey encircling the entirety of the complex.

"Bienvenu á Poitou," Eleanor said under her breath, taking it in. Every battlement was hung with tapestries and flags in preparation for the coming tournament. Just inside the large inner bailey was a camp of a thousand knights and their support staff, tents dotting the massive field in every direction. The trio recognized some of the crests, though most were likely Aquitanian knights. The delicious smells of roasting meat, stews, and fresh baked bread filled the air as vendors from the city hawked their wares around the encampment. Far across the lawns Eleanor could see the tournament arena, larger than any she had yet set foot in. There was a full grandstand for spectators.

"We should find Lord Otto first," Alec suggested. Richard had told them a little about Eleanor's liege lord, but he was hard to picture. Richard obviously thought highly of the man, his nephew. At the gates of the castle itself, they presented themselves and entered yet another walled enclosure. After showing a letter sealed with King Richard's crest, they were granted entry to the castle itself. Eleanor's eyes widened at the expanse of the massive hall they were led into. It was only partially constructed. During the tourney the building supplies were stored to the side and massive wooden tables had been crammed in for the feasts. But even in its partially completed state, the massive domed ceiling overhead stretched up fifty feet. The details of the stone columns were painstakingly matching. And massive windows, still awaiting their glasswork, stretched toward the ceiling to light the hall with a bright glow.

"Bienvenu, à la Salle des pas Perdus," a voice welcomed them. "This is my grandmother's project. Or at least one of them."

The three of them turned and bowed their heads to none other than Lord Otto himself. They were caught off guard for a moment by his age. He could not have been older than his early twenties, Eleanor's age. Despite this, he looked like a perfectly capable lord. He was tall with dirty blond hair. His features had a rugged handsomeness like his Uncle Richard's. "My Lord," Eleanor ventured, "It is our greatest pleasure to meet you. I am Lady Eleanor nee Levan d'Aquitaine, and this is my new husband, Sir Alec Earnblaec of Neroche, and my friend Sir Wilfred Fyr Hors."

"Ah, welcome," Otto answered. "I thought perhaps you might venture here. Reclaiming your ancestral lands here in Poitou! Quite the scandal you've caused all across France. And England from what I'm told. A woman, riding in tournaments. And being knighted. And you," he turned to Wilfred, "One tiny melee and my uncle raises you from a squire all the way to our ranks of knighthood. I would have loved to see whatever deeds you performed that day to impress him so. It took me years of training until he deemed me ready," Otto chuckled. "And then I have England's famed tournament champion himself, Sir Alec Earnblaec. I wonder, I have heard your – wife is she now? – bested you once before in a tourney. I do wonder if she could do it again? I am so looking forward to you all competing in my tourney tomorrow. But of course, you must all be exhausted. Are you fit to compete?"

Alec started to speak, but Eleanor quickly cut him off. "I am, my lord. How could I miss my first tournament as a true knight?" Alec's jaw muscle twitched, but he kept silent.

"I as well, my Lord," Wilfred also replied. His eagerness to prove himself was written all over his face.

Alec nodded his head to Otto, unable to conceal his frown. "I, too, look forward to it, Lord Otto," he said and straightened.

"Good, good," Otto said. "After tomorrow we will feast! And we will talk."

"My lord, we have a letter for you. From King Richard." Eleanor handed him the folded paper with its wax seal.

Otto narrowed his eyes as he read but otherwise remained expressionless. "I know this property you come to manage for me. We have much to talk about." He smiled a youthful grin that didn't quite reach his eyes. "Until then, enjoy Poitiers." Otto smiled to himself and carried on down the hall. Eerily, they could not hear his footsteps on the stone floor, such was the vastness of the room.

"Lord, I can't decide if I want food or sleep more," Eleanor whispered as Otto disappeared.

"Where are we going to stay?" Wilfred asked.

"Pray there's room somewhere in the city. Or that we can buy some tents of our own finally. I don't care if it's used and in someone else's colors at this point." Alec led the way back out of the castle. They shaded their eyes from the bright sun outside the main gates. As they adjusted, they noticed the small group of men loitering along the wall.

"We heard she had come to Poitiers. And there she is."

"My, but she is pretty, don't you think?"

"Lovely. But with a sword on one hip."

"And a dagger on her other." Eleanor glared at the knights congregating outside the castle gates. "Gentleman, we will have time enough to fight tomorrow, and you can have your fun analyzing my form all you want then."

"Didn't mean any harm, my lady. We just thought you were a myth."

"She exists." Alec's tone ended the conversation.

The knights smirked, but continued on their way, whispering amongst themselves.

Alec took Eleanor's hand and pulled her away from Wilfred. "We're going to find food. And we need to talk." Wilfred shrugged and headed toward the town.

When they were further from the crowds, Alec whispered, "Eleanor, what were you thinking, agreeing to fight tomorrow? You are in no condition to fight. You were injured only weeks ago." Alec dropped his voice. "And the baby. You can not take another blow."

Eleanor shook her head. "I know. I'll just have to be careful. I have to at least make a showing, or no one will take me seriously. If I am to lord over any part of this dutchy, I need to gain the respect of my peers, and this is the quickest way. I'm not far along," she insisted and glanced at the faint bump of her abdomen. "It should still be safe. Far safer than actual battle would be. And that is what I hope to avoid. Don't forget, Montag is free now and heading this way. I wouldn't be surprised if he competes tomorrow. If he can scrape the funds together after that ransom."

"What if *I* have to fight against you?" Alec hissed. "I have a reputation too, Eleanor."

"Are you afraid you'll lose?" she teased.

Alec glared. "I don't want to hurt you."

Eleanor's smile faded to seriousness. "Alec, we don't have a traditional relationship. You have to separate me from the category of wife sometimes, or neither of us will survive this. What if we were called to battle? I would have to go. So would you. And you can't neglect your other men-at-arms to rescue me if something goes wrong. Same tomorrow. You joust like we always joust. You fight like we've done a thousand times before and don't you dare hold back."

"What more do you need to prove, Eleanor?" he questioned. "You're free of Lezay. I've promised to protect you and traveled hundreds of miles to help you regain your land. I can handle our peers. You have a husband now. You don't *have* to be a knight anymore."

"Is that what you think?" Eleanor asked incredulously. "Alec, this was never a petty dream for me. I've worked so, so hard for this. Why would I give it up now?"

"To be a wife. A mother," Alec insisted, his tone lowered on the last word to a hiss.

"Is that why you married me?" Her heartbeat quickened as sweat broke out on her palms.

"Isn't that why any man marries? For a wife and a mother of his children? Not to have to worry about some half-crazed fiend with a sword!"

Eleanor's eyes went wide. "Now I understand. Your eagerness to marry me, what happened after the ceremony . . .what we did . . ." Eleanor felt a heat in her center as she recalled the intense pleasure that had left her thoughtless and clinging to Alec like a shipwrecked maid in a stormy sea. And he had clung to her as if he was the one drowning. Had it all been one of his acts? "This wasn't about helping me maintain my independence, my title. This is about you finally having me under you. Subservient. *Obedient,*" she emphasized. She shook her head. "I'm such a fool. For years now I've seen through your smooth talk. I thought you had changed, but you . . .you are good." She laughed coldly and shook her finger at him. "You. Are. Good."

"Eleanor—"

"No, Alec. Save it for after the tourney. I'm tired and I'm hungry and I have a fight to prepare for tomorrow." She walked away into the crowds, looking for a food vendor.

Chapter Thirty-Nine

Eleanor navigated the hall, her jaw tight against the pain. After a long day of tournament, her side felt as if the healing of the past few weeks had never happened. She held her wine away from her and winced as a fellow knight bumped into her, completely oblivious of the lady with a sword on her hip in his drunken pursuit of his "fair maiden." She shouldered between another throng of nobles, all drinking and chatting together. It was no wonder La Salle de Pas Perdues was so vast. It needed to be to accommodate this volume of a crowd. Most of the castle was full. Today's competition had been far more intense than even Eleanor had expected. Across a dozen different events, a thousand men had competed. And one woman.

Finally reaching the edge of the most celebratory attendees, Eleanor sank onto a bench at one of the long tables, watching the group as they danced and drank and laughed. Two young knights passed by, elbowing each other as they saw her. They feinted swordplay, with one clutching his ribs in a mocking show of pain. She glared at them, and they laughed as they wandered back into the crowd.

She drank another long swallow of wine.

"There you are." Alec sat across from her. "Why aren't you out celebrating?"

"I don't exactly have much to celebrate, do I?"

"It wasn't that bad."

Eleanor raised her eyebrows.

"You think I wouldn't be the first to tell you that you were an embarrassment?" Alec looked at her sternly. "You weren't. You aren't. If you were, they would be beating you up in some back stairwell right now." Alec shook his head. "As much as I didn't think you should compete today, what you've done has proved you deserve your title."

Eleanor chuckled. "Are you admitting I was right to compete after all?"

Alec smirked. "You let your own body answer that."

Eleanor shook her head and looked back into the crowd, resting her head on her propped fingers. She was exhausted. She was sore. The day's fights had tested her skills to the max, but she had emerged intact and though not victor, marked a place for herself solidly in the middle rankings of fighters.

Alec rapped his knuckles on the table. "Come. I have someone I want to introduce you to." Begrudgingly, she stood and followed him back into the mass of people, following Alec's broad back to break the crowd.

"Lady Eleanor, I would like to introduce you to my liege, Lord Cenric."

Before her stood a man almost as tall as Alec, though with greyer hair. His tunic was embroidered in silver thread and dyed a deep royal blue: high nobility. He smiled at Eleanor with curiosity. "My, my, Sir Alec. She's even prettier up close."

Eleanor nodded to him politely. "I've heard a great deal about you, Lord Cenric. It's a pleasure to meet you finally."

"My lady, the pleasure is all mine. I've been forced to watch you from a distance for over a year now, and I've seen you slip in and out of roles like a snake sheds its skin. First as a lady." His eyes twinkled as he glossed over the more obvious words for what she had acted as. "Now today I watched a knight. You fought well, my lady. Bravely. I can see the influence of your instructor in your style. And his instructor in turn." Cenric shot an amused look at Alec. It was he, after all, who had given Alec the majority of his own training.

"I dare say she would have continued on longer if her companions hadn't forced her to yield by dragging her out of the arena," a second man added.

Alec rolled his eyes. "Lord Hamilton, she could barely stand."

"She would have kept on waving that sword from her knees if she had to!" Hamilton laughed.

Cenric clapped Alec on the back. "You better teach your next student how to yield. Surviving to fight again is a rather useful skill to own." They all laughed. Even Eleanor couldn't help but smile. "I would have liked to see you joust, Lady Eleanor. But then again, from what I hear, I may not have become tournament champion if you had."

A man stepped in, clearing his throat. Eleanor's smile iced over. Raoul.

"Excuse me, gentlemen. Lady Eleanor, may I have a word?"

Eleanor flashed a smile at Hamilton and Cenric. "Pleasure to meet you both. Hopefully we meet again soon. Perhaps in England." She followed Raoul a few steps away.

"How dare you?" she hissed, planting her feet in the midst of the crowd. "After what you've done, I have no desire to talk to you. Why are you even here? Can I have no respite from you and Montag?"

"You need to get out of here."

"What?"

"He's been talking to Lord Otto. I don't know what he's plotting. You need to go."

Eleanor shook her head, incredulous. "I am far past the point of running now, Raoul. What do you know?"

"He knows nothing," Alec cut in, appearing at Eleanor's side. He glowered at Raoul. "I agree with your cousin, Sir Raoul. You shouldn't be here."

Raoul returned Alec's icy glare. "Don't say I didn't try to warn you." He spun on his heel, heading in Montag's direction toward the far end of the hall. Eleanor's heart pounded as she noticed that her uncle was in fact deep in conversation with Otto, and both of them were smiling amicably at some joke.

Eleanor smoothed her hands down the front of her skirt. "Where's Wilfred?"

Alec pointed a few tables away, to where Wilfred was chatting away with a captive audience of nearly ten other men, one foot resting on the bench casually as he gestured wildly with his hands. His horsemanship had put him second only to Alec and Cenric in the joust, and nearly every knight was envious of the fiery Harlequin. Wilfred was one of them now, and he was surprisingly at ease with it. How could he not be, with conversations dominated by horses and tournaments?

Eleanor smiled faintly. "It does seem he was born for this, doesn't it?" She glanced at Alec. His face was unreadable as he watched his half-brother. Eleanor slipped her cup of wine back out of Alec's hand and took another swallow. It was dulling the aches from the fight, but she was being careful not to repeat her mistake from the last celebration they'd attended.

Two teenage noble women walked by, giggling as they shot glances at Alec. He ignored them.

"I heard one of the ladies tried to slip you her token." Eleanor took another sip of wine to cover her amusement.

"I didn't accept it."

"No. She's rather bitter, you know. Seems you had her convinced once that you would pursue her betrothal."

"That was well before everything changed. Before I even left Castle Homme."

"Did you inform her of your marriage?" Eleanor's voice was teasing, though she tried to hide her smile.

Alec turned to her, clearly not sharing her amusement. "She would have made a lovely, obedient wife with a huge dowry and some of the best familial connections in the country."

Eleanor gaped at him. "I'm—I'm sorry. Alec—"

He turned away from her, working back into the crowd.

Eleanor watched him, suddenly acutely aware that she was alone in a crowded room. It had never bothered her before, but today it did. She gritted her teeth in frustration and again made her way through the crowd back toward an empty table. She resumed her seat, head in her hand, watching human to human interaction in all its forms.

Lord Otto navigated the crowd with ease, sharing a casual word with all his guests. He commanded attention, and he had a look about him that gave Eleanor the impression he was ambitious enough to seek that attention. He looked over at her, which he'd done several times that night.

Carefully Eleanor kept his gaze. Whatever it was, he should come talk to her already. He smiled lightly at her with amusement and excused himself from his conversation to approach her. He filled his mug with ale from her table, then sat beside her, joining in her quiet observations. They kept the silence for a while.

Finally, Otto began, "That was quite the show today. You have skill, m'lady."

"Thank you, my lord," she replied. She knew he wasn't there for small talk.

"Why didn't you finish him?"

She started slightly and looked at him. "Excuse me?"

"There was one moment in the sword event where the knight was refusing to yield, yet you had your sword at his neck. Why didn't you deal the blow?"

Eleanor sucked in her breath. It had been the mistake that weakened her. In her moment of hesitation, the knight had leaped to his feet and thrown a blow with his fist to her injured side. She had recovered enough in the moment to force his yield, but the mistake had crippled her for the next match. "If I had taken that swing, I would have killed him."

"Sometimes tournaments are deadly," Otto mused. "Would you back down in a real fight?"

"I haven't yet, my lord."

He nodded, sizing her up. "So I've heard." He turned back to the crowd, and she followed his gaze to Montag.

"Lord Montag came to me about two months ago. He told me about your tournament. He described you as ruthless. Even foolhardy. He warned that you may possibly return to claim your lands. And here you are. Without my Uncle Richard's order, I may have been hesitant to grant an unknown woman such a right to lands, but you've been smart. You have King Richard's blessing, thus an order to me. You now have a title, which I must admit shocked me. And you competed in my tourney, and though not won, I will admit you did admirably." He looked at her, and his gaze seemed to penetrate her in a way no other person's had. "You have me in a difficult place, Lady Eleanor."

Eleanor looked back at the crowd to escape his gaze.

"Your lands are intact. Montag burned the manor years ago, before my time. When Montag was here last, he sought to rebuild the property himself, requesting that I allow him to act as your advisor. I get the impression though that you two do not have as civil of a relationship as he claims?"

"You could say that." Eleanor frowned.

"I do, however, want that patch of brambles producing again. We need sheep, cattle, cropland. There will be a campaign in the near future, and I am stockpiling supplies. I want it farmed. Can you do that without Montag's help?"

"Of course," she answered without hesitation.

"Then I shall tell him to return to his own estates," Otto said simply.

Eleanor stared at him. "Thank you, my lord." Quickly she added, "What else do you need from me?"

Otto thought carefully, choosing his words. "I know Sir Alec is indebted to his own liege lord. Lord Cenric if I'm not mistaken?"

She nodded.

"He should stay with you for now, help you rebuild. But eventually duties to his own liege will necessitate his return to England. You are a knight, and if you are to remain as such, you must manage your estate independently." Otto frowned at her. Eleanor raised her chin and gripped her cup tighter to hide the quiver of her fingers. "You have been given the title. You will choose the role. But you must deserve to keep it."

"Understood," she replied.

"Good," Otto said and straightened. "Eventually you will have other duties as well, should I need you. I'm eager to uphold our connection with Alsace, via your uncle. Perhaps you can help with that."

Eleanor swallowed hard but nodded.

Otto stood to go, then hesitated. Slowly he leaned toward her and dropped his voice. "Your condition is not to be a distraction from your duties I hope?" His eyes flicked uncomfortably to her womb to clarify his words.

Eleanor's eyes went wide. "How do you know?"

"Answer me."

"No, sir. Of course not."

"I will avoid dispatching you into conflict for a few months. You have plenty to do in that time. You may remain discrete. But then I expect you to be in the condition you were at the tournament in Sarum, *not* in the condition you were today." Eleanor nodded quickly, her heart pounding. "Enjoy your evening, my lady."

As he walked away, Eleanor downed the rest of her wine in one swallow. She shuddered slightly. Whether good or bad, that man was intense. She never wanted to be on his bad side.

Chapter Forty

September 1197
Levan Estate, Aquitaine

E leanor pushed a vine out of the way as she waded through a patch of briars. Seventeen years of abandonment could do quite a bit of damage to a property. She *thought* she was standing in the barn yard of the Levan estate, her father's home.

"Do you see the foundation at all?" she shouted into the thicket to Alec and Wilfred. Their three new squires held their horses on the main road while the three of them delved into the thick to find the old ruins.

"Nothing," Alec shouted back.

"Maybe a well over here?" answered Wilfred. "Yes! A well!"

They bushwhacked in the direction of his voice into a clearing around the old well. Eleanor sighed. "Wrong well. This is the old well. The really old well. I remember a newer one. It was bigger. I remember mother scolding me never to go near this one. And that means the house was . . ." she pushed through the thicket on their right. "Found it!"

They followed her onto a faint trail, the grass tall and weedy, thorn bushes lining the path. In front of them stood a pile of stones. Eleanor ran up to the old foundation. Home. She stepped onto the stone steps of the front entry and stopped. The rest was gone. Two stories of a stone shell were all that was left. The charred beams of the roof, or what was left of them, lay in a pile on the ground amidst the crumbling rubble. Saplings had latched hold here and there and were already working on turning the old manor-house back into a forest.

At least she'd been warned.

Alec let out a low whistle. "Didn't leave much for you, did he?"

Eleanor shook her head. She turned. The stable was to their left, in much the same condition. Nothing was left of the villagers' houses but lumps of rotten boards. Had anyone lived? Had they all moved before Montag's destruction came? They had not met anyone on the roads here since the last fief back, where they'd only briefly stopped to meet the neighboring lord. He hadn't been very friendly. In fact, he'd seemed rather disappointed in losing some of his best hunting grounds.

Eleanor asked the obvious, "Where do we even start? And with winter coming."

Wilfred was the first to cut in. "Well . . . we should make a road."

At first Eleanor could only blink at him, stunned at the simplicity of his statement as it clashed against her overwhelmed, spinning mind. Then she started laughing. Once she started, she could not stop, though she knew there was no joke. All the tension of the past weeks burst within her, and in the simplicity of that moment, she could only laugh. Eventually Alec and Wilfred laughed along, or at least at her, until she calmed down once again. Then they picked up their tools and set to work clearing brush and chopping trees to rebuild what once had been the road into Levan Manor.

As the men worked, Eleanor watched Alec as he swung the axe, his muscled back sweating through the thin linen of his shirt. She dragged the last of the fallen branches out of the way and approached him while he stopped to rest. Wilfred was working further down the road, and Eleanor knew now was the first moment in weeks she had to talk to Alec alone.

He glanced up, back against a tree, his arms resting on the axe. "Of all the things you've made me, I never thought I'd be a builder, Eleanor. I could be at a tournament right now."

"Winning prizes. Horses. Women," she finished for him. Her tone was light, but her face showed her conflicted emotions. "Look, I just wanted to tell you it was worth it."

"What was?"

She avoided his gaze, the words awkward on her tongue. "Marrying you."

Alec's eyebrows went up in surprise.

She sighed in frustration and rubbed her forehead. "Alec, I don't know what to make of what I'm feeling right now. I know I don't always listen to you, and I know you had plenty of other options for brides. I'm not an ideal wife. Just . . . I guess I'm trying to thank you."

Alec sucked in his breath and let it out very slowly. In a panther-like motion he pushed off the tree and stalked toward her, stopping so close that the fabric of their clothes brushed. Her heart pounded as she stood there in his shadow, his scent a mix of sweat and pine. "Say it." He looked down his nose at her, that palpable confidence he'd exuded since the day she met him radiating off of him like the heat of summer.

She had no idea what he was talking about. "Say what? I'm sorry?"

He shook his head in impatience. "Stop apologizing when you don't even know what you're apologizing for. Say what you're feeling!"

"I'm . . . tired?" She looked utterly bewildered.

He suddenly crushed his lips to hers, her mind spinning. When he pulled away, she was somehow chest to chest against him, her hands twined in his hair. Awkwardly she moved to take a step back and restrain herself, but he held her hips tight to his own. "Say it," he whispered.

Eleanor looked up at his pleading eyes, knowing now what he wanted. What she could not give. She blinked away tears, panic rising within her, though she knew there was no reason for it. The edges of the woods began to blur. It was so unfair to him. He was so steady. He had followed her this far. Defending, supporting, protecting . . . but he was too close. This could not be more than a practical relationship. How could she trust him? And he didn't even know . . . God he didn't know the child wasn't his. Couldn't . . .trust . . .

She blinked her eyes open. The damp forest earth was right under her nose. Then something pulled her away from it. Arms. That's what they were. Alec's arms. She closed her eyes again. Everything was still spinning. Trees and leaves. Orange and red and yellow leaves. He shook her slightly. Slowly she blinked her eyes back open.

"You look terrible," she said quietly, for the look of horror he had etched into his face didn't suit him at all.

"What's wrong? Are you okay?" he rushed.

"Why am I on the ground?"

"What happened?" Wilfred appeared.

"She went down cold," Alec answered. "I think I caught her before she banged her head. Is it your side, Eleanor? Is there another injury from the tournament?"

Eleanor pushed herself to a sitting position and felt the color returning to her face. Lots of it. "I'm fine." She pushed them both away. "I just need a drink." She pulled herself to her feet slowly, and when they held her steady, she walked in the direction of the well, leaving the men staring after her.

They spoke quietly amongst themselves for a moment, then she saw Wilfred headed her way.

"You really alright?" He took the rope for the well bucket from her, pulling it up with ease.

She nodded.

"This isn't the first time that's happened, is it?"

"Only once before. A while back. I don't know what's wrong with me."

"When, Eleanor?"

She took a deep breath. "When I first met Edmond." She shook her head. "Well, when we re-met at least. At a tournament over a year ago."

"I'm sure that brought on a rush of emotions."

"Yes . . ." her voice trailed. She splashed water on her face from the bucket Wilfred offered her. "I guess I'm just weak."

Wilfred shook his head. "Not weak. You handled riding into tournaments, even into a full out melee, without hesitation. Without faltering. You fought through pain. There's just one thing you can't handle . . . yet."

Eleanor looked at him curiously.

"Love, Eleanor. Love."

Chapter Forty-One

December 1197

Levan Manor, Aquitaine

Eleanor strode quickly through the manor, an arm over her heavy belly. Her two maids, Collette and Marin, stood in the kitchen stacking wood next to the hearth. The fire blazed bright against the damp cold of winter. The ladies glanced up at her as she passed and opened the newly hewn oak door for only a few moments before shutting it again. The blast of cold air was laced with snowflakes. She stood there a moment, her hands on her hips.

"Have you seen Alec or Wilfred?" she asked, her brow furrowed.

"They both were headed to the stable a while ago," Collette replied. "You want me to go check?"

"No, no. Just tell them to come up to the hall if you see them." She again crossed the kitchen and started up the stairs, hesitating in the entryway. "Marin, please bring your husband up when you see him. I have another project for him, too."

The woman nodded. For reasons unknown she was mute, though her exuberant carpenter husband usually could be counted on to chatter enough for both of them.

Eleanor worked her way up the stairs, a hand now bracing her lower back. The past few months had been a complete whirlwind as the manor came back together. They had a small team of tradesmen and carpenters as part of the household now, and with Lord Otto's financing, the entire project had come together quickly and smoothly. The interior finishes would have to be slowly worked through the winter, and even now the men were erecting new cottages. By spring, they should be ready to start working the land as Otto had requested.

As Eleanor entered the hall she breathed in the rich smell of newly hewn wood. She sat on a bench at one of the rough tables near the fire. She picked up her embroidery, which was going terribly, and set it down as the baby kicked. She was restless, just like the child. After so many busy months, it felt wrong to be still.

Heavy footsteps approached. Without looking up she said quietly, "It won't be much longer than a month or two."

Alec stood in front of the fire, warming himself. "Collette said you wanted to see Wilfred and I?"

"The stables. Will we have enough hay and grain for the animals through the rest of winter? Should I send a rider out to locate more? And the fencing, did they get it done yet? And—"

"Eleanor, Eleanor. It's all under control. You have a good household."

She exhaled.

"What's really wrong?" Alec sat beside her, elbows on his knees as he looked at her.

"I just . . . I feel like I'm not doing anything."

"You are growing my child, and that is plenty."

She bit her lip. She had to tell him. She had to tell him now.

They turned as they heard Marin's husband Godwin enter the hall. Marin was on his arm guiding him, her face impassive. He was rattling on to her about something, loudly. Marin motioned toward Eleanor, and he shifted his attention.

"Oh, my lady! What a fine day it is outside! The snow just fluttering along on the breeze with the sparkle of diamonds. What may I do for you, my lady?" Godwin bowed theatrically.

Eleanor smiled weakly. His enthusiasm was exhausting. "We have more animals coming in. The manure pile is going to have to be relocated to where we have more room."

"I'm on it, my lady." He again bowed and led an expressionless Marin out, again blabbering on to her.

Eleanor shifted her weight uncomfortably. "Where is Wilfred?"

"He's leaving for Poitou." Alec shrugged.

Eleanor sighed, and the sound of hoofbeats outside pulled her from her bench to the window. Sure enough, her fellow knight was again headed off on some noble mission. Today he was mounted on yet another fine stallion, a gift from some lord he had helped, his new armor shining in the sunlight as the flurries floated around him. She felt two strong arms encircle her gently as Wilfred cantered out of sight. "He's going to give me quite the challenge when tournaments start up again. Everyone wants the help of The Fyr Hors. Imagine how many tournaments he'll be called to compete in." Alec's lips grazed her neck. "You're deep in thought today."

She leaned back against him. Partly she was jealous, longing to be as valued as Wilfred and Alec among her peers. The other part of her was flooded with relief that she was finally settled in her own estate, running things with the confidence and capability her parents had dreamed she would possess. "I feel like I am on top of a mountain, with everything I've dreamed around me."

"Good."

"It *is* good. But where does life go from here? Things can fall very quickly from on top of a mountain. I feel like I'm going to lose it all again." She felt Alec stiffen at her words. Slowly, she turned to face him, frowning. "What?"

He brushed the whisps of hair that framed her face, and she saw the telltale twitch of the muscle in his jaw. "King Richard has called us back to Normandy."

She sighed. "And there it is."

"It shouldn't be long."

"Alec, I can't travel like this. I certainly can't fight like this."

"He doesn't expect you to."

"I stay. Again?" Eleanor inhaled slowly. "He did warn me I would have to run this place independently." She wrapped her arm around her belly. "We're getting so close though. What if I *do* need you here?"

"You know I have to go," he insisted. "You have time. He says we will only be gone a few weeks."

"It will be longer, and you know it. And with both you and Wilfred away . . ." She didn't have to add her fears that Montag would return while they were defenseless.

"You will be fine. He's snowed in, trapped in Alsace, hundreds of miles away. We'll be back before you know it."

Eleanor stood at Alec's side and joined his watchful gaze out the window. "I feel like this is a test of Lord Otto's. He wants to challenge my independence when he knows I am most vulnerable."

Alec pulled her to face him. "Test though this will be, Lord Otto also trusts that you will succeed. And so do I."

Eleanor closed her eyes and steeled herself. "When do you leave?"

"I will meet Wilfred in Poitiers tonight."

Begrudgingly, she let him go. She still couldn't voice her fear that the child would come weeks earlier than even Alec expected. She knew that option had never crossed his mind. He had never asked her about timing. That was strictly in the category of something men didn't have to worry about. And besides, with Edmond it was only once. Eleanor put a hand to her belly as the child kicked. In the beginning she had been sure it was Alec's. But with the size of her stomach, the frequency of the child's kicks, everything the midwives had told her to watch out for had happened very early.

Alec and Wilfred were only gone a few days when Eleanor had a visitor. A lone woman on a grey horse, a bundle strapped around her chest, rode up to the manor looking thoroughly exhausted. A few of the workers exited the manor, weapons at hand. It was snowing, and in the dead of winter. The woman must either have the plague or be crazy or both. Eleanor watched from the window and the men pointed down the road, telling the woman to ride on. But the woman was adamant about something. Gesturing, pleading, and stubbornly refusing to move on. Eleanor grabbed her cloak and sword and went out into the snow.

Up close, the palfrey was skin and bones, an ancient little horse well past its prime. The woman was still bundled that Eleanor could not see her face, but she could hear her imploring the men. They all turned to Eleanor.

"She says she won't leave until she speaks with you," the hunter Gregory said.

"Eleanor!" the woman gushed. "Please, Eleanor!"

Eleanor looked at her closer. "Marie?" The woman pulled her scarf down, her nose bright red, her cheeks stained with tears, and her blue lips trembling with cold. "Marie!" With horror Eleanor realized the bundle was a baby, only a few months old. "Good God, woman! Come! Come inside!" She quickly took the baby from Marie's arms so she could dismount. Seeing Marie struggle, Eleanor ordered, "Help her! Help her! Take care of this poor horse. We need to get them all fed and warm." Gregory lifted Marie clear off the saddle, placing her on her feet. Her knees buckled, and he instead picked her right up and carried her after Eleanor into the house.

In the kitchen, Eleanor rushed to the fire, every maternal instinct in her flaring. The baby was quiet, too quiet. She felt its little chest and the breath beneath her fingers. Still alive. But cold. Gregory set Marie on a stool by the fire, her teeth chattering away.

"Gregory, get blankets for them. Get Collette and Marin. Please." Eleanor's eyes pleaded urgency, but Gregory was already throwing more wood on the fire and gone.

Eleanor held the baby as close to the fire as she dared, trying to share her body heat as well. She glanced at Marie. "What on Earth are you doing here, Marie? In the middle of a snowstorm. Where is your husband?"

Marie leaned against the warm stones of the hearth, cloak tight around herself, soaking in the heat. She still shivered, but her teeth didn't clack together anymore. "He threw me out."

"Threw you out!"

"I didn't know where else to go, Ella. I heard you had reopened your manor. That you needed workers. I will work Eleanor!" There was an edge of desperation in her voice.

"But why . . .?" They were interrupted as Collette and Marin flew down the stairs. Collette immediately swung a kettle of water onto the fire, as Marin wrapped blankets around Marie. They took the baby out of his damp traveling blanket and tucked him into a dry quilt. Eleanor protectively held him between her and the fire's heat.

Collette handed Marie a piece of bread. "What on Earth are you doing out here, darling?"

Marie shot Eleanor a glance.

"She came to work," Eleanor offered. "Ladies, this is my friend from England, Marie. She was part of Alec's household. Marie, meet Collette and Marin. Collette is the wife of Gregory, the man who carried you in."

Marie tried to smile as she shivered.

Collette knew better than to ask too many questions. "Oh, dear, you picked a terrible time to travel. But welcome! It will be nice to have another woman around here, right, Marin?"

Marin nodded.

Collette swung the kettle back off the fire and poured the hot water into a ceramic mug, to which she added some spiced wine. "Here, this will warm you up." More certain that Marie was going to be okay, she turned her attention to the baby in Eleanor's arms. "He – she? –is adorable."

"He," Marie offered quietly, smiling.

"How old is he?"

"About three months."

Eleanor looked down at the boy's delicate features. He squirmed a little now. He must be warming up. Three months? She'd been right back in Petite Andelys when she'd last seen Marie. She had not been only a little pregnant then. Marie did not have to finish explaining what had happened with her husband. Eleanor suddenly understood. Apparently, Jorge could do math just like everyone else, and healthy babies simply did not appear after only five months of marriage. Obviously, he was not on board with raising another man's child. Eleanor paled a little as she stared at the boy's face. What if Alec could do math, too?

The baby started to cry and immediately Marie reached for him. Eleanor reluctantly yielded him and watched as suddenly Marie was no longer cold or hungry . . . only her child mattered as she quickly allowed him to nurse. Motherhood was such a beautiful thing. Eleanor's breasts ached suddenly, and she hugged her womb as her own baby kicked. She stood. "Marie, we will make a place for you upstairs. I am happy to have you as part of our household."

Marie leaned contentedly against the stones of the hearth. "Thank you," she mouthed to Eleanor, a faint smile on her lips. Her relief was unmistakable.

Chapter Forty-Two

Late January 1198
Levan Manor, Aquitaine

Two weeks later, it started. First there was a little blood. By that evening, her back was cramping, and she retreated to the private room in the uppermost floor of the manor, under the eaves. As she paced before the warm hearth along the side of the manor, a stab of pain forced her to let loose a shriek that echoed through the manor. Her maids came running.

Collette was concerned. "It's too soon," she cautioned, lines riddling her face with more pain than what Eleanor was experiencing. She stoked the already bright fire and tidied the organized room.

Eleanor knew Collette was the most experienced mother in the manor, as evident by the two small children playing far below them in the kitchens. She winced as another wave of pain coursed through her, mercifully less intense than before. "Collette, how long will this last? Is this child coming now or is this—augh!" Eleanor doubled over with pain.

Collette wrapped an arm around her. "My lady! Oh, we need to call the midwife now."

Eleanor nodded, a hand on her back as she straightened again. She felt oddly dizzy. "I think I'm going to lie down." She stumbled a step, Collette and Marie catching her arms and guiding her.

"Her water just broke," Marie whispered to Collette.

Eleanor glanced down in embarrassment at her wet clothes.

"Get her down to her shift, then put her to bed. Get clean linens. I'm going to tell Geoffrey to get on the road to the midwife's cottage." Eleanor was dimly aware of Marie and Marin bustling around her. Within a few moments she was tucked into the bed, but the pain was increasing in intensity. She pushed the blankets back off, curling into herself as another wave of pain brought tears to her eyes.

"Marin, can you get the linens, please?" Marie asked gently. The silent woman was staring at Eleanor with a panicked expression, while Marie was pouring water from the pitcher. As soon as Marin ducked out of the room, Marie whispered into Eleanor's ear, "Please be honest with me, my lady. Are you full term? Has it been three seasons since you came to be with child?"

Eleanor looked at her young friend with a twinge of panic. If the child was Edmond's she likely was. But they had only had one night together. Surely it must be Alec's, in which case it was early, too early. She could not admit her doubts to the young maid. She took a breath as another contraction took her, letting silence be her only answer.

Marie must have sensed her thoughts, for she smiled gently. "Can I tell you a secret, my lady?"

Eleanor nodded, temporarily distracted.

"My child was not my husbands." Marie smiled.

"I knew that already." Eleanor started to laugh but was overcome by another wave of pain. When she caught her breath, she turned to the maid, who watched her with concern. "Does Wilfred know?"

Marie nodded, a tear leaking from her eye. "It's more complicated than just that, my lady."

Eleanor laid a wrist over her forehead, the warning of another contraction beginning to twist in her core. She breathed deeply. "Wilfred will be back soon. With Alec."

Marie looked at Eleanor with worry. "My lady, I need to know so we can better help you. If the child is too early, it will not survive and if necessary, we will do what we must to aid you. I know from my mother there are things we can do for a mother whose child will not survive, but not for a child that has a chance to live. If anyone understands an early conception, it is me. I do not judge. But I can't advise the midwife *unless you tell me.*"

Eleanor glared at the girl, a mix of emotions burning through. Marie was both friend and serf, equal and commoner. Eleanor was not used to being the lady of the household, but she would have to be if her household continued to question her thus. Marie looked away, blushing. Eleanor softened her gaze and sighed. "I do not know."

"That is all I need to know." Marie rose and refreshed the water in the damp cloth. Collette and Marin burst back into the room, just as another contraction hit Eleanor and she curled into a ball in pain.

"Good God," Collette froze in horror.

Eleanor followed her gaze down to between her legs and felt a wave of dizziness wash over her. There was blood everywhere, so much blood. She looked to Collette in panic.

Marie appeared at her side. "Lay back down, my lady. You're going to be fine."

"There's too much . . ." Collette stammered, fidgeting with the linens. Marin had shrunk back against the wall.

Marie grabbed Collette's wrist. "Collette, she is going to be fine. Now tell me what we need."

Eleanor's eyes blurred as another wave washed over her, the pain ripping and stabbing all at once. Was this thing trying to claw its way out? Their voices became a distant babble as she was propped into a better position. Soft hands were on her legs and then gone.

"Is this normal, to feel distant?" Eleanor asked the women. Their images blurred before her. As her eyes refocused, she could see the alarm in their faces.

"We need the midwife. God help her." Collette crossed herself. "There is nothing I can do." She sat next to Eleanor's bedside and clasped her hand. After a while she started to hum a hymn, which in Eleanor's panicked state was oddly comforting. They settled into the rhythm between the contractions.

After what seemed like an eternity, the door burst open and the midwife came in, disrobing from her winter garments as she walked. She took in the scene before her with practiced eyes, then started shouting orders. "You, girl, get hot water. Oh good, it's here already. Add this to it. Now go get more. You, get her knees up. Here, drink." A cup was pressed to Eleanor's lips, and she obeyed, sipping the bland tea.

"Raspberry leaf," the midwife muttered. "May make things worse before they get better." She handed another small satchel to Collette. "Mix this with more warm water. We'll give it to her after."

Eleanor clamped her legs together as she felt the midwife's hands on her legs. She stared at the woman with wide eyes.

"You want this baby in or out?" the strong middle-aged woman asked.

"Out," Eleanor said quietly.

"Then let me in."

Eleanor relaxed her legs, looking away from the stranger that probed where so few had touched.

"My name is Sara, my lady," the midwife said, her tone softer now, soothing. Eleanor was grateful for the distraction. "I knew your mother, a lifetime ago. She was a sweet woman."

"You remember my mother?"

"Aye." Sara's words went silent, her forehead furrowed in concentration and concern. After a moment, the midwife cursed under her breath. She wiped her hands and looked up at Eleanor. "It will be soon now. It is going to be hard. I understand they call you the Knightess?"

Eleanor nodded.

"Show me how brave you are."

Within minutes the contractions intensified, and Eleanor bore down with all her might, teeth grinding. Her sweat beaded on her brow. In a moment of reprieve Eleanor asked, "Is it always like this?" She gasped for breath, her limps trembling from exertion, a film of perspiration like dew covering her body.

Marie and Collette shared a look. The midwife gently assured, "You're doing great, my lady."

In the next contraction Eleanor felt the baby move, and the midwife jumped into action, carefully guiding. As Eleanor strained with the effort, the midwife wiped her own sweaty brow with a wrist, fingers bloody. Eleanor felt a release, then a flood of warmth between her legs, hot and surprisingly wet. The baby was quickly passed to Collette as Sara calmly yet urgently issued commands to the maids. A cup was pressed to her lips, and again Eleanor drank, sputtering on the now bitter brew. She felt Sara's hands between her legs, but before she could ask what was happening, the scream of an infant cut the room, giving her a sharp moment of clarity.

Marie gave Eleanor's shoulder a squeeze. "You have a son!"

Eleanor's eyes closed with a contented smile for a moment, then fluttered open again. She was dizzy. The pain was easing, but the room was a bit blurry. "Can I see him?" She tried to look for him and could not see. The room was going black. She thought she felt a small weight on her chest, but she could not make her arms reach for it. Blackness engulfed her, and she did not have the strength left to fight it.

Faintly Eleanor became aware. She was weak, so weak. She could not get the attention of the fuzzy figures across the room.

"I did everything I could for her. I left more of the Shepard's Purse on the table there. Use it again in the morning, and tomorrow night if she lasts that long. Please, let me know how she does." Sara shot a worried look back to the bed at her patient.

Marie pleaded, "But you've had women pull through with this, right?"

Sara watched Eleanor, her eyes concerned. "A few," she conceded. "But not many. She lost a lot of blood."

Silently she took her leave, leaving Collette still holding the baby and a worried Marie wondering what to do next.

"We need to send word to Alec," Marie admitted. "Wherever he is. If something happens to her . . ."

"I know," Collette said, her voice cracking. "I'll tell Gregory. We'll send someone."

Eleanor's eyes closed again slowly, yielding to sleep once again.

"What?" Marie exclaimed, waking Eleanor.

"Shhh!" Collette whispered harshly. "She's gone. The baby's gone. I have everyone looking for them. Her husband knows nothing. He's a mess. He's been looking all night, thought she got lost in the woods yesterday. He didn't know we've been missing the baby, too."

"Wha-what's going on?" Eleanor whispered with the rasp of an unused voice.

"Oh God!" Marie said and rushed back to the bed. "Thank God! My lady, we've been so worried about you. How do you feel?"

"T-tired," Eleanor admitted, blinking her eyes wearily, and slowly trying to pull herself upright. The world spun again.

"Easy there!" Collette said, and the two ladies helped her move a little.

"What happened? Where is my son?!" The anxiety weakened her further, and she had to close her eyes.

Marie gently explained. "You've been out for two days, m'lady. You lost a lot of blood in the birth. You still need to heal."

"My son?" she again asked.

"Shhh," Collette coaxed. "Rest and heal. We'll bring you some soup in a few minutes."

Eleanor could not fight them. She let sleep take her once again.

Chapter Forty-Three

Eleanor laid in bed, blinking at the ceiling. She felt like she was trapped in a prison. Her body was her prison. It would not let her out of bed. It would not let her run away. There was little natural light in the attic, just a narrow archer's slot on either end of the stone walls, but the space was vast. The roof slanted sharply over her bed, and she imagined it would fall in and crush her. She'd drunk and eaten little the past few days, only what Marie and Collette could coax into her. She closed her eyes and nestled deeper into her blankets, willing herself to die. The ache inside her echoed to her bones.

She longed for her child, but all Marie would say was that he was gone. She'd fought to get out of bed, longing to look for him, but that had only ended with her splayed on the floor with bruised knees. Delirium had taken hold, and she envisioned the manor burning. It was hot, so hot. Then the roof closed in, suffocating her. Now the last few days it was just emptiness, loneliness in the attic. She heard the staff go about their lives in the main hall below. Marie and Collette checked on her frequently, even encouraged her to come down now. But she wouldn't talk to them. Why talk to them if they wouldn't tell her where her child was?

Heavy footsteps sounded on the stairs. Was it Death, come to finally take her?

She heard a man let out a slow breath and step closer. She closed her eyes and pretended to sleep. A man was not what she wanted.

"Eleanor," Alec whispered softly.

She furrowed her brow and blinked her eyes open again. Was she dead now?

He laid his hand on her shoulder. She felt that. He pushed her hair out of her eyes. She felt that, too. She blinked some more and slowly tried to pull herself up in the bed to get a better look at him. Her abdomen twinged in pain, though nothing like what it had done the last few days. But she felt it.

She wasn't dead.

"Alec?" she whispered in disbelief.

"I'm here now, Eleanor. I'm so sorry." Gently he pulled her into his arms, and slowly she curled her own arms around him. She let her body lean into him, feeding on his warmth, his strength. He kissed her forehead, and she thought she felt a wet tear on his face.

"Alec," she breathed. She held on to him, caught in the blurry bliss between her delirium and reality. But eventually he had to pull away, and it pulled her mind harshly back into reality.

"You're back," she said, struggling to organize her thoughts.

"Yes. Wilfred too. I'm so sorry I had to leave you during . . . this."

"They won't tell me where he is," Eleanor stubbornly pointed out.

"Yes, I know."

"You know!" she almost shrieked.

"Shhh . . ." Alec coaxed. "No secrets. We're going to figure this out now, together."

"Figure out what?"

"How to find our son."

"Where is he?"

"I don't know."

"You said you knew!"

Alec became exasperated. "Eleanor, no. Maybe you aren't ready to talk about this yet. Go back to sleep."

"No! I want my child!" The pulse of blood rose hot in her veins, her voice shocking her ears by its volume.

"I can't talk to you like this," Alec said calmly and stood to leave.

Eleanor tried to grab him and fell out of the bed in a twisted mess of sheets. The impact shocked her to her senses, and she broke into tears. Alec instantly was at her side, and he pulled her to her feet and into his arms. He kissed the top of her head, pulling her tight. "Eleanor, I need you to calm down and listen to me. Can you do that?"

Eleanor nodded, wiping her tears. He steered her to the edge of the bed and sat them both down, keeping her hands locked in his. He took a deep breath and began.

"Do you know how long it's been since you gave birth?"

Eleanor thought hard, but really had no idea. It was all a blur.

"It's been two weeks. I'm sorry I couldn't get here sooner, but you know how long it takes to travel to Chateau Gaillard and back. We came as fast as we could when they told us. From what your ladies tell me, you've had a rough time of it. You lost a lot of blood during the birth, more so than after the melee with Lezay and Montag outside Paris. You remember that, don't you?"

She shuddered a little but nodded. She remembered the birth, too. Painful, but something went wrong afterwards. She remembered her child's screams.

"They said I had a son," she insisted.

"You do. A healthy boy," Alec answered.

She sighed in relief.

"After the birth you were too weak to take care of him. Marie nursed him. Then you became feverish, delirious even . . . or so they tell me. They tell me the fever broke a few days ago, and you are stronger now. How do you feel?"

Eleanor flexed her fingers and legs. She did feel stronger. Weak and a little sore, but not incapacitated like she had the last few weeks. Had it really been that long? She nodded.

"What I have to tell you next is going to be hard, but I want you to promise me you will stay calm. I promise you, we are going to figure this out, but we need to do it rationally. Understood?"

She again nodded.

"Eleanor, Marin took your baby. A few days after you gave birth, she and the child were both gone. The staff here, including her husband, have been looking for them ever since. As is your liege, Lord Otto of Poitou. Do you understand what I'm saying?"

"Why?" was all Eleanor could say.

Alec furrowed his brow, worried she was going to lose herself to hysterics again.

"Why would she take him?" Eleanor insisted but stayed calm. She let Alec's steady energy ground her.

Alec shook his head. "I don't know, but I have my suspicions." He took a cautious breath, studying her reactions. "I think she was working for Montag."

Eleanor's eyes went wide. Montag? Kidnap her child? And use one of her own staff to do it? It was such an outlandish way to get back at her that she actually believed it was possible. After all, none of his other plans had worked.

"Is my son alive?"

"We have no reason to believe he's not. A lone woman and babe have been seen in several towns, indicating she is headed to Alsace. We have friends following her. I made the decision to come straight here, to you." Alec shot a worried look over her. "I think Marin was planted here at the manor all along. Wilfred and I interviewed her husband. Turns out they met only days before they came here. He claims love at first sight, and I believe him. But I don't think she shared the feeling."

Eleanor leaned into Alec and put her head on his shoulder.

"Why would Montag do this to an innocent child?"

He pulled her into him. "At least we know he wants the child alive. If not, Marin would have killed him here. We're going to get him back."

"What are we going to do? Lay siege to Chateau Brunstein itself?"

"If we have to." Alec spoke without hesitation, the firmness of a warrior in his tone.

Eleanor looked hard at him, surprised at how strongly he felt.

He kissed her gently. "Don't forget, Eleanor. He's my son too."

Eleanor's blood ran cold for a moment. He sensed her shiver and pulled away to look at her.

"What?" Alec asked.

"Alec . . . he may not be yours." Eleanor looked away from him and braced herself for his explosion. After the last few days, she was still questioning how much she wanted to live, so if he wanted to kill her, let him get it over with now.

But Alec was only still beside her. "Of course he's mine," he ventured.

Eleanor shook her head. "He was too early. It would have been before you and I—it would have been back when Edmond and I . . ." She stopped, tears welling in her eyes. Guilt poured from her. She didn't want to hurt him. He'd been so good to her, and now she was going to take away what he'd wanted most.

Alec let out a slow breath and stayed perfectly still while Eleanor trembled beside him, tears streaming down her face. Long minutes passed that way, until finally he spoke, his voice rough. "No, Eleanor. The child came early. He is mine. You are mine. And we are going to get him back." His kissed her roughly on the forehead. "I'm going to send the women up to help you get cleaned up. You need to come down to the main hall for dinner. We're going to get your strength up again. I want to ride to Poitou as soon as you are strong enough."

As he left the room, Eleanor let out a sob. Grief. Regret. Hope. They were powerful feelings pulling in every direction. But one overwhelmed them all. A new emotion, one so great it threatened to break her. Love.

Chapter Forty-Four

G ingerly she descended the stone staircase down into the great hall of her manor. Her legs felt weak, but they held her. Collette took her arm to steady her when they reached the bottom. Eleanor smoothed her palms down her skirts, her figure already slim again after two weeks of little nourishment. Marie and Collette had insisted she wash and even did up her hair. She knew she looked a fraction of her former self, but they were right, she did feel better when she looked better. And the crazed woman she had woken up as that morning could not have looked worse.

Alec approached her and gently took her arm from Collette, guiding her over toward the great table in front of the fire. All of her workers nodded to her and smiled, welcoming her back. She felt as if she were a ghost, returned from the dead. Over the next few weeks, she would learn that in many ways, she was.

Wilfred came over to her and embraced her gently. "My lady," he said, stepping back with a courtly bow. Eleanor rolled her eyes at him and took the mug of ale that he offered with a smile. He sat across the table from her, with Alec at her side. The rest of the manor resumed what they had been doing. Eleanor stared after Marie as she took her own child from where it played with Collette's children and carried him down into the kitchens. The apologetic look Marie shot to her did little to dampen the sudden ache in Eleanor's chest.

Wilfred caught her attention by rapping on the table in front of her. She looked back to him. "How do you feel?" he asked.

Eleanor shrugged. "Tired. Sore. Weak." Heartbroken. Angry. There were many more words she wanted to add. "How was Normandy? Everything alright with King Richard?"

Alec replied, "Politics as usual. Turns out our Lord Otto has a claim to the German crown. He had a meeting with Richard and a select few vassals to discuss how to go about taking said claim."

Eleanor let out a low whistle. "That is news. Interesting."

"We thought so, too," Alec said. "That is why he is so keen to keep Montag close. We were in Petite Andelys when they told us you had had the baby and it was kidnapped. We immediately informed Lord Otto of our suspicions, and he sent men to Alsace to investigate. He doesn't trust Montag. Not only does Montag support

King Philip of France, but he also supports King Philip of Swabia's claim to the German throne, not Lord Otto's."

Eleanor put her head in her hands, weary. "I just want to see my child," she whispered. She had not even gotten to hold him yet.

Wilfred took her hand. "Eleanor, we are going to get him back."

"I'm not strong enough. It could be weeks yet until I am ready."

"Lord Otto is already started on the search," Alec pointed out. "We'll know where they are by the time you are healthy again. So focus on getting your energy back. Drink that, then we'll get you some soup."

"I'll get some now," Wilfred offered and left Alec and Eleanor alone.

Alec wrapped his arm around her. "I missed you," he whispered in her ear. "I'm so sorry I wasn't here for you."

Eleanor allowed herself to lean into him. "You had to go," she said simply. "About earlier, what I said . . . Alec, I'm so sorry. I didn't know . . ."

"And we never will know," he cut her off. "I told you, he's mine." The kiss he lightly placed on her head clarified that indeed, she was his as well.

That night when she went to bed, she took off Edmond's ring for the first time since she'd put it on. With a tear in her eye, she kissed it and gently slid it through a knot in the floorboards. The thud echoed as it settled into the dark cavern between the floor and the ceiling of the room below. She knelt there on the floor a moment. Now he would forever be part of her manor, just as he would always be part of her. He'd given her the courage to do the impossible. But just as Alec had gotten Lezay out of their bedroom, she now had to get Edmond out, too. Alec had laid his claim on her and the child. She could no longer let him continue competing with a ghost.

Chapter Forty-Five

Noir pawed the ground impatiently. The earth was muddy from melting snow and ice, and it splashed up his legs. She knew how he felt. She was ready to go, too. She'd lost two months recovering from childbirth. The good news was she was fully recovered, and they knew where her son was. He was in Alsace, with Montag.

Eleanor tightened her gauntlets and checked her sword belt for the dozenth time. They were riding to Alsace by way of Les Andelys to avoid Paris and King Philip. Lord Otto travelled with forces from the German provinces in the North. This was not just about her son, though he had turned out to be the catalyst. Otto was laying the framework to take the German crown, and Montag was to be either bribed or forced to join his side.

This was what Eleanor and Alec had dreamed of a year ago, and here it was happening.

"Ready?" Alec asked, riding up next to her.

"Where's Wilfred?" she asked, impatient to be on their way. The squires were mounted behind them, one holding Wilfred's horse. He shrugged.

Then they saw him, striding from the barn, his face anxious. Marie trailed after him. "Wilfred, don't you dare do this to me again! Don't you dare!" she shrieked. Their audience raised their eyebrows at each other. Wilfred turned back to her and said something in a hushed tone, then again turned toward his horse. Marie broke into tears.

"Women," he muttered under his breath.

Eleanor looked back and forth between the two of them, then sighed in exasperation. "Wilfred, stay here."

"What?"

"Stay. Here. Someone has to look after the manor. We can't leave it completely defenseless, especially since Lord Otto is abroad as well. And Marie needs you. Your child needs you. There will be time again for battle."

Wilfred's mouth opened and closed. Marie wiped at a tear, glaring at Eleanor.

"I told you, my lady. Wilfred is too good to be like that." She wiped her eyes with the heels of her hands, forcing a brave face. Wilfred stared at her, wide eyed. "Will, I've apologized more times than I can count. If you don't love me, say it, and I'll be on my way."

Wilfred opened and closed his mouth, his face red as the group watched their struggle. "I—"

"Say it!" Marie stomped her foot, her fists balled.

"Fine! I love you, Marie of Neroche! Will you marry me?"

Marie's eyes went wide. "Really?"

Wilfred threw his hands in the air, rolling his eyes. Marie suddenly squealed and rushed into his arms.

The squires hooted and everyone laughed. Marie wiped her tears and looked up at him imploringly. Wilfred scooped her off her feet in one of the most dramatic kisses Eleanor had ever witnessed. She beamed at her friends. Wilfred and Marie were still entwined together as the five riders rode away, leaving catcalls in their wake.

Eleanor twisted in the saddle until Wilfred and Marie were out of sight. When she turned to Alec, her expression was more conflicted. "I hope she has an easier time getting rid of her first husband than I did mine."

Chapter Forty-Six

Riding to Alsace was like Déjà Vu for Eleanor. She'd longed to attack Montag since she'd left as a girl. A dozen different ways she'd dreamed up how to make it happen, but the reality had always been impossible. Never had she imagined that she would be making this ride to rescue her son. Now, somehow, because of a decision of passion months ago, she was riding to Montag, armored as a knight, titled as a knight, and with the strength of an army to back her. This new reality was both dream and nightmare. She felt strong, and anger fueled that strength. The month of careful conditioning and care had re-motivated her not only to be at her best, but to live. She had a child, and he was worth the great fight she had avoided the last decade.

She, Alec, and their squires made it through the forest path in record time. With a brief visit to her friends at the Abbey St. Catherine, they were on the last stretch . . .weaving through the mountain passes into Les Vosges where Montag had his mountain fortress. There was little open farmland here, as Eleanor remembered. There would be no jousts over large fields as there had been at Paris. As they rounded a final bend in the road, they saw the siege camp of Lord Otto. He'd amassed a fearsome following, and Eleanor hoped it was all for show. Carefully they made their way through the army, and many stared at her. The German lords in particular had only heard stories of her, not seen the knightess in full battle attire.

Otto himself sought them out. "You are just in time," he said, face lined with frustration and greasy hair askew. "I am meeting with Montag in mere minutes to try to come to terms. He's been most stubborn thus far. All I want is for him to join our alliance of German lords. And of course to get your son back." He added the latter as if an afterthought.

Alec's jaw muscle pulsed, but he and Eleanor handed off their horses to the squires and followed Otto into a tent toward the front of the encampment. They could see Montag riding across the field toward them. Eleanor laid a hand on Alec's arm, for once the one to quiet *him* as he clenched and unclenched his fists. "We must try to do this civilly first," she reminded him. "All I want is my child back."

Otto and Montag greeted each other cordially but coolly in the middle of the tent. Eleanor and Alec hung back. Otto explained his terms and his reason for them in what Eleanor thought was a very convincing argument.

But Montag steadfastly refused. He gave them until morning to get away from his manor and go home, or Eleanor's child would be sent back to them in pieces. He sneered at her as he made the remark, and she shook with anger. She felt the tension in Alec beside her. But they were trained to hold back from a fight when necessary. And thus they did. Worse still, he insisted to Otto that the Chateau was stocked to withstand siege for months . . .months he knew Otto didn't have if he was to invade the rest of Germany.

As soon as Montag had ridden back to the Chateau, Otto exploded in an uncharacteristic rant. Eleanor soon realized she was not the only one infuriated by Montag, nor the only one who had struggled to find her place. Otto not only had claim as King of Germany, but also had a claim as Holy Roman Emperor, both titles which still remained elusive to him. It seemed the politics of the world were never ceasing. And that more people wanted to settle things with the death of innocent lives than by compromise.

But first she had to rescue her son. The anger and adrenaline sharpened her mind as she sat there in Otto's tent, thinking over every possible plan she had ever come up with to get back at Montag. And then she remembered the simplest way she had succeeded in evading him. As a child she had been forbidden to play with Raoul and Edmond, so she had to sneak out of the castle when they went riding or wanted to sword fight. There was one passage she was sure only she and Raoul still knew about, that led from the belly of the castle's dungeons to a cave in the backside of the fortress. If she could get to that cave, she could get in. And she could get her son.

Quickly she told Alec and Otto her plan, and Otto instantly agreed. With the child off the table as a bargaining chip, Montag may be more apt to agree to Otto's terms. Montag knew he was outnumbered by Otto's army, and Otto was willing to wager that Montag's stores of supplies must be lower after the long winter than claimed. The stealthy invasion held little risk to Otto himself.

"How soon can you get in?" Otto pondered.

"Tonight," Eleanor said firmly. "Why wait?"

"Sounds perfect."

Alec ran a hand through his hair. "Are you sure only two of us, Eleanor?"

"We can move faster and quieter. I considered going alone. I'm the one who's gotten in there a hundred times—"

"You are not going alone." Alec leaned across the table toward Otto. "Do you want us to raise the gate while we're in there?"

Otto shook his head. "Not this time. If Montag doesn't yield to me by morning, I'll send in the entire army through Eleanor's tunnel. We will be ready out here, but

I'm afraid I can't offer you much assistance if things go wrong."

"We'll be fine," Alec insisted, confidence pouring from him in his anticipation.

"Don't kill Montag unless you must," Otto instructed. "If possible, I want him alive. I need his allegiance."

Eleanor nodded reluctantly. She knew that would be near impossible, but if they could make it in and out of the castle without being spotted, there was a chance.

Getting to the cave that night was easy. Eleanor knew how to skirt the towers so they would be hidden from view. At the entrance to the cave, she took a shaky breath and looked at Alec. "You ready?" she asked.

"Lead the way," he gestured forward. "Eleanor, wait." He pulled her back to him and kissed her, hard. She kissed him back, willing him to know her soul but not wanting this to be the moment to tell him. "Be careful," he whispered as he pulled back, and silently drew his sword.

She drew hers and whispered, "You too."

The cave connected to the manmade tunnel into the castle with an iron door. By some miracle, the key still was in the lock, almost as if someone had left it for them. It put Eleanor even more on edge, but silently she crept through the passage and up the stairs, feeling along the wall to guide herself, not willing to risk light. The trap door into the dungeon was also open, and the lower rooms of the castle empty.

"Where would they have him?" she whispered to Alec, every nerve on edge, trying to reach out and feel her son.

"Where would Montag be?" he asked.

"He has a study, part of his private rooms. That is where he usually met with advisors, conducted business." She nodded. That room had a view of the entire countryside. He could see everything from up there. That is where he would be. It was also at the top of the tower, protected by a staircase that spiraled its way to the top. Once on that stair, one could be cornered from both ends with no escape. She could only pray he was alone.

Silently she led Alec through the castle. They saw a few people, but they were not noticed. It was as if the household didn't know there was an army on their doorstep. Eleanor hoped that the army she knew Montag did have was preoccupied with watching the western walls that faced Otto's army. Eleanor heard a baby cry and froze, looking at Alec in alarm. She felt the familiar surge of energy light every nerve on edge.

"You don't know if that's him," Alec pointed out. "If I were Montag, I would have that child in my sight. We have to find him first."

Eleanor nodded reluctantly, looking longingly down the hallway toward the kitchens, where the sound came from. If they didn't find Montag in his study, they would go there next. They reached the stairs and slowly started to climb, swords in hand. Eleanor stopped as she heard a noise above them. He was in there. Her heart pounded, and she pointed upwards to indicate to Alec what she heard. He nodded to her that he was aware. Silently he stepped around her on the narrow stair, leading them upward the last few steps, their ears straining to gain what knowledge they could. Eleanor knew there was a door at the last stair, and she prayed it was unlocked.

Not only was it unlocked, but ajar, and the room looked vacant from what Alec could see. He silently took the last steps to the door. Eleanor hung back, her nerves ablaze. He looked around, then stepped into the room. Eleanor saw him flinch for just the briefest second, but it was too late. Montag had hammered a blow across Alec's shoulder that could well have broken it, even through his mail and gambeson. Alec stumbled to the floor with a shout. Eleanor leapt up the last stair and blocked Montag's sword as it came down toward Alec's head as he scrambled to regain his feet. Montag parried blows at her quickly, giving her no time to think. She reacted on instinct and kept him at bay. Alec, his left arm clutched at his side, hammered a blow at Montag's knee that brought him a moment's hesitation, allowing Eleanor to spin away from him, kicking the door shut behind her. Deftly she locked it behind her and pocketed the key. No one was getting out of this room until this was finished this time.

Alec circled Montag, sword at the ready, as Eleanor closed in on him from the other direction. She glanced around the room: empty. "Where is my son?" she demanded.

Montag laughed coldly but evaded the question. "Niece, so good to see you."

Alec attacked, his hurt arm still at his side, and Montag parried with him in a quick succession of blows. He slammed Alec in the face with a half thrust and blood spurted from Alec's nose. She slammed her sword against Montag's sword arm, and he growled, but she could tell his mail had done its job. As Alec wiped blood from his eyes, Eleanor fought to keep ahead of Montag as he advanced on her, backing her into a corner. She threw a candlestick at him, and he yelled in rage as the hot wax splashed across his face. It gave Alec the opportunity to hammer into his sword arm, and Montag dropped his sword. He chuckled.

Alec wondered if the man was half crazy, and in that moment, Montag grabbed the blade of Alec's sword with his gloved left hand and slammed it into him. Alec fell back, surprised, and had to let go of the hilt. Montag flipped the sword in his hand to grasp the handle with his right hand and swung hard, right into Alec's side. Alec doubled over and Montag slammed the hilt into Alec's head, and he crumbled.

"Alec!" Eleanor screamed and ran madly at Montag. But she froze as he laid the sharpened point of the sword at Alec's throat. She stayed in her tracks, furious.

"There's nothing stopping me from taking his life," Montag cooed. "Just like with Edmond."

Eleanor fumed, her eyes locked on Montag's.

"Should we make it slow? Like we did with him?" He nicked Alec's cheek with the sword. Alec didn't stir as the red blood welled, though Eleanor could still see his pulse pound in the vein in his neck, the vein that Montag again laid the blade against. Montag continued his taunt. "I had no idea you were involved with Edmond, but his silence despite my persuasions told me otherwise. Yet it seems you also feel something for this man, too. Husband to you now, I hear. Still I wonder, what was wrong with the husband I chose for you all those years ago? All you had to do was be a good girl and none of this would have happened. Edmond would be alive, and your Alec would stay alive."

For the first time in her life, instead of her uncle's words controlling her and weakening her resolve, they stirred the fire within Eleanor. She felt a steadiness come over her as she kept her sword raised, every nerve alive. "Tell me one thing, Uncle. One thing. You have worked my whole life to take everything from me. My family. My friends. My honor, freedom, now my son and my husband. Tell me why. What did a little five-year-old girl do to deserve this? What did my son do to deserve this? We are blood, Uncle! Blood!"

"Yes, Eleanor, we are blood," he hissed, eyes narrowed like a serpent. She noted his hand waivered with the sword, for once distracted. "And I have always taken the bond of blood to heart. I protected my sister through a hell you will never know. I tried to shield her from the brutal realities of life, of men. But she was a fool, and she ran away to marry a fool. They called it love, but it weakened them both. Because of your father she is dead. So why, you ask? Because I promised her on her deathbed that I would not make the same mistakes with you as I did her. I swore to make you stronger than her, without laying a hand on you. And you know I never have, until this day. You know it." He glared at her with a black stare that a few years ago would have made Eleanor cower. She studied him, but did not argue, for his words were true. Except for the jousts where *she* had charged *him*, he himself had never laid a hand on her.

Montag plunged ahead, as if a floodgate had been opened. "I taught you to ride and let you see the world. I gave you work to make you strong; I kept you away from those who would fill your mind with foolish stories. All you had to do was listen. Obey. Do your duty to the family. Respect the blood your mother betrayed. But you . . ." He chuckled. "You've been the biggest failure of our line. I gave you a husband, and you ran away. You became an adulteress, a whore, and now have brought a bastard into the world, all the while pretending that you are as good as a knight! You are a woman! You are weak! You can not fight me and—"

"Explain Lezay!" Eleanor shouted, cutting him off.

Montag was silent.

Eleanor said quietly, "You never laid a hand on me, Uncle, not that there was affection either. That I could have lived with. And then there was Lezay." Her sword hand trembled slightly, still at the ready. "Montag, do you know what he did to me?"

"A marriage bed is hardly . . ."

"It was no ordinary marriage bed, and you damn know it! You heard me screaming! You did nothing! Nothing!"

Montag was silent. Slowly he lowered his sword.

Eleanor's voice again went quiet. "Why?"

Montag for once didn't have control of the emotions that flitted across his face. Sadness, anger, curiosity. He finally settled with pity. "I denied him your mother." He paused for a moment, letting his words sink in. "I owed him. She owed him."

"And I was payment for this debt?"

Montag nodded.

Eleanor's stomach churned in disgust.

Montag continued, "And since you never properly paid the debt to the Lezay family, now your son will. As Lezay has no heir, I've arranged to have the boy raised with Lezay's kin."

Eleanor was horrified at the thought of any part of Lezay's family being near her child, much less raising him. "You have no right!"

Montag's evil glint came back into his eyes, and he suddenly swung his sword at her yet again. Eleanor jumped out of the way, knocking her hip on the table next to her. The pain brought her back to full awareness and her body acted instinctually. There was a sharp crack as Eleanor slammed her sword down hard on the angle between Montag's shoulder and neck. She hit mail, but flesh too. She didn't hesitate and threw in the next blow, low to his knee, then smashed the hilt of her sword like a hammer into his face. He hit his knees and reeled in shock for a moment. When he burst to his feet, she was ready for him. The blows came quick and hard, but Eleanor focused as she did in the tourneys. He made a forward jab toward her, but she twisted away, using the opportunity to drive a two-fisted stab straight into his stomach with all her might. She felt the mail tear and thrust again, harder. It gave, and she felt the blade tear into muscle. She stepped back, readying her sword once more, but her uncle swayed slightly.

"Where is my son?" she gritted her teeth. "This can end here between us, Montag. Just tell me where my son is, and we'll be gone."

Montag chuckled, and blood appeared at the corner of his mouth. "I've often heard that it's underestimated how much strength it takes to kill a man."

"Where is he?" Eleanor glanced down and saw Alec stir. Montag saw the movement, too. He was only an arm's reach away, which was no distance at all for the longsword he still held in his right hand. He twitched, maybe it was even involuntary, but it was the end of Eleanor's resolve. She swung hard and true at Montag's exposed neck, her sword sinking deep. She looked away as he gurgled his last breath, his blood pulsing onto the wooden floor until suddenly it stopped.

Shaking, she knelt by Alec, wiping the blood from his face. He blinked at her, dazed. The blow to his head had been impressive and his collar bone was broken, but the cuts weren't deep. She shook him.

"Alec . . .Alec! We have to get out of here." She spotted a cup of ale on Montag's desk and splashed it into Alec's cuts. He roared upright, immediately grabbing his head as though it would break.

"Alec, we have to go!" she hissed. She pulled him up. She couldn't carry him alone, but if he could stagger, she could get him out.

"You okay?" he mumbled.

"Yes."

"He dead?"

"Yes."

"Where's . . ." his voice trailed.

"I don't know. We have to find him. Alec, listen to me, you have to help me, or we aren't going to get out of here. Alec!" she patted his cheek as he swayed against her again. "Damn it. Alec, please!" she pleaded, and kissed him, ignoring the blood.

He stood up a little more.

"Alec, I need you . . ." she whispered. He stood a little straighter still, steeling himself, fighting through the fog of his head injury and the pain he must have in his shoulder. She watched him take internal account of his injuries, summoning adrenaline to overcome physical limitations, one by one. She exhaled as she saw the familiar spark of anger in his eyes. He was a fearsome sight, bloody, bruised, yet standing there as if going into battle anew. "Alec?" she asked tentatively.

"I'll be okay, for now at least," he said solemnly. He knelt to pick up his sword, and she braced to catch him, but he stayed steady on his own. "Let's find him and get out of here."

Eleanor led the way down the stairs, trying to be as quiet as she had been when they'd come, but knowing she rushed. They made it to the bottom without incident. She turned right down the main hall and rushed into the kitchens, where they'd heard the baby cry earlier. A stout, grandmotherly type sat by the fire, a bundle in her arms. Eleanor crept in, taking account of the room. It was empty but for the pair by the fire. Her mail made the faintest clank and suddenly the woman jumped up. "You can't have him!" she shrieked, running for the large butcher knives on the kitchen counter. Then she hesitated. "Eleanor?"

"Madame Brigitte?" Eleanor asked hesitantly.

"Oh, Eleanor!" the woman sighed in relief. "I hoped you'd come for him."

Eleanor quickly went up and hugged her old friend, tears streaming down her face. "Is he mine?" She stared at the tiny, dark-haired baby for the first time. His delicate features were so peaceful as he slept, lips pursed in some deep dream, that Eleanor was afraid to touch him.

Madame Brigitte nodded. "Oh, he's yours. I swore I wouldn't let Montag take him from me. Not if my life depended on it. I saw you in him as soon as he came to our door. The Le Bruns stamp their children well. Oh, Eleanor—" She took in her and Alec's bloodied appearance. "Take him. Take him and go. Get out of here. I never saw you."

Eleanor sheathed her sword so she could take the sleeping child, tucking him against her heart in an awkward but desperate embrace. He murmured against her chest before returning to his deep slumber. "Thank you," was all she could whisper.

"Footsteps!" Alec warned.

"God speed," Madame Brigitte whispered, hurrying back to her chair at the fire.

Eleanor guided Alec down a secondary stair from the kitchen to the cellars. They were running now, Alec leading the way. He snatched the last torch from the brazier in the cellar, holding sword and torch together with his good arm, leading them deeper into the dark, ancient levels of the castle. As they got to the door to the cave tunnel, he froze. A shadow of a man danced in the torchlight before them, his features shadowed like an evil creature born from the depths of the dungeon.

"Who is it?" Alec asked, his voice firm.

"I figured you would come this way," Raoul stepped out of the shadows, sword drawn. His face had shrunken to boney prominence, his eyes dark hollows. His once-solid frame was draped in baggy clothes. Yet his stride was as purposeful and solid as ever. The wiry sinews and veins of his arm led to a sword-hand that did not waver from the sharp point of metal that pointed directly at Eleanor. "I see you found him." He nodded at the baby Eleanor held tight in her arm.

"Raoul, what is this?" Eleanor asked impatiently.

"I'm supposed to kill you. He'll kill me this time if I don't."

"It's time you decide to be your own man, Raoul. You make your own choices. You fight under your own orders," Eleanor said, even as her eyes calculated the distance to the tunnel door. She knew Alec was still weak, and she couldn't fight with a baby in her arms. Though she would if she had to. "Let us go, Raoul."

"You make it sound so simple, Eleanor. Right and wrong, black and white. But there is so much grey in between."

"Let the light shine on the grey, Raoul. That is the only way to see the truth. And that is all that really matters." She hesitated. "Raoul, you are my cousin, and once were my closest friend. I know you are a good man. You can change this. All of this. You can be lord of this manor, choose who your allies are. You have it in you."

Raoul's sword arm dropped. The turmoil etched in his face was evident even in the torchlight. The dark circles under his eyes seemed to darken yet more in the dim light. He looked like a man on a walk to the gallows. "I can't do it, cousin. Just like I couldn't face you in battle outside Paris." She remembered wondering where he had been. "I am weak," Raoul continued. "Weaker even than you."

"No!" Eleanor insisted, her fingers tightening around the child in her arms. "Raoul, mercy is never weak. You are going to be a strong, fair ruler."

"I will never live to be a ruler of anything, Eleanor. Go. Remember me."

Alec edged toward the door, and Eleanor followed him, tears in her eyes. The shell of Raoul merely stood there watching them, his arms slack at his sides. "Raoul," Eleanor ventured as she hesitated at the door. "Montag is dead. I killed him." She bit off the words "I'm sorry." Alec was the one who taught her not to apologize for decisions she had made in the moment, and now she understood why. She saw Raoul straighten, and she hurried down the passage after Alec.

By the time they emerged from the cave into the starlit meadow, the castle was echoing with the sounds of horns and shouts; Montag's small army knew they had escaped. Alec extinguished the torch and left it. They could see Otto's encampment in the distance bursting into action, readying for an attack. As Alec strode confidently forward in the dark, Eleanor lagged behind and finally stopped.

Suddenly she was shaking from head to foot, her heart pounding.

"What is it?" Alec whispered, returning to her side, sword still in hand. He glanced around with alertness.

"I . . . I killed a man," Eleanor breathed. Her trembling worsened and her knees threatened to give out as the adrenaline crash burned through her system. The child in her arms fussed as she held him tighter in fear that her arms would fail her. "Here, take him, Alec. Take him."

Alec sheathed his sword, but instead of taking the babe, he wrapped his arm around them both, steadying them with a gentle strength.

Eleanor sobbed.

Alec kissed her forehead.

"Eleanor, you saved my life tonight. And our child's. And your own."

She sobbed harder, but the trembling had stopped.

"Eleanor . . ." Alec said gently, lifting her chin with one finger so he could look her in the eye. Her tears sparkled in the light of the stars. "You did . . ."

She cut off his words, blinking away tears as she held his gaze. "Alec, I love you."

He was still with shock for a moment, studying her. Before he could reply, she pressed a passionate kiss to his lips that tasted of sweat and blood. It was the best kiss either of them had ever had. As he pulled away, Eleanor leaned her forehead against Alec's strong chest, breathing him in, willing to be part of him. Her eyes closed as she felt him and the child against her. Alec's breathing steadied her heart, and despite the chaos clamoring on the wind, she took the moment of reprieve for the beauty of it.

"I've loved you longer," Alec whispered, and Eleanor realized he was right, noting all he had done for her since they had met, the risks he himself had taken. Love: such a formidable force. She had survived eight years alone, but with Alec by her side, life had bloomed into something completely different. Eleanor did not care to think to the future and how their lives would evolve further, not at that moment. There was only the sound of the crickets, the stars above their heads, the breeze on her tear-stained cheeks, and the thrum of three hearts beating in their own melody.

They lingered in each other's embrace, a moment of peace impenetrable even to war.

Epilogue

S ir Raoul de Brunstein ignored the pounding coming from the other side of the door. He'd been ignoring it for hours, choosing instead to sit in his father's tower study, slouched in a chair, observing the bloody corpse before him. For corpse it was indeed, though it had the visage of the man who had fathered him.

He had weighed his options through the night, and if the light pinking the room around him was any indication, the man pounding at the door was right, and he was running out of time. He'd had a plan when he'd woken up the day prior, if one could call the nightmare-laced closing of his eyes sleep. The plan was what it always was: stay alive, obey Montag.

His cousin had changed all that last night.

Montag was dead. Raoul was his own man, she had said. He could make his own decisions, she had said. He had not killed the woman who held a sword, as Montag had ordered. He had not hidden the babe he was told to protect and keep from her at all costs, including his own life. No. Eleanor, her child, and even her husband were alive and well and waiting outside the gates of Brunstein with an entire army backed by a man determined to be king, whether claim be true or not.

Raoul had many choices this dawn, as he blinked away darkness, the rose light sharpening the image of the dead man before him. He was now the rightful Lord of Brunstein, heir to one of the most expansive tracts of land in Alsace. No one, save the woman who had killed the former lord, had even a distant claim to this title, and she undoubtedly had no interest in it. He knew her well enough for that. That meant his first decision would have to be to accept this title and with it, the responsibility of governing a princedom pulled on every side by different interests. War was in their future. He could smell it. He knew he had the skill to protect Brunstein and the estates, but it would come at a price.

He had allies. Or should he say, his father had allies. They would take kindly to him if he continued to work in their best interests, as Montag had. To disobey could be deadly or worse, complicated. Which led to the second pressing decision of the day: did he want to start upending the organization of things? His allies did not accept Lord Otto as the rightful King of Germany. He was a French noble who knew nothing of their affairs . . .or so they said. But to not accept Otto brought immediate war upon his castle. He was far outnumbered, their stores were low after a long winter, and quite frankly he had no desire himself to fight the man who promised riches and protection to those who allied with him. Having a king as a friend was a good thing, and Raoul was inclined to believe this man was going to succeed in claiming that title in the near future.

Raoul sighed, rubbing his forehead with a hand, the first movement he'd made in hours. His corporeal form was coming back to life. The fire cracked in the hearth, only remnants of coals remaining. He let his arm fall back to the table next to him, the crinkle of parchments alerting him further. Alarm coursed through his veins, triggered more by the simple pages before him than the pounding at the door or the army outside the walls. At least this decision was easy. No one must know. His attention peaked as he scanned through the short pile, committing the contents to memory. In a swift motion he scooped up the writings and threw them into the fire. The hearth immediately blazed bright again. Raoul threw in a few small logs to ensure the parchments would burn completely, then did a final scan of the room.

His father's sword within reach of his dead hands, and for a moment Raoul considered taking it. But why? Surely it was a fine sword, but his own was made for him and of equal quality. Sentimental value? No, Montag had been a cold beast, not father. No, Raoul decided, he would let the sword be buried with the man. Someone else could take care of that, just like they would take care of carting the corpse down to the front gate, that Lord Otto may look upon the former Lord of Brunstein as proof of his demise.

There was one thing he would need though, as proof of all these decisions he was making. He steeled himself and touched the cold hand of the corpse, stiff with death, and yanked the gold signet from its finger. Raoul ignored the fact that it was streaked with dried blood. He was going to have far more blood on his hands as lord, no matter how hard he tried for peace.

Eleanor did not know what wheels she had set in motion. How long would they have? A few years? A few months? Then the fury of Le Brun would be back. Did she even know he existed? She couldn't. That was a family secret buried deeper than the bodies of their ancestors.

He steadied himself with a breath, noting the pounding on the door was intensifying. He would have to protect her, Raoul realized. That was another, surprisingly easy decision. The easiest way to do that would be to claim Brunstein as his own and manage the elaborate political maze that it was. He grinned to himself, thinking of the game *that* would be. The second-best thing to do would be to ally with her allies, particularly the powerful ones that would also compliment his fief. Lord Otto would be a good man to start with, and Raoul had the opportunity today to make a good impression.

With a last look around the room, he went to the door, unlocking it and throwing it open. The man on the other side looked wide-eyed at him, panic in every feature.

"Sir!"

Raoul pointed over his shoulder with his thumb as he descended the stairs, already past the stunned man. "Get help to move him. Bring him to the gate."

He continued through the grand castle to the gates himself, his face set as he passed his ready army, who waited for his cue to begin firing their arrows and trebuchets on the massive force outside their walls. The leaders fell into step behind him, their queries ignored. Raoul motioned for the gates to be raised, squinting into the sunlight that now sliced through the valley, the shadows of his enemy at his feet. He walked alone out to the waiting throng, eyeing the standard of Lord Otto.

Lord Otto stepped out to meet him, and there in the field outside of Chateau Brunstein they agreed to a peaceful alliance. Lord Raoul le Brun would support Otto in his endeavors, and remain lord of Brunstein. It was a new dawn for Alsace.

Lord Raoul had decided.

Historical Note

Historical fiction aficionados, forgive me for my generous use of creative license. I will herein explain some of my manipulations of the past and my reasonings, as well as the historical truths that inspired this story. The medieval era is truly a fascinating period, an era about which we know just enough to excite yet not enough to limit imagination.

◻First and foremost, I must address the tournaments. In this book you see the tournament being held in three formats: the "ring-style" tourney, the full-contact joust, and the melee. Some of the research I acquired early on proved to be completely false. For example, I was fascinated by a claim that the ring-style tournament was being used in the early medieval period due to the reduced risk of injury. They made the point that armor was still very weak in the twelfth century, which is true. Plate armor was not yet in use, and chainmail had limitations. Years later, I learned the ring-style joust did not come into popularity until the 1500s. In the twelfth century, the common format of a tournament was an oft-deadly melee,

with dozens of men in an arena at one time. I made moves
to correct this in the storyline, but for the heart of the
tale—a woman riding in the joust to best the men that
oppressed her— it was too late. The ring-style joust had to
stay.

□During the reign of King Henry II (1154-1189),
tournaments were outright banned in England due to
their brutal nature. Some say the ban was partly from
the raucous behavior of the knights as they traveled the
countryside on their way to tournaments, yet others
blame it on the deadliness of the tournaments themselves.
Later bans by the Catholic church in the early thirteenth
century support this latter notion, and so strong was this
position that knights killed in tournaments were denied
Christian burial. It would be a century more before the
joust as we know it in popular culture emerged in all its
glory, with armored knights charging into contact jousts.
Eventually, the joust was so popular that it alone would
make up the tournaments, and the other events faded into
obscurity outside of the battlefield. The melee-style and
contact-style tournaments were brutal no matter how you
put it. If one follows those who fight Modern Medieval
Combat today, you will see their injuries are plentiful
even with full-plate armor and some modern steel-making
technology. And rules.

Therein lies something I did try to stay true to form
with, as the rules at each tourney, at each location, in

each country, could change. What events (sword, joust, pike, club, etc.), what they fought to (yielding or the more civil counting blows), and even the awards (gold, horses, armor) varied. In the cases of melees and other events where the losing knight was forced to yield, he did in fact give up his armor, horse, and a substantial ransom. A chivalrous victor would ask what the knight could afford and charge that so as not to make the loser destitute. For the victors of any style tournament, huge fortunes could be won. Though not explained in depth, this is how I made poor knight-errant Sir Alec rise to power, as well as common-born Wilfred.

Wilfred's rise to knighthood was not unheard of in this early medieval period. True, most knights were made so by inheritance, solidified by their apprenticeship under fellow knights, before earning the ordination into knighthood themselves. Parents would put a lot of trust in having their sons raised under the most prestigious knights, not only for the skill-set their sons would need to survive but for the influence and connections they would need to further the family's power. However, this period included the last decades in which a man could bypass the limitations of nobility and by pure show of skill and worthiness, earn the title of knight. It did not happen often, but it did happen. In fact, it caused some tension between the blooded nobility and the newly titled. Old nobility was not keen to share land or inheritances with the newcomers.

From what we know of ordination ceremonies, those of this era had a great deal of ceremonial custom woven into them, yet they were not yet as elaborate as they became centuries later. To be ordained by someone as high as the King himself was uncommon and held a great deal of weight and importance. I let King Richard knight Wilfred and Eleanor so that no one could question their titles. They had to be accepted, at least formally.

Yes, I know. A woman could not be a knight. Creative license generously taken. Yet indeed, there are records of women who rode to battle and took up weapons. Eleanor's story of Lady Adelaide of Tuscany is a true rumor. Philippe Contamine's book War in the Middle Ages holds the interesting line that "The participation of armed ladies...was considered, when everything is taken into account, as fairly normal, given the fact that many feudal customs gave them a formal right to succession" (241). If we talk about female warriors across the scope of history, there is a list pages long. They did exist. They were formidable, and some even commanded armies. I let Eleanor fall somewhere along the lines of the legend of Lady Adelaide, where she fights on occasion with great skill, while also embracing her role as a woman.

The roles of women in the late twelfth century are something I challenged in this novel. I feel there is a general stereotype that women, particularly the nobility, were as dainty and sheltered as they were in more recent historical eras, such as the Victorian age. What we know of the medieval period just doesn't support this. There are numerous accounts of women managing fiefs or entire countries while their men were away on crusade. Women were expected to work to support the manor. Yes, they had the dual responsibility of raising the children, but they were also contributing members of society and were treated as such. I imagine it had to be a supportive strength similar to the women during World War II. I made Eleanor a bit on the rougher side, which is in large part due to her unique upbringing, which I explore more in future books.

In marriage, a man had just as little ability to choose a spouse as a woman. The negotiations were undertaken almost entirely by their families, in order to benefit the family as a whole. Now if two individuals had no family, they sometimes had a little more freedom. Not always, as sometimes the girl would be given into a fellow noble's care until she was of age. Eleanor's marriage to Lezay was perfectly legal, thus why she was completely trapped, unless she had chosen to enter a nunnery, which was its own process. Eleanor's engagement to Edmond as a child would also have been commonplace.

Then there are the clandestine relationships. I found sources that claim that mistresses were more common in this era than whores. It was a show of status if you could afford to maintain one, which is in part why Alec agrees to Eleanor's plan to "bolster" his reputation. The flip side to this was the church's vehement position against both adultery and sexual immorality. It was fighting against courtly visions of chivalric love, while trying to prevent an entire generation of people locked into loveless marriages from committing the grievous sin of adultery. The Archaeology of Weapons by R. Ewart Oakeshott makes for interesting reading on chivalric love. Oakeshott claims, "Ladies were encouraged to find the emancipation of illicit intrigue, and were carefully instructed in the devious ways by which their husbands could be outwitted" (187). I must give credit to the line that inspired this entire story, though it's historical accuracy should be questioned. The National Jousting Association website says, "It was considered downright disgraceful—absolute treachery—for a lady to refuse her favors to a knight who had fought in her honor."

I estimate that the distances traveled throughout this novel were feasible within the times frames I give. A typical horse averages about fifteen to twenty miles per day, though exceptionally fit horses like Noir and Harlequin could probably do upwards of fifty. For comparison, a modern endurance horse can cover one hundred miles in less than ten hours. That said, a horse that would function as travel mount, tournament mount, and battle mount would have been rare. Most knights would have at least two horses, one to travel (a rouncey) and then their battle-trained destrier. They could also have a fast, light charger for tournaments or a quiet palfrey for their servants or wives to ride. Since my knights are starting off poor and for the sake of fluidity, I only wrote them one main horse each.

With the exception of King Richard the Lionheart, King Philip of France, and Lord Otto of Poitou, my characters are fictitious. King Richard was building Chateau Gaillard at an exceptionally rapid pace through 1196-1198 in order to thwart his cousin King Philip who kept trying to retake his dutchies. Richard is often credited as architect and spent a great deal of time there in those years. Lord Otto was Richard's nephew and Count of Poitou from 1196 forward. During the timeframe of this story, he was indeed making moves to claim the German throne, which he eventually did in June of 1198. A few years later, he also became Holy Roman Emperor.

The quest by Lord Otto to save Eleanor's son by sieging Lord Montag is completely fictitious, though technically as an Alsatian noble at this time, Montag would have owed the King of Germany his allegiance. Unlike today, where Alsace is part of France, the area was pulled back and forth by both French and German influence. The nobles within this area were very powerful and independent, as Eleanor calls them, "princes". I tried to demonstrate this with Montag and Lezay's relations with several kings. They are friends with the King of France, the King of England knows about them, and the future King of Germany wants their allegiance.

The last thing to note is that most of the castles and manors I mention are real, with the exception being the Levan estate in Aquitaine. Sarum is now a ruin, though in the twelfth century it was already a centuries-old fortification booming with activity. Decades after this story, the move from Sarum to Salisbury began. Castle Neroche was a hunting lodge already abandoned by Alec's time, though likely standing. Paris was a mere town, with Louvre Castle (now Louvre Museum) a fortification on its northern outskirts. Chateau Gaillard is now a ruin. Montag's castle in Alsace, Brunstein, was inspired by the ruins of Fleckenstein castle, which dates from prior to 1174. Leuwenstein, Lezay's home, is another ruin a short distance away. That area of Les Vosges really does seem like it has a castle on every hilltop and maintains its wild beauty.

Fictional though Eleanor may be, I hope she has stimulated your imagination as we followed her on her quest to break away from the limitations society placed on her. Thank you for reading, and I hope you will enjoy more of Eleanor's adventures in the stories to come.

Bibliography and Recommended Reading

Contamine, Phillip. <u>War in the Middle Ages</u>. Presses Universitaires de France, 1980.

Goubert, Pierre. <u>The Course of French History</u>. Franklin Watts, Inc., 1988

Oakeshott, R. Ewart. <u>The Archaeology of Weapons</u>. Lutterworth Press, 1960.

Acknowledgments

I won't admit to you how long this book has been in the making, but it is my amazing beta readers and critique partners at Critique Match that brought it to light. Thank you so much for your encouragement and vital assistance. You made this a better story, and you made me a better writer. The same must be said for my editor, Gail Delaney, who demonstrated the absolute necessity and value of a professional pair of eyes. Finally, thanks to Emily and Katie, who put up with the earliest versions of this book and encouraged me to keep writing in the first place. I can't wait to hear what you thought of this version.

About Author

When J.A. Stein isn't dreaming up stories of centuries past, you can find her training horses like those in her stories. Or perhaps you won't find her at all, as she frequently disappears into America's stunning wilderness to chase adventure. She loves to read anything that has a plot and makes it a goal to write stories that can't be put down.

This is her debut novel. In 2023 it won second prize in the Royal Dragonfly Literary Awards.

Reviews of this book are greatly appreciated. To follow upcoming releases and receive bonus content, please subscribe to the free newsletter at www.authorjastein.com. Looking for social media? You won't find it. Stein is a firm believer that time is better spent reading a book than a news feed. Then there is more time left over to experience your own story. That said, we will pretend YouTube isn't social media. See channel @AuthorJAStein.

The Story Continues...

Sometimes the monsters are only shadows of bigger monsters.

In 1199, Lady Eleanor de Levan and Sir Alec Earnblaec have finally settled into a life of peace. That is, until a chance encounter in a marketplace resurrects old ghosts and leaves Eleanor scrambling to piece together more of her past.

Twenty-seven years prior, Lady Igraine le Brun betrayed her family to marry for love. As Eleanor's parents' love story is revealed, so are the layers of loyalty binding Igraine to Lord Montag, the brother she will one day entrust her only child to. Family secrets are revealed that are tangled with love, betrayal, and echoes of a monster who is stepping out of shadow.

***

Lady Eleanor de Levan worked hard to consolidate her new role as wife and mother with her adventurous spirit. When the winter of 1199 reaches its icy fingers towards Aquitaine, her peace is cut short. A mysterious messenger warns her that danger is coming, then dies. The fiery knightess within Eleanor steps back into the light.

As the threats rise, she and husband Sir Alec Earnblaec set off to find answers as to who these shadowy men are and what they want. One by one, members of her family's dark Order are revealed, each with their own danger and agenda. They are willing to divide the couple by any means, including Alec's past. When Eleanor sees through his half-truths, Alec will be reminded how she earned her nickname English Winter.

Will the love Alec and Eleanor have fought so hard to forge be able to withstand the onslaught of forces seeking to divide them?

Also see Stein's novels set near her Pennsylvania home, **The Last Farm** *and* **Patch Town.**